C000131471

The Three Great Loves of Victoria Turnbull

BOOK TWO

A PROMISE UNMADE
The Geordie

A heart-rending marriage story full of passion, betrayal and the healing power of love.

ISABELLA WILES

Other books by Isabella Wiles

THE THREE GREAT LOVES OF
VICTORIA TURNBULL SERIES

A Life Unstarted - A novella (Prequel)

A Flame Unburned - The Kiwi (Book 1)

A Promise Unmade - The Geordie (Book 2)

A Star Unborn - The Celt (Book 3)

ξ‫כ‬

Join Isabella's online reading club:
facebook.com / groups / IzzysReadingBees

☐ facebook.com / IsabellaWiles
☐ instagram.com / isabellawiles_author
☐ tiktok.com / @isabellawiles_author
☐ bookbub.com / authors / isabella-wiles
☐ goodreads.com / Isabella_Wiles

To Angela,

Through good times and bad,
thank you for always being there.

Words cannot express how much I love and appreciate you.
Plus you know far too many of my secrets to not be friends for life!
xxx

Contents

Author's Note

My stories include many themes, some beautiful, and some ugly and painful. My intention is never to sensationalise trauma – many of us have wounds – but rather, through the safe medium of story-telling, to give them air, so that our collective societal stitches may heal.

This particular story includes themes around infidelity, sexual assault and suicidal thoughts, and at the back of this book you'll find contact details for organisations that can offer support, if you're at all worried your own stitches may tear open.

Also some readers may notice some spellings or meanings of words differ from their own everyday use of the English language; this novel is written in British English (interspersed with some Kiwi and Geordie slang) which befits both the setting and the characters of this story.

Finally, please do share your comments and feedback on my Facebook Page, follow me on Instagram, or Tik Tok and ensure you sign up to my newsletter to be the first to hear about new releases. Your encouragement inspires me to keep writing. I have lots more stories in me which I can't wait to share.

Much love,

Izzy x

Get a FREE Victoria Turnbull Novel

For a limited time, to celebrate the launch of *The Three Great Loves of Victoria Turnbull* series, you can get an exclusive free ebook of the series prequel novel *A Life Unstarted.*

Claim your free ebook at www.isabellawiles.com

A chance at a new life, a past that refuses to stay buried, and a dangerous encounter that threatens it all.

Victoria is excited to get her new life started, but paradise quickly turns to hell during a weekend trip to Istanbul. Forced to confront her inner demons, she must find a way to save her friend and herself before it's too late, in this fast-paced origin story.

Claim your free ebook at www.isabellawiles.com

Prologue

Leeds, England. May 2005

*M*y hands shaking, I grip the steering wheel of my luxury 4x4. Checking for oncoming traffic, I pull out of the multi-storey car park and join the line of cars snaking their way along the Leeds inner ring road.

When I turned up for the meeting this morning, even though I wanted them to say yes to my proposal, I was ready for some push back and never expected them to be so enthusiastic about my ideas. It feels as if I'm finally on the receiving end of some good luck, and the dark cloud that has been hanging over me has finally lifted.

Is this small victory the end of one enormous, tortuous roller-coaster? This positive outcome a small but significant step forward in the next chapter of my life?

This deal will inevitably change the trajectory of my business, and the course of my life. About fifty percent of new businesses fail within the first three years, and with what we've just been through, today's good news means we can look forward to positive business growth.

I can't wait to share the news with my employees.

I pull up at the pedestrian crossing to give way to those waiting patiently at the side of the road. Watching the crowd of people filing numbly in front of my car, I catch my breath.

It can't be? But it is: it's him!

My eyes follow him as he ambles, unaware, in front of me. The last person on the entire planet I'd expect to see walking in front of my car. The sight of him again after all this time causes me to freeze in my seat, the windscreen in front of me the only barrier between us as he saunters past a few feet away. Never, on this day of new beginnings and fresh starts, when it feels as if something massive has just shifted in the ether, did I expect to be confronted so directly with my past.

I remain frozen but for the continuous and intense shaking of my hands on the steering wheel. I hold my breath.

He shouldn't be here. He should be on the other side of the world, focusing on his new life, as I am on mine. What on earth is he doing in this northern industrial city where neither of us has ever lived, or, as far as I'm aware, has any connections?

I take in his familiar gait and relaxed manner as he steps up onto the opposite kerb and watch out of my rear-view mirror as he turns left down the pavement, walking away, still unaware of my presence.

If I don't act now, this moment will be gone forever, and I may never see him again. Is there a reason the universe presented him here, directly in front of me, today of all days? On a day when I feel like I'm gliding into a new era of my life, why have the planets chosen this moment to collide and serve up my past?

If I ever wanted closure, or answers to my unasked questions, I realise that *this is it*; I must seize this opportunity before it is gone forever.

I quickly check my reflection in my rear-view mirror, running my tongue over my teeth, and smacking my lips together to even out my lipstick. Satisfied with my appearance, my tyres screech in protest as I yank the steering wheel to the kerb, stopping abruptly at an awkward angle. Horns honk around me, but I don't care. I leap out, cup my hands around my mouth and shout his name.

He's about a hundred yards away now, the muscles in his strong, wide shoulders rippling under his cotton shirt as he continues to walk in the opposite direction. But the familiar pitch of my voice calling his name must resonate. He stops and turns, tilting his head as if confirming his mind is not playing tricks on him and that it really was the familiar sound of my voice he heard.

He spots me amongst the flow of passing pedestrians moving around me, smiles widely, and quickens his pace back towards me. The adrenalin and buzz I felt from my earlier business meeting returns and intensifies as I realise this is it: the moment we never had when we broke up.

I have no idea what he will say, what questions I'll be brave enough to ask, or what will happen as a result of us bumping into each other again. Seeing him so unexpectedly and in such an odd way feels as if greater forces have reunited us.

But why?

As he approaches, I suck air into my lungs and attempt to organise the tumultuous thoughts racing through my mind. His smile grows the closer he gets.

"Hi," he says, running his hand through his hair. "Well, this is a pleasant surprise. What on earth are you doing here?"

"I could ask you the same thing," I reply, taking in the slim gold wedding band on his left hand.

Part I

Chapter 1

VICTORIA

9 years earlier, North-East England, April 1996

"Rise and shine," my mother chimes, pulling back my bedroom curtains and allowing the midday sun to flood my room.

"Oh, fuck off," I groan like a petulant teenager, squeezing my eyes shut and pulling my pillow over my head.

"Language Victoria! I'll not tolerate that kind of vulgarity whilst you're living under my roof."

I sigh into the underside of my pillow and mime along with her well-rehearsed lecture:

"If I've told you once, I'll tell you again... my house, my rules."

"I know, Mam. I'm sorry," I muffle like an embarrassed ten-year-old.

It's not her fault I landed in a crumpled heap on her doorstep three months ago with nowhere else to go.

She plonks herself on the end of my bed and strokes the outline of my leg. "I'm worried about you, poppet."

I say nothing and pull the pillow tighter over my head, hoping its familiar scent will quell my inner self-loathing. It doesn't. I brace myself for what I know is coming next.

"It's been months now, sweetheart. Don't you think it's about time you pulled yourself together? Got back out there, put more effort into finding a job, any job, even something temporary? You need a reason to get up in the morning. It's not healthy the way you're carrying on. Moping around all day with your curtains closed."

Frustrated, I jerk the pillow away from my face. "It's not like I haven't been trying, Mam. You know how many hundreds of CVs I've posted. But no one's hiring. At least not around here. I could always leave again, if that's what you want. Go back to London. I don't want to be a burden," I spit, my tone laced with sarcasm.

"That's not what I'm saying, sweetheart, and you know it. Me and your stepdad have loved having you back at home."

I exhale. As much as I hate everything about my life right now, the thought of heading back to London has my gut twisting into knots. When I last lived there, I wasn't happy. I lived in a tiny flat in a crummy area where the restless rumble of the buses kept me awake at night, and in the heat of summer opening the windows only invited plumes of pollution into the hobbit-sized home I shared with my now ex-boyfriend. I had no option but to commute well before dawn, and as my office was underground in the bowels of a bank, for a large part of the year I lived without sunlight.

No, it's hopeless. I need to face facts. I'm nothing but a sad excuse for a twenty-six-year-old. A washed-up singleton with nowhere to live other than her childhood bedroom under her parents' roof. I have no job, no prospects, and no income. How did my life turn into such a shit-show? This wasn't the plan.

I pull the pillow back over my face and squeeze my eyes even tighter shut, trying to ignore the burning at the back of my throat as I swallow down my tears.

By this age I expected to be on the cusp of settling down. Laying the foundations for the rest of my life. If not engaged, then at least making a commitment to the person I envisioned becoming the father of my children. Buying a house together. Having fun trans-forming it into a home. My career reaching the middle rung of the ladder.

Somehow I'm back at the beginning of the Monopoly board. I've inadvertently *'not passed GO'* and *'not collected two-hundred pounds'* and ended up in *'Life Jail'*. Meanwhile everyone else's lives are carrying on around me while I'm slipping further and further behind. I'm stuck in *'Jail'*, with no way to re-enter the game until I somehow *'roll a double'*.

"Come on, Victoria," my mother continues. "You're better than this. You have Fenwick blood in your veins, and we Fenwicks never give up. We fight for what we want, even when we're backed into a corner."

I roll onto my side, hugging my pillow.

I know what I want — I want Chris. But at the same time I know loving him almost destroyed me.

We tried so hard to make it work, but we were stuck in a never-ending cycle of unrivalled passion followed by hurtful actions, unimaginable pain, then a passionate reconciliation. Leaving him is the hardest thing I've ever done; my empty body aches for him every waking moment.

Opening my eyes, my gaze falls onto the wooden box, its lid inlaid with an enamel ballerina, that sits on my dressing table. Inside it and underneath the lifetime of letters I've held onto from friends and family, lie the tentative tendrils of my last connection to him. The few letters we exchanged in the early days of our relation-ship, when he had to go home to his native New Zealand. Each scrap of wafer-thin blue Airmail paper scrawled with words of love and longing.

I slide my hand over my empty womb. Oh, what have I done?

"Come on, Victoria." My mother pulls back the duvet. "You need to get up. And I can say this because I'm your mam and I love you: sweetheart, you stink." She stands up. "And I know you won't want to greet Mel smelling like that."

"Mellie? But she's not due until next weekend."

My mother lets out a long sigh. "Victoria, it's already 'next weekend'. She's due in about twenty minutes, so you'd better hurry." Her eyes travel over the piles of discarded clothes and mess strewn over every square inch of my bedroom floor. "And tidy your room. I'm sure you won't want her to see you like this."

I wait until my mother's left the room before I groan and throw my pillow at the back of my bedroom door.

But she's right, I don't want Mel to see me like this, especially when her visit is the one thing I've been looking forward to.

෬

"Eeeeeeeeeeeee!" we both shriek in unison half an hour later when Mel arrives.

"You're actually here." I squeeze the outside of her arms, my face splitting into a wide smile as hers does the same. Just her presence instantly lifts my mood.

"Of course I'm here. God, it's so good to see ya, Chook," she says in her familiar Kiwi twang as we fall into a warm embrace.

When Mel had asked if she could come north for a weekend to see me, of course I'd gushed and said 'yes' immediately. I've missed her almost as much as I miss her brother, but I'd accepted that leaving Chris meant leaving our friendship behind as well. Or so I'd thought.

"Come in, come in." I pick up her bags and usher her into the kitchen. "Tea?"

"Yes please. I'm gasping."

"Well hello, Melanie. It's lovely to see you again." My mother pulls Mel into a hug.

"And you," she replies. "It's been too long Mrs. T."

"Indeed."

"Thank you for having me this weekend. I've been dying to catch up with Vicky."

My hands shake as I flick on the kettle. The last time I saw Mel was on the beach in Auckland, the morning of my dramatic escape from the North Island. She was super supportive when I told her I was dumping her brother, but it strikes me she may have an ulterior motive to her visit. Is she digging for dirt that she'll feed straight back to Chris?

'You're my best friend and I'll always support you, but he's my blood. No matter what happens, if I was ever forced to choose sides...' Mel once warned me.

"Let's go upstairs." I raise an eyebrow in my mother's direction, acknowledging my mam's flapping ears.

"Good idea. We have tonnes to catch up on. Not least my news." She thrusts her left hand out and wiggles her fourth finger.

"Aaaaah!" I scream at the sight of her sparkling engagement ring. "YOU ARE KIDDING ME! Okay, we need to go upstairs right now." I grab both mugs. "I want to know EVE-RY-THING."

Chapter 2

*S*pill," I instruct, as we flop down on the bed together. "I want *all* the details. Starting with WHO?!"

"You don't know him, but he's called Karl."

"And how long have you been seeing this Karl?"

"I wasn't trying to hide him from you, you were on the other side of the world when things started to get serious, but we've been official for seven months now."

"Seven months?! How the hell have you managed to keep him a secret all that time? You sly old goose—" I stop dead when I accidentally use Chris's old pet name for me.

Mel doesn't notice. "I didn't intend to. I just didn't want to make a song and dance about it, in case I jinxed it. Plus, you've been kinda pre-occupied with your own relationship drama these last six months," Mel continues. "I didn't think it was right to rub my relationship bliss in your face when your world was clearly falling apart."

I suck in a deep breath. Don't cry, don't cry, don't cry.

"And what does this Karl do?" I ask, keeping my emotions under control — just.

"He's an accountant."

"AN ACCOUNTANT?!" I almost spit my tea across the room. "But they're all boring. I never would have pictured *you*, of all people, with an accountant."

She laughs. "Well we all have to grow up some time. These days I'd rather spend my Saturday nights curled up with him watching crap telly, than gallivant all over the place partying like we used to."

"Bloody hell! Someone's managed to tame my wild Kiwi friend. So come on then — how did he propose?"

"It was after I came back from New Zealand. That month apart actually did us the world of good. Made us realise we never want to be apart again."

"And? How did he do it? Was it all unicorns and rainbows?"

"Not quite, you soppy old romantic, although he did do it on Valentine's Day. I thought he was only taking me out for a nice little meal at our local Italian, but when the puddings turned up, suddenly there's a bottle of champagne and he's down on one knee holding out this beaut." She wiggles her ring finger under my nose again.

I pull her hand towards me so I can inspect her rock more closely. A single solitaire: it glitters as I turn it in the light. "And have you guys thought about a date?"

"Summer 1999. Which I know is three years away yet. But I've always thought you should either have a long relationship and a short engagement or, as in our case, a short courtship then a long engagement. Plus, we're saving up for a deposit on a house and, from a purely practical perspective, I need to give my rellies as much notice as possible if they're going to fly over."

"So you'll do it over here then? Or are you thinking you'll do something in New Zealand at a later date?"

"Actually, neither. We were thinking maybe somewhere in Europe. Possibly Spain. It's cheaper, plus it means everyone can have a mini-holiday."

"Ooh, how exciting." I clap my hands together like a child who's just seen the number of presents left by Santa.

"Well, when else are our families likely to have the chance to hang out and really get to know each other. It may be the only time they all meet. So if we're there for a week, we'll make it a big family affair."

I lift my chin. "It sounds perfect. I'm so happy for you, Mel."

"Thanks." She crinkles her nose. "I can't wait for you to meet him. He's so kind and sweet… and *dead* sexy."

"Oh yeah? Good in the sack then?"

"Oh-my-good-god, Vicky." She places her hand over her throat. "You have no idea."

Actually I do, I think to myself. One thing that was undeniable with Chris and me was our sexual chemistry. He took me to places I never thought possible, and in doing so created a need within me that only he could satiate. A part of me that I've only been able to reach, *through him.*

"Say no more." I raise my hand before she goes into any more detail about her sex life. "I hope he takes good care of you. You deserve it, Mel." I raise my mug in a toast. "Here's to the kind, sweet, and *very* sexy Karl."

She clanks her mug against the side of mine. "So, what's been going on with you?"

"Not much." I shrug.

"You've lost weight."

"Not through trying."

"Since you've been home, have you picked up with old friends?"

"Kind of. Nessa's been great."

"Your old friend from school?"

"That's her. And my cousin Julie has dragged me out on a couple of occasions. But everyone's busy with their own lives, so it's only ever at the weekends."

"So how else have you been filling your time?"

I shrug and nibble at a hangnail on the side of my finger.

"I see. And how have you been feeling, generally?"

I gesture around my room. "I would have thought it was obvious, Mel."

"Don't be too hard on yourself. You've just had a massive break-up and moved back from the other side of the world. I'd be worried if you didn't feel shit. You're in love rehab."

"Maybe, but it feels like the wheels of my life have completely fallen off and I can't find the energy or motivation to do anything about it."

"And that's to be expected. As long as your wheels don't stay off permanently. At some point, you have to renter the world."

"That's exactly what my mam thinks. She's told me… in no uncertain terms, that I've had enough time to wallow and should be focusing on finding a job and getting my shit together." I break eye contact and dip my head, my tears always only a couple of blinks below the surface. "But I'm scared."

"Of what?" she replies softly.

"That if I focus on *moving forward* I have to forget him, and I don't know how to do that. I don't know if I *want* to do that." I drop my head into my hands. "I just miss him, Mel. So much. You've no idea."

I don't add that I've had to stop myself on more than one occasion from buying a one-way ticket back to New Zealand.

"Hey, hey." Mel takes my hands in hers. "It'll all be okay. I promise. Obviously it still hurts. You wouldn't be human if it didn't. You loved him, but you will get past this. I know you will."

Looking at her with bloodshot eyes, I ask the question that's been burning at the back of my throat for three months now. "How's he doing, Mel? Tell me… honestly."

Mel rolls her lips inwards and presses them together. "Same as you really. He was inconsolable for the first few weeks. Full of remorse. Wanted the chance to win you back. But he's slowly coming to terms with why you left and that you're not coming back. He's realising that sometimes loving someone means letting them go."

My shoulders shudder with staccato sobs as I give in to the heavy wet tears that leak out of the corner of my eyes and roll, unabated, down my cheeks.

"There, there. Let it all out." Mel soothes, rubbing my back. "I can't tell you how sorry I am that things didn't work out between you and my little brother, but I'll say the same thing to you as I said to him… and I know it's a terrible cliché, but you *will* find somebody else. You both will. Everyone knows how much you both tried to make it work, but for whatever reason, it wasn't right, and that's really sad. But the best thing you can both do for each other is stay focused on moving forward. Your life's not over, Vicky. Far from it. It might not feel like it now, but it's just getting going." She allows me a moment to collect myself. I blow my nose and wipe away my tears before she continues, "Are you still journaling? Writing down how you feel?"

"Not consistently. To be honest, everything I seem to write at the moment is so depressing. Whenever I read it back, I end up feeling worse."

"Hmmm. It can feel like that sometimes. But trust me, there will come a time when you look back and you'll not recognise the person who wrote those things. You'll be a new you — in a good way."

"If you say so." I give her a weak smile.

"See, that's better. Now tell me, what's the plan for tonight?"

"We're going out with Nessa and Julie."

"Perfect. That's exactly what I would have prescribed. A chance to get glammed up and head out on the town — or the *toon* — as you seem to say in this part of the world. You never know, you might get lucky."

"God no. I couldn't think of anything worse."

"Oh, lighten up. It's not like you're looking for a husband or anything, but the guaranteed best way to get over someone is to get under someone else."

"Me-el!" I slap her arm, a smile creeping across my lips. "What are you like?"

"There she is. My old pal. Drinking partner extraordinaire. Wearer of the sauciest LBDs and sexy Louboutins. Wingwoman and provider of the best Yum Yum hangover cures — ever!"

"We did have fun, didn't we?"

"Hell yeah we did. And tonight will be no different. Right, crank those tunes on and let's get ready. Newcastle's not going to know what's hit it."

Chapter 3

*T*he wind bites as we turn the corner. The four of us: me, Mel, Nessa, and Julie, our arms linked in unison, like a line of Tiller Girls teetering down Dean Street in ridiculously impractical stilettos. The bitter north-easterly that whips up the River Tyne slaps our bare arms and legs, punishing us for baring so much flesh, forcing us to hunch over and tuck our chins into our chests.

"Jeez, it's cold," Mel says.

"Welcome to The Frozen North," Nessa replies, laughing. "But it's still against *Geordie Law* to wear a coat."

Turning right onto Sandhill, the iconic Tyne Bridge looms protectively above us. Its uplights illuminating its famed curve. Smaller in scale, but built to the same blueprint and by the same North-East steel makers who erected Sydney Harbour Bridge, its distinctive green arch links the cities of Gateshead on the south bank of the Tyne, to Newcastle on the north. Looking around at the familiar sandstone architecture of my home city — a city I willingly left four years ago without a backwards glance — believing my future lay elsewhere, I never expected to walk these cobbles again. But with my girls holding me up, a warm familiarity seeps through my extremities. Like a hot toddy at the end of crisp winter's day, and my breath settles inside my body.

Perhaps this is where I am meant to be. Perhaps this is my 'home.'

This may not be the future I'd envisioned for myself, but who knows what may lie around the corner.

A particularly strong gust of wind blows our skimpy skirts up around our waists and a gaggle of lads on the opposite side of the street wolf-whistle in our direction.

"Ya'll right lasses?" one of them shouts, his vowels singing in the familiar upbeat rhythm of a thick Geordie accent.

"Yes. We're fine thank you," Nessa shouts back, smoothing her flame red hair back into place.

"Are you sure?" the ringleader on the opposite side of the road shouts. His arms open wide and hips thrust forward. "You look like you need someone to warm you up."

"No — you're all right, thanks," Julie shouts back this time.

"They're very forward around here, aren't they?" Mel giggles.

"Only the knobheads," I reply.

"Come on, Tor." Nessa links her arm through mine as the bouncer unclips the security rope and we clonk our way up the stairs into The Quilted Camel.

"Tor?" Mel quizzes, catching up with me.

"I know, it's been Nessa's nickname for me ever since we were at school," I whisper back.

"It suits you." Mel playfully nips my bum, making me jump.

Pushing through the fire doors at the top of the stairs, we walk into a wall of sound and the distinctive smell of stale alcohol mixed with sweaty bodies disguised with aftershave and expensive perfume.

"My round," I shout over the blare of Nirvana's *Teen Spirit.* "Same again?"

Everyone nods.

"Four double vodkas and coke please," I yell into the barman's ear when it's my turn.

He nods and fills four glasses with ice before flaring the vodka bottle into the air and filling each glass from a great height.

Once ready, I give him a ten-pound note and smile my thanks. "Keep the change." He nods, and slides the drinks across the bar top.

Clutching three of the glasses together in a makeshift triangle I head off in search of the girls. They've drifted over to the windows, where a perfect view of the bridge is illuminated through the Jacobean pitted panes. They've been joined by a group of men; my gut tightens. I had hoped tonight would be just us girls, but Newcastle is such a small city it's impossible to *not* bump into someone you know.

One man has his arm around Nessa's waist, and the other two are chatting animatedly with Julie and Mel. I recognise Nessa's boyfriend, Anth, the guy who has his arm around her waist. They met during Fresher's at Leeds Uni, and even though I'd left the North-East by then, I've met him a few times when I went to visit Nessa at uni. The other two men, I've never seen before.

One is well over six-foot-four and towers over the rest of the group. A goth, judging by his long hair tied back in a pony-tail, and the studded belt looped twice around his hips. He's wearing a black Radiohead T-shirt with the sleeves cut out. My eyes hover over the Newcastle United Football Club crest tattooed on the top of his left arm.

The other guy is facing away from me. Slightly shorter in stature but still at least six foot tall, he's wearing tight black trendy trousers that hug his perfectly ripe arse, and a lime-green shirt, which, judging by the shape of his shoulders, hides a strong back. I notice he has a cluster of thin leather straps wound around his right wrist. The epitome of cool.

Holding the drinks aloft, I weave my way through the crowd and Julie spies me walking towards her and smiles, causing the lime-green shirt guy to turn and look over his shoulder. Keeping his chin angled towards the floor, he looks at me over the top of his pint glass, and his lips curl into a flirty smile.

He's wearing a monochrome tie with an image of James Dean printed down its front.

Holy crap. This guy could have stepped straight out of the pages of *GQ* magazine.

Mr James Dean's eyes bore into me like hot lasers, causing an unexpected flutter to dance in the pit of my stomach, and my legs to turn to jelly. I miss my step and stumble, but with ninja reflexes he leaps forward and catches me by my elbow.

"Whoa there. You don't want to be dropping them," he says rescuing the middle drink out of the precarious triangle I'm clutching.

"Thanks," I reply, passing the other drinks out to the girls.

They nod their thanks while continuing their conversation with the goth.

"Where's yours?" Mr James Dean asks, the deep timbre of his voice plucking at my heart like a harp.

"Back on the bar." I look over to the other side of the room.

"Don't move," he instructs before disappearing into the throng.

With one long arm he reaches between a new line of punters and grabs my drink.

"Here." He passes me my glass, before chinking his pint against the side of it. "Cheers."

"Thanks," I say a second time, feeling as if I've grown extra arms and legs. I can't remember the last time I spoke to a stranger in a bar and I've forgotten how to behave.

He's devastatingly handsome. A strong square jawline sits beneath chiselled cheekbones and very deep-set dark eyes. Almost the colour of onyx. His hair is jet black too, cut fashionably short at the sides and styled with gel on top.

Leaning forward, he asks, "And where have you just landed from?" Each word a hot puff in my ear.

All my senses switch on and my breath catches in the back of my throat.

"Sorry, I don't know what you mean?" My stomach clenches.

How can he possibly know my history?

"You don't get a tan like that…" he points to my deeply tanned shoulder, "…unless you live on a sunbed, or you've just been away on holiday. And you don't strike me as the sunbed type."

I may have been home a few months now, but my Antipodean tan is still burnt deep into my skin. I wonder what else he can see. Are all my wounds this visible?

"It's a bit of a long story," I reply, my eyes darting around the room. Looking for the emergency exits.

"Well it's a story I think I'd like to hear," he says, his lips pulling into a smile, revealing dimples in each of his cheeks. "Don't worry. I don't bite," he adds when I don't say anything further. "Let's start over. Hi. I'm Craig. Craig Fenwick. I work with Anth."

"Sorry. What did you say your name was?"

"Craig. Pleased to meet you. And you are?"

"Victoria Turnbull. Most people call me Tor. But I meant — what was your surname again?"

"Fenwick. Why?"

I shake my head, smirking. "You've gotta to be kidding me."

"No. Why? Is there something wrong with being a Fenwick?"

"Absolutely not." I throw my head back laughing. Relaxing at last. "Well Craig Fenwick, it's very nice to meet you."

He raises his glass. "Likewise." He holds my eye contact while he takes another languorous sip of his pint, but I look past him and catch Mellie's eye. She beams back at me, nodding, and winks.

*

Whether it was intentional or not, my girls seem happy to leave me chatting to Craig for the rest of the night. But every time I look away from Craig's dimples, I spy either Mel, Nessa, or Julie's eyes on me. Supervising us from a safe distance.

Wobbling on vodka-filled legs, at one point I nip away to the ladies and don't remember much about the evening after that, until I feel Mel's firm hand on my shoulder, extrapolating me away from Craig's lips when our taxi has arrived.

"Time to go," Mel instructs in a tone that screams *non-negotiable.*

"U-huh," I mumble.

"It really was lovely to meet you," Craig says, dipping his head to kiss the back of my hand before Mel has dragged me too far away.

'U-huh." I beam, my cheeks hurting from smiling.

My final image of Mr James Dean is him leaning nonchalantly back against the wall of the club, his head dipped, his eyes tracking me as we leave, before he shakes his head and bursts out laughing as I lose my footing, stumble backwards through the doors and land flat on my arse.

Fucking brilliant!

Chapter 4

I can't believe you have to go already. It seems like you've only just got here." I pull Mel into a hug as we stand together on the platform at Durham train station the following afternoon.

"See, time flies when you're having fun. Let's do it again, and soon."

"Definitely."

"Maybe you can come down and see me next time. I can introduce you to Karl. And I know Mich misses you too."

Mel makes reference to her older sister, Michelle, who was also a really close friend when I was dating their brother.

"I miss her as well. I hope she can understand why I haven't been in touch. I was just too battered and bruised and needed to distance myself from any ties to Chris."

"Of course. She gets it."

"But seeing you this weekend has been really nice."

In fact, it's been more than nice, cathartic even. I didn't realise how much I needed it.

"Good… and sucking face with a tall, dark, handsome stranger in a nightclub doesn't hurt either."

"*Me-el.*" I lightly slap the back of her hand.

"Well it's true. I told you the best way to get over someone is to get under someone else. Have some fun, Vicky. You deserve it."

A flush creeps up my neck at the blurry memories of my amorous encounter with Mr James Dean. I have to admit, Mel was right: a bit of harmless flirtation, and locking lips with a tall dark handsome stranger, did feel nice.

A voice booms over the tannoy, announcing the imminent arrival of the 14:40 to Kings Cross.

"Time to go." Mel slaps the outside of her thighs with straight arms as the train trundles into the station. Seconds later the air is filled with the sound of train doors clanking open, whistles blowing, people shouting, rushing towards the exit or hauling their luggage on board.

"It's been soo good to see you." I hug Mel again before she climbs onto the train and I slam the door shut behind her. She leans out of the open window.

"Take care, Vicky." She reaches down and air-kisses both my cheeks.

"I will."

"And you must let me know how it goes with Mr James Dean."

I shake my head, laughing. "It was nothing, Mel. Forget it. He didn't even ask for my number."

"It didn't look like nothing from where I was standing. Maybe you should track him down. It wouldn't be hard if he works with Anth. He seemed nice. Remember what I said, the best way to get over someone..." She taps the side of her nose with her index finger.

"Yeah, yeah. Definitely time for you to go." I step back as the guard blows their whistle.

We wave. Blow kisses, then in the blink of an eye the train disappears down the tracks, taking my friend with it. I'm left on the station platform, where the first cherry blossom of the season swirls around my feet like fallen confetti at a wedding.

RⱭ

There's something about the tinny echo, that rattles around the roof of the old swimming baths as I cut through the water, that I find familiar and comforting. After dropping Mel off I decided to go for a swim, her visit, combined with my encounter last night, has stirred up some confusing emotions.

My limbs propel me forward as I focus inwardly on my breath.

In. Out. In. Out.

Every time my thoughts try and run away with me, I consciously refocus on my breathing.

What the hell was I thinking last night? How did we go from talking about football and our favourite films, to our lips connecting?

My thighs burn as I increase my pace. My need to submerge in the water and cleanse myself accentuated after my thoughts drift back to Chris.

I touch the side, turn, and go again.

In. Out. In. Out.

It's been so long since I've been kissed. It felt strange. Unfamiliar and familiar all at the same time.

I dip my chin below the waterline, allowing the pool water to invade my mouth. I taste the chlorine before blowing out the excess on my next breath.

His tongue inside my mouth, searching for mine to caress. Me kissing him back, my body reacting instinctively. Our hips closing the gap between us as we come together.

I reach the shallow end, plant my feet on the floor, and run my fingers over the top of my rubber swimming cap.

The feel of his hands nestling on my waist; the weight of them. Before they cup my face. Holding me like a precious jewel.

I push off again.

In. Out. In. Out.

My hands limp by my sides before finding their place around his neck. The ripple of muscle beneath my fingers. Air sucking urgently in through our noses as the kiss continues. A spark igniting between my legs. A groan. From him or me? Maybe both of us?

The side of my face touches the water as I sweep an arm overhead.

Kick. Splash. In. Out. In. Out.

My back pushing up against a wall. Firm and grounding. His hips pressing into mine. His tongue in my mouth. The spark between my legs burning hot. His lips on mine again. His hands holding my face. I groan.

A swimmer passing in the other direction causes a counter wave to slap my face and I accidentally inhale a mouthful of water. Spluttering, I come to a stop, my flow broken. I tread water and cough, clearing my airway.

I catch my breath and continue on.

Did it mean anything?

In. Out. In. Out.

Should I take Mel's advice? Have some fun? But he didn't ask for my number, is that a sign? Surely if he wants to see me again, he needs to make some effort. But even if he does, do I want to see him again?

Touch the side. Turn. Go again.

He could easily find me. He'd only have to ask Anth and Nessa for my number. But what would I do if he actually called?

Splash. Kick. Splash. Kick.

Maybe I should let it go. Accept it for what it was. A drunken snog on a girls' night out. It's too soon after Chris anyhow to open myself up again. Oh, but those eyes. And those dimples. But am I over Chris? Mel said he only wants what's best for me and he's realised that loving me means letting me go. But do I want him to let me go? Or am I secretly hoping he will still fight for me? Would *he* want me to find someone new?

In. Out. In. Out. Touch the side. Turn. Go again.

But remember when it was good, how good it was. Soo good. His tongue inside my mouth. His hands on my body. His scent invading my nostrils. Chris's scent. Craig's scent.

In. Out. In. Out.

What if he doesn't fight for me? What if he doesn't call?

In. Out. In. Out.

Craig. Chris. Chris. Craig.

In. Out. In. Out.

Touch the side. Turn. Go again.

Mel nodding her head and winking. 'The best way to get over someone is to get under someone else.' Mel cupping her mug of tea. 'He was inconsolable after you left.'

In. Out. In. Out.

Jesus Christ!

"Aaaaahhhhhh," I scream into the water which swallows my anguish before the sound reaches the surface.

Gasping, I tread water again while I catch my breath and focus on my heartbeat, consciously trying to slow it down. Blood pumps in my ears as my heart thumps inside my chest. Like a caged animal rattling the bars that keep it from being free.

I resume my stroke. In. Out. In. Out.

My breath much calmer.

Enough, Vicky. Enough.

Splash. Kick. Splash. Kick. Touch the side. Turn. Go again.

I don't have to do anything. Whatever happens now is my choice. But my mam's right. I need a purpose. A reason to get out of bed in the morning. Maybe I could do some volunteering while I keep searching for a job. I'm sure one of the charity shops would appreciate my help. Yes, that's what I'll do. If nothing else, it'll get me out of the house.

In. Out. In. Out.

I feel better instantly. My mind now focused on something within my control. Volunteering. It may not be a long-term plan, or solve my money problems, but at least it's something productive. Meanwhile everything else is not important or can be forgotten. For now, at least.

Chapter 5

2 weeks later

*C*ome on in." Nessa ushers me across her threshold.

"Here. Another one for the fridge." I pass her the bottle of wine I'm holding.

"Head that way. Everyone's in the kitchen."

"Everyone? I thought it was just us girls?" I scratch at a dry patch of skin on my arm.

"It is. The boys have gone to The Red Lion. Apparently, we all talk too much and interrupt the football."

I exhale and follow Nessa through to the kitchen, where around the table, drinks already in their hands, are Julie and another woman I don't know.

"You remember Becca?" Nessa asks.

The stranger is more petite than me, with a sweet, heart-shaped face, dark brown eyes and matching long dark auburn hair.

"Hi," she says in welcome, and the sound of her voice triggers a sliver of a memory I can't quite place. "I'm Rebecca Bell. We used to dance together."

I snap my fingers and point in her direction. "That's right. I remember now. You were in the junior troupe when I was one of the Big Girls." My brain floods with fun memories of local am-dram productions of *My Fair Lady*, *Oklahoma*, and the annual pantomime where we both trod the boards as pupils of the local dancing school.

"Nice to see you again," she says.

"And you," I reply, nodding and pressing my fingers against my smiling lips.

"Here." Nessa passes me a glass of wine. "Sit." She points to the empty chair around the kitchen table, before clearing her throat. "There's a reason I've asked you all here today, girls. I've something to tell you all."

"Oh, God," Becca groans. "You've not dumped Anth have you? You guys are the poster couple for *relationship goals*. If you two fuck it up, then there's no hope for the rest of us."

"Quite the opposite actually, Becks." Nessa raps her fingernails against the side of her glass of Lambrusco. "I'm surprised you haven't noticed."

"Oh my good God... Nessa!" I grab her left hand, inspecting the ring on her fourth finger. A single square diamond mounted on impractically high shoulders. "That must be at least a full carat. And wow, what a stone. That's got some serious fire."

She takes her hand back and admires her engagement ring. As if seeing it with new eyes.

"Maybe. But I wouldn't know, or care."

"It's lovely," Julie says sighing, her hand over her chest. "Congratulations."

"Yeah, your boy done good, Ness. Come on. Tell us all the deets," Becca adds.

"It was all fairly low-key. We had a run up to Bamburgh last weekend."

Nessa refers to the seaside village on the Northumberland coast.

"We went for a nice walk along the beach, before we circled back through the dunes below the castle."

We all lean forward, eyes wide, hanging on her every word as she retells the story.

"I'd stopped to look at the view out towards The Farne Islands, and when I turned around, there he was — down on one knee. Right in front of the castle."

"Aww," we all chime in unison. "How romantic."

"He knows that beach is my happy place so it was really thoughtful."

"But what did he actually say?" Becca rushes her words.

"Gave some mumbled speech about how I complete him. How he never wants to be without me. That sort of thing. I don't remember exactly, only that it made me cry."

"And you said 'yes' immediately?" Julie asks.

Nessa pauses and her eyes flick upwards from one side to the other as she searches her memories for what actually happened. "I'm not sure I did, you know. I think it was more a frantic snot-filled nodding followed by a big hug."

"Well, massive congratulations to the both of you." I raise my glass. "Vanessa. My oldest friend. May the pair of you continue to make each other as happy as you've been since the moment you both met. Here's to one of us having found their Prince Charming."

Everyone follows my lead and raises their glass. I take a sip of my drink and the bitter liquid pools in my stomach, together with a renewed sense of loss. Two of my closest friends have achieved their *happy ever after* in the past few weeks and, as delighted as I am for Mel and Nessa, their engagements are yet another reminder that my life has careered off course. If I'd stayed with Chris would I be looking at a sparkly ring on my left hand sometime soon? Who knows?

Ding-Dong. The front doorbell interrupts my melancholy and brings me back to the present.

We all look at Nessa, expecting her to know who is at the door. She shrugs and goes to answer it.

Seconds later, four mildly drunk men, led by Anth, rush into the kitchen and my gut flips over.

He's here. I don't want him to be here. This was just meant to be 'us girls'.

"Stag-dooo!" One of Anth's friends throws his head back and howls like a wolf.

"I gather Anth has told you then?" Nessa laughs as the men flood into the kitchen, rooting through the fridge and pulling out cans of beer.

"Has he ever. Stag-dooo," the short stocky bloke hollers a second time.

"Oh behave," Becca says, smacking stocky bloke's stomach with the back of her hand. "Tor, have you met my Mark?"

Only a few inches taller than his girlfriend, what Mark lacks in height he makes up for in bulk. Clearly a gym bunny, judging by the size of his biceps peeking out from the bottom of his T-shirt, the thickness of the ropes of muscle in his neck, and the outline of his torso, he leans down and gives Becca a peck on the lips.

"Mark, this is Tor. Julie's cousin and an old school friend of Nessa's." Becca introduces me.

"Nice to meet you." Mark grabs me by my waist and plants an unexpected kiss on my cheek. His breath tinged with the sour smell of beer. "Has anyone ever told you two you look like sisters?"

"Yes Mark. You're not the first." Julie laughs. Her oval face and piercing eyes are framed by the same long blonde locks as my own, except she has bright blue eyes, whereas mine are vivid green. "I see you've been enjoying yourself this afternoon," she adds.

"Stag-dooo," he howls a third time. Earning him another gentle slap from Becca.

"But why are you lot all here?" Nessa stands with her hands on her hips. "You said you wanted to watch the match in the pub." Nessa eyeballs Anth.

"Yeah well, once I shared our news, the guys decided they wanted to come and congratulate — I mean annoy — you all as well," Anth teases, landing a light kiss on her lips. "You don't mind, do you?"

"Well, you're all here now," Nessa says, resigned. "Tor, you've met everyone else, haven't you?"

"Yes I think so." I give a tentative wave to the two guys loitering in the opposite corner of the kitchen. The same two guys who joined our group the other night in The Quilted Camel.

The goth, who I was told afterwards goes by the nickname of Clarky, is wearing more or less the exact same outfit as when I first met him on the quayside. Drainpipe black jeans, winkle-picker shoes, a studded belt, and his long hair tied back in a ponytail.

Standing beside him, two bottles of beer in hand, is Craig, wearing the same black trousers and James Dean tie he had on the night we met, only this time instead of a green shirt, he's wearing a blue Ted Baker one.

Craig catches my eye and mouths, '*You good?*'

I nod, feeling my cheeks blush red hot.

He winks at me before breaking eye contact and pulling Nessa into a hug. "Congratulations Ness. You two thought about a date yet?"

"God, no," Nessa replies. "We're saving our pennies for a new bathroom first."

"And let's not forget it took me five years to actually propose." Anth gives Nessa an affectionate kiss on the cheek. "We'll do it when we're ready."

"So she's not up the duff then?" Mark blurts, earning him a hard stare from Becca.

"Oi, behave."

"No Mark. No plans for any bairns yet," Nessa replies.

"Alright-y then," Anth says, looking at his watch and changing both the subject and the energy in the room. "It's almost time for kick-off."

Everyone tops up their drinks and we all pile into Nessa and Anth's front room. The girls sit on the sofas while the boys sit on the carpet and lean back against any available surface. The room falls silent as the game begins and we watch Liverpool take on Manchester United in the FA Cup Final. Although a major rival to Newcastle United, all the boys are rooting for Liverpool. Hoping they can stop Man U from '*taking the double.*' Manchester United having stolen the Premier League title from Newcastle only last weekend. A bitter loss that all the boys are still pissed about.

As our little crowd cheer and boo every touch, out of my peripheral vision I track Craig's every move. My energy drawn to his like a magnet. I study his relaxed demeanour. His easy camaraderie amongst his friends. The incessant teasing. The deep timbre of his laugh. The way his eyes lift at the corners when he laughs.

Every time he turns to look at me, I quickly dip my head and avoid his gaze. On one hand it's nice to be noticed, but on the other, I feel as if my skin is inside out.

At half-time, I disappear to the toilet, and when I come back out, he's standing against the wall opposite, clutching two bottles of Smirnoff Ice.

I look down at the alcopops in his hands.

"It's all I could find." He shrugs, his lips pulling into a wide smile.

Oh, those damn dimples.

"Fancy joining me outside? I'm not really interested in the half-time analysis."

"Ok-ay." I thrust my hands into my jean's pockets and roll my shoulders forward.

"Come on." He jerks his head in the direction of Anth and Nessa's back door and I follow him out into the garden.

Chapter 6

*C*raig leads me across to a picnic table in the corner of the garden. Using the top of the wall he prises the caps off the two bottles, before passing one to me.

"It would be better if it were champagne, but still… cheers." He chinks his bottle against the side of mine.

"Cheers," I repeat before allowing the cool lemony vodka mix to slide over my tongue. It's surprisingly refreshing.

"Better than champers." I smile and watch as his eyes crinkle in the corners.

"I don't believe that for a second. You strike me as the kind of girl who appreciates the finer things in life."

"What makes you say that?"

He shrugs. "Call it a hunch."

"So, if I'm such a snob—"

"Whoah. I didn't say you were a snob," he cuts me off. "I said you strike me as someone who appreciates the finer things in life. And given the choice, would much prefer a bottle of Moët than this cheap shit."

"Eurgh…" I shiver. "Can't stand the stuff. Moët, that is. Far too bitter. No, if it's going to be champagne then it has to be Verve Clique, or better still, Bollinger."

Realising I've just confirmed his exact summation of me, we both dip our heads and giggle.

"Okay. Point taken," I confirm.

"See," he says. "No one I know could tell the difference between a bottle of Lambrusco and any brand of champagne, never mind tell the different champagnes apart. You're not like anyone else I've met before."

I momentarily break eye contact, distracting myself with another sip of my drink.

"Is that the only tie you own?" I point at the black and white image of James Dean that hangs down the front of his shirt.

"No, but it's my favourite." He runs it through his fingers, before it falls back into place.

There's another slight pause in the conversation, before he continues. "Can I let you into a little secret?"

I meet his gaze.

"I was the one who persuaded the lads to come back here and watch the match. I was hoping you might be here."

"So if you knew you wanted to see me again, why didn't you ask for my number? Either the night we met, or from Anth and Nessa?"

"Would you have given it to me?"

I shrug. "You'll never know. You never asked."

"Maybe I thought you'd judge me."

"Judge you?"

"Think I was some horny guy on the drink, hoping to score."

"Are you? A horny guy who goes out drinking, hoping to score?" I tilt my head at the question.

He fits the profile. Good-looking. Confident swagger. Cooler than an iceberg. The definitive lad about town.

"Have I ever had a one-night stand?" he continues. "I'd be lying if I said 'never', but chasing bimbos doesn't interest me."

"What does interest you then?"

"Sharing cheap alcopops with beautiful *and* interesting women. Especially those who know how to kiss, and who say 'yes' when I ask them out." He smirks.

His eyes hooded, he looks at me across the top of his bottle and my insides turn to jelly. I blink in quick succession, attempting and failing to shake off the memory of our kiss.

"Or maybe you didn't ask for my number because you're full of shit and were secretly hoping that after sucking face you'd be saved the embarrassment of ever seeing me again."

"Spunky. I like that," he says, not missing a beat. "But if that were the case, then why would I have persuaded everyone to come here this afternoon?"

I laugh nervously but feel my shoulders drop a smidgeon. His persistence, despite my initial brush-offs, appeases my initial fear that he's more interested in chasing tail than actually building a connection with someone, or more specifically… with me.

"Even if you hadn't been here today, I wasn't worried. I knew I'd see you again. It was just a matter of time. Especially after *that* kiss."

"Do you have lots of girls on standby then? Waiting to see which ones you happen to bump into again?"

"Something like that," he teases, taking another sip of his drink.

Oh, those bloody dimples.

"You're very confident, aren't you?" I tilt my head again. "Some might say cocky?"

He laughs. "Maybe. But I'm more interested in knowing more about you." He presses his lips together and slowly shakes his head. "I haven't even begun to scratch the surface with you have I, Tori Turnbull?"

Tori?

For all my nicknames — Vicky, Goose, Tor — no one has ever called me Tor-*i*. Until now.

I'm not sure if it's an honest mistake or whether he's purposefully given me a personal moniker that he can claim as his and his alone. Either way I don't correct him and instead allow the new nickname to settle in my gut.

"Tell me something about yourself. Something I don't already know," he asks.

"How can I do that when I don't know what you've been told?"

"Okay, so let's play a game. You ask me what I think I know, and if I get it right, you take a drink. And if I get it wrong, I take a drink. And if you don't want to answer… you take a drink."

"Alcopop drinking games — classy." I snigger. "Okay then. Where do I live?"

"Easy-peasy. Here. In Derwentside." He turns his palm upwards.

"Oh no, I'm not accepting that. Too vague. Take a drink." I point to his bottle.

He takes a sip.

"I've been told you've not long moved back to the area after being abroad and are currently staying at your parents'. I believe your plan is to move into Julie's once you're back on your feet."

"Wow, the grapevine has been busy."

"Yes they have and that's one for me." He points to my bottle and waits until I've placed my Smirnoff Ice back onto the table, then continues, "Okay, your turn. Ask me something you don't already know about me?"

I rest my chin on my steepled fingers. What do I want to know? Everything. I know nothing about Mr James Dean, except the gooey feeling inside my guts when he looks at me like that.

"If I did, I think I'd be drunk very quickly. But then, maybe that's your intention."

He throws his head back and laughs. "I'm really boring, honestly. Born and raised by two loving parents, who were childhood sweethearts and are as much in love today as the day they first met. I went to school locally. Don't have a qualification to my name. Die-hard *Toon* fan. And when I'm not trying to impress a really beautiful girl with this shit," he holds up his bottle, "I normally drink Newcastle Brown, or a decent pint of lager."

My cheeks glow red hot and I take an urgent sip of my drink to give my face a chance to cool down. "Well I'll give you a tip for next time," I say eventually, once I've regained my composure. "If it's not champagne, a decent bottle of Pinot Grigio will do just fine. Or if it's hard liquor, then a vodka and Diet Coke is my poison of choice."

"Duly noted. So, there's going to be a next time is there?"

"Maybe."

"So what else do you want to know? What have the gossipmongers not told you? And divn't tell me you girls haven't been yacking."

"Sorry to disappoint you... but you've not been top of my conversation agenda."

Which is not strictly true. In the taxi home after our night out, and after Mel had had to peel my lips off his, Nessa told me he was a director at the software company where Anth works. And in fact, it was on Craig's recommendation that Anth was able to get a job there.

"Oh wait. Nessa did say something about you being a corporate big shot." It's my turn to tease him now.

He shrugs. "A director — yes. Corporate big shot — I wouldn't even know what that means. I've only ever had one job. I left school and went to work for this local GP who had the idea of writing a piece of software to automate his appointment system. I've always been interested in coding. Taught myself in the evenings when I should have been doing my other schoolwork. Anyway, I was chuffed to find a job doing the only thing I was good at. It was only a two-doctor practice, so really small. Me and this other guy wrote and developed the software. It was only ever meant to be a side hustle for the doc, but he marketed it to a few other practices and it kinda took off. When he retired, he sold the IP to a bigger software company, and me along with it. Roll forward another few years and the same thing happened. Each time I gained a promotion and more responsibility. It's not long happened again. New owners, another promotion, more responsibility. Somehow I've ended up being a director of the biggest medical software company in the U.K. But I don't feel like I can take credit for it. It's not like I planned it or anything. It all just sorta happened."

"Then you must be good at what you do. Nobody is given rewards without paying their dues."

"Partly true. Some people are born rich. Arrogant bastards."

I take a hasty sip of my drink.

"And do you have family? Brothers or sisters?" I ask, wanting to move away from the topic of being born with privilege.

He stiffens. "It's complicated."

"How so?"

"It just is." He shrugs, dismissing me with his tone.

"Okay then, but that's not a proper answer." I point at his bottle. "Take a drink."

He picks it up and shakes it, but it's empty. "Wait here. I'll see what else I can rustle up. Anth must have some half-decent stuff stashed somewhere."

"Shouldn't we be going back in anyhow? I'm sure the second half must have kicked off by now."

"Only if you want to, but I'd rather stay out here and carry on with our game."

"What? You'd rather be out here than watching the second half of the FA Cup Final?"

"Yes I would." He smiles. "Mind you, it'd be a different story if it were Newcastle on the pitch."

"Of course. Go." I flick him away with my hand. "Bring more booze."

He disappears through the back door and Nessa appears at her kitchen window. She gives me the okay sign, her eyebrows raised in question, and I reply with a flat hand which I wobble from side to side, as if signalling *maybe*, but then seeing the worried look on her face, I smile and give her a thumbs up. She wipes fake sweat off her brow and disappears again.

Craig returns with a bottle of Sauvignon Blanc and two wine glasses. "Look what I found hidden in the back of the fridge. It's from New Zealand, so should be good."

I suck in a deep breath and momentarily close my eyes, reliving my trip through the beautiful Marlborough wine growing region. Why is the universe throwing me reminders of the memories I want to forget?

Do you not want me to move on?

"You okay?" he asks, passing me a glass of Marlborough.

"Absolutely. But you lost the last round and therefore owe me a drink." I point at his glass.

He obliges, before asking, "So how come you're not working? You don't strike me as the lazy kind, and you're clearly intelligent. I would have thought you'd have walked straight into a job the minute you moved back here."

"Well, before—" I pause, not wanting to reveal too much. Any talk about my life *before* risks opening up a conversation I'm not yet ready to share. "Before I went abroad I worked in Business Travel. But at the moment, I'm applying for anything and everything — currently unsuccessfully. I have an impressive pile of rejection letters that only seems to grow by the day. I've nicknamed it the *never-ending pot of porridge*. I'm a slave to the *Chronicle*'s Thursday evening job pages. But you know what the economy is like up here. I can't even get an interview, just lots of *'we'll keep your details on file and let you know'* responses. However, I've just started volunteering in the Oxfam shop in town. So far so good. It gets me out of bed in the morning." He tops up my drink, as I continue. "It's funny. I know with my C.V. and experience, I could walk into any Business Travel job down south — but I don't want to move back to London."

He raises his eyebrows in question.

"Nope, not answering that one."

"Then you know the penalty," he teases.

"Gladly." I sip my wine, which tastes polished and smooth after the cheap, sharp lemony vodka mix. "I fancy a change of career though. I'm ready for a new start. Perhaps something in marketing. Office Management. Sales. Something like that. I've got transferable skills but until I catch a break I'll be helping out at Oxfam and living at home with my parents."

"Maybe I could help? Pass your C.V. onto some people I know."

He leans forward and touches my fingers and the instant our flesh touches, a spark of electricity shoots up my arm. Both of us take a sharp intake of breath and for a nanosecond, the world stops turning.

After an almost imperceptible pause, I pull my hand away.

"Thanks, I appreciate the offer… but it's not going to help you get into my knickers." I close my eyes and throw my head backwards. "Eurgh! I have no idea why I just said that. Ignore me."

I do not want anyone inside my knickers right now. Or do I?

"Not that I don't think you're fanciable or anything." I drop my flushed cheeks into my palms. "Oh God, I'm making it worse. Forget I said anything."

When I open my eyes again, he's come around to my side of the picnic table, straddling the bench like a cowboy in a saddle. The scent of his musky aftershave invades my nostrils as he leans forward on both hands.

"Well, first off, I've never said I want to get inside your knickers, so that's a massive assumption." His mouth pulls into a wide smile; he's clearly enjoying this. Revelling in my faux pas. "Especially when I haven't even asked you out — *yet.*"

"I just thought, after our drunken snog the other night, and now this…" I circle my wrist in front of me. "Whatever *this* is. I'm a bit out of practice."

"I wasn't drunk," he says solemnly. "The other night. At The Quilted Camel. I wasn't drunk. Were you?"

I shrug.

"Can you remember what it felt like… when we kissed?"

I can tell he wants to touch me again, but instead he holds my gaze. His eyes are so dark. Two powerful onyxes that penetrate my soul, making my tongue thicken and stick to the roof of my mouth. I don't say anything and instead nod slowly.

We stay very still. Our breath falling into sync.

"Because I remember every moment of it," he whispers.

He leans forward and flicks a tendril of hair behind by shoulder, before cupping my jaw with his palm. Lifting his other hand he caresses my face and brushes my cheekbones back and forth with his thumbs. I remember now: this is how he held me when he first kissed me in the darkened corner of The Quilted Camel. Instinctively I tilt my head and soften into his right palm.

"Who are you?" he whispers. "You're like some mythical creature that's dropped out of the sky and landed slap bang in my lap."

I place my hands over the top of his, my gaze dropping to his lips. His very kissable, pillowy lips. I swallow hard and watch his Adam's apple bob in his throat as he does the same, then unconsciously rolls his lips inwards and slides the tip of his tongue from one side to the other.

"When did it get dark?" I breathe.

The temperature has dropped — but I don't feel cold. My insides are on fire. I fear if he kisses me again, I may internally combust.

Very slowly, he edges his face towards mine. Closer. Closer still. Until I can no longer breathe. Our lips are only millimetres apart now and I feel the gentle warmth of his out breath on my face. The sound of my beating heart thumps inside my ears. I close my eyes, anticipating the feel of his lips on mine, but instead he dips my head and leaves a soft imprint in the middle of my forehead.

"You're absolutely mesmerising, Tori. I've never met anyone like you. I hardly know you, but I know enough to know that this could be something really special. Please may I have your number? Not that I want to get inside your knickers or anything — at least not yet anyway. Maybe we should have a date first."

I hear the humour in his voice but, puce with embarrassment, I keep my eyes closed. "Okay," I whisper. "But right now, there's something I want you to do for me."

"Anything," he whispers back, his breath warm on my face.

"Please leave."

I feel him pull back slightly.

"When I open my eyes… " I say, keeping them firmly shut, "… you won't be here and you're going to save me the embarrassment of looking into your face when I know I've just made a complete and utter tit of myself."

He laughs and gently kisses the tip of my nose. "Okay. If that's what you want."

"It is. You can get my number off Nessa." I keep my eyes squeezed tightly closed. "I'm going to count to three and when I open my eyes, you're not going to be anywhere near here. Is that okay?"

"Absolutely." I hear the playfulness in his voice.

"One," I say quietly as he kisses my closed right eyelid.

"Two." This time he kisses the left, and the spark between my legs intensifies. I suck in an urgent breath and swallow hard.

His hands, still cupped around my face, hold me still while he waits for me to complete the countdown.

Meanwhile, I'm wrangling with a turmoil of thoughts that whizz through my mind.

What the hell am I doing? Maybe I should tell him that I don't think this is such a great idea. I'm not ready for this.

But what more do you want? You're as ready as you'll ever be. Say three, Vicky. Just say it.

But when I do — he'll be gone.

Only temporarily.

Then what?

Wait and see.

I draw in a deep breath and feel my lungs expand with air. Eventually, my voice hardly audible, I whisper, "Three."

I feel his lips connect briefly with mine, in the lightest of touches — then he is gone.

Chapter 7

*T*he next morning my mother answers the doorbell, before shouting up the stairs, "Vic-tor-ia. It's for *yo-ou*."

As I pass her in the hallway, she smirks. "Someone's popular?"

Standing on the doorstep is a delivery driver holding the most beautiful bouquet of Winchester Cathedral cream roses, together with a gift box of Bollinger champagne.

Taking the bouquet and champagne from the courier, I open the card.

> *Tori,*
>
> *I can't wait another day before seeing your beautiful face again.*
>
> *Let me take you out for Sunday Lunch.*
>
> *I'll pick you up at 12.30*
>
> *Craig x*
>
> *P.S. Still not interested in what's inside your knickers.*

Angling the card inwards to hide the blush that creeps up my neck, I rush upstairs shouting down to Mam, "I'm going out. Don't worry about saving any dinner for me. I'll eat while I'm out."

"Nice wheels," I say, trailing my fingers over the black quartz paintwork of Craig's Audi A4 when he pulls onto our drive at 12.30 p.m. sharp.

I managed to sneak out of the house without my mother requiring a formal introduction, but I see her peeking out from her bedroom window. Judging by the smile on her face, she approves.

"Thanks," he says, holding the passenger door open for me. "I only picked her up on Friday. Another perk from my recent promotion."

"If she's new, you'll not have had a chance to break her in yet."

"I haven't. Let's see how many miles we can get on the clock today, shall we?"

"Is this the 1.8 Turbocharged Petrol Engine, or the Diesel Quattro?" I ask once Craig's settled himself into the driver's seat.

He laughs, revving the engine. "How do you even know the difference?"

"What can I say — I like cars. Even if I don't have my own wheels at the moment, this one here is a real beauty." I curl my palms over the edge of the cool black leather seat underneath my bum. "I noticed your alloys — gorgeous."

Craig changes gear and glances at me out of his peripheral vision. "Wow. No disrespect, but most girls lose interest if it's not in their favourite colour."

"None taken. I happen to have spent a lot of time around someone who dealt in luxury cars. I listened and learned. Plus owning a car has always been important to me. Driving reminds me of my grandfather."

Craig glances in my direction.

"He taught me to drive."

"Ah." He raises his chin in understanding.

"I became a real enthusiast once I'd had the chance to drive some proper fast cars. For the record, Audis are my favourite. Beautiful tight steering. Especially the Sports models like this beaut here. Much nicer than Beemers or Mercs. In my opinion, only Porsches can top this for driving experience."

"Well, well, well. I never realised my girl is a petrolhead."

I jerk my head back. "My girl?"

"Are you anyone else's right now?"

"No."

"Well then. Unless you object."

I dip my head as my insides do an involuntary flip.

"So let me get this straight. You're claiming me as *your girl* even though this is our first date?"

"Yes... unless you count sneaking off into the garden yesterday as a first date."

"Nope. I was at Nessa's already. You just hijacked me."

He leans over and squeezes my knee. "So if this is our first *official* date, we'd best get the day started, hadn't we? We've still got a lot of firsts to tick off."

"Let's just see how today goes, shall we?" I say, picking up his hand and plonking it unceremoniously back on his own thigh, both of us smiling.

The road ahead opens up and, indicating and pulling out, he easily cruises past the car in front of us. I slide deeper into the seat, allowing my head to loll backwards, close my eyes, and smile.

෨

Ten hours later I'm now behind the wheel, driving us home after the most marvellous unplanned day that rolled on and on.

First he took me for Sunday lunch, as promised. Choosing a country pub buried deep in the green hills of the Derwent Valley, far away from prying eyes or local gossipmongers. After lunch he led me on a leisurely stroll along the River Derwent — a tributary that flows into the Tyne ten miles east from here. We lazed in a meadow of bluebells, chatting under the shade of an old oak tree, and by early evening neither of us were ready for the day to be over, so we headed back into Newcastle for pizza, followed by a spontaneous trip to the cinema where we watched the new release of *Romeo + Juliet*, staring Leonardo DiCaprio and Claire Danes.

Once the lights went down and the film started, Craig threw his arm over my shoulders and pulled me into him. Being wrapped in his embrace felt easy and natural and what I've been needing. A feeling of togetherness. Two halves of a jigsaw puzzle.

When the film reached its climactic ending and Juliet woke to find Romeo dead beside her, before then killing herself, Craig quietly passed me a hankie so I could dab the silent tears that had rolled down my cheeks.

Once back in the car park, he'd held out his keys. '*Wanna drive us yem?*' he'd asked, using the Geordie slang for 'home'.

'What about the insurance?'

'I'm a director of the company. Anyone over the age of twenty-one can drive any of the company cars with my permission.'

I didn't have to think twice.

'Toss 'em here. Let me show you what this baby's really capable of.'

A few miles from home, Craig leans across the central console and lays his hand on my thigh as I drive hard into a sharp corner. Outside, a kaleidoscope of light from a small copse of barns, now converted and sold as luxury homes, whizzes past in the pitch black, their brittle carboniferous limestone walls shining slick and wet.

"Careful Tori. We don't want to have an accident."

I tighten my hands more firmly around the leather steering wheel.

"Don't worry. Her grip is amazing."

I simultaneously slam my left foot to the floor whilst ramming the gearbox down into third. The engine screams like a horse wanting to gallop but being held back by a too-tight martingale. Pulling out, I floor the accelerator, overtaking a much slower car in front.

"So, we're not going for the 'let's run her in for the first few thousand miles' philosophy I take it," he says light-heartedly, but his voice is laced with concern.

"Sorry. I'll slow down now. I just wanted to get past *Driving Miss Daisy* back there." I change back up the gears and the engine returns to a more sedate purr.

Turning briefly to look at him, I ask, "What did you think of the film?"

"Do you want my honest opinion, or the polite version?"

"The truth — always."

"If I'm honest, it was a bit weird."

"Hmm. I promise we can go and see the remake of *Mission Impossible* next time. Tom Cruise is supposed to be amazing in it. That's assuming there's going to be a next time…"

"Oh, there will be. I guarantee it."

He looks at me and out of my peripheral vision I catch a glimpse of his smile. A warm gooey feeling settles in my stomach. Today is the most relaxed and comfortable I've felt in months.

"I suppose this evening has reconfirmed one thing for me," he continues.

"What's that?"

"I'm not a fan of Shakespeare. Hated it in school, hate it still. Definitely an acquired taste."

I throw my head back and laugh.

"I appreciate it was an attempt to make Romeo and Juliet *cool*," he uses air-quotes to emphasise the word cool, "but to my uneducated brain it was still Shakespeare. Ninety minutes of gobbledygook. If I hadn't of been with you, I would have walked out after five minutes."

"Well I loved it, and I very much appreciate you suffering it for me." It's my turn to reach across the central console and squeeze his thigh.

A comfortable silence falls between us as my mind drifts back to the film. Then from out of nowhere, a valve releases behind my eyes and heavy wet tears leak out. Craig notices immediately.

"Hey, hey. What's up?"

"I was just thinking about the movie. It's so compelling. *'I never saw true beauty before tonight'*. You've got to wonder who broke Shakespeare's heart for him to have written such powerful prose."

"It really got to you, didn't it?"

"Yes. Every time. It's such a tragic tale. But the artistry was incredible. Did you notice how most of the classic scenes involved water? Their first meeting, looking at each other through the aquarium. Or the balcony scene — how they ended up in the pool together. That all makes sense to me. Even without Shakespeare's words you could tell how much they loved each other. The intensity of their desire — enveloped in water."

He turns his head, listening.

"Most people think of fire when they think of passion, but I think water is equally as powerful. Well, actually the duality of water and fire together. The yin and the yang. Just thinking about the swell of the ocean, or the intensity of a blazing fire makes my heart beat faster."

Instinctively my hand finds my throat. My own dormant desires wanting to break free. But it's been so long since I've connected with my own inner pool of passion, I've forgotten how to access that part of me. I'm not sure I can on my own.

I glance briefly at him, and see his eyes are stretched wide open. He twists in his seat and reaches across the gearstick, touching my leg with both of his hands. Needing to strengthen the connection between us.

"Sorry, just ignore me. I'm rambling. What can I say – I'm a hopeless romantic."

"No. Keep talking. It's interesting. I don't think I've ever had a conversation like this with anyone — ever." His lips pull into a wide grin, the outline of his dimples silhouetted against the passing lights outside.

"The purpose of art is to stimulate the senses. I don't know if that was the intention of that particular presentation of Shakespeare's classic, but that's how I interpreted it." I pause. "Did you catch the director's name?"

"I remember it was a weird one. Buzz somebody or other."

"Baz Luhrmann?"

"Yes, I think that was it."

"That makes sense. He's Australian. Started out in musical theatre. I wondered if whoever was behind it came from a theatre background. It had that kind of vibe."

"If you say so."

"I just love the story — full stop. I love every interpretation that's ever been done. *West Side Story* is my all-time favourite musical and Romeo and Juliet is my favourite ballet. The music is so powerful."

I hum the first few lines from the infamous *Dance of the Knights* from Prokofiev's ballet score, tapping my fingers on the steering wheel in time to the pulse.

"Hmm, whereas when I hear that, I think of Sunderland coming out onto the pitch at Roker Park."

"Oh yeah! I'd forgotten about that." I chortle. It's an unfortunate coincidence that one of my most favourite pieces of ballet music is also the tune played at every Sunderland home game. In this region, football is most people's religion, and you're either red and white or black and white, depending on which local team you support. "I have a completely different image in my head," I continue. "I can almost do the choreography from memory. In the original Russian version of the ballet, that scene is actually called *The Cushion Dance*, as the noblemen drop to their knees on cushions as part of the courtship of their ladies. When it was introduced in England it was re-choreographed by Sir Kenneth MacMillan, and the cushions were left out. I actually prefer the original Russian choreography, but you have to catch The Kirov or The Bolshoi when they do an occasional short run in London to see it live. Having said that, I was lucky enough to see the Royal Ballet version at The Royal Opera House a couple of years ago. It was spellbinding."

My mind flits back to the memory of that night. My boss at the time, Edwin Astor, having invited me to join him and two other business associates at Covent Garden.

"Remind me to be on your team at the next pub quiz," Craig quips.

"Sorry, ignore me. I know nowt about nowt really. It's just my dancing background; when it comes to the Arts, particularly the performing arts, I can get quite passionate."

"That and cars?" he jokes.

"That and cars."

"Whereas, by contrast, the only live stage show I've ever seen in my artistically sheltered life, is *Rocky Horror*."

"A cult classic," I chuckle. "And one of the few stage shows I've never actually seen. Never had the guts to go. I hear it's an absolute riot and everyone gets dressed up."

"I'll take you," he says easily. "It comes on tour every couple of years. But be warned, nothing can prepare you for the sight of Clarky in a basque and suspenders."

"I can only imagine," I laugh.

A comfortable silence falls between us again, the only sound the rhythmic squeak of the windscreen wipers.

"I thought I had a love like that once," I say, my gaze fixed firmly on the road ahead.

"What? Like *Rocky Horror*?"

"No," I breathe, my emotions bubbling up once again. "An all-consuming, passionate love. A love like Romeo and Juliet. A love that was impossible to deny. A love that should have transcended all barriers and overcome all obstacles." I reach down and change gear. "But it turned out not to be."

"What happened?" he asks, softly.

"I left. I had to — it was that… or die. Or so it felt. I don't mean to sound overly dramatic, but it was almost too powerful. I ended up lost. Like falling into a bottomless well." Tears sting at the corner of my eyes and I wipe them away with the pads of my fingers.

"Were you still in love with him when you left?"

I nod silently.

"Then it must have taken superhuman strength to leave."

"It did."

"And now? Are you still in love with him now?"

I suck in a deep breath and slowly shake my head. "No, not now. Even if I could, I don't want to go back."

"Any regrets?"

"Some," I say softly. "But I can't change any of that now. And I learnt a lot about myself in that relationship."

He sits quietly, listening.

"It has been hard and there were days when I questioned my decision to leave. But I realise now I was grieving. Not for him, per se, but the fantasy of him. For what I wanted our relationship to be, when in reality things were *very* different. It was over long before I actually left."

I turn and give him a small smile.

"I can't say I've ever experienced anything as powerful as you've just described, but I hope to one day. Without the heartbreak obviously."

I breathe out a short puff of air through my nose in agreement.

"Thank you for today, Craig. It's been amazing. More than I think you'll ever know."

I can't remember the last time I felt so comfortable in a man's company.

"I get the feeling it's been a long time since anyone made you a priority."

I turn briefly to look at him and nod silently.

He lifts my free hand away from the gearstick and kisses the back of my fingers.

"This is not something I usually talk about Tori ... but I feel there's something about me, about my family, that you should know—"

But before Craig has a chance to finish his sentence the world slips into slow motion, like we've slipped into Romeo and Juliet's swimming pool and we're underwater. Everything outside speeds up and we're trapped in the middle of a spinning tornado as I lose control of the car.

Chapter 8

*W*e're out of control and unable to stop, the car having aquaplaned across a deep puddle and lost its grip.

My hand smacks against Craig's chest as my body lurches left, pulled off-centre by the centrifugal force. I try desperately to control the skid, holding onto the steering wheel with my other hand, but the back-end of the car has jackknifed and we're spinning like a toy that's flown off a Scalextric track. Spinning, spinning. Powerless to stop.

Craig has one hand braced on the dashboard, the other on the roof. "Take your feet off the pedals," he shouts. My panicked braking only intensifying the skid.

The car is now travelling at speed backwards, across the oncoming lane, and we're fast sliding sideways towards a very solid stone wall on the other side of the road. I squeeze my eyes shut, anticipating the impending crunch. But as violently as the skid started, we come to an abrupt stop millimetres from the hard stone wall.

I'm not sure what feels longer, the out-of-control skid, or the moments sitting in the dark afterwards. The only sound inside the vehicle the urgent, shallow in-out of our breathing, punctuated by the rhythmic squeak of the wipers and the soft pitter-patter of rain that continues to fall onto the windscreen.

Rivulets of water snake their way down the side windows and the car engine purrs quietly under the bonnet; like a lion who has just roared loudly, but is once again sitting quietly waiting to pounce.

Leaning forward, I rest my forehead on the steering wheel and let out a long exhale.

Craig switches on the hazard warning lights. The flash of the red triangle in the middle of the dashboard increasing the tension inside the car.

"I'm so sorry, Craig. You warned me to slow down and I didn't listen."

"You're right, I did, but it's okay. We got lucky. But you need to move, Tori. And quickly. We're sitting ducks here."

A glare of headlights appears in the rear-view mirror, followed by a hideous screech of tyres as a car rounds the corner behind us and slams on its brakes. We brace ourselves, expecting to be rear-ended, but the car swerves around us, thankfully into an empty oncoming lane — missing us by millimetres. Blaring its horn in protest, it disappears into the darkness as quickly as it appeared.

"Now, Tori. Drop us into gear and go." Craig's voice is deep and authoritative.

"I'm not sure I can," I whimper

"Look at me. L-o-o-k at me," he enunciates.

I do as he says.

"Breathe with me. In ... and out. In ... and out. That's it. You can do this."

"I can't," I whisper. "I'm so sorry, Craig. But I can't."

"You can. I know you can."

When I don't move, he commands, "Come on. We don't have time for a debate. The next car that comes round that corner is going to smash right into the back of us. You need to move ... NOW!"

"Can't you take over?" I snivel.

"I will. But not here. It's too dangerous."

Still frozen, he reaches for my face. Holding me safe in his palms. "It's going to be okay. I promise. Keep breathing. Left foot on the clutch. Left hand on the gearstick. You can do this."

As if on autopilot I press my foot to the floor and drop the car into gear. Craig turns and looks behind us.

"All clear. Just pull away gently. You're doing great."

I gingerly accelerate, but my foot slips and the car lurches, and stalls.

Tears sting in my eyes, and my throat burns from withheld sobs. "I can't do this, Craig. I can't. Please take over."

He yanks the handbrake on. "I can't. Not yet. You can do this. You're my girl now, remember. And my girl is fearless and can do anything she wants. One step at a time. Take another deep breath. Turn the ignition, and let's go."

I return the gearbox to neutral, and restart the engine.

"All clear," he says having checked behind us again. "Go now. Take your time."

This time I change up the gears from first, to second, then third without any problems. I shiver, regaining my composure, and swipe my hand underneath my nose, wiping away the tears and snot that have collected there.

"Over there." Craig points at the Parking Zone sign that appears out of the darkness. "Pull in and I'll take over."

I indicate and half a mile down the road, pull into the layby.

Even before we've stopped, Craig is out of the car and running around to my side. Slowly I unbuckle my seat belt and slump over the steering wheel again. Craig opens the driver's door and pulls me up into his embrace. The bulk of his muscles almost squeezing the breath out of me.

I release the sob that was lodged in the back of my throat as I cling to him. The rain soaks through our clothes, and the pitch-black countryside around us smells damp and earthy.

"I'm so sorry," I say over and over. "I'm such a bloody idiot. I could have killed us."

"Hey, hey. It's okay. We're both okay, aren't we?"

"But I was so stupid. I shouldn't have been trying to impress you. I should have been more careful."

"I know. But you're safe now. I've got you."

He holds my head between his hands and tilts my face towards his. I blink hard against the falling rain.

"Tori Turnbull you are the craziest, smartest, most bullheaded, amazing woman I've ever met. Never think you have to do anything to impress me, okay? Just be you."

Before I've had a chance to absorb his words he leans down and presses his lips onto mine. He tastes of popcorn and Coke, and his aftershave smells of spice and woodsmoke, and the minute our lips connect a thunderbolt of lust lights the spark between my legs, causing my knees to give way. I inhale sharply as his arms envelop me tighter still as he deepens his kiss. His tongue parts my lips and licks its way into my mouth. Instinctively I soften into him, relinquishing myself to his strength and desire. Reaching up I nestle my arms around his neck, feathering my fingers into his hair, and dive head first into his kiss.

The primal needs that had been lying dormant in my core surges through my body. That deep pool of water surrounded by the burning flames of my desire has risen up from the depths of my soul.

Craig slides a hand down over my bum and grabs a handful of flesh; I instinctively tilt my hips, allowing him to feel more. Willingly giving myself over to him. He releases a deep guttural groan as his own desire intensifies.

I don't know how long we stand kissing by the side of the road in the pouring rain, but my body doesn't register the cold. The water runs in rivulets down my neck, my back, and in-between my breasts. My drenched top clings to my body as Craig's shirt does the same, outlining every curve of his muscular torso. With my eyes closed, all I'm aware of, is the feeling of him all around me. The taste of him on my lips. The smell of him invading my nose. His hands on my body, his strength enveloping me.

Only moments ago I almost killed us, yet I've never felt more alive — or safe, and I don't want this feeling to end.

Eventually he pulls back from our kiss, holding my head in his hands, and smooths my hair away from my brow. "I'll drive us the rest of the way."

My shoulders drop and I release a sigh. Yes please. I'm done with having to be strong on my own all of the time. Please take over. Are you the one to stop my world from spinning out of control? Are you the one I'll be able to lean on when I need to?

He kisses the end of my nose. "Let's get you home, before you catch your death of cold."

He walks me around to the passenger side, opens the door, and I slide into the seat. Buckling myself back in. Once we're back on the road, he retunes the radio to Jazz FM and cranks up the heaters.

Only later do I remember he was about to tell me something about his family.

Part II

Chapter 9

CRAIG

*L*ush wheels," Mark comments as he climbs out of Craig's Audi when the pair arrive at The Red Lion a couple of Saturdays later. "Hear that?" Mark has one hand cupped around his ear as he slams the car door shut with the other. "That's the sound of German engineering, that is. No other sound like it in the world."

"Thanks mate. She drives like a dream." Craig presses his key fob and the headlights flash as the central locking *bleep-bloop*s.

"I can't ever imagine owning a motor like this." Mark hunkers down by the near-side wheel, running his hand along the paint-work, admiring the Audi's lines.

"Aww, but you love your van," Craig teases.

Being a sparky, Mark has the use of his company van. Useful when anyone needs furniture shifting, but it's hardly an executive saloon.

"You're definitely going up in the world, mate. Good on ya."

Mark has to stretch up as he swings his arm over Craig's shoulders, guiding the pair inside the pub. The barmaid, one hand wrapped around the beer tap, nods her acknowledgement as the pair walk inside. Ignoring the queue at the bar, the two friends find a quiet table underneath the dartboard in the back corner and turn their chairs around, sitting on them back-to-front and resting their arms over the backs.

"Thanks. Yeah, I never thought I'd own a car like that either. It's not the norm for people like us," Craig replies, even though his meeting this week with the new chairman of the board, Jack Walker, has made him think about his future career prospects at the company. If everyone else believes in him, maybe it's time he did as well. Who's to say he couldn't have anything he puts his mind to? The world is his oyster, or so Jack told him.

"True," Mark agrees.

Knowing their son had potential, Craig's parents drummed a solid work ethic into him from an early age. All they wanted was for their son to — as they described it — *get out*. And now they couldn't be prouder. A company director, a steady income, his own home, and now a flashy company car. If only he would complete the set and settle down with a nice bride, pump out a couple of bairns, then his mother would stop nagging him.

"Some days I have to remind myself where I started," Craig says. "It's easy to forget that you and I are the first in our families to work above ground."

"Yeah, except I still spend my days crawling around on my hands and knees rewiring people's kitchens, whereas you get to sit in your lofty white tower and count all your money."

"Something like that," Craig laughs.

The barmaid plonks two bottles of Newcastle Brown Ale down in front of them, having already added the cost to their ongoing tab. The special treatment they get when their local is busy an advantage of being regulars.

Craig lifts his bottle and takes a sip while Mark nods his thanks in the barmaid's direction. She smiles before turning her attention to the next impatient punter.

"So how's it going with the new bird?" Mark raises an eyebrow.

Craig shrugs. "Don't be getting ahead of yourself. It's early days."

"Oh, don't play cutesy with me. We all saw you sneak outside during the Cup Final. Then someone told me they'd seen you in The Derwent Walk Inn the day after. Seems you shared a nice cosy Sunday lunch together. Then Nessa told my Becca that you've been to the pictures — twice."

"Bloody hell. Can nobody do anything in private round here?"

"You know how it is. Small town syndrome," Mark laughs. "You were bound to get caught."

"So it seems."

"So what's the craic? Is it serious?"

"I haven't decided yet. Like you said, my life seems to be on the up 'n up at the moment. The last thing I need right now is a bird tying me down."

"Yeah, maybe. But you could do a lot worse than *that* bird on your arm. You know who she is, don't you?"

"I have a feeling you're about to tell me."

"Becca says she doesn't really know her that well because she's a bit younger than Tor, but you do realise she's related to the Fenwicks? Not your lot, the other ones. The ones *with* money."

"U-hum." Craig doesn't react, but that would explain her reaction in The Quilted Camel the night they met, when he told her his name. She told him her surname was Turnbull, so he didn't make the connection. In the few dates they've had, she's told him she's an only child, brought up by a single mother who re-married a few years ago, so at no point did he have any suspicion she could be related to *those* Fenwicks. His family had to scrimp and scrape, and go without for most of their lives. Whereas if what Mark says is true, she would have grown up with privilege, opportunity, and a cushion of wealth beneath her. That would also explain her refined tastes and knowledge of art and the like.

"And she's not bad to look at either," Mark adds. "You shagged her yet?"

Craig takes his time in answering. Slowly slipping his beer. He wipes his mouth with the back of his hand. "I'm not sure that's any of your business, Mark. But no, I haven't shagged her — *yet*."

Craig's mind wanders back to their last heavy petting session, in the car, after they'd been to the pictures during the week. Their second 'official' date. Things got pretty heated and he's certain if the setting had allowed they would have ended up in bed together ... but he's not sure if either of them are ready. He senses she's extremely fragile. Like a delicate bird whose wings are not quite healed and if they were to leap from the nest too soon, they'd fall and break. He's happy to wait.

He's always happy to wait.

Mark watches the micro emotions roll across Craig's features.

"Jeez, I've not seen you so besotted with a chick since Clare."

Craig's only other long-term girlfriend. An on-off three-year relationship which ended over twelve months ago.

"So do you think this *Tor* is sat on a big fat trust fund and is going to buy us all a yacht one day?" Mark laughs.

"Even if she is, who's to say you'll benefit?" Craig jests.

"Because you'll leave it all to me in your will. But her parents do live in a massive house and she did go to the same school as Nessa. Proper posh it was."

Mark's right. Although Craig's not been inside Vicky's parents' home, he has picked her up from there and it is intimidating. Double garage, large orangery running down one entire side of the building. Cherry trees a go-go in the garden, and aesthetically trained roses growing up the façade. What the hell is she going to think if he ever introduces her to his parents?

"Well the rest of the family are stinking rich," Mark continues. "More money than you or I could ever dream of having – rich. Play your cards right mate with her and you'll be set for life." Mark gives Craig a celebratory slap on the back.

"And like you say, she's not bad to look at either." Craig laughs, while the cogs in his brain whirr faster than they have since first meeting Vicky. A big house doesn't always mean financial abundance, it can just mean a massive mortgage, but this conversation with Mark has made him think.

"I'd hang onto that one if I were you. And remember your mates in your will." Mark slaps Craig on the back again.

Chapter 10

*S*mells delicious, Mam," Craig says, leaning against the doorframe of the tiny galley kitchen in his parents' pit bungalow. The inviting aromas of cooked beef, roast potatoes and tangy cauliflower cheese filling his nostrils.

He watches as his father carves the beef joint, while his mother adds flour and boiling water to the meat juices in the roasting tin and makes up the gravy. There's only room for two people in the tiny space, otherwise he'd be in there, helping.

Four weeks after Craig and Vicky first met, despite Craig's nervousness at introducing his new 'friend' to his parents, they've accepted an invitation for Sunday lunch. They may not have officially labelled their relationship, but to everyone else it's clear things are moving fast.

After Mark's revelation and learning that Vicky's mother is from the *other* Fenwick family, Craig's senses are on high alert.

Will she think less of me? he'd thought to himself on the drive over knowing that Vicky is about to see first-hand how different their upbringings were.

"Can I do anything to help?" Craig asks his mother.

"The roasties are ready." She points to the oven. "Can you take them to the table please?"

Donning a pair of oven gloves, Craig dutifully carries the hot dish through to the main room, where Vicky is standing in front of the fireplace. Her eyes travelling over the myriad of family photos on the mantel.

"You're the double of your dad." She points to a silver framed photo of Craig's parents on their wedding day.

"Maybe. If you lose the Teddy-boy quiff and sideburns." Craig gives his girlfriend a quick peck on the cheek.

She glances at the dining table, set for five. "Are we waiting for someone else?" she asks just as Craig's mother walks into the room, carrying the jug of gravy.

Craig locks eyes with Vicky, slowly shakes his head and mouths, '*Later*'. She bobs her head in acknowledgement.

"You have a beautiful home Mrs Fenwick." Vicky smiles at Craig's mother.

"Well that's very kind of you, and we're delighted to have you here." She smiles warmly at the younger woman. It's been a long time since her son brought someone home. "Now sit — please." Craig's mother bustles. "We don't want all this good food to go to waste now, do we?"

Vicky makes to take the seat in front of her, but Craig's mother shouts, "NO! Not there."

"Oh I'm so sorry." Vicky leaps back upright.

"Sorry, I should have told you. Take this one here." Craig's mother smiles and points to the chair between herself and her son.

Vicky gingerly sits back down, fearful of making another honest mistake.

Craig's father arrives with the plate of carved meat and takes his seat at the head of the table, leaving Vicky wondering why there is still an empty place setting that no one is allowed to sit in. Craig's father says grace, before everyone passes around the tureens of food. Heaps of roast potatoes, broccoli, carrots, cauliflower cheese, mashed turnip, and sprouts, and of course Yorkshire puddings and beef, all covered with lashings of thick, tasty, home-made gravy.

"Well isn't this lovely," Craig's mother says. "It's so nice to have company to entertain, isn't it Bob?"

Craig's father looks up blankly from the ladle of vegetables he's spooning onto his plate.

"I was just saying to the young 'uns, how lovely it is to have people to entertain."

"Uh-huh," Bob replies, balancing a piece of meat between the carving knife and fork. "So tell me, lassie, what is it you do?" he asks Vicky.

Oh, here we go. Craig closes his eyes and internally cringes.

When he called his mother and asked if he could bring his new 'special friend' over for Sunday lunch, he had to hold the handset away from his ear as she'd squealed her delight back down the line. Whereas the light behind his father's eyes was snuffed out many years ago and nothing and no-one has been able to reignite it.

Vicky laughs nervously before she answers. "I think the polite term is *professionally resting.* I moved back to the North-East five months ago, and I've been on the hunt for a new job ever since."

"So, what you been living off?" Bob asks.

Craig coughs into his napkin, and Vicky's cheeks turn pink with embarrassment.

"I'm living back with my parents while I re-find my feet."

"So you're sponging off your folks, or the state, or both? Good to know where my taxes are going," Bob huffs. "In my day, if you didn't work you didn't eat. It was that simple."

"Actually," Craig dives in to rescue his girlfriend, "Tori has a second interview this week, the day after Bank Holiday Monday. With a tele-marketing agency. As a manager."

"Yes, fingers crossed." Vicky holds up both sets of crossed fingers.

"But while she's been looking for work, she's been volunteering at the Oxfam shop."

"Oh?" Craig's mother's ears perk up.

Dropping her head, Vicky replies, "Oh, it's nothing really. Just helping out for a couple of days a week. There's only so much *profes-*

sional resting anyone can do before going completely insane." She giggles nervously. "But hopefully if all goes well next week, my career will be back on track. Actually Craig helped me get the interview. It's not even a role that's been advertised, but he knows someone there and passed my C.V. onto them."

"Well isn't that nice." Craig's mother beams at her son.

"Even though she was born in the North-East, Tori's spent most of her life travelling and exploring the world," Craig says, puffing his chest out. "Lived a bit in New Zealand, and London before that. She has reams of qualifications, unlike someone I know… " he adds, laughing at his own self-deprecation. "She just needs someone to give her a break."

"Well, good luck with the interview," Craig's mother says. "I'll have my fingers and toes crossed for you." Slicing into a roast potato, she continues, "New Zealand, eh? That sounds very exotic."

"It's a gorgeous country," Vicky replies. "If a very, *very* long way away."

"I bet. The furthest we've ever been is The Lake District, or the caravan park down in Scarborough. Isn't that right, Bob?"

"Explain something to me," Bob pipes up. "If you managed to escape this shithole of a town, what in God's name made you come back?"

"Manners, Bob. Not in front of company, remember." Craig's mother raises a warning eyebrow in her husband's direction.

Craig's back stiffens. He's still in the dark as to all the details of why Vicky returned from the other side of the world, but he knows it involved the break-down of the relationship she talked about in the car on the way home from the cinema that night.

Unfazed by Bob's tone, Vicky answers Craig's father. "Well I think it was inevitable really. No matter how far you travel, there's always a part of you that's anchored to the place you were born. There was a time when I couldn't wait to — as you describe it, Mr Fenwick — *escape.*"

"Call me Bob." Craig's father smiles and Craig lets go of the breath he was holding.

"But actually, having left the area and seen something of the world," Vicky continues, "there really is no place like home."

"Well said." Craig's mother smiles in Vicky's direction. "Sometimes you don't appreciate what you've got until it's gone."

"Exactly." Vicky returns Craig's mother's smile.

Craig reaches in front of Vicky and places his hand over the top of his mother's. Something unsaid passes between them.

"You should hear the list of places Tori's travelled to... it's never-ending," Craig adds.

"Oh hardly." Vicky blushes. "But then that's partly the advantage of having worked in the travel industry. The pay wasn't great, but the perks were fabulous."

"That, and it helps when you have money and means." Bob smiles smugly. He's done his homework on his son's new friend and knows exactly which side of the tracks this girl comes from.

"How's work, Dad?" Craig asks, desperately wanting to remove the tension from the atmosphere.

"Same old, same old. If it wasn't for that bitch, Maggie Thatcher, I'd still be doing an honest day's graft for an honest day's pay. Instead I'm stacking shelves for a living. Them bastard Tories have no idea the damage they did when they shut the mines and ripped the heart right out of our community."

Vicky takes an urgent sip of her drink.

"Now, now Bob. Nobody wants to hear your opinion on those matters," Craig's mother tempers.

"But it's true. They should be in jail for what they did. The whole bloody lot of 'em. And that John Major's not much better either. There's a change coming. Mark my words. The sooner Blair gets voted in, the sooner we can get this country back on its feet."

"Okay, Dad," Craig interrupts. "Enough with the politics. Tell me how your veggie patch is coming on."

"Your parents are lovely," Vicky says later, as they climb back into Craig's car.

"Thanks, but you have to forgive my father. He can get quite opinionated, as you probably gathered. Sadly there's a lot of men like him around here. He's a proud man, and when the coal mines closed it broke him. Dad's from the generation that provided for their family, so when he wasn't able to do that anymore, it destroyed him."

"I can imagine. Was he involved in the Miner's Strike?"

"Was he ever. He was a union rep, so right in the thick of it. Mam helped run the soup kitchen, even though during the winter of '84 we hardly had anything to eat ourselves."

"Wow. I was only fourteen years old when it was all going on. I had no idea how hard it was for some families. I suppose, my family not being in mining, we were protected from the harshness of it."

"Whereas I lived it. I think it's fair to say that our experiences growing up couldn't be more different." Craig leans over and reaches for Vicky's hand, lifting it to his lips and kissing the back of her fingers.

"Does that bother you? Our differing backgrounds and upbringings," she asks.

"If I'm honest, I was worried that you'd be too posh for my family but you seem to have passed the first test with flying colours."

"Hmm. I wouldn't describe myself as posh. I once had a boyfriend who *I* would describe as proper posh. Went to Eton. Then Oxford. His father worked in The City and they had a massive house on the outskirts of London. Whereas — yes — you and I have had different types of upbringings and I've never experienced some of the harshness that your family lived through, but just because my upbringing was more financially comfortable than yours doesn't mean I don't envy some of the things you had."

Craig turns briefly, eyeing her through his peripheral vision.

"Your parents are still together whereas I never had that growing up. My mother didn't remarry until I was fifteen. Surely what matters more is the things we have in common.? Not how much money our families had in the bank when we were little."

"And what is it they say, opposites attract?"

"Exactly. On paper some sceptics might think this shouldn't work. Yet here we are."

"You're right." He offers Vicky a small smile. "What other people think of our relationship—"

"So, we're in a relationship now, are we?" Vicky teases.

"Yes. I think we are," Craig replies solemnly. "I know I don't want to be in a relationship, with anyone else."

Craig checks his rear-view mirror and flicks on the indicator, preparing to turn the car towards Vicky's parents' home.

"Erm," Vicky mutters. "How would you feel if I stayed over at yours tonight?"

Craig looks sideways at his girlfriend.

"If that's okay with you?"

"Of course it's okay. But won't your parents be worried?"

"They're away for the weekend."

"Well then. What are we waiting for?"

He checks the rear-view mirror then swings the car into a full U-turn and heads back in the direction of his house.

Chapter 11

*T*he soft glow of the bedside lamp throws delicate shadows up onto the wall of Craig's bedroom. They're standing facing one another, their eyes locked onto each other's faces. Each of them searching for hidden truths from deep within their souls. They're both hesitant, neither of them wanting to be the first to lead the other down that sacred path.

"Are you sure?" Craig whispers. "I'm happy to wait if you're not ready."

"I'm ready," Vicky breathes. "Are you ready?"

He nods.

Very slowly Vicky reaches around her back and unzips her dress, which falls seamlessly away from her body, pooling in soft folds around her feet. Craig's breath catches in his throat at the first sight of her perfect form, encased in only a delicate pink lace bra and matching G-string. Instinctively he reaches for her, his arms enveloping her tiny waist, closing the gap between them as his lips seek out hers to kiss.

Their lips meet in the softest, most tender of touches, as if they both know they're approaching the moment that, once travelled together, can never be undone.

Craig tastes the remnants of the red wine on her tongue, which licks and twirls with his own, and the exotic scent of her Coco Channel Perfume rushes up the inside of his nostrils.

Reaching for him, Vicky pulls his shirt out of his jeans, her hands running gently up and down his spine; the feel of her fingertips on his skin sends a fire-bolt of desire into his groin. Lost momentarily in the feeling, Craig is jerked back into the present when she lightly scratches her fingernails down his back, causing a fresh ripple of desire to shiver over his skin. He sucks air in fervently through his nose as she pushes her soft form up against his hard torso. They may have taken their time before consummating their relationship, but he senses these are experienced fingers exploring his body.

"You'll need to show me what you like and don't like," she whispers, nibbling his ear.

"Likewise," he replies, nuzzling her neck.

Craig takes Vicky's hand and leads her towards the side of his bed. Holding his gaze, her hands find their way to his chest; beginning at the top, she undoes his shirt buttons with the same care as if she were unwrapping a special gift. She peels the cotton from his body, allowing it to fall to the floor. Tracing the outline of his shoulders, she threads her fingers through the dark down of chest hair that covers Craig's pecs and upper torso.

"I can shave it off… if you don't like it."

"No, don't. I like it. It's manly… and it's part of you."

Craig tilts her face towards his, kissing her more urgently now. Their hands travelling over the surface of each other's bodies. Each making a mental map of the new terrain they're exploring together.

Vicky's fingers travel downwards, feeling their way over Craig's taut obliques, coming to rest on the waistband of his jeans where, at the front, his obvious desire bulges and begs for attention.

He breathes in sharply as with one hand she encircles and palms his erection over the top of his Levis, gently squeezing his shaft and rubbing her thumb over the protrusion of his penis.

Yes, this is a woman who knows her way around a man's body, he thinks to himself.

Threading his fingers through her hair, Craig deepens his kiss, his desire rising with every passing moment.

Craig reaches around Vicky's back and with one hand expertly unhooks the clasp of her bra. Pulling back from their embrace, their gaze locked onto each other, he watches her slide the straps down her arms and cast the slip of lace to one side, allowing the perfect swell of her breasts to break free. He stands entranced, watching them bob gently with the natural movement of her body as her arms reach for him again, her fingers nestling into the nape of his neck.

Craig can't take his eyes off her.

Her pale breasts are accentuated by the deep tan lines that run across the top of each mound, before her tan disappears down into her cleavage where it melts into the deep golden sheen of her flat stomach.

A groan of desire escapes from deep within him.

His eyes hooded, he instinctively bends his head and takes a taut, dusky rosebud into his mouth, running his tongue over the pert tip.

"Oh my God." Vicky arches her back and throws her head up to the ceiling, and Craig has to steady her as she sways off balance.

His tongue still working its magic on her nipple, she reaches for him. Undoing his belt, she slides her hands inside the back of his jeans, her eager fingers grasping his bum. She slides his jeans free from his hips and they drop with an audible clunk when his belt makes contact with the polished floorboards of his bedroom floor.

Fully expecting her hands to finally free his straining erection from his Calvin Klein's, instead she pauses and takes a step back, sitting down on the edge of the bed.

Slipping a finger inside either side of her G-string, she hitches her bum off the mattress and slides the delicate lace from underneath her. Seductively she peels her knickers down over the length of her thighs, then her knees, kicking the slip of lace free once it reaches her slender ankles. Now completely naked, her polished bronze skin glows in the soft lamplight and contrasts against the pale triangle of untanned skin just visible where her thighs meet.

"Finally time for you to see what's inside my knickers," she says, purring like a temptress.

Craig kneels on the floor, resting his hands on her thighs, and replies gruffly, "Show me."

With manicured fingernails she traces a path down to each knee, before she leans back and slowly spreads her legs, offering Craig a full frontal of her gorgeous feminine glory.

Her own eyes also hooded with desire and her voice laced with longing, she says provocatively, "Brazilian? Or I can shave it off, if you don't like it."

"Never," Craig replies, hastily climbing up onto the bed, straddling her, his hands stroking the side of her face. "You're perfect just as you are."

&

They both lose track of time as over the next few hours they explore each other's bodies. Kissing, teasing, and sucking as they go.

Writhing with longing, eventually Vicky whispers in Craig's ear, "I need you in me."

"Do you need me to wear anything, or are you on the pill?"

"No, not at the moment. Have you got some condoms?" she asks, breathlessly.

Leaning over to his bedside drawer, Craig pulls out a square silver wrapper. Tearing it open with his teeth, he rolls the condom on before Vicky reaches down and guides him into her soft warm folds. Her heat envelops him instantly and at the moment of their coupling, both of them release deep guttural groans of pure pleasure.

Instinctively they begin to move in unison, their hips grinding and rocking together as their passion intensifies.

Their pace and rhythm increasing, Craig feels himself fast approaching the cliff edge as Vicky writhes and rocks beneath him.

"Oh God, you're so tight," he moans.

"Kiss me." She pulls his face towards her, connecting their torsos once again as Craig interlaces their fingers while his lips smash onto hers.

He closes his eyes, anticipating his release when suddenly something *twangs* between them.

"What was that?" Vicky asks, freezing instantly.

"I'm not sure. Are you okay?" He slides his hand under her bum so he can deepen his next thrust.

"Was it the condom? Has it snapped?"

"I don't think so. Maybe."

"Craig, no. You need to stop."

"I'm not sure I can. Oh, God. Here it comes," he moans.

"NO!" Vicky screams.

But before he is able to understand what's happening, everything slows down, as if they've both slipped underwater again.

Vicky places both her hands firmly on Craig's chest and pushes him off her, seconds before he explodes all over the now empty sheets in-front of him.

Bereft, confused, and deeply embarrassed, seconds pass while Craig kneels listlessly at the bottom of the bed, his ejaculate lying in a wet pool in front of him. The condom had indeed split.

What the hell? His mind struggles to refocus.

A few more moments pass, each feeling like agonising minutes before he looks up.

Holy shit!

Curled up at the top of the bed, Vicky is shaking uncontrollably. Her knees pulled into her chest, her eyes glassy and lost, she's rocking back and forth like a terrified child.

"Hey, hey, hey. It's okay." Craig scuttles towards her and she recoils, burying her face into her knees.

Ever so gently, he reaches for her chin, lifting it so he can see her eyes.

"I'm so sorry. I should have stopped. I'm so sorry I didn't. Can you ever forgive me?"

Her unfocused eyes stare right through him, her breathing tight and shallow. He grabs a tissue and wraps the useless condom in it, before peeling back the duvet and pulling it over the both of them.

"You must know, I'll never intentionally hurt you. I'm so sorry I was such an idiot before. It'll never happen again. I promise."

At this, her jaw still quivering, her eyes refocus; looking into her face Craig feels a stab of pain as acute as if someone had speared him right through his heart. He has difficulty catching his breath.

"Oh my goodness. Come here pet."

He pulls her into the crook of his armpit and although still tight and tense, this time she doesn't pull away. Minutes pass, all the while Craig shushes her, gently stroking the outside of her arm and kissing the top of her head.

Eventually she turns and buries her face in his chest and the shaking and quivering is replaced by uncontrollable sobs that erupt from deep inside. Her tears gather in his chest hair but he says nothing, instead he continues to hold her as the pain leaves her body in great wracking shudders.

Only when her sobs begin to subside does he eventually ask, "Do you want to talk about it? I maybe wrong but I don't think this is just about what's just happened."

Sitting up and exhaling, she meets his gaze. "I'm so sorry."

"You're sorry? I'm the one who's sorry."

"It's okay. I know you should have stopped, but I'm not upset because you didn't, or you couldn't. It's just that..." she trails off.

Relief floods Craig's veins and he smooths Vicky's hair away from her face. She looks into his eyes, and he watches as her face dissolves once again into an ugly cry. Her features crumpled by a sadness that makes his heart bleed for her.

"Hey, hey, hey," he says again. "Whatever it is, it can't be that bad."

"Oh, but it is," she whimpers.

They remain locked in each other's arms. Craig lovingly holding her. Giving her the time and space she needs to release her pain.

"Whatever it is that has hurt you, I promise you, I can empathise."

Wiping her nose with the back of her hand, she meets his gaze again. "Oh?"

"There's a reason my mam always sets an empty place at the dinner table."

He looks down and places a light kiss on her lips.

"It's for my older brother. Robert. Their firstborn. Named after my dad."

"I noticed the other child in your parent's photos and assumed he must have been a relation. A cousin maybe? You all look so alike, but you've never said you have a brother."

"That's because I don't anymore. He died."

Vicky's hand flies up to her mouth. "Oh, I'm so sorry."

"It's okay. It was a long time ago. Eight years now. But my mam and dad, and I suppose to some extent — me, have never gotten over it."

"I'm not surprised. And I assume, that empty place at the table, that was his?"

"Correct."

"How did he die?" she asks, then realising she may have over-stepped, back-pedals. "You don't have to tell me if you don't want to."

"No, it's okay. He had a car accident. Side-swiped by the other vehicle."

"Oh my goodness, that's horrific."

"It was. The only blessing was that he didn't suffer. His skull smashed against the seat belt holder. You know the bolt, by the door, that fixes the seat belt to the chassis of the car."

She nods.

"Smashed into the side of his head and he died instantly. Wasn't another mark on him."

Craig pulls Vicky tighter into him. "It was the hardest thing I've ever lived through. I was seventeen, he was twenty-one. Still had his whole life ahead of him. A part of me died that day, and not a day goes by when I don't think about him."

"I'm so very sorry, Craig."

"So you see, I recognise your pain. Something triggered you, because even if the condom had failed and I'd come inside you, it wouldn't have been the end of the world, would it? If you'd been worried about dates and stuff, I would have taken you to get the morning after pill. But this is something deeper isn't it? What on earth has happened to you, my darling?"

Craig watches as his girlfriend's features crumple once again into ugly tears. This time he holds her face in his hands and rubs his thumbs back and forth over her cheekbones in his familiar way.

"Whatever it is, it'll be okay. You can tell me. It might make it a bit easier."

She sucks in a deep breath, composing herself once again.

"I need you to promise me something."

"Anything."

"You can't ever take any risks with me. With contraception, I mean. I can't ever get pregnant. At least not by accident."

"Oka-ay." Craig's Adam's apple bobs in his throat as he swallows hard. "Are you saying you don't ever want any bairns?"

She shakes her head. He waits for her to explain further, but when she doesn't, he continues. "Help me out here. If you're open to the idea of kids, but don't ever want to get pregnant, is there a reason you shouldn't get pregnant. Is it dangerous for you?"

He watches as his girlfriend's chest rises and falls as she inhales and exhales a deep breath. "The thing is ..." she stutters, "I lost a baby."

Craig's eyes stretch wide open. "Oh, pet. Come here." He pulls her back into a hug.

"It was so hard, I didn't think I would survive. I don't think I'm over it and I'm not sure when I'll be ready to feel *being pregnant* again. Just the thought of possibly falling pregnant again, especially by accident." she pauses, "I'm not sure I'll ever get over what I did..." Her eyes stretch wide. "I mean... get over what happened."

"Was it Chris's?"

She nods.

"Is that why you left him? Left New Zealand and came home?"

She shakes her head. "It happened before we went to Christchurch. When we were living in London. New Zealand was meant to be our chance to start over. But our relationship was irreparable by then. Something like that changes you. When it happened, he emotionally checked out and I went through it all alone."

"But surely, you had friends and family to lean on?"

She shakes her head. "No one knew. Only Chris. And now you."

"What? Not even your mother? Or Nessa? Or Julie?"

"No. No one. I went through it all alone."

He stays quiet for a moment, allowing that revelation to settle. "Oh that's terrible. But I think you're stronger than you give yourself credit for. Thank you for telling me and I promise I won't take any risks. And even if something like that were to happen again, I promise I'll never abandon you, and I'd be there for you. But don't worry, we can take the pressure off if you'd prefer. There's lots of ways to be intimate. I'm happy to just hold you. Being close to you is enough for me." He squeezes her extra tight as if to make the point. "And I know it's way too soon to even think about starting a family, but I am open to the idea... when the time is right, of course."

She continues to cling to him like a baby koala, as he continues, "I've never really talked to anyone about how I felt after my brother died either. It's funny, after the accident my entire world collapsed. I stopped thinking about the future because what's the point when it could all be ripped away in a heartbeat? Might as well live for the moment, eh? Since then everything in my life has just sort of happened. But now I've met you and you've turned my world upside down, Tori. And for the first time in a long time, I've started to fantasise about what my future might look like... with you in it."

Vicky dips her head, a small smile spreading across her lips.

He rolls his fingers down the outside of her smiling face. "And for the first time in my life, I have thought about how great it would be to become a dad. Not now, obviously, but further down the track. I'd love a little girl. A princess of my own. A proper little daddy's girl."

Craig expected his words to offer Vicky comfort, but instead she collapses into his chest and sobs again. He looks down at the curve of her eyelashes, her tears like shining beads on the end.

"Me too," she says eventually when her sobs subside. "I was nowhere near ready when it happened with Chris, and even though I…" she falters before continuing, "before I lost the baby it made me realise that I do want kids… someday. But I worry that I've screwed it up. That that might have been my one and only chance to become a mother."

"Hey, hey," he soothes. "But it wasn't your fault. You did nothing wrong."

She turns her head away from him, but he hooks a finger under her chin and forces her to look into his eyes.

"These things happen. Losing a baby under any circumstances is hard. Doubly hard without any support, which it sounds like you didn't have. But you'll have your chance again — I know you will."

"I hope so, Craig," she snivels wiping her eyes clear. "I sincerely hope so."

Chapter 12

VICTORIA

*O*kay, keep your hair on, but don't you think closing the curtains is a bit extreme?" I say the next day, when Craig reaches behind his humongous telly, which he's told me '*cost a cool five grand*', and draws the living room curtains, blocking out the warm May sunshine. "Are you sure this is how you want to spend your Bank Holiday Monday?" My eyes follow him around the room as he prepares for our *Star Wars* marathon. "Won't the lads be expecting you in The Red Lion?"

"Maybe, but I'd rather be here with you." He leans over and kisses the end of my nose, before padding across the floor in his bare feet to switch on the answerphone.

Settling back next to me on the sofa, he plonks a large bowl of cheesy nachos on the three-foot square pine box which doubles as a coffee table and storage for his VHS collection of *X-Files* and *Buffy the Vampire Slayer*. His final act of preparation: adding four bottles of Budweiser and a bottle of wine for me, to the cool box full of ice he's placed next to the sofa.

"Settling in for the long haul?" I laugh.

"I simply cannot allow myself to date anyone who's never seen *Star Wars*. How's that even possible?"

"It's called growing up in an all-female household. But then I could ask you how you've never been to London's West End?"

"Touché." He raises his bottle of beer. "Something we'll need to rectify sometime soon." He kisses my shoulder before sliding the film into the video player. "Buckle up pet, you're about to enter a galaxy far, far away." He slumps back onto the sofa. "Okay, young apprentice, let's do this."

The TV screen initially goes black, then the unmistakable John Williams soundtrack starts up, followed by the famous opening crawl of text that climbs up the screen:

A long time ago
in a galaxy far, far away …

"Here we go." He smiles, lifting his beer to his lips.

Ro

Seven hours later, my *Star Wars* cherry thoroughly popped, the final credits from *Return of the Jedi* scrolling up the screen, Craig disentangles his legs from mine, lunges across the floor and switches the TV off.

I stand up and stretch, before following him across the room as he throws open the curtains. "Bloody hell, when did it go dark?" He pulls the curtains shut again and instead rests his hands on my waist. "*Soooo*, what did you think?"

"Do you want my honest opinion, or the polite version?"

"The truth — always." He mirrors my words from our first date after we'd been to see *Romeo + Juliet*.

I shrug. "Not really my genre, but now I know that stormtroopers are the bad guys. I always thought the Jedi were the enemy."

"I give up." He throws his hands up in the air in mock offence.

"Don't. I did enjoy it, and I'd watch paint dry if I was watching it with you."

"Another drink?" he asks.

"Yes please." I follow him through to the kitchen where he collects another bottle of wine from the fridge and pours us fresh glasses.

"I still remember going to see the first one with my dad and my brother." He pauses, and coughs into his closed fist. Composing himself. "Sorry. I never normally talk about Rob, but you seem to have uncorked something. I've said his name more in the past twenty-four hours than I have in years."

"But surely the more you talk about him, the more his memory lives on?"

"We went to see the first one when I was seven. Rob, eleven. And I'm not sure I can describe what it was like. The special effects blew my mind. I remember ducking in my seat during the battles. I was convinced the spaceships were going to fly out of the screen. Rob and I didn't stop talking about it for weeks. God, I miss him." He slouches his shoulders and pinches the bridge of his nose.

I park my glass on the kitchen island and throw my arms around his neck. "It's not the same, but I do know what it's like to miss a family member. It's like a hole in your heart that no amount of time can ever completely heal."

Holding me at arm's length, he cocks his head to one side. "Who've you lost?"

"My father."

Over the next few minutes I share with him how I allowed my biological father to drift from my life when I was nine years old. How our relationship had been strained after my parents' divorce, and how I was too young to appreciate the adult drama at play. I explain how he lived at the opposite end of the country, which didn't make visitation easy. And eventually I share with him how I put the phone down on him after he'd gotten hold of my school report and berated me for my below-average grades. How betrayed I was by his actions. Then how I refused to reply to any of his letters or birthday cards after that.

"I thought I was doing the right thing." I drop my head. "By then my mother had remarried and I had a loving stepfather who essentially adopted me as his own. Maintaining a connection with my father felt like a betrayal to both my mam and my stepdad. As if continuing to love my dad would somehow invalidate my mother's pain and my stepfather's love."

"But surely that's not your cross to bear?"

"I see that now." I crumple my mouth. "But through a nine-year-old's eyes it felt like the right thing to do. I believed by shutting him out I was removing the cause of my greatest pain. But I was wrong. As I've gotten older, the hole in my heart only gets bigger, not smaller, and I think about him all the time. So you see, on some level, I do understand what it must be like for you to miss Rob."

"Where is he now?"

I shrug. "I have no idea. He could be dead for all I know."

"So look him up. It can't be that hard."

"I don't know where he is. Only his name and the part of the country he lived in fifteen years ago. Who's to say he hasn't remarried. Possibly had more kids. If I crawl out of the woodwork now, I'll likely be nothing more than inconvenience."

"But you're still his daughter."

"I know. But maybe that's not enough?"

"Why would you say that? You're his blood. He's your father."

I look into Craig's eyes, and freeze. He reads the fear that crosses my face.

"I don't get it. What's stopping you?"

I take my time in answering. I've thought about the possibility of finding my father for over fifteen years.

"I'm... not sure," I stutter. "It's a whole can of worms that once opened can never be resealed. I know rekindling a relationship with him would hurt my mother and most likely damage our relationship — potentially irreversibly. Their divorce was horrific, and she harbours as much hatred for him today as she did back then."

"But what about you? What is it *you* need?"

I suck in a long breath. "To stop wondering *'what if.'* To have some closure. But I've long since accepted it's too risky."

"How so? From where I'm standing I don't think you've got anything to lose. If you wait too long, as you say, you might find out he isn't here anymore. Then how will you feel?"

"But what if I do find him and then he rejects me — like I did him all those years ago?"

"Then you'd know. But I very much doubt that'll happen."

"Perhaps, but a part of me is also angry that he didn't fight harder. No matter how difficult it became. If he really did love me, surely he wouldn't have walked away. I'm not sure I could handle it if he didn't want anything to do with me. I've had so many men abandon me, or leave when I've needed them the most–" I cast my eyes down and bite my lip.

He comes and places his hands on my hips. Grounding me. With one finger he lifts my chin, and our eyes meet.

"I'm here now, aren't I? Look, I can't tell you what to do, but all I will say is this… if I had a chance to spend just one more minute with Rob, I'd take it. So what if you find out he doesn't want anything to do with you, or he's a compete arsehole? You'll still have closure and can move on. But what if he's waiting every day, wondering if today is the day you'll find him. And surely, despite their own feelings, your mam and stepdad can respect that?"

I press my lips together, before taking a slow, considered sip of my wine.

"I think you should live for the now, stop worrying so much about the 'what ifs', and stop trying to overthink the consequences. If Rob's death has taught me anything, it's that everything can change in a heartbeat. There are no certainties in life. Take the chance now, before life slips away."

My gut bubbles with an unexplained emotion. "I think you're right, Craig. Despite the risks, I think I need to know one way or the other. But I still have no clue where to start."

"I can help if you want? It's not strictly legal but we have access to the largest database of medical records in the U.K. If he's registered with a GP, we'll find him."

My chest suddenly feels lighter and I realise this is what I've needed for a long time now. Certainty.

"So is that a yes?"

My bottom lip quivers as I nod my head.

"Aww, come here. Don't be nervous. This is exciting. I'll get my team on it first thing tomorrow morning."

Chapter 13

I got the job," I squeal, running into The Red Lion the following Friday night, brandishing my offer letter in one hand, and holding Craig's with the other.

"Oh, that's excellent news. I gather the interview went well then?" Julie says, air-kissing me on both cheeks. Craig heads to the bar.

"Couldn't have gone any better. I got a sense they would have offered me the job there and then, but needed to check my references and stuff. I've been biting my nails all week waiting to find out."

"My spare room is ready and waiting for you, whenever you're ready."

"Uh-huh," I reply, my gut clenching. "But I've something else to tell you," I lean into Julie's ear and whisper.

She looks at me, her eyes stretched wide open.

"Later." I wink.

Craig returns from the bar with a bottle of Newcastle Brown Ale and my usual vodka and Coke. He presses his freezing cold beer against my exposed back and I shriek, then laugh as a secret smile passes between us.

"And let's not forget, we're off to pick up your new wheels

tomorrow as well," Craig announces to the group who are all observing our open flirtation.

"What are you getting, Tor?" Nessa asks.

"Now don't baulk, because I know I should buy a sensible Ford Fiesta or something like that, but I kinda feel if I don't do this now, I'll never get the chance again. Plus the deal that Craig's negotiated means I can totally afford the finance." In my peripheral vision I spy Craig puffing his chest out as he looks on fondly. "People — you're looking at the owner of a brand new MG in British Racing Green."

"No friggin' way," Becca exclaims.

"Soft top or hard top?" Clarky asks.

"Soft top."

"Because of course what you need in the frozen north is a car with two seats and no roof," Anth says, laughing.

"It has a heater," Craig interjects. "And there are such things as hats and scarfs, you know."

"I've always fancied a silly car at some point in my life, and now…" I glance up at Craig's smiling face, "well, now seems like the right time."

Our conversation from last weekend, about taking chances before they slip away, is already making me bolder.

"You're turning into quite the power couple, aren't you?" Mark says. "One of you in an Audi, the other in a snazzy little sports car."

Craig slides his arm protectively around my waist.

"Meanwhile I have to sit shotgun in the side of a dirty old van." Becca rolls her eyes and everyone laughs.

Over the next few hours the conversation bounces around as everyone offloads their news from the previous week. Glancing from one face to the next, it's almost impossible to comprehend how much my life has changed in the five short weeks since meeting Craig.

For three months, I buried my head under my pillow. I was sad, skint, and single. Fearful of the world beyond my bedroom.

Convinced everyone could see my wounds through paper-thin skin. Yet stood next to Craig I'm stronger, braver, and bolder than I've ever been. I'm about to start a new job in a new career as an account manager for a marketing agency. I have a new car, and through Nessa, Julie and now Craig I've been accepted into a ready-made friendship group. *And* I'm in a relationship. Something that three months ago wasn't something I could have imagined, yet here we are. I feel so lucky to have found someone who's so kind and considerate, funny and down-to-earth. In the time I've known him he's done nothing but build me up and shown me how much I mean to him.

The group have begun to refer to us as a couple.

Craig and Tor.

Tor and Craig.

It feels nice, and for the first time in a long time, it feels right. *I feel right.*

៚

Standing side by side in the ladies loos, Julie and I lean across the sinks as we look into the mirrors and apply a fresh slick of lipstick.

"So what was the *something else* you wanted to tell me?" Julie asks, smacking her lips together and checking herself in the mirror.

I pull a folded piece of A4 paper out of my handbag.

She reads it, then meets my gaze, confused.

"I've found him. After all this time." I point at the paper. "Can you believe it?"

"Who?"

"My dad. That's his address and telephone number."

She inhales sharply. "No way."

Julie and I are cousins on my mother's side, and her father — my uncle — and his family lived in a different part of the country when we were all growing up, so she's never met my birth father.

"How on earth—?" she asks.

"Craig. I told him what happened and he put someone in his team on it."

"Gosh. That's amazing. But I'm curious: why now?"

"I think about him all the time. It eats away at me. He's become like some mythical creature, and a part of him is part of me, so it feels like a part of me is missing as well. I was so young, any memories I have of him are all smudged. Like an out of focus photograph."

"I'm not surprised, you weren't even two years old when your parents divorced. But still, why now? What's been the catalyst?"

I shrug, but say nothing.

I can't share with her that since learning about Rob's death, it's made me realise I can't allow my fears about the future, haunt me anymore.

"It just felt time to rip that plaster off, you know?"

"Have you spoken to him?"

"God, no. Craig only gave me the details tonight."

"Okay. And when you do, have you thought about what you might say?"

"Erm… no. Not really. I'm still in shock that I actually have an address and telephone number for him. Obviously, I've imagined for years and years what I might say if this moment ever came, but now that it's here…"

She hands me back the piece of paper and I study it, as if looking at the address and telephone number can somehow tell me the right next step.

"I still can't believe all I need to do is make the call, and I'll hear his voice again." I feel a lump building at the back of my throat. "I hardly remember what he looks like, and the last thing I remember hearing him saying was my name over and over, as he pleaded with me not to hang up."

That memory still haunts my dreams. At the time, my nine-year-old self had had enough of being the by-product of a vicious divorce, and stepping away from the parent I had the least amount of contact with seemed like the only way to survive.

"Jules… I'm terrified of what comes next." I half-smile at her, even though my eyes glass over.

She rubs the outside of my arms. "Of course you are. That's to be expected. But don't forget this'll be a massive shock for him too. His memories of you were of you as a child. You've got the luxury of processing all of this before you act on it, whereas it'll come out of the blue for him. Don't be surprised if he's full of regrets."

"For not keeping in touch?"

"Possibly, or just acknowledging the years that you've both missed out on. The best you can do is try to focus on the future and the relationship you can build from hereon in, not dwell on what you've both lost."

As a trained psychotherapist, I appreciate Julie's words of wisdom.

"My biggest fear is that he won't want anything to do with me. I mean, I was the one who pushed him away."

"Yes, that is also a possibility. But you were nine years old, Vicky. A mere child. You had no way of understanding the consequences of your actions."

"I'm so scared," I say, snivelling through staccato breaths.

Julie pulls me into a hug. "Of course you are. This is huge."

"What should I do? I don't know what to do."

"Only you can make that choice. But whatever you do decide, I'll be here in support."

I rummage through my bag and pull out a tissue. After I've blown my nose and straightened my make-up, I give Julie a tentative smile. "Thanks Jules."

She rubs the outsides of my arm again and changes the subject. "But on a lighter note. Things seem to be going well with Craig."

I meet her eye. "Yes they are. He's actually a big softie underneath all that image."

"What image?"

"You know, edgy. Streetwise. I never thought I'd be cool enough for someone like him. I've got about as much edge as a circle."

"Edgy?" She laughs. "I know it's an old cliché, but it's not what's on the outside that matters. It's what's inside that counts."

"Exactly. He's even holding back from... you know."

"No, I don't know."

"Well, when we're in bed together, he's really affectionate and stuff. But he'd rather kiss and snuggle and isn't pushing me to do anything more than that."

"Oh?"

"Which is so refreshing. My relationship with Chris was so sexual. At first it was fun, well more than fun actually. It was potent and powerful, but eventually it became the only way we could connect. Whereas with Craig, it's just so lovely to be affectionate, without any of that added pressure."

"Ok-ay," Julie replies, unable to hide the scepticism in her voice. "So you haven't slept together yet?"

I pause. Technically we have. The one time the condom broke but since then, our intimacy has changed. Our connection now is more emotional than physical.

"Not in the traditional sense," I say.

"Well, as long as you're both getting your needs met, that's all that matters. Intimacy can come in many forms, including intercourse, which for some couples is the deepest form of intimacy. But not always."

"I know. And it'll come. I'm not worried. For now I'm happy with where we're at."

"Good." She picks up her bag as I tuck my dad's details back inside my handbag.

"I don't know about you, but I'm ready for another drink."

"Lead the way," she replies.

Later that evening, when Craig drops me off at home, I rush up to my bedroom, open my wardrobe and lift out the ballerina box. Unlocking it, I carefully slide the paper with my father's details inside, before replacing the lid once again. I flump back against my pillows and exhale.

Always wondering if he was out there, but not knowing where exactly, meant I was trapped in a never-ending purgatory. Always wondering, never knowing. But now I know exactly where he is and there's been a shift inside of me. Even without reaching out to him something has changed within me than can't ever change back.

I have a father, and he's alive.

But now being faced with the very real prospect of reconnecting with him and crossing that bridge is more terrifying than the not knowing, always wondering.

Closing my eyes I pinch the bridge of my nose. Hugging a pillow, I look up at the ceiling. Unable to settle, I pick up the box and shove it back in the bottom of my wardrobe, underneath a shoe box, and slam the door shut.

It takes me a couple of minutes to regain my self-control; once my breath has settled inside my body again, I know what I need to do.

Nothing.

For now at least.

At least not tonight, or tomorrow, or even the day after.

It can wait. He can wait.

Until I'm ready. Whenever that is.

Chapter 14

4 weeks later, Saturday 29th June 1996

*A*nother?" Nessa points to the empty champagne flute in my hand.

"Yes please," I reply, and she heads off in search of the nearest waiter.

Nessa, Becca, Julie and I are enjoying a girls' day at the races at Gosforth Park, while the boys spend the day defending their place in the regional paintballing championships. They're hoping to better last year's bronze medal.

"Hurry up." Becca totters in from the outdoor viewing balcony, in heels so high she's almost *en pointe,* yet she still only comes up to my armpit. "The next race is about to start. I've got twenty quid on the favourite." She jerks her head in the direction of the track outside.

"Coming." I smile, wrapping my arm around her shoulders and walking back outside onto the terrace and into the blazing June sunshine. Julie and Nessa follow a few steps behind, carrying four fresh glasses of fizz. Our elbows sharpened, we push through the crowds and line up along the balcony railing. Down below, the horses prance and snort excitedly as their jockeys jostle them into their starting gates.

The Northumberland Plate is an extravagant event, one of the highlights of the North-East social calendar, and everyone dresses for the occasion. We're all wearing vibrant block coloured cocktail dresses in bright coral pink, cobalt blue, and regal purple, and I'm in a satin claret-red figure-hugging number, matched with a coordinating Jackie-O style pillbox hat. I feel like a million dollars, even if my outfit has cost most of my first month's wages.

The final horse is wrestled into its box and a heartbeat later the starter pistol cracks, the stalls clank open, and the stallions thunder down the track at full pelt. Their jockeys and whips flying in the air as the sound of their hoofs hitting the soft turf pound past. Everyone shouts and jeers, and some racegoers grab their binoculars for a better view as the race leaders' curve around the top of the elliptical track and disappear down the back straight.

"Come on!" Becca yells.

Julie checks her programme. "What colour's yours Becks?"

"Blue and white."

Looking between the programme and out onto the track Julie shakes her head, laughing. "Half the field are blue and white."

"Blue with a white 'V'. There... that one." She points at a particular jockey, bunched up with a couple of the others at the front of the pack, wearing a light-blue satin jersey.

"Come on, ya great big hoofer!" Becca yells at the top of her voice, earning her a few hard stares from the snobby crowd around us.

Julie and I snigger into our programmes.

"Becca!" Nessa shushes her. "Honestly, we can't take you anywhere."

But Becca is not listening, her entire focus on the race playing out in front of her, and as the leaders turn the last corner and gallop down the final straight, her horse begins to edge ahead.

"Come on," I cheer.

"What's its name?" Nessa asks.

"Aluminium," Becca replies, without taking her eyes off the race.

"Don't you mean Al-mu-himm?" Nessa chuckles.

"Whatever. Look, he's in the lead!" Becca jumps up and down. "Come on... you can do it." She throws her clenched fist into the air. The jeering around us intensifies, everyone wanting their favoured horse to win.

Then out of nowhere another jockey cracks his whip and a grey stallion begins to close the lead on Becca's bay colt. Within a few more strides the two horses are jostling for the lead, each of them nosing ahead of the other on alternate strides.

"Nooooo," Becca shouts.

"Come on Aluminium," I shout along beside her, and Nessa shakes her head laughing.

We all hold our breath as they gallop over the finish line in a dead heat. The stadium falls silent; everyone's eyes turning to the screens while we wait for the photo finish. Then a deafening roar is released from the crowd, as an equal number of people groan and tear up their betting slips. Becca's horse is crowned the victor. Winning by a nose.

She punches the air. "Go on! Get in their son!"

"Well done," I say. "How much did you win?"

"No idea."

"What were its odds again?"

"Eleven to four."

I quickly do the calculation in my head. "Seventy-five quid, including your original bet. Not bad for a punt."

"Too bloody right."

I may have only known Rebecca for a couple of months, as long as I've known Craig (if you discount the brief period when we both danced together as children), but along with Nessa and Julie she's fast becoming one of my favourite people. Honest, down-to-earth, good fun and big-hearted, she reminds me a lot of Mel. They're both the kind of people who aren't afraid to tell it like it is, without fear of other people's judgement. I wish I could be more like that.

"Don't lose that." Nessa points to the betting slip in Becca's hand.

"I think I'll go and cash it in now."

"I'll come with you," Nessa replies. "I want to put a bet on the final race."

I glance at my programme and look down the names of the horses for the final race of the afternoon. The big one — The Northumberland Plate. However, knowing nothing about racing, we've spent all day choosing our horses based on their colours, or which ones have the craziest names.

"Ness, would you put fifty quid on Double Bounce for me?" I ask.

"Fifty?"

"Yeah, why not." I pass her the cash. "It kinda feels like the vibe of my life right now. You know, bouncing back."

"There's also a horse called Double Splendour in this next race. You sure you don't feel more Splendiferous than Bouncy?" she asks.

"Hmm. No. Double Bounce resonates more."

"Because of course, we always increase our chances of winning based on how a horse's name *resonates* with us." Becca rolls her eyes.

"Like you know anything. You were just calling your last one after a man-made metal," Julie interjects, and we all laugh.

"Exactly. But who cares. It still won. What matters is we're all here. Poshed up and drinks in hand."

"I'll drink to that. *'To good friends and having fun.'*" I raise my glass as the other three girls all follow suit.

Everyone drains their glasses, then Becca and Nessa head off to the betting booth. Julie opens her mouth to speak, but her mobile rings inside her handbag, interrupting her. She looks at the screen and crumples her brow before hitting the *call accept* button and saying, "Hello?"

I wave her empty glass in front of her nose and mouth *'Another?'* She nods, her phone clasped to her ear. Heading back inside I wander towards the free bar and I'm turning around, a fresh glass in each hand, when I see her rushing over, a worried expression washed all over her face.

"Leave them, Tor. We need to go."

"What? Now?"

"Yes, now. Paul's downstairs. He's come to collect you."

"Paul?"

"Paul Clark."

I've only ever heard Clarky called by his nickname, or sometimes as *The goth*. I never knew his real name was Paul — until now.

"Come to collect me?"

"Yes. No-one could get hold of you," Julie continues. "He's driven here and he's downstairs right now, waiting for you."

"Why? What's going on?"

"Have you checked your phone?"

"No."

Putting down the two champagne flutes, I pull out my own mobile. A Nokia 1610, purchased only last weekend after a trip to the Vodafone shop with Craig. Another luxury I can now afford since starting my new job, but a gadget I've yet to master. Only a handful of people have — as my mother describes it — this newfangled technology, so rather than keep bum-dialling Craig by accident, which I've already done multiple times this week, I prefer to keep it switched off when I'm not using it.

I press the *on* button and the screen lights up with a list of missed calls. They're mostly from Craig, but also another number I don't recognise, presumably Clarky's. Now I'm worried.

I put the phone to my ear preparing to listen to my messages, whilst asking Julie, "What's happened? Has something happened to Craig?"

"Not quite." Julie grabs my arm. "Come on. I'll come with you and explain on the way."

I hang up the phone before I've had a chance to listen to any messages as Julie drags me out of the room.

"What about Nessa and Becks? We can't just abandon them."

"They'll be fine. We'll find them on our way out and explain.

Come on. We need to hurry." She links her arm through mine and ushers me down the grand staircase.

Julie climbs into the back seat of Clarky's Golf GTI and I sit up front.

"Hi," I say to a stony looking Clarky who's still dressed head to toe in full combat gear.

When he doesn't offer up any explanation, I look between him and Julie on the back. "Is anyone going to enlighten me?" My pitch involuntarily increasing as my throat constricts.

Clarky slams the car into gear and pulls away. "Craig's in a bit of a bad way, that's all."

My hand flies up to my mouth. No, please God, don't let anything have happened to him.

"Don't worry. It's nothing like that. He's not been physically hurt, but it's not been a great day—"

"Why? What's happened? Just give it to me straight."

"It's Rob's birthday," Clarky replies flatly, while he weaves through the traffic on the A1.

"Oh. I didn't realise."

"Most people don't. It's not something he generally talks about."

That may be so, I think to myself. But why didn't he tell me? These past few weeks he's let me blab on about my new job, my new car, and how excited I was for this day out, when all that time he's been thinking about his dead brother's birthday coming up. I'm not sure what words of comfort I could have offered him, but I would have tried. As much as I've opened myself up to him, clearly there are still some things he's keeping private from me.

"Those of us who knew him *and* Rob," Clarky continues, "keep a mental note. I knew it might be on his mind today, but he was particularly depressed this morning. Add in a high-pressured, albeit fake, combat set-up, a dismal result, not to mention lots of shouting and the sound of gunshots going off, and he's pretty shaken up. I've not seen him this bad since the actual accident itself. He went a bit mental on the field, then shut down completely. None of us have been able to get through to him. When he eventually broke down the only thing he wanted was you." Clarky turns and gives me a small smile. "That's why I came for you sooner rather than later. Sorry to bust up your day. But I thought you'd want to see him if you knew."

"Yes, of course. You did the right thing."

"It can't be easy," Julie pipes up from the back seat. "Even after all this time."

"There's two days a year we all secretly keep an eye out for him. Rob's birthday, and the anniversary of the accident. The last few years he hasn't been as bad — which is why I think we were caught by surprise today."

"Where is he now?"

"The lads have taken him home. I have a suspicion by the time we arrive he'll be two sheets to the wind."

"Because alcohol always makes a bad situation better," Julie tuts.

"Agreed." Clarky looks through his rear-view mirror and meets Julie's gaze. "So, the sooner we get there, the better."

Clarky indicates off the dual carriageway and points the car towards home, while I turn and look out the window.

I'm the tonic he craves. I smile inwardly. As much as I'm not taking any pleasure knowing he's emotionally distressed, there is a part of me that is pleased knowing that he's asked for me. It demonstrates how much we both mean to each other. Even in the relatively short time we've known each other.

"I don't get it," Craig says a few hours later from his end of the bath.

After we'd arrived at Craig's house and Julie was satisfied that Craig wasn't about to throw himself under a bus, everyone tactfully left.

We fell into each other's arms the moment we were alone and I held him while he grieved. Allowing his well of emotions to overflow. Shouldering his burden as my own.

His combats still soggy from paintballing, his knuckles red raw, I suggested we slip into a nice warm bath. To soak his bruises, and not just the ones on the outside.

"What don't you get?" I meet his gaze.

"You've had your dad's details for what — a whole month now — and you've not done anything about contacting him."

I stay quiet. How do I explain that when you've harboured the void for more than half your lifetime, the wound may be painful but it's also familiar, and not knowing what it will feel like once that uncertainty is taken away is more frightening than putting up with a dead hole inside of you.

"What's stopping you?"

"I don't know." I cover my breasts with my arms, suddenly feeling self-conscious.

"We've been through this. I know you're scared. But when I was thinking about Rob today — it would have been his twenty-ninth birthday — almost fucking thirty, man, I got so angry. More angry than I think I've ever been since he was first taken from us."

I watch as his pupils dilate, and the muscles in his jaw twitch. I stay quiet, wondering whether his anger over his brother's death is about to turn on me. I've been here before; my body tenses. Everything on high alert. Is he about to lash out, just like Chris once did?

He looks me dead in the eye. "I would *love* to be in your situation, Tori."

"My situation?"

"To get back the person I've lost."

I watch as Craig's eyes glass over with unshed tears. I relax, the tension passing. He may be angry at the world for taking his brother away, but he's not angry at me.

"I'd give anything to have one more day with him. I just miss him so much. He used to tease me something rotten and I miss the sound of his laughter. When he wasn't winding me up, we would gang up on Mam and Dad. We had this whole secret language."

He drops his head and I reach forward and stroke his leg.

"I can only imagine," I say softly.

"But that's the thing. You *can* imagine because you know exactly what I'm feeling, except you have the opportunity to reverse it, and I don't. That's what I don't get. And that's why I was so angry. If our roles were reversed, I would have made that call the minute I was given the opportunity."

I suck in a deep breath. "But our situations are not the same, darling. You had someone taken away from you, someone you knew, someone who was a part of your life, someone who you loved and who loved you in return."

A single tear rolls down Craig's cheek and his bottom lip quivers.

"I'm so sorry. It's unfair that you lost your brother, and I'm so sad for you, but my fears are about the future not the past. You know that if you had the opportunity to see Rob again, you would pick up where you last left off. Whereas I've never really had a relationship with my father. Other than a few fleeting traumatic visits when I was a child."

I look away, as a tsunami of memories crash over me. Me as a toddler being dragged away from my mother on Christmas Eve to go and spend the holidays with him, essentially a stranger. Crying for hours and hours in the back of the car, looking out of the back window, waiting for my mother to rescue me, which of course she was powerless to do. My final image of her, the anguish etched into her own face knowing there was nothing she could do to take away my pain and reverse what the courts had ordered. Or the confusion that came later, when I enjoyed my time with him, questioning if that was *allowed*, or if I'd somehow betrayed my mam when I'd arrive home again and the pain of my absence was still present.

"Come here." Craig motions for me to turn around. I lie back between his legs and he kisses my shoulder. "We're a sorry pair of saps aren't we?"

I lean my head against his shoulder and wrap my arms over the top of his. The weight of them against my waist comforting me. Our breath falls into sync. *In. Out. In. Out.*

"Whatever you do, I'll always support you," Craig says. "But surely you can't ignore the chance to heal your past?"

I let out a long exhale, my breath wobbling as I empty my lungs. If I do this, my mother can never know, at least not yet, until I've found out what kind of relationship he might want, or not want.

"I'll ring him tomorrow," I whisper, my eyes closed. "Give me a chance to think about what the hell I'm gonna say. *Hi Pops. Remember me? Your long-lost daughter* — seems a bit crass, don't you think? Plus, I'll need to nip back to my mam's and get his details. I've hidden them in my bedroom."

"I kept a copy… just in case."

"Of course you did," I say, smiling.

"I know this is hard for you, Tori. But I think you're doing the right thing. I'm proud of you."

The sound of the landline ringing shrills through the house.

I lean forward but Craig pulls me back into him. "Leave it. Let the answerphone get it."

We listen to the *beep* of the answerphone kicking in and the pre-recorded message playing, then the giggles and shrieks of Becca and Nessa. It sounds like Julie and me bailing on them hasn't affected the rest of their day. "*You won you lucky git! Your nag romped home in The Plate. But unlucky — we've got your betting slip and have spent all your winnings in The Red Lion! Ha ha!*"

Craig shakes his head and laughs. To see him happy again, I know I would forfeit any number of winning bets.

Chapter 15

$\mathcal{T}$he following night I finally pluck up the courage, and with shaking fingers punch out the digits of my father's telephone number.

What if he doesn't want to know me? What if I turn out to be an uninvited inconvenience in his neat and tidy life? What if I'm not enough? What if he hangs up, just like I hung up on him all those years ago? My thoughts tumble over each other as I listen to the line connect, then instead of a normal dial tone at the other end, the phone emits a violent screeching noise.

I blurt out a laugh and hang up.

Craig looks at me. "How way man? Why'd ya hang up?"

"It's a fax machine. The telephone number you have must be his fax number."

"So write him a fax. Think about it. This could be the perfect way to reintroduce yourself, without the shock of him picking up the phone and hearing your voice. This way, you can really think about what you want to say."

I follow Craig up into the attic and sit on the opposite side of his desk as his pen hovers over a sheet of blank paper.

"Okay, so what do you want to say?"

I bite my bottom lip. "Pass it here."

Don't freak out when you read this...It's Victoria.
I wondered if you might like to meet up.
To leave the past behind and look forward instead?

I sign off with my contact number and draw an 'x' underneath my signature.

"Here. Send it. Before I stop myself." I pass the paper to Craig.

He spins round in his chair and punches in the number. We hold hands as we watch the paper message slot through the machine.

No going back now.

That was a month ago.

I stare out of the window as the train trundles into Paddington Station. The guard announces our imminent arrival and I check my reflection one last time, sliding my tongue over my teeth and smacking my lips together to set my lipstick.

On one hand, I want to create a perfect first impression, but surely it shouldn't matter to him what I look like, and this is hardly a first impression is it? More like a reboot.

My hands shake as I pack away my stuff, but as the train jolts to a stop I drop the contents of my handbag all over the floor.

"Bollocks!" I mutter under my breath as I scrabble around on my hands and knees hastily gathering up my stuff from the sticky train floor.

What if I don't recognise him? It's been so long. What if he doesn't recognise me?!

The only image I have of him is a photograph of my parents on their wedding day, which I secretly stole from a box in Granny Fenwick's attic when I was a teenager. Over the years I've studied every grainy black and white pixel of that image. Searching for clues. As if a static photograph of a stranger could somehow fill in the missing pieces of my identity.

Regardless, with his arm linked through my mother's, he looked extremely dapper in his sharp grey morning suit and top hat.

Studying every contour of his beaming face I've often wondered if either of them knew then that their marriage would be over before it really got started?

Walking down the platform and towards the exit, I force my shoulders back and lift my head high, wanting to trick my nerves into submission. And that's when I see him. Just beyond the ticket barriers. His features an older version of the face I remember. A more mature looking and male version of me.

Dropping my bags, I rush into his waiting arms and we cling to each other. All my cautious hesitation evaporating the moment he held out his open arms to me. His face streaked with tears.

A few silent minutes pass before he kisses the top of my head and mumbles, "Oh, Victoria. It's so good to see you again. "

*

An hour later and I'm kneeling in prayer, inside one of the most magnificent places of worship on the planet: Westminster Abbey. My hands clasped and my eyes closed, I remain mute, the man in the pew beside me both a stranger and strangely familiar. Even though I've tried hard not to have any expectations for what I might feel today, my gut is rolling with a cacophony of confusing emotions.

Does he also feel a part of him has been missing all these years? Like he too has had a limb torn from his body?

It feels strange kneeling next to the man without whom I would not exist, whilst also acknowledging I've managed to reach the grand old age of twenty-six without any guidance or support from him. Unlike my mother and stepfather — the parents who've raised me and to whom I feel a continued obligation to be a kind and loving daughter who lives up to their expectations — I owe this man nothing.

Still, it doesn't stop the child within me desperately wanting to be worthy of his love and acceptance.

It was his suggestion to start our daddy/daughter 'date' with a lunchtime service in the majestic cathedral. I've yet to fathom whether he chose this activity to give us something to do whilst we get used to being around each other, or whether he wanted to cleanse his sins before we got into any intense conversations.

Although I attended Sunday school as a child, I've not been inside a church for years, but it's surprisingly cathartic. The ethereal sounds bouncing off the stone walls and wrapping around me like a spiritual cloak. We watched quietly as the ceremonial procession glided regally past us, their white robes hovering just above the hard stone floor, as if levitating along like a line of holy *Doctor Who* daleks. On the final verse of the choristers' arrival the rousing euphony from the Harrison and Harrison organ, its pipes now fully open, physically passed through my body as the angelic tones of the choristers' descant floated on top of the thunderous vibrations of the organ music. The sound swirling up into the rafters seventy metres above, seemingly dissipating through the solid stone roof and directly into the heavens. It's impossible not to be uplifted by the experience.

Despite my Christian upbringing I've never considered myself particularly religious, my beliefs being more spiritual but not tied to any one faith. Still — my eyes glass over as we stand side by side and begin to sing the opening hymn. My father's surprisingly bass voice booming out next to me, drowning out my delicate soprano.

My breath catches in the back of my throat as the first lines of Hubert Parry's lyrics cut through me like a knife:

Dear Lord and father of mankind,
Forgive our foolish ways;

My jaw simultaneously pains with disappointment, while my blood boils with anger and my heart aches with hope.

Why did he not fight for me? Was I not worth it?

But some of my anger is also directed at myself.

Why did I put the need to appease my mother over the need to continue a relationship with him?

But how could I have realised that that decision would have such a profound impact on my identity in later life?

I need him to forgive me too.

I've dreamt of this day for so long. As if meeting him again would erase all my pain and heal all my wounds, but even in the short time we've spent together I've already realised he's not Santa Claus or the mythical mystery idol that I've spent years fantasising over. He's just an ordinary man. Nothing more, nothing less.

Then as we reach the final verse of the hymn and sing together...

Breathe through the heats of our desire
Thy coolness and Thy balm;
Let sense be dumb, let flesh retire;
Speak through the earthquake, wind and fire,
O still, small voice of calm.

...I can only mumble the final reprise, '*O still small voice of calm*', as in that moment my father has reached for my hand to hold. His fingers intertwining with mine as our eyes remain firmly focused on our hymn books. He squeezes my hand, and in that moment my heart fills to capacity, my internal turmoil stills, and somewhere deep inside of me a quiet voice whispers, '*Victoria, you are loved.*"

I exhale.

My father and I may hardly know one another, yet through our interlocked fingers, I feel him.

I feel his pain.

I feel his sorrow.

I feel his remorse.

And I feel his love and the bond between us. A tie that stretches far beyond any superficial level of knowing one another. We're connected in a way that can't be explained logically. And for rediscovering that, I'm immeasurably grateful.

℞

Later that evening, I arrive home and, stepping down onto the platform at Durham train station, my heart lifts when I spy Craig waiting for me, clutching a small bouquet of white roses.

"You look exhausted," he says, kissing me and taking my luggage.

"I am," I croak.

"How was it?"

"Emotional, but also cathartic. However I haven't got the energy to talk about it now. I just want to go home."

"Of course. Back to your mam's, or do you want to crash at mine?"

With everything that's been going on, I've still not had the opportunity to move my stuff into Julie's spare room, so I'm still 'officially' living at my parents' whilst 'unofficially' spending the majority of my time at Craig's.

I meet his gaze with tired eyes, and all I want is for him to take care of me.

"Yours, if that's okay. I'm not sure I've got the energy to deal with my mother tonight."

She's bound to quiz me about the training course I attended during the week, which provided both the perfect opportunity and cover story for arranging the meet up with my father. Only Julie and Craig know where I've actually been today.

"Come on. Let's get you home and into a nice warm bath."

I rest my head against his shoulder as he wraps one arm around my back and leads me out of the station.

Chapter 16

*B*etter?" Craig kisses the end of my nose the next afternoon, after I've updated him on the previous day's events.

"Absolutely." I smile, nestling into his armpit as we snuggle up on his sofa. "I didn't expect to see so much of myself in him. It's all a bit strange."

"I can only imagine, but I'm here for you. Whatever you need."

"Thanks, Craig. I couldn't have done this without you or your support."

"You hungry?" he asks, changing the subject.

"Umm. A bit." I untangle my limbs from his, and follow him through to the kitchen, gathering up our used mugs on the way. Opening the dishwasher I place the mugs on the racks while Craig disappears down the back stairs to the cellar.

Craig's home is a large Victorian villa, spread over four floors and complete with the remains of servants' quarters in the attic. Modernised and extended, it still retains two magnificent marble fireplaces in the main living spaces, and smaller cast-iron ones in three out of the five bedrooms. Decorative coving and picture rails run around every wall, and the main living room has an original ceiling rose. The rooms are flooded with light from the large bay windows in all the reception rooms, so large they're split into three panes of glass. It's a huge house for one person, but a brilliant house for entertaining.

I'm still baffled what possessed him to buy such a big house to live in on his own, especially when he's previously told me, '*He stopped thinking about the future after his brother died*'. Maybe, somewhere deep in his unconscious, he was thinking ahead when he bought it. Imagining a future wife and a rabble of rug rats to fill it up. My heart warms at the thought.

I'm leaning over the kitchen island, reaching for a handful of peanuts, when Craig returns through the back staircase, wine in hand. He presses the bottle up against my bare midriff, making me jump. A trick that is becoming his signature move.

"Oi, gerroff. Whaddya think you're doin'?"

He's slouching, a cheeky twinkle in his eye. We lock eye contact and both of us register the suppressed desire that passes between us.

"Nothing," he replies, his eyes hooded, his Levis hanging off his hips in a way that makes me want to rip them off him. "I thought I'd put these in the fridge up here... for later."

We've been dating three months now, and following our disastrous first attempt to consummate our relationship, we've still not crossed that line. When our intimacy reaches that critical point, I've willed him to take the next step, but he always backs down. What started out as a respectful gesture is fast becoming a barrier to deepening our connection. Everything else about our relationship is perfect, but I still want to be desired. To be loved — fully.

He puts the bottles in the fridge then comes and rests his hands on my waist, causing a ripple of desire to dance across my skin. Instinctively I shuffle my stance, my legs parting slightly as I lean back against the cool marble worktop. Secretly wishing he would pick me up, plonk my arse on the surface behind me, rip my pants off with his teeth and ravish me right here and now. But before I have the chance to turn this moment of connection into anything more, he looks away.

"I thought I might knock up a curry. Wanna help?" he asks.

"Okay," I exhale.

"I'll mix up the marinade, if you don't mind prepping the chicken."

"Of course," I smile.

I grab the necessary utensils and begin chopping the chicken breasts into cubes. Meanwhile Craig mixes yogurt with fresh lemon juice, crushed garlic, grated ginger and a whole host of spices.

"There's something I've been meaning to tell you," I stutter while we work side by side.

"Oh?" He raises an eyebrow.

I pause. "I've been to the doctors."

He stops mixing his ingredients and turns to look at me. His stare burning into the side of my skull. "Why? What's wrong?"

"Nothing, but I've gone back on the pill." I turn and look at him. "After the last time, I thought it was best. No chance of anymore condom mishaps." I look past him, focusing my gaze on the rolling hills on the horizon. "I just thought you should know, you know — for when the moment's right."

I hold my breath.

He says nothing; a few long moments pass in agonising silence.

Shit! Why did I have to say anything? Now he's going to feel pressured.

He turns his attention back to his marinade, staying silent, but playfully bumps his hips into mine.

"Oi, give over." I brandish my knife in mock threat. Following his lead to defuse the tension with playfulness.

Smiling, he holds out the bowl of marinade and I scrape the chicken into it. Using his hands, he mixes it together, covers the bowl with cling film and places it in the fridge.

I'm rinsing my hands when he comes up behind me, planting his feet firmly on either side of mine, hemming me in as he leans his full body weight up against me. Just the weight of him, pressing me into the cold ceramic sink, turns me on, and a pool of heat unfurls in the pit of my stomach.

"So, you're back on the pill then, are you?" he whispers, his hot breath tickling my ear.

I hold my breath, again.

Waiting for his next move, I remain stock-still. Waiting for him to kiss the nape of my neck, or nibble my ear, give me a signal that he wants to take things further, but instead he slides his arms under my armpits and plants two masala-mix handprints on my boobs, ruining my T-shirt.

"Aww, we're playing this game are we?" Sidestepping him, I flick water into his face.

"Ahh, howay man," he protests, unable to wipe his eyes clear, his hands still covered in the masala marinade.

"Can't take it, then don't dish it." I chase him around the kitchen island holding my glass of water and flicking it at him as he tries to escape.

What ensues is a messy play fight of yogurt masala marinade and water hurling, until we are both covered in a messy concoction of burnt-orange streaks and wet patches. Our hair stuck to our scalps. Our arms and chests covered in splatter marks and handprints. I press my fingers into my side, pushing against the stitch that's formed from laughing so much.

I see that he too is holding his waist, bent double and catching his breath. Seeing my chance I make another dash around the island, but he doubles back and this time catches me, grabbing me around the waist. I scream loudly in mock fear.

"Oi. Put me down," I shriek, my legs flailing as he lifts me off my feet and pins me up against his huge American fridge.

Leaning into me, my head turned to one side, my cheek and torso pressed up against the cold, hard metal, he whispers, "It's what you deserve, you naughty, *naughty* girl."

A thunderbolt of desire rips through me as the deep timbre of his voice reverberates in my solar plexus.

He pants against my cheek. Our bodies breathing in and out in sync, each exhalation sending ripples of pleasure down into my groin, where my heat now throbs white-hot. How can he not realise how sexy he is?

He spreads my arms wide, splaying me against the fridge and smearing the smooth metal surface with masala-mix palm prints from our sticky fingers. His hard torso pushing against my back. Fisting my matted hair he holds me still, and I willingly surrender. The void within me aching to be filled, and, judging by the hardness I feel pressing into my butt cheek, he too feels the same desire.

I hold still, waiting for him to make the next move. Praying that he won't diffuse our passion with humour. My out-breath causes a cloud of condensation to cling to and then contract off the brushed grey metal; out of the corner of my eye I spy the muscles in his forearm twitch and flex as we remain pressed together against the cold, hard surface. Not wanting to lose any heat out of the moment, or fearful that he'll back down, I fight my own instincts to turn around and pull him into a kiss and instead remain still, sensing that he's fighting his own internal battle.

In my submission I'm mentally willing him to take things further, wanting him to know that I offer no resistance.

I'm yours Craig. All yours. Take me now.

All the while our breath, visible against the brushed metal of the fridge, remains the only movement between us.

Eventually, I whisper, "It's okay, Craig. I'm okay. I want this. I want *you.*"

Releasing a soft growl he turns me around and slams me back up against the fridge, kissing me hard. Our hands and clothes still a messy mix of tikka masala marinade, we run our fingers up and down the length of each other's bodies. I slide my hands inside his black T-shirt, smearing his back with my sticky fingers while he urgently pulls my top up and over my head. Throwing it to the floor, he looks at me as if for the first time. Pushing me back against the fridge again, he smashes his lips against mine and I gasp as my back makes contact with the cold metal.

I follow his lead and pull his own T-shirt up and over his head. Our lips reuniting again, his chest hair tickles my skin where our torsos press up against each other, and his musky scent rushes up my nose.

I want desperately to run my hand down to his hardness, still safely cocooned inside his jeans. I want to touch him, stroke him, caress him. Show him my appreciation for his own desire, but still I hold back. Only touching him where his hands have touched my body. We've been here before and not managed to take things to the next step; I want this time to be different.

Our lips still locked together, he picks me up and I wrap my legs around his waist as he carries me the few paces across to the kitchen island. Placing me down, I cup his face and kiss him hard. Searching his mouth with my tongue.

Without pausing for breath, he pulls down one of the cups of my bra and takes my nipple in his mouth. I throw my head back and gasp at the shock of it. His tongue twirling and encircling the tip which tightens instantly at his undivided attention.

"Oh God," I moan.

He gives the bud a gentle nip with his teeth and I lean back further as a rush of heat shoots down, stoking the burning flames in my groin.

"Keep going. Don't stop," I say urgently.

Locking his eyes with mine, he dutifully obliges, continuing the delicate dance with his tongue, while he watches my reaction out of the corner of his eye.

My legs part, seemingly of their own desire, and I fist his hair. Holding him. Guiding him. Once he's satisfied my first nipple has been sufficiently teased, he pulls down the other side of my bra and turns his attention to my other rosebud, covering it with his mouth while his hand now cups my other breast. Running his thumb back and forth across its tip, he continues to turn me on. I run my fingers through his sticky matted hair and close my eyes. Lost in the ripples of desire that pulsate through my core.

He releases my breasts, pauses, before reaching for my face. Cupping my jaw in his hands, his thumbs gently stroking my cheeks.

A moment of stillness in the heat of passion.

No, please don't stop, I want to shout. I want him — No, need him — to fight and win his own internal battle.

Taking one of his hands in mine, I kiss his palm, tasting the concoction of salt and spicy yogurt mix that clings to his skin.

My voice hardly a whisper, I ask, "What is it? Why have you stopped?" I see tears glisten in the corner of his eyes. He holds my gaze as he strokes the circumference of my face starting at my brow, feeling his way over my cheek bone, before lifting my chin between his thumb and forefinger. I see fear skate across his features.

"Whatever it is... you can tell me," I whisper.

He's cracked wide open, exposed... vulnerable.

"It's going to be okay, Craig. I promise. I want this. I want you."

He looks deep into my eyes. "The thing is, before we go any further, there is something I must tell you."

My gut contracts, while I wait for him to continue.

"This means more to me than just sex, Tori. Ever since the day we met you've managed to wheedle your way into my heart. And now that you're there, I don't ever want you to leave."

I breathe hard, grinning from ear to ear, my own chest cracked open as if he's unlocked the door to a birdcage and set me free. I'm flying, weightless, and nothing can hold me back now. I feel light as air.

"I love you, Tori. I'm *in* love with you," he says, smiling so wide his dimples form pockets of cuteness in each cheek.

I inhale a rush of emotion, like a tsunami rising up out of the deep pool of still water within my soul, and my eyes flood with tears.

"I love you too, Craig."

He envelops me in a boorish hug. "I was worried that this would be too much for you. That it's too soon. You've been through so much, and I never want you to feel obligated to me. But I wake up every day so happy that you're in my life. *My girl.* What the hell did I do to deserve you?"

"I feel the same." I stroke his hair as he buries his face in my stomach. "I wasn't looking for love when I came back from New Zealand. But you've shown me what I was missing and I've fallen completely and utterly head over heels for you too."

"There's something else I want to say — but I don't want to scare you."

"Nothing could scare me now. Unless you have a secret love child or a Thai bride you've not told me about." I laugh.

"Don't be daft." He gently pulls my bra back up and over my breasts, giving me back my modesty. "You know how you have a bottom drawer in my bedroom?"

I nod.

"Which is a complete mess by the way. Your stuff is spilling out onto the floor, and I can't remember the last time I saw my bedroom chair."

"I know. I'm sorry"

He laughs and tucks a tendril of hair behind my ear. "I think you're trying to stuff too much into that one drawer."

"I'm sorry. I will tidy it up."

"What if you didn't have to?" Tidy it up, I mean."

I cock my head to one side.

"What if you also shared my wardrobe, my bathroom, my kitchen and my bed? Do you think you'd have enough space for all your stuff then?"

"You mean move in?"

"Why not? I have a big house and no one to share it with. And you're still living out of boxes at your mam's. Don't you want to put down some roots? Make somewhere your real home? I promise I won't say a thing when you cover the place with cushions and scented candles."

I fake punch him in the ribs and he pretends it hurts.

"Seriously though, Tori. I want to be with you. You want to be with me. Let's just remove any barriers to us being together."

"But I've promised Julie I'll move into her spare room. I think she was looking forward to the little bit of extra income."

"I'm sure she'll be fine about it. And if she's that desperate I'm sure she could advertise for another lodger. I get the sense she was only offering you a spare room so you could move out of your parents' and have a bit more independence."

I press my lips together and jut out my jaw. "Okay mister. You've persuaded me and I think you're right. I'll call Julie in the morning. She's probably wondering why I've been putting it off for so long."

"Brilliant. I'll get Mark to help me shift all your stuff as soon as he's free." He plants a light kiss on my lips and lifts me off the island, cradling me in his arms like a baby. "Now, where were we? Come," he says authoritatively, carrying me towards the stairs. "You and I are about to play a game of *'hide the sausage.'*"

"Your wish is my command," I laugh. "But I hope we're heading to the shower first."

"Sex in the shower. You horny little devil. Another first for me. And with you as *my girl*, I suspect it won't be the last."

"And one more thing," I say as he runs up the stairs with me in his arms. "If I'm moving in, then the toilet seat stays down."

"Okay, got it," he laughs, kissing me again.

Part III

Chapter 17

VICTORIA

18 months later, Friday 20th December 1997

I look up and scan the forty or so expectant eyes. Holding my plastic cup aloft, I suck in a deep breath, clear my throat, and a hush descends over the team in front of me.

"Well I think we can all agree that 1997 has been a tough but successful year, and I want to thank each and every one of you for your loyal and valuable contribution."

Today is the last working day before the Christmas holidays and this is my opportunity to thank my team before everyone scatters home to their families.

1997 has indeed been a super successful year for me personally. Twenty-one months on since I stumbled across the floor of The Quilted Camel and Craig leapt forward to steady me, his large Victorian villa feels as much my home as his. Not long after I moved in, we began redecorating from top to bottom, and true to form, I've feminised his once bachelor pad. Filling it with pointless scatter cushions and scented candles. And as promised, Craig has learnt to replace the toilet seat after using it.

In the past year and a half, both our careers have continued to soar. My decision to take a management role in an outsourced marketing agency has proven to be a wise move. I've discovered I have a natural flair for the sector, and I've uncovered a new passion.

Both Craig and I bust our balls Monday to Friday, then come the weekend, we play harder still. Saturdays are spent hanging out at The Red Lion, or the boys head to St James' Park if Newcastle are playing at home, while the girls get together at someone's house, before we all head out into town to party. Sundays are more relaxed and my kitchen has become the epicentre for the 'day after' gatherings, as we munch on bacon sandwiches and slurp never-ending mugs of tea, picking over the escapades from the night before. Often the dissection of the previous evening's antics is as much fun as having lived it first time round.

Someone at the back of the room smiles at me and I raise my plastic cup of shop-bought wine and continue my team address. "Knowing how hard everyone has worked, I shall gladly overlook the extortionate amount spent on pizza and beer that appears to have been charged to my expense account over the past twelve months." A ripple of laughter. "I know how many extra hours and weekends you've all put in when our backs were up against it." Glances and smiles are exchanged amongst the crowd. "Who can forget that infamous Monday morning, finding Michael fast asleep over the top of the printer."

Someone standing next to the aforementioned Michael gives him a slap on the back. "That's only because his mam threw him out and he doesn't have a home to go to," someone heckles.

"I have no doubt..." I raise my hand to *shh* everyone again. "But the facts speak for themselves. We've grown our client revenue by twenty percent and our gross margin to a very healthy seventy percent. We've successfully taken on more campaigns than any other division, delivered the highest results and revenues for our clients, and achieved the highest levels of client satisfaction in our recent customer survey." I take a breath. "Results like these do not happen by accident. They happen when a hard-working team, with a fantastic culture and a great work ethic, place the client at the heart of everything they do, and won't accept anything other than *exceptional* as their baseline."

I pause, allowing for more backslapping and handshaking amongst the crowd.

"Regardless of what the sales team have thrown at us, we've delivered. Regardless of the unrealistic expectations of our clients, we've delivered. When senior management have asked us to find new ways to eke out more profit, we've delivered. Every time, we come up trumps and I couldn't be prouder."

I pause again, allowing my praise to settle. My gaze travelling around the room I spy Nessa peeking around a pillar at the back. She holds up a suit carrier and winks.

I nod my acknowledgment before continuing, "I'd like to be able to tell you that 1998 will be easier... but you know us. We won't stop until we're the largest outsourced telemarketing agency in the country. So let's neck this horrendous poison that's masquerading as some sort of wine..." I grimace as the sour liquid insults my taste buds, "... and agree that that's the last time we send Michael down to the shop to buy our Christmas booze!"

More laughter and backslapping of Michael. "And for those of you joining us on the Quayside for some proper drinks, then I believe the cabs are waiting for us downstairs. Merry Christmas everyone!" I raise my cup and everyone copies me and chimes, 'Merry Christmas' in return.

I emerge from the ladies fifteen minutes later and bump into the one person I'd rather not see right now — my boss. The managing director of the company.

"Err, hi, Victoria," he says, his eyes scanning me from head to toe. "I was hoping I'd catch you before you left."

"Really? I was hoping the complete opposite," I reply, tugging at my skirt. "Black Eye Friday," I add, by way of explanation.

"No need to explain." He waves a hand in the air, chuckling to himself. "I was hoping to see you as I have something very important to discuss with you."

A ball of dread lands heavy on my chest. One of my team dropped an absolute clanger with a client a few weeks ago and I've had to work hard to not only correct the mistake but also recoup the relationship.

"Merry Christmas." My boss passes me a white envelope with my name on the front.

I look at him, wondering if I'm meant to rip into it now, or keep it for later.

"Open it." He gestures with a wave of his hand.

I tear into the envelope and scan the letter inside. My hand flies up to my mouth as I absorb its meaning. "Are you sure?" I meet his gaze.

Laughing, he replies, "You have to be the only employee who would question a promotion. It's time we made good on our promise of a directorship. You've more than proven yourself. And yes, I'm absolutely sure. Your contribution this past year Victoria, has been massive. So, enjoy your Christmas bonus, and welcome to the Senior Management Team."

He holds out his hand and I shake it enthusiastically. "Thank you so much. I'll not let you down. I promise."

"Well, now you have another reason to celebrate this evening." He steps aside, as Nessa and I skip past him and out the building.

In the taxi, Nessa squeezes my knee. "Well done, Tor. You must be over the moon."

"Thanks. I am," I reply, fumbling with my phone as I punch out a text to Craig:

You'll never guess what?

He replies almost immediately:

What?

Guess who's just had a chunky pay rise and been made a director? We're on the same money now. Who'd have thought it. No more being a kept woman ... haha. Love you T x

That's awesome. You deserve it. You've worked so hard. At this rate, I'll be able to give up work and become a kept man! Haha. See you soon. C x

Nice try. But I can't ever imagine you as a house husband. I still reckon you'll make CEO before me. I have ovaries, remember.

True. But I'm still super proud of you. See you in a bit. x

I stare at my phone as Nessa asks, "Everything okay?"

"Totally." I smile.

But I'm left pondering whether he meant, *true* — he'll make CEO before me, or *true* — he'll never be a house-husband, or *true* — I have ovaries, so at some point his career will overtake mine when we have kids.

Chapter 18

CRAIG

*C*raig steps out of the taxi, followed by Anth and another couple of members of his team, and is almost mowed down by a Christmas fairy, a reindeer, and a couple of elves who charge past.

The town, as always on Black Eye Friday, is heaving. Five, six deep at every bar. As the last Friday before Christmas, it's renowned in Newcastle as one of the biggest nights out of the year, and one guaranteed to send someone home with a black eye, which is how it acquired its name.

Some of the tamer revellers wear reindeer horns or have a length of tinsel wrapped around their necks. A nod to the festive spirit that ripples through the streets. Craig unconsciously hums along with the cheesy Christmas tunes that drift out onto the street, together with a puff of sweaty condensation, every time a pub door opens to admit new drinkers, or to allow revellers back out onto the pavement.

After buying a couple of rounds for all his subordinates in The Akenside, then Chase, the majority of Craig's team drift off into smaller groups, leaving Anth, a software developer called Dave, and a customer support agent called Amanda, to follow him into Offshore 44.

They manage to nab a window booth where through the bevelled panes of Jacobean glass they have a ringside view of both the action inside the pub and the drunken antics outside on the street.

Sliding along the padded bench, Craig shuffles up next to two older guys who occupy the corner. In their sixties, mostly likely retired miners, they stick out like two sore thumbs in their flat caps and plaid shirts.

"Phwoar... canny bit of stuff that one there," says one to the other.

Craig whispers into Anth's ear, "They look like they've just been let out for the afternoon."

"That'll be you and me one day," Anth sniggers.

"Nah. I'm Peter Pan. Never gonna get old," Craig replies.

"Blimey, get a load of the norks on her," one of the old timers says, nudging his friend to look in the direction of a particularly busty partygoer. "Oh, just imagine Eric, burying your nose in them. You might not get out alive."

Anth giggles into his closed fist.

A gust of cold air blasts into the bar, followed by two stunning girls who dance and shimmy their way into the middle of the crowd. One a redhead with wavy shoulder-length hair, the other a stunning blonde with a long straight bob. Their glittery Christmas fancy dress outfits are topped off by Santa hats, complete with a jingle bell on the end. Their faces tipped to the ceiling; they're singing at the top of their voices. Bopping along in time to the music, they're oblivious to the numerous pairs of male eyes who have clocked their arrival.

One of the old guys turns to his mate. "Cor, what I'd give to be forty years younger. I'd march straight over there and buy them two a drink."

"Ya reckon, Eric?" his mate replies. "Which one would you go for?"

"The blonde. She looks right up for it."

"Yeah, but you know what they say about redheads. Fiery."

Seizing the opportunity, Craig turns to the men. "You reckon you'd be in with a chance… if you were forty years younger?"

"Definitely. We had both looks and charm back then. Didn't we Eric?"

"Well, me and my mate Anth here might not be as good looking as you two," Craig winks at the old timers, "But Anth… whaddya reckon? Do you think if we went over there, we could charm those two lovely ladies?"

"Pah! I'd like to see you try," Eric challenges. "We'll watch your drinks. Off you go. I can't promise I won't laugh." Eric gesticulates in the direction of the girls.

"Come on, Craig. We've got this." Anth slaps Craig's knee and the pair stand up.

Shuffling out of their seats they step down from the raised booth and elbow their way through the crowd. Their two other colleagues, Dave and Amanda, suspend their conversation and watch their bosses stride purposefully towards the two women.

Anth plums for the redhead and Craig chooses the blonde. Tapping them on their shoulders, both women turn around and smile in recognition, before each man pulls them into a passionate kiss. The girls throw their arms around the men's necks, and Craig dips Vicky backwards, Humphrey Bogart style.

Out of his peripheral vision, Craig catches a glimpse of Eric's jaw, which has fallen to the floor.

Craig taps Vicky on the bum. "You look amazing… oh newly promoted director of client services," he whispers. "We're sat in the window seat, come and join us when you're ready."

"Will do, babes," she replies breezily.

Returning to the table, Dave and Amanda high-five Anth and Craig as they shuffle past.

"You jammy buggers," Eric says, sliding Craig and Anth's drinks back across the table.

"What can I say? When you've got it, you've got it," Craig teases.

"Oh it's not fair," Amanda pipes up. "Don't worry boys, they were only winding you up. Those are their girlfriends."

"Fiancée, actually," Anth corrects her, raising his index finger in the air.

Craig pretends to be annoyed. "Aww, why'd you have to go and spoil the fun? I reckon Eric and his pal here thought we had magic pulling powers."

The old guys smile in unison. "Well you young 'uns fooled us good and proper."

"Yup, there was me thinking *you pair of jammy bastards*," Eric's friend laughs.

Vicky and Nessa arrive back from the bar, fresh drinks in hand. They slide into the booth, sitting on their respective boyfriend's knees.

"Hello stranger, fancy meeting you here," Vicky says, landing a peck on Craig's lips. "How's your night been so far?"

"Better now I've bumped into you."

"Has Craig told you about Tor's promotion?" Nessa says to Anth.

"No?" Anth turns and looks at Vicky.

"Oh, it's nothing really." She flicks her hand, not wanting to draw unnecessary attention to herself.

"Hardly." Craig beams. "She's just been made a director."

"Wow. Well done you," Anth replies. "That's awesome."

"Thanks." Vicky dips her head. "I'm really chuffed."

"And so you should be." Craig kisses her shoulder.

"It will mean more travel and time away from home. But the money's good." Vicky adds.

"So who's going to keep the home fires burning, when you're off travelling or doing whatever?" Amanda chimes in.

Vicky turns and glares at her, confused by the blatant dig. "I think Craig is more than capable of looking after himself when I'm not there. He doesn't need me to cook his dinner and iron his shirts, if that's what you're implying."

"I'm not implying anything, only that I know some men prefer a woman to be home when they are. It makes them feel more... well, manly."

"In the 1950s perhaps? But I'm pleased our relationship is not like that. Is it?" Vicky looks for Craig's support.

"Too right. You've earned this and I couldn't be prouder." He lands another peck on his girlfriend's lips. "Right, sup up everyone. Time to move on."

The crowd muster towards the door, Anth holding Nessa's hand, Craig with his arm thrown over Vicky's shoulder, and Dave reaching for Amanda's hand to hold, but she flicks it away and follows on behind.

Chapter 19

*C*raig thought his mother would burst when he'd asked if he could invite Vicky to Christmas dinner. Last year, their relationship still being relatively new, they each returned to their parents' homes to eat Christmas dinner, but this year they want to be together. Therefore, after spending the morning with Vicky's parents, the pair have relocated to Craig's parents' house for the afternoon.

Despite Bob's initial scepticism that Vicky was nothing more than a freeloader, he's come to realise how hard-working and driven she is. Especially now her career status has matched his son's. More importantly, he's appreciative of the positive impact she's had on both his son and his wife. And as Vicky has become more accustomed to Craig's family, she's learnt to subtly acknowledge then ignore the rituals Craig's mother refuses to relinquish. The extra place setting at dinner. The cards on the mantle marking Rob's birthday. The extra present under the Christmas tree that will never be opened. And Craig loves her even more for this.

"Let me help you with those Mrs. F." Vicky begins stacking everyone's empty dinner plates, which she carries through to the tiny galley kitchen.

"That's so kind of you," Craig's mother replies.

Craig knows this Christmas has been especially hard for his parents. Seeing him here with Vicky is a stark reminder that there should have been five round the table today, possibly six, if Rob might have also found love. Who knows, maybe if he hadn't have been so cruelly taken from them nine years ago, there might also have been nieces and nephews crawling around the floor, or playing with the tinsel on the tree.

"Leave them, Tori," he hears his mother's voice drift in from the other room. "I can do them later. Now I think it's time for presents."

The two women rejoin the men in the lounge, and Vicky sits on the floor by Craig's feet, as he takes the only armchair. His mother sliding into her normal spot next to her husband on the small two-seater sofa.

"As you're down there, do you want to do the honours?" Bob asks Vicky.

"Of course, but let us give you your presents first." Vicky takes the gift bag Craig has slid around from the back of the armchair.

Craig's parents each open their gifts. A bottle of whiskey and some gardening tools for Bob and a gift voucher for a local beautician's together with a gift box of smellies for Craig's mam.

"Oh this is lovely," Craig's mother says.

"Merry Christmas, Mam." Craig kisses the older woman on her cheek. "I thought you could treat yourself. Get your nails done, or have a massage."

"And this is great. Thanks, son," Bob says.

"And thank you," Craig's mother says magnanimously to Vicky, who's sitting quietly watching the ritual unfold.

"Actually we have something else for you." Vicky exchanges a conspiratorial smile with Craig.

"When was the last time you and Dad had a holiday?" Craig asks.

"Like we have money to fritter away on something like that," Bob snorts.

"Exactly. Which is why we both want you to have this." Craig passes his mam an envelope. She opens it and gasps, her hand flying up to her mouth.

Looking over his wife's shoulder, Bob rips the Hoseasons gift voucher from her hand. "This is really generous, son. But we couldn't possibly accept it." His pride, as ever, overruling his heart.

Take the fucking money you stubborn old boot, Craig thinks to himself. I've been known to piss that amount up against the wall, in a single weekend of drinking. Just take the sodding five hundred quid.

He meets his father's steely gaze and the older man bobs his head.

Perhaps he heard me, Craig smiles inwardly.

"Don't be silly, Bob. It's our gift to the both of you." Vicky tries to appease Craig's father, unaware of the unsaid words passing between father and son. "Craig and I talked it through and we want you to have it. You haven't had a holiday since—" Vicky stops dead. "Well, anyway, Hoseasons are a great company and have some lovely parks over in The Lake District, or you could take a trip to Devon or Cornwall. If you avoid the school holidays, that should stretch to two weeks in a nice caravan." She kneels up and kisses Craig's mam on the cheek.

Clasping Vicky's hand, the older woman replies, "Thank you pet. This is really lovely and way more than we could have ever afforded. Say thank you, Bob." She digs her husband in the ribs and he mutters a 'thank you' under his breath. "Now it's your turn. Vicky, would you mind?"

Vicky dutifully crawls on hands and knees under the tree and collects the gifts labelled for herself and Craig.

She rips into her present which contains a couple of novels. The latest Danielle Steele and a new book by an unknown author, Helen Fielding, *Bridget Jones's Diary*.

"I've heard about this." Vicky reads the blurb on the back. "All the girls at work are raving about it. It's supposed to be really funny."

"That's what I've heard as well. Maybe I can borrow it back off you, for when we go on our little holiday."

The two women exchange a smile, while Craig rips into his gifts. A pair of comedy socks, a couple of pairs of Calvin Klein trunks, and another gift which he holds onto. Turning it over and over, he already knows what will lie inside.

When will she stop?

"Mam, thank you, but make this the last one, okay?" The older woman's eyes glass over and Craig slides the unopened present into his back pocket. "It's been ten years now. And I miss him as much as you both do. But we can't keep living in the past."

Vicky sucks in an urgent breath. She's never heard Craig bring up his brother's death in front of his parents.

"I know, son," Bob says softly. "And nothing we can say or do will ever bring him back. All we can do is continue to honour him. We're just so thankful we still have you." The older man reaches out and clasps his son's hands. A rare expression of physical love from the deeply stoic older man.

"And we're also thankful to have a gorgeous daughter-in-law." Craig's mam beams at Vicky, but Craig coughs into his closed fist and Vicky looks awkwardly down at the carpet.

"I think you might be getting a bit ahead of yourself there, Mam."

"I don't understand what's taking you so long. You've been together what — nearly two years — by then, me and your dad were long-married, and Rob was already on his way."

"I know Mam, but things are different for our generation."

"Someone once said to me, you should either have a long relationship and a short engagement, or a short relationship and a long engagement, and I think we're heading towards the former, Mrs. F."

"Well don't take too long about it. I want to be around to enjoy my grandkids."

"And that's my cue to put the kettle on." Craig stands up and heads into the kitchen.

"See what you can do, Tori." Mrs F. leans forward and pats Vicky's hand. "If anyone can persuade him, you can."

Chapter 20

*W*hat was in the gift from your parents?" Vicky asks later that evening while lying in the crook of Craig's armpit, the pair of them sipping Bailey's over ice while *The Vicar of Dibley* Christmas special plays on the TV in the corner.

Craig retrieves the still-wrapped present and tears into it. "It'll be another one of these." He points to the numerous leather straps bound around his wrist. "Can you help?" he asks, holding out his forearm, as Vicky ties the leather band around his wrist. "These three were Rob's. He was wearing them when he was... you know."

Vicky reverently touches the leather bands. Rolling her index finger over them one by one.

"I asked if I could have them, rather than let him be buried with them. I suppose I needed something of his to hold onto. To keep him close. Especially in those first few weeks and months."

"I get it." Vicky wraps her arms around Craig's waist, resting her head on his chest. "That's why I never take this off." With one hand she rolls her fingers around the antique heirloom, the Masonic orb that once belonged to her grandfather that she wears around her neck. "Whenever I'm feeling a bit wobbly, I hold onto this."

"My dad says your grandfather was an amazing man."

Vicky jerks her head back. "They knew each other?"

"Not directly, but let's face it... everyone around here knew *of* your grandfather, or at least his companies."

It was impossible not to, Craig thinks.

"I loved him so much." Vicky sniffs hard. "I often wish I could talk to him again. Now that I'm an adult. It wasn't until I was a lot older that I realised the reputation he had. Growing up, to me he was just *Grandad*. Kind, funny, and extremely hardworking. It's only as I've gotten older that I've appreciated the influence he had, not just on our family, but also the wider community. After he died, Granny received letters from people we never knew, who wanted us to know how he'd helped them out. With advice or mentorship, sometimes money. I spent hours in front of the fire, with Granny, writing thank-you notes. I look at your dad, and he's cut from the same cloth as my grandfather was. Hardworking, stoic, proud."

"Yeah, but your family seem to have done a lot better financially than mine ever have."

"True. But he never let any of his success change him, and coming from nothing, he never took it for granted. Like your dad, all he wanted was for the next generation to have an easier ride than he did. That's why he paid for my education. There's no way my mother could have afforded to send me to that school otherwise. And he bought me my first car, but that was only because by then he'd passed all his shares over to my two uncles once he retired. That meant my cousins were all given company cars on their seventeenth birthdays and he didn't want me to be the odd one left out. Plus he taught me how to drive. Those are some of my best memories of him."

So that's where all her grandad's money went... down the male bloodlines. It dawns on Craig that despite her family connections, Vicky is not sitting on a secret trust fund she hasn't told him about. Oh well, no chance of retiring early. We'll just have to make all our own money. But then, if Private Pratice Software is ever sold... Craig's mind flicks back to a recent board meeting when Jack Walker proposed the long-term exit strategy for the company ... I'll be the one sitting on a canny little nest egg.

Keeping his thoughts to himself he raises his right arm. "Yeah, well, my mam's ended up turning this into a grief-remembrance ritual. As if by giving me a new strap each Christmas it somehow keeps her close to Rob. But it only reminds me how many years it's been and makes me miss him even more." Craig strokes Vicky's hair with the flat of his palm. "It'll be ten years this year. Which is insane."

Vicky rolls up, lying along the length of his legs while she walks her fingers up his bare stomach. He discarded his shirt when he lit the fire earlier. "Thank you for inviting me to your parents' today. It's been lovely to be part of your family tradition, even if it will always be tinged with sadness."

"Any special days always are, but you being there made it feel... well, different."

He looks down at her and his body floods with desire. God, she is soo beautiful. What did I ever do to deserve her?

Vicky notices the change in his demeanour and unconsciously moistens her lips.

"Merry Christmas, *My Girl*." Craig pulls her up onto his stomach so he can lean his forehead against hers. They remain connected for a few long moments, their eyes closed, neither of them speaking as their breath falls into sync. Their chests rising and falling as they soak up the love that passes between them.

"Today felt like the beginning of a new chapter, rather than just another sad Christmas without Rob. Thank you for that."

How I would love for him to have met you, he thinks. I know he would have loved you as much as I do.

Craig fills his lungs with air then releases a long exhale, which comes out staccato as he wrestles with his emotions. An inner battle reconciling his pleasure in the present with his pain from the past.

How can I be this happy when it's all my fault...

Vicky notices the micro emotions flash across Craig's features and she reaches up and caresses the side of his face. "I've never felt like this with anyone else," she whispers. "Loving you is so easy,

Craig. You always make me feel so calm and I can be myself around you."

"Likewise." Craig tilts her chin and gently kisses her.

Their lips tingle at the moment of connection. Gently, reverently, slowly, they both take their time, savouring the moment as their lips brush together. Craig tastes the remnants of Baileys on her tongue, and Vicky threads her fingers behind Craig's neck, inhaling sharply through her nose as their kiss deepens.

Pulling back momentarily from each other, the glow from the crackling fire throws shadows around the room and illuminates the sides of their faces. Craig unclasps Vicky's hair claw and her hair tumbles down around her face. Her naturally straight locks messed-up with kinks from being tied up all day, but he smooths down her tresses with his fingers, flicking the ends over her shoulders. Reaching for her face, he cups her jaw, rolling his thumbs back and forth over her cheekbones.

"God, I love you. You've never looked more beautiful. If I could bottle this moment I would."

"Then you should." She makes the shape of a square with both thumbs and index fingers, as if looking through a camera lens. Holding them up in front of Craig's face she inhales deeply then closes her eyes. "There. I've made a picture memory for us both."

Craig smiles.

She keeps her eyes closed and he leans forward and kisses her right eyelid. "One," he says, his voice hardly a whisper. Then he leans forward again and lands a light imprint on her left eyelid. "Two."

She flutters her eyes open, and he notices the worry lines etched into her brow.

"What's wrong?"

"Don't ever leave me," she says urgently, her voice strained.

Craig crumples his brows together like a stitch. "Where on earth did that come from?"

"The last time you did this, I asked you to leave on 'Three'. I don't want you to leave me — ever. Promise me."

He releases a long exhale and wraps his arms around her. "Whatever makes you think I would? I'm not going to go anywhere."

"I know. It's just … our lives are so perfect right now, I worry that something bad's going to happen."

"Close your eyes," he says softly.

Vicky does as she's instructed.

"One," he says again, landing a gentle kiss on her right eyelid. "Two," he whispers, kissing her left.

She rolls her lips inward, anticipating his next move.

"Three," he breathes, before angling her head towards his once again and gently brushing his lips against hers.

They inhale simultaneously, filling their lungs with air, and Craig grips her waist, laying her down so that she's now underneath him. They deepen their kiss, their tongues licking and twirling together, and Craig feels himself go hard.

Vicky's hands reach around the bulk of Craig's back, her fingers trailing up and down his skin while his hands feel their way around the outsides of her shoulders and down her arms.

Their fingers, finding each other's, clasp together, before Craig holds their intertwined hands above Vicky's head as he leans into her, his hardness pressing against the front of his trousers.

Pulling her hands free, Vicky rips her dress off over her head and wriggles her way out of her black winter tights, dumping them on the floor next to his socks and shirt. She reaches for his belt, but he stops her and instead stands up. Reaching one arm around her back, the other under her knees, he lifts her off the settee and lays her gently on the hearth rug in front of the fire.

"I don't want you getting cold."

She smiles and slowly closes then reopens her eyes.

The logs crackle and spit next to them as Craig leans forward and gently peels the strap of Vicky's bra down her shoulder. She tilts her head and leans into his hand, as if chasing it down her arm along with her bra strap. He leaves a trail of butterfly kisses across her collarbone, continuing across the nape of her neck and across to her other shoulder. Using his teeth, he peels her other bra strap from her body. Vicky fists his hair and arches her back, her body begging for his attention.

"My, my. We are an impatient little minx tonight, aren't we?" he teases.

"I just want you so badly," she breathes. "It's been too long."

Craig's lips continue to move over her body, but his mind whirrs like a spinning top while she writhes and moans beneath him.

It wasn't that long ago... was it? A few weeks maybe. Definitely no more than a month. Or has it been two?

Since overcoming condom-gate Craig is aware that Vicky's sex drive is way higher than his. He feels bad every time he rejects her, fakes a headache, or opts for a cuddle instead of sex. But what with the pressure at work and everything...

"Then we'd better make sure tonight counts, hadn't we."

Snaking his way down her torso, he grips her knickers with his teeth and peels them down over her thighs. She kicks them free at the same as she undoes her bra. Tossing it aside to join the growing pile of discarded clothes on the floor.

Craig locks his eyes with hers, before he lifts both her legs over his shoulders and buries his head in-between her thighs.

Vicky lets out a little yelp as his tongue begins to work its magic. Circling and teasing her nub as he simultaneously slides two fingers inside her. She covers her face with her palms as Craig's fingers penetrate the deepest part of her, stimulating her G-spot. All the while his tongue licks and sucks her clitoris, tasting her sweet elixir.

"Oh God..." She writhes and bucks beneath him. "I need you in me," she whispers, her arms reaching down his torso. Attempting to hook her hands under his armpits and pull him back up her, but he resists. His mouth remaining firmly connected to her feminine altar.

"Craig, let me feel you. Let me see you," she pants.

But he continues to ignore her pleas to reveal himself and instead focuses his intention on her pleasure alone. He feels her legs begin to twitch and knows that she is close.

"Just relax," he mumbles, sliding a third finger inside her. "I'm fine."

She fists his hair, her hips rising and falling as she reaches the precipice, then with one almighty moan, her entire body begins to shudder and contract. Her eyes roll into the back of her head, and a satisfied smile settles on Craig's lips.

Once her orgasm has subsided, Craig wipes his mouth with the back of his hand and shuffles up to lie next to her. Wrapping one arm around her waist, he kisses her cheek. "See, now doesn't that feel better?"

With one hand over her eyes, the other on top of Craig's as he cuddles her, she replies, "Yes it does."

"Merry Christmas. Santa Claus told me you were on his Good List and deserved an extra special present this year. Did you enjoy it?" He chuckles.

She rolls towards him, burying her head in his chest as he holds her, and she wonders how it is possible to feel both loved and simultaneously spurned. Satisfied, yet somehow... not fully satiated.

"Yes. Thank you, I did," she lies.

Chapter 21

VICTORIA

1 week later

*O*utside the kitchen window snow falls silently, muting the sounds of the few passing cars. Mostly taxis, the only vehicles that are still on the road, due to the bad weather. I wrap my fingers around my glass of wine and, illuminated only by the neon light of the streetlamps, look out of the window. My eyes follow the shapes of first the symmetrical rows of Victorian terraces, past the irregular road layouts of the modern housing estates on the outskirts of town, up towards the black and desolate moors beyond. In summer the vast open hills are transformed into a rich carpet of vibrant purple heather, but right now they are bleached white under a layer of thick snow that twinkles in the moonlight.

Others may find the vast openness of the treeless landscape wild and bleak, but I find the moors comforting and freeing. I remember how cramped and hemmed in I felt living in London. The perpetual rumble of traffic, the suffocating pollution and cramped living conditions. I felt like an irrelevant speck in a city of millions from which there was no escape. Whereas now, no matter how stressful my day has been, within half an hour of leaving my office in

Newcastle I can stand at my kitchen window and look out over the wild and vacant hills rising up to meet the horizon. On clear days, I love nothing more than flipping the roof down on my little MG sports car and heading out for a few hours, throwing her into the tight and twisty lanes that criss-cross their way over the Derwent valley into Teesdale beyond the ridge to the south, or over into Northumberland if I turn her north.

Today, it may be cold and Christmassy outside, but this only highlights the warmth and love that envelops me within these walls. Two New Year's Eves ago I was camping with Chris and his brother's family, on the opposite side of the world in New Zealand. A truly beautiful setting but an emotionally wretched time in my life. But that night began the journey that led me here.

I hear a squeal from behind me as someone opens the door between the kitchen and the dining room, and a blast of music interrupts my thoughts.

Nessa and Becca both rush into the kitchen laughing, and frantically open cupboards.

"Where do you keep your kitchen roll, Tor?" Nessa asks.

"In there." I point to the tall cupboard in the corner of the room.

"Mark's jus' managed to open a can of Stella an' spray it all up the wall," Becca slurs.

"Don't worry. Better in there than in the front room. I'd have gone ballistic."

Our lounge has just been decorated.

"I'll get it." I reach up and retrieve the kitchen roll. "Here," I add passing it to Becca.

She runs off and Nessa and I follow her into the chaos. I jump into the middle of the crowd dancing beneath the glitter ball we've hung from the chandelier. The skimmed but not yet painted walls, and stripped but not yet polished floorboards, making this the perfect place to host a rowdy New Year's Eve party with our lot.

"What time is it?" someone shouts.

"Five minutes," Craig hollers back over the din of the music. "Anyone who needs a top-up, go and grab it now."

Someone switches the stereo to live radio, while there's a mad dash in and out of the kitchen as everyone tops up their drinks.

Once the New Year countdown starts, we all gather in a circle and join in from ten down to one, before a roar of 'Happy New Year' rises up from the crowd and a mass hugging and cheering envelops us all.

More champagne corks are released into the air.

More party poppers explode, showering the room with streamers and confetti.

More beer is spilt as everyone cheers and hugs.

Craig pulls me into him. "Happy New Year, Tori," he says, his eyes glinting with happiness.

"Happy New Year." I beam in return, before we kiss.

Then, before I know it, my glass is lifted out of my hand and someone is crossing their arms through mine as, back in our circle, we all sing a drunken rendition of Auld Lang Syne.

I look around the room at everyone's smiley happy faces, and like the snow falling softly outside, a contented feeling settles in my gut. I can't ever remember a time when I felt this content and happy.

I'm so blessed.

I squeeze Craig's hand, and he squeezes mine in return.

⟨⟩

The next morning I grab the frying pan and make a start on breakfast. The bacon sizzles and shrinks in the hot pan, its smoky aroma snaking its way through the house. I pop four slices of bread into the toaster, drop two bags of English Breakfast Tea into the pot, flick the kettle on and tip freshly ground coffee into the Krupp's, which gurgles and spits into life. My bare feet pad quietly across the warm kitchen floor while I prepare to feed the sixteen or so bodies left strewn around the house, like fallen soldiers at the battle of Waterloo.

I hit 'play' on the stereo and The Spice Girls fill the room.

I flip the bacon in the pan and dance along to the beat of the music. Enjoying this moment alone before the chaos resumes.

Mark is the first zombie to appear. He trundles into the kitchen in a crumpled AC/DC T-shirt and yesterday's jeans, sniffing the air, his hands raised protectively over his ears.

"Jeez Tor. Do you have to have it that loud? My head's banging."

"Well it got you moving." I laugh as he stands in front of me, simultaneously scratching his five o'clock shadow with one hand and his balls with the other.

"Help yourself to orange juice, tea, or coffee if you prefer… and there's paracetamol, for your headache." I point to the selection laid out on the island. "Then, do you see that roll of bin bags?" He nods. "Take one. Fill it up with empty cans and any other rubbish you find. Bring it back here and your reward is a bacon sarnie."

He shakes his head, laughing at my meticulous planning. "Unbelievable."

"What can I say. Before I was in marketing, I used to be in travel. Details mattered. Get something wrong and someone ends up in the wrong country — which I did to some poor sod once."

"No way." He gulps down his mouthful of orange juice.

"Yup. I sent some poor bugger to Muscat instead of Dubai."

He coughs into his closed fist.

"I know, right? Fortunately, he was one of my regulars and saw the funny side of it. I booked him on the next flight to Dubai, pulled a favour with the airline and got him an upgrade, but I do remember the only thing I could think of to say when he'd called me to tell me I'd sent him to the wrong country was, *'But you got on the plaaaaaane!'*"

Mark grips his sides, laughing.

"I had this image of this guy clutching his boarding pass, wandering through Terminal 4 at Heathrow, looking at the gate information and thinking, *'Well it must stop off at Dubai on the way. Victoria wouldn't get it wrong.'*"

A female voice with a distinctive Kiwi twang butts into the conversation. "I remember that!"

Mel has staggered into the kitchen, followed closely by her fiancé, Karl. I was over the moon when she said they would come and spend New Year with us.

"I thought you'd be sacked on the spot," Mel adds.

"Probably should have been."

"But then, the number of times I rolled in hungover—"

"Or still pissed," I interject, laughing.

"Agreed. How I got through Monday mornings when I look back now—"

"Strong coffee and Yum Yums, I seem to remember."

"They were good times, weren't they?" She hugs me from behind, resting her chin on my shoulder as I flip the bacon.

"Indeed they were."

Mark pours Karl a coffee and the pair start a conversation over on the other side of the island.

"But it's lovely to see you settled and happy," Mel says, "Who knew your destiny was only one good night out away."

"And what about you. Karl's lovely. Just what you need."

"Yeah. He's a keeper."

As if on cue, Karl passes Mel a fresh mug of coffee.

"Thanks, Goose," she says to him and an involuntary shiver rips through me.

Becca, Anth, Nessa, Julie, and Clarky all stagger into the kitchen together. Like moths drawn to a flame, the smell of coffee and bacon having drawn them out from wherever they'd crashed. They collectively mumble for tea, coffee, or headache tablets, wiping sleep out of their eyes and scratching their heads as if they have lice. Everyone looks like shite and no-one cares. It's great.

The noise level vamps up. The sound of the music overlaid by the clatter of cups being pulled from kitchen cupboards and the chatter of easy conversation, recounting tales and highlights from last night's frivolity.

If 'love' could be a sound it would sound exactly like this.

Clarky makes a play for a bacon sandwich and I slap his hand away.

"Not until you've filled an empty bin bag with rubbish."

Picking up the roll of bin bags, I begin tearing them off. Dishing them out before sending the troops on their way. Led by Anth, their reluctant moans and groans follow them out of the kitchen like an apocalyptic swarm of zombies fading off into the distance. Turning my attention back to the growing pile of toast and cooked bacon, I chortle inwardly.

Out of my peripheral vision I spy Craig. He's leaning casually against the door frame, arm raised, watching me cook. I swallow hard as my eyes take in the gorgeousness of my man. His eyes hooded with desire, he locks his gaze onto me and flashes me one of his cocky smiles, making my insides melt like an ice lolly left out in the sun.

Oh, those damn dimples.

Bare chested and bare footed, his Levi's hang invitingly from his hips. His unkempt bed hair is begging to be ruffled and my hands desperately want to run over his taut torso, feeling the definition and firmness of his chest.

As if reading my mind, his pecs twitch as he shifts his weight. I purposefully turn away from him, pretending that my task of buttering toast and flipping bacon requires much more of my attention than gawping at him. Undeterred, he comes up behind me, wrapping his arms around my waist, and nibbles my left ear in that way I love so much.

"Surely those rules don't apply to me," he whispers, his breath hot against my skin, causing an involuntary shiver to ripple through me.

"Oh yes they do. No exceptions."

"Well maybe I don't want to play by the rules," he replies as I lean back into him.

He pulls me in tighter, lightly kissing my neck, and I reach one hand behind me to touch his face. He turns his head and plants a gentle kiss on my palm.

Leaving the fish slice in the pan, I turn around and throw my arms around his neck. Looking deep into the jet-black irises of his eyes the world around us falls away. I no longer hear the music, or the bacon sizzling in the pan, or notice the snow that continues to fall softly outside — I only see Craig and feel his love.

"Welcome to 1998," he says kissing the tip of my nose.

"Gosh, since meeting you it feels as if time has sped up. So much has happened. It makes me wonder what this year will bring."

He shrugs. "Who knows?" he says, bending his head and kissing me tenderly.

"Ahem." I hear someone fake cough behind us. Looking over Craig's shoulder, I see Amanda, the girl from his office, standing on the step that leads up into the hallway from the kitchen.

We also invited a couple of people from his team to join us last night, but they all left around one in the morning. I can't remember why Amanda didn't go with them. Something about her taxi not turning up, I think. I'm not sure how long she's been standing there, but I suspect it's been long enough to witness our intimate and private moment.

Her long dark hair hangs loose and damp over her shoulders and judging by her shiny skin, she's already showered.

I can't quite put my finger on it, but something about this girl grates on me. Wait, is that my T-shirt she's wearing? What the hell!

Seeing my eyes scan over the T-shirt, she tugs at the bottom. "Oh, Craig gave it to me. I didn't have anything else to sleep in. He didn't think you'd mind."

"Sure. Whatever," I hiss through gritted teeth.

Just peeking out below the bottom of the T-shirt are a pair of skimpy black lace knickers. The see-through mesh triangle at the front revealing a pubis as smooth as a baby's bottom.

"Jeez, put some clothes on girl," I mutter into Craig's neck.

She walks brazenly across the kitchen and pours herself a glass of juice, exaggerating the need to stretch and causing the T-shirt to ride up, revealing two perfectly pert butt cheeks at the top of endlessly long slim legs, all fully exposed thanks to the G-string that cuts up her backside like the dimple in a perfectly ripe peach.

Turning back around, she smiles coyly in our direction. "Sorry guys, I hope I wasn't interrupting anything."

I ignore her, hoping she can sense my annoyance.

I want Craig to tell her that she *was* interrupting and to go and put some damn clothes on, but instead I hear him reply in level tones, "No it's fine. I was just helping Tori with the bacon."

"Ahh, is that what that was?" she mutters, loud enough to be heard.

I watch as she walks away and find I have to clench my fists to suppress my childish need to run up behind her and give her one almighty wedgie up her perfectly peachy arse.

Chapter 22

6 months later, June 1998

I fiddle with my phone as I wait outside Newcastle Central Station, underneath John Dobson's iconic stone portico. Checking to see if Craig's left me any voicemails. He should be here any minute. I'm so excited for this weekend.

Looking up I see Craig's black Audi weaving through the taxis and my heart skips a beat.

"Quick, jump in!" Craig hollers as Becca throws open the rear passenger door. "I'm not supposed to stop here."

Jétèing like the ballet dancer I always aspired to be, I throw my work bag into the footwell and land in the back seat next to Becca. Leaning through the gap in-between the front seats, I give Craig's shoulders a quick *hello* squeeze.

"Hi Tor," Mark says from the other front seat. "You good?"

"Yes thanks, but I'm *sooooo* ready for a weekend away." I catch Craig's eye through his rear-view mirror and he gives me a conspiratorial wink.

Mark rubs his palms together. "Right Craigy-boy. Let's get this show on the road."

Craig flicks on the car's indicator and turns right onto St. James' Boulevard, the famous St. James' Park football stadium towering above as we drive past.

"Aww, the Holy Grail," Mark sighs. "I swear if I could live in the middle of the pitch I would."

"You and every other nutjob diehard supporter." Becca rolls her eyes and we all laugh.

A few minutes later, and clear of the city congestion, the A1 Great North Road opens up in front of us. Craig turns on the cruise control, cranks up the tunes on the radio, and slides his Oakley Romeo sunglasses up the bridge of his nose. Pulling out into the fast lane we speed off towards the coast.

"Let's hope the weather stays like this." Becca looks through the car window at the cloudless blue sky.

"Fingers crossed," I reply.

"If it stays dry, how about a barbecue on the beach tomorrow night?" Craig says.

"It can piss down for all I care," Mark replies. "It won't keep me out of the hot tub."

"I love a good hot tub, but nothing compares to sitting in an actual hot pool, especially in the rain," I say.

"Hot pools?" Mark quizzes.

"In New Zealand. Over there they laugh at us with all our artificially heated spas when there are hot rivers and thermal pools all over the country."

"Well I never," Becca replies. "But Mark, I'm not sure I packed your trunks. I didn't realise there was going to be a hot tub. I definitely packed shorts, but not swimming costumes."

"Don't care. I'll climb in naked."

"I'd better warn the neighbours," Craig teases.

"What? In case they clap eyes on my ginormous knob?"

"Don't make me laugh," Becca interjects. "There's more chance of your eyebrows frightening the neighbours than your teeny-weeny willy."

"Oh, let's not chastise the poor lad for what he was born with. I mean it's not his fault he has such little hands," I tease as Mark rolls his eyes.

Over the last two and a bit years I've learnt that the constant ribbing is a form of currency between this tightly knit friendship group.

"She's got you there mate. Or should I say, *Little Hands*." Craig uses a knee to steer while he does his best impression of T-Rex fingers.

"Yeah, yeah. All right. Take the mick all you want, but it's my beer in the boot and you'll not be having any of it if you carry on like this. I'll take the whole bloody lot of it into the hot tub with me and the rest of you can *do one*."

Becca reaches from the back seat and places a hand on Craig's shoulder. "Seriously though. It was really great of you and Vicky to shout us this weekend."

"No worries. You guys brought the booze," Craig replies.

"Courtesy of Mark's dad's Costco account," Becca adds.

"Doesn't matter." Craig swishes his hand in the air. "There's no tally between friends."

R

"This is amazing," Becca squeals as she steps through the front door of the rented cottage. Racing across the room she looks out of the lounge window. "It has a perfect view of the castle."

The quaint two-bed fisherman's cottage backs onto Bamburgh village green, a small rectangle of canvas covering the cricket pitch, ready for tomorrow's match. On the other side of the outfield, perched high on a dolerite outcrop, and forming a protective barrier between the village and the sea, sits the impressive castle. Once the capital of Bernicia, a small kingdom of what now is South-East Scotland and North-East England in Anglo-Saxon times, the castle has been extended and renovated over time. The castle we see today was rebuilt by the Normans in the 12th century after it had been flattened by the Vikings before that.

"I know. That's why we picked it. It doesn't get any better than this." I smile across at Becca.

"And what's all this?" Becca points to a champagne hamper in the middle of the coffee table.

"That's my fault," Craig says, carrying in a crate of beer. "I thought we could spoil ourselves." He bends and lands a kiss on my cheek. "Put the champers in the freezer. It'll need chilling. Then once Mark and I have finished unloading, I'll light the log burner."

"But it's the middle of summer." I laugh.

"Don't care." Mark appears at the door. "Me — man. Me — make fire." He adopts a caveman stance.

"Fair enough. We'll open the windows if it gets too warm." I shrug.

"That's the spirit," Craig says. "It'll make it more romantic," he adds, whispering in my ear.

A couple of hours later, our bellies full of food and our mood mellow from booze, everyone is basking in the warm glow of the fire. Mark coughs into his hand, before he untangles himself from Becca and stands up. "Stay there pet. Back in two ticks."

Becca looks quizzically across the room but we both shrug and shake our heads.

Craig gives my knee a little squeeze. *Here we go.*

Mark reappears with a large box, almost the same size as him, tied up with a shiny red bow.

Rebecca's face lights up.

"I know it's your birthday on Monday," Mark says, "but I wanted you to have this now."

"Are you sure? I don't mind waiting."

"Are you flipping kidding me?" I squeal and clap my hands like a sea lion. "Get it open, girlfriend."

Mark places the box on the floor and Becca pulls on the end of the bow. She lifts off the lid and peers inside. "Oh, very funny," she groans and lifts out... another box, only marginally smaller than the previous one.

The next box is sealed with Sellotape, and Mark pulls out a Swiss army knife and passes it to Becca. She slits open the tape and pulls out... another box.

"Oh, ha-ha," she says sarcastically.

"Anyone for a top-up?" I rush around and top up everyone's glasses.

Craig and I both know we could be here some time.

Becca repeats the unwrapping of the next parcel only to reveal another one inside. Then another, and another, and another. About six or seven parcels in, the box has been reduced to a size that fits onto her lap. All around lie piles of discarded wrapping paper and empty cardboard boxes. She's been unwrapping for around fifteen minutes or so and has just revealed a shoe box.

"A pair of Nikes — really, Mark?" She laughs.

"Maybe. Maybe not," he replies. "Open it and see."

Becca unwraps the next layer and lifts out the box inside — a metal biscuit tin — welded shut. "Oh, howay man. How am I supposed to get into this one?"

"Figure it out," Mark teases.

"Tin opener!" I leap up and, clambering over all the wrapping debris, retrieve a tin opener from the kitchen drawer.

Becca jimmies her way through the metal to reveal... another box.

She groans and we all laugh.

Sitting back on Craig's lap, I whisper, "Do you think she's figured it out yet?"

He raises his eyebrows and presses his lips together into a thin line. "I don't think so."

"When will it *end?*" Becca throws her hands up in the air in mock frustration, before ripping through to the next box, the next one, and the one after that, before she freezes.

She looks from inside the box, to Mark's face, then back inside the cardboard box again.

I hold my breath as my fingers fly up to my face as I try desperately to contain my squeals of excitement.

Mark reaches inside the last parcel, lifts out a black velvet ring box and slides onto the floor in front of his girlfriend.

Craig squeezes my waist, and I can't help letting out a tiny high-pitched squeak.

Mark clears his throat. "Rebecca Bell. It was eight years, four days," he checks his watch, "and nine hours ago, when I first saw you striding across the refectory at college with all your hairdressing classmates. It was love at first sight. At least for me. You don't remember that day, as you and your mates gave me and all my sparky pals the cold shoulder."

"Oh, I remember." Becca beams.

"But by that Christmas I'd worn you down and you'd agreed to go on a date. Even if it was only to stop me pestering you."

Becca nods her head in agreement, her eyes twinkling with happy tears.

"That first date led to a second, and then a third, and before I knew it, we were going steady and I was the happiest man alive. I know I can be a miserable twat at times, Becca, and I know I don't always show you the love you deserve, but I can't tell you how grateful I am that you continue to put up with me every single day."

He sucks in a deep breath.

"I want you to continue putting up with me every single day for the rest of our lives. I promise I'll do my best to *not* piss you off, and try my hardest to make you feel as happy as you make me feel every day. Rebecca Bell, will you do me the honour of becoming my wife?" He opens the small black velvet box, revealing a ring in the shape of a delicate flower made up of tiny diamonds. Becca gasps.

"Marry me Becca ... *please*," he adds at the very end, as if he's not a hundred percent certain she will say 'yes'.

But he needn't have worried. With both her hands over her

mouth, Becca nods her head vigorously and breaks into happy sobs. Mark reaches for her shaking finger and slides the ring onto it.

Both Craig and I break into applause and lunge across the room to embrace the newly engaged couple.

"Did you know?" Becca asks me.

I nod my head. "Not about all the boxes. That was all Mark. But we helped him plan the getaway. He wanted to do something special for you."

"Bravo." Craig slaps Mark on the back with one hand, while he shakes his hand with the other. "Well done mate. I'm proud of you."

"How can I ever thank you both?" Becca asks us.

Craig leans down and gives her a peck on the cheek. "No thanks needed. We're just happy for you guys."

"Right, where's the champagne?"

I run to the freezer and pull out the special bottle and pass it to Mark. "I think you should take it into the hot tub."

"Good idea." Mark winks at Becca who is still admiring the new ring on her finger.

"You two should enjoy a bit of alone time," I laugh. "Especially if you've both forgotten your trunks."

෨

We leave Mark and Becca to celebrate on their own, meanwhile Craig throws another log into the wood burner as I look through the cottage's VHS collection.

"That went well," I say as we both settle back onto the sofa. "I'm really pleased for them. They've been together such a long time."

I release a long sigh and meet Craig's gaze.

Since Craig first asked me to move in with him, we never seem to talk about our relationship anymore. I know he loves me, yet all the other couples around us seem to be engaged and planning the next phases in their lives — Nessa and Anth, Mel and Karl, and now Becca and Mark — but I have no idea if we're still heading down that track. I'll be twenty-seven next month. The clock is ticking.

"What's up?"

I bite my lip. "Seeing Mark's beautiful proposal tonight has made me think about us. You know, when you might think about making us official."

"I thought we were official, *My Girl*. You're not seeing anyone else, are you?" he teases.

"That's not what I mean, and you know it."

"Yes, I do know, but we're happy as we are, aren't we? Why would we want to change anything when everything is already so good?"

"Because I would like to be married — one day. And I'm not saying I want to get married next week, or next month, or even next year. I just want to know we're on the same page, and that we'll get there someday. And in enough time for us to think about having a family."

"Of course we will. I'm never letting you go." He pulls me into him and kisses my hair. "The only future I picture is with you, Tori. I suppose I just don't feel the same urgency as you do. Both of us are so focused on our careers right now, I didn't think you'd want to be pinned down by marriage and ankle-biters."

"I get that. It's just…"

"What?"

"Oh, I don't know. It's just that without a ring on my finger there'll always be a part of me wondering if you're really choosing me, or if you're with me because you haven't found anyone better."

"But you know that's not true." He holds my chin between his thumb and forefinger.

"How do I?"

"Because you are the most important thing in my life. I don't need a ring on your finger, or mine for that matter, to know how much we mean to each other."

"I know; it would just be nice, that's all."

"What if we make our own promise to each other?"

I tilt my head. "Okay, I'm listening."

He pulls me up onto his lap so that we're facing each other. I stare directly into the dark pools of his eyes.

"My darling Tori, I promise to love you — always. I promise to always choose you. To be there when you need me and... to marry you and give you babies. One day."

Tears spring to the corner of my eyes. "You really mean that? You're not just saying it because you think it's what I want to hear?"

"Of course not."

"Oh, Craig. That's all I needed. I can't wait to tell the girls. They'll be so excited."

"Erm... I'd rather you didn't."

"But why?"

"Think about it. From their perspective, nothing's changed. And we don't want to take anything away from Mark's proposal. Just think how excited Becca's going to be when she retells the events from this weekend. You don't want to take that away from her, do you?"

"You're right. It wouldn't be fair on Becca — or Mark — if we announced our engagement as well."

"Well I wouldn't quite call it that," he chuckles.

"So if this isn't an engagement conversation, then what are you saying?"

"I'd call it a... 'love promise.'"

"A love promise?"

"Yes. Regardless of what we say or do to appease the outside world, I don't need to conform to society's rules on relationships; what's more important is that you and I both know we promise to love each other, forever."

"I'll take that," I say, my face splitting into the widest of grins. "I don't need a diamond on my finger to show the outside world what you mean to me. I love you. You love me. And that's what matters."

"Exactly. I knew you'd understand," he says, pecking me on the lips. "See? Sealed with a loving kiss."

Chapter 23

5 months later, November 1997

J'm really sorry, Tori," Craig says at the other end of the telephone. "I know I promised I'd be home early tonight, but we're still dealing with this utter shit-show. I can't leave until I know the team are on top of it."

"Okay," I sigh. "But you have to be here by 7.00 p.m. — latest. Don't make me host this dinner party alone."

"I'll do my best. *'Okay, tell them I'm on my way'*," Craig shouts to someone in the background. "Sorry babes. Gotta go."

"Okay then. See you soon," I reply into the handset, but the line's already dead.

"Everything okay?" a voice behind me asks.

Turning, I smile at my friend Tim, who steps down into the kitchen, coffee cup in hand. Tim and I have been friends for over five years. Ever since he was Mel's landlord before she and I moved in together. By then he'd moved up to London and we all remained in contact. His parties were legendary. Similarly to my friendship with Mel, Tim and I may not see each other anywhere near as much as we used to, especially since I've moved back north and his career has gone international, but on the infrequent times we do catch up, it's easy to pick up where we last left off. Which normally involves him teasing me — usually about my choice in boyfriends. He's like the big brother I never had.

"Yeah. Craig's just stuck at work," I continue. "They've not long taken over another business and his team are migrating all the customers onto their software platform. It's been a total nightmare." I look around the kitchen surfaces, stacked high with ingredients and kitchenware. "I had hoped he'd be here to help."

"Then let me."

"Thanks, Tim."

೧ು

"Here, let me do that," Craig says four hours later, taking the oven gloves from me and kneeling down in front of the cooker. "You go back next door. Make sure everyone's glass is topped up." His tone more commanding than questioning.

"Are you sure?"

"Yeah. Someone needs to watch these soufflés and make sure they come out right."

"But I'm more than happy to stay."

I don't add that I'd really wanted to serve up the final pièce de résistance. It feels unfair that I won't get to take the final curtain call. Especially when I made them.

"No. Leave it to me. You've put masses of effort into tonight; let me do this one. Go and enjoy the craic." He gestures towards the dining room where, judging by the peals of laughter filtering back through to the kitchen, everyone is having a great time.

Biting the inside of my cheek, I grab another chilled bottle of wine from the fridge and head back next door, my heels click-clacking across the kitchen floor.

Everyone is seated around our beautiful wrought-iron, glass-topped and *very* expensive designer dining room table, purchased in last year's January sales. We decided on a dramatic deep crimson paint colour for this room, and we've hung a huge chandelier from the restored ceiling rose and added a dramatic wrought-iron mirror, one that matches the table, and placed it in pride of place above the black marble fireplace. It took forever to remove the layers and layers of paint and restore the original marble to its former glory. A couple of oversized prints and, second only to the kitchen, this is now my favourite room in our home.

I slide into my seat, next to Nessa, but everyone else's attention is on Tim, who is holding court at the opposite end of the table. In front of me is a pile of empty dishes which, I assume, Nessa has kindly gathered up now that everyone has finished their main course.

Anth leans in, waiting for Tim to deliver his punchline — something about gweilos in Hong Kong, at which point the room cracks up.

"That's crazy," Anth says across the table to Nessa. "I've never been to Hong Kong but it sounds fascinating. Maybe we should consider Asia for our honeymoon. Whaddya think pet?"

"A great choice," Tim adds. "Especially if you combine it with a beach break in Thailand. I'd recommend Phuket, or Koh Samui. You can get a five-star resort for buttons. And I'd do it that way round. Hong Kong first, then go to a beach to relax."

"Sounds perfect," Nessa chimes in. "I'm not sure I could sit on a beach for a whole two weeks. I'd get bored."

"Me too," Anth confirms.

At the mention of Hong Kong, my mind wanders back to the time I visited with Chris, in what was meant to be a holiday to bring us closer together, but turned out to be the first major red flag in our relationship. I unconsciously rub my neck, the memory of his rage as fresh today as the moment he had his hands around my throat.

"You okay?" Nessa whispers in my ear while reaching under the table to squeeze my hand. I nod my head and take another sip of wine.

Satisfied I'm okay, she turns her attention back to Anth. "I think we should check it out."

"We will. But first we need to agree on a date." Anth picks up his glass and takes a sip, eyeing Nessa over the top.

Nessa rolls her eyes. It's a standing joke. No one is expecting them to make things official anytime soon, not when they are already considered the 'old marrieds' of our group.

"You two need to start by choosing a *year*, then work backwards from there." I roll my eyes.

"We'll get round to it. Eventually." Nessa smiles affectionately at her fiancé. "Or we could take the honeymoon before we tie the knot."

"Or we could just get married out there." Anth smirks.

"Don't you flippin' dare," I exclaim. "There's no way you're gonna deprive us of an outrageous party!"

"We won't," Nessa says. "You'd never let us live it down."

"Too bloody right," I reply.

"Ever the party animal. I have fond memories of you tap dancing across my very expensive parquet flooring, dressed head-to-toe in sequins." Tim raises his glass in my direction, and I smile. The memory of one of Tim's many parties settling warmly in my gut.

"If you do decide to come out to Hong Kong, for any reason, make sure to drop me a line." Tim hands Anth his business card.

"Thanks. We will." Anth slides the card into his top pocket.

I stand up, reaching for the pile of dirty plates, but before I have a chance to leave the room, Amanda — the customer services team leader from Craig's work — who has contributed nothing to the conversation all evening, leaps up out of her chair.

"I'll take those through, Tori," she says authoritatively, reaching over and grabbing the plates before I have a chance to object.

Her words slap me around the face like a wet fish. I stand stock-still watching her flounce off towards the kitchen. Only Craig (and by extension his mother) call me by that nickname. My really close friends call me Tor, and to everyone else I'm Vicky, or Victoria.

How bloody dare she!

Over her shoulder she adds a throwaway, "You look after everything in here; I'll make sure Craig's got everything he needs." The muted tones from the stereo continue to play softly in the background. The lyrics from the current tune cut through the chitchat of our guests and punch me right between the eyes.

It's the Beautiful South's big hit, *Don't Marry Her Have Me*, one of my favourite songs, but the timing of the lyrics seems poignant. Defeated, I flop back into my chair.

"Remind me why she's here?" Nessa asks quietly in my ear, while Tim and Anth continue their animated conversation at the opposite end of the table.

"To be honest, Ness, I have absolutely no idea. Craig made some excuse about feeling guilty for all the late nights she's pulled lately. I think he considers her a work wife."

"Hmmm..." Nessa's eyes narrow. "As long as she's not more than that."

"Maybe if Craig told her Anth was invited, she thought it would be more of a work thing. Or a bigger crowd. Like at our New Year party." I shrug.

"Maybe," Nessa says, taking a sip of her wine.

Tim addresses me, breaking into my thoughts. "Victoria, I appreciate your persistent attempts to convert me to the poor and unrefined white grape," he holds aloft his empty glass, "but really — have you still not learned that those of us with a more developed palette prefer the more mature red variety."

I reply with an equally sarcastic delivery, "Our cellar used to rival the George V, but all we have left is the dregs our *other* friends haven't drunk."

"Ha-ha. Very funny," Tim replies, smiling.

It's unlikely anyone else around the table would pick up on the reference to the world-famous Parisian hotel, famed for its wine cellar. I've never actually been there myself, but back when I worked in travel, I've sent plenty of business travel clients there. Anth and Nessa laugh politely nonetheless.

I make to stand up, my chair scraping across the floor, but Tim is already on his feet.

"Don't worry. I'll get it." He leans over and pecks my cheek as he walks past.

Nessa leans into me. "He's lovely, by the way."

"I know. He's a great friend. Even if only a friend from afar these days."

"True friendship never dies." She clasps my hand under the table again. "Just look at us."

Tim's frame fills the doorway, and instead of stepping down into the kitchen he stops dead and jerks his head back. I hear him release a hardly audible, "Oh."

He remains frozen on the step, as if he's forgotten what he was going into the kitchen for.

I stand up. "Dear God, Tim. You'd forget your head if it wasn't screwed on. Go and sit back down. I'll get the wine."

I'd already opened a new bottle of Malbec a few hours ago and left it to breathe on the kitchen island.

Tim turns sharply and embraces me. "No, Victoria. You stay exactly where you are. You deserve to enjoy the rest of your evening. I'll get it."

Releasing me, he turns again, clears his throat loudly and steps down into the kitchen.

Chapter 24

*E*verything alright?" I ask moments later when Tim reappears, bottle of red in hand.

"Absolutely," he says, brushing my question aside. "Anyone for Malbec?"

"I will, thanks Tim." Anth holds out his glass.

"The soufflés must be ready by now," I mutter to no one in particular.

"Trust me, everything is under control. Just sit back and relax." Tim says, his glare pinning me to my seat.

"Well, I can't until I know my puddings are alright."

Ignoring him, I stand up and push past Tim, but just as I'm about to step down into the kitchen, we're all plunged into darkness. The room goes silent, the stereo also muted by the untimely power cut.

"Well, this is interesting." Tim giggles in the darkness. "Dinner in the dark. I didn't know this was the plan, Victoria."

"Ha-ha, very funny. Sadly, this happens a lot." I peer into the pitch-black kitchen. "Talk amongst yourselves," I say to the group. "Back in a bit. *Cra-aig*, are you checking the fuse box?" I shout into the darkness.

"I'm about to." I hear him rummaging through our kitchen man-drawer. "It's definitely just us. The streetlights are still on and I can't hear any house alarms going off."

"Top drawer. Left-hand side," I instruct, knowing he'll be looking for the torch.

"Got it." A beam of light appears in the far corner of the room. Through the partial light I can see Amanda's outline next to Craig.

"What a bloody nightmare. Can you believe it?" I say, trying to lighten the atmosphere which feels noticeably heavier in the kitchen than back in the dining room.

"Not to worry. I'll fix it." He disappears down the back stairs into the cellar, taking the beam of light with him and plunging us back into darkness, which seems even more pronounced now that my eyes have been robbed of the torchlight.

"At least the soufflés are out of the oven," Amanda says.

"Oh good. Have they risen?"

"They looked okay a moment ago," she replies.

"Let's hope they don't collapse before we can serve them. But this is par for the course when you live in a big old house like this."

"Yeah, you've really fallen on your feet haven't you, Tori? Craig's a great catch and his house is lush."

"Yes he is, and yes it is. We're both very lucky," I say in response to her last two statements, whilst ignoring her first.

"Well you are."

"I am what?"

"Lucky," she says defiantly.

Who the hell does this woman think she is? She's lucky the lights are currently out, otherwise I might just swing for this tramp.

"Amanda, why are you here?" I ask directly, annoyed that I can only make out her face in silhouette and can't read her features.

"Well, that's a bit rude, don't you think Tor-*i*."

This time she exaggerates the 'i' and I can hear the smirk on her lips as she says my name. She knows she's overstepping an invisible line and is enjoying pushing the boundaries.

"I thought I was an invited guest at your over-the-top, must-impress-my-posh-friend-from-London dinner party."

As much as I want to lash out I choose the moral high ground and retain my composure, muttering quietly, "... only because Craig invited you."

The bloody gall of the woman. How dare she judge me. Tim's a friend. One I've not seen in ages, and if I want to throw a civilised gathering, showing off my best crockery, serving up my best wine, and cooking my little socks off to impress everyone — not just Tim, then surely that's my prerogative. It's not my fault this ignoramus has no taste for the finer things in life. Just because I have, doesn't give her the right to judge me.

I realise my murmurings must have come out louder than I intended when she spits in response. "That's right, Tori. I'm here because Craig invited me. I know you don't like me. Why? I have no idea — nor do I care, but Craig and I are good friends and you're just going to have to get used to it. Just like you're asking Craig to get along with your posh friend from London, you have to put up with me." I see the outline of her silhouette change as she crosses her arms. "That's the thing about loving someone, isn't it? You have to accept every part of them, including their friends."

I suck air in loudly, Amanda's words piercing me as sharply as a wasp stinging the end of my tongue.

My friends are a reminder of how far I've travelled, whilst he's hardly been more than ten miles outside our home town. My friends are a reminder of the different cultures I've experienced and all the adventures I've had, whilst his life has largely revolved around work, football, and weekend drinking. My friends like Tim can distinguish between the different grapes of a Muscato and a Merlot, whilst Craig would drink wine if it was on draft. My friends enjoy discussing opera, or the ballet, whilst the only theatre he's ever been to is *The Rocky Horror Picture Show*. I really don't care about any of this, but other than on our first date, I've never asked him how he feels about our differences now. I've just assumed he's okay with it. And as annoying as Amanda is, she has a point. I suppose it does go both ways; if I want him to accept my friends, I too must extend that same courtesy to him — even if I can't stand the woman.

There's a loud click as the electricity comes back on and everything whirrs back into life. Amanda and I both blink hard, our eyes readjusting to the bright light. Seconds later Craig reappears, his black shirt covered in cobwebs. I step forward and run my fingers through his hair, displacing particles of dust that disappear into the air.

"My hero," I say exaggeratedly, brushing the last of the cobwebs off his shoulders. If I were a lioness I'd be peeing in a circle, marking my territory.

"Aww I'm not so sure about that, Tori," Craig dismisses me, shrugging off my affection. "I just had to find the right switch and flick it back on."

"Isn't that all it ever takes, Craig?" Amanda drawls. "Finding the right switch to flick?"

Chapter 25

*L*et's get theses soufflés served before they spoil." I try to lighten the mood.

"Erm, I think it might be a bit too late for that," Amanda says.

I turn around and my heart sinks. Next to Amanda is the oven tray containing six white ramekin dishes, still in their water bath. Only, instead of six perfectly risen chocolate soufflés, the porcelain dishes now contain a soggy brown eggy mess.

"Oh dear," she says triumphantly. "They must have collapsed while we were waiting. I promise you they had risen when I lifted them out."

I can't speak. I know it's only a bloody soufflé but part of me wonders if she's purposefully sabotaged them, my eyes travelling over the small paring knife on the worktop beside her.

"Never mind babes," Craig offers. "I'm sure they'll still taste nice."

"I doubt it," I sob. "We can't serve these."

"Oh, I don't know. It *is* Friday the thirteenth after all," Amanda says flatly, as if the ruined soufflés are some kind of joke.

"Don't take it personally darling. Vanilla ice-cream, fresh raspberries with some chocolate shavings will do just as well." Craig opens the fridge and collects the ingredients for an alternative 'emergency' dessert.

"I'll leave you two to it," Amanda says, flouncing back to the dining room. My jaw set, I watch her leave, wishing my eyes would turn into lasers so I could burn a hole in her arse.

ᖇᗴ

"Well, I think that went pretty darn well. Don't you?" Craig asks after we've gone to bed.

Nessa and Anth have gone home. Tim is comfortably tucked up in our larger guest bedroom, and I've put Amanda in the single bedroom, next to ours at the front of the house.

'It's so expensive for her to get a taxi on her own, this way she can stay and have a drink and drive home in the morning,' was Craig's seemingly logical reasoning for offering her a bed for the night.

"Apart from the ruined puddings?" I reply light-heartedly but still disappointed that what should have been a triumphant climax turned into a half-hashed rescue.

The ruined soufflés had become a talking point for the rest of the evening. Tim, bless him, attempted to taste one. Faking 'mmm' noises, as he swallowed down the disgusting soggy mess.

'It definitely tastes better than it looks, Victoria,' he'd said magnanimously.

'Well, to be fair, that's not hard. They look bloody awful,' I'd replied with a half-smile.

"What a shame," Nessa had chimed in.

"Yup, this is one dinner party I'll definitely remember," Anth had laughed. "Gawd knows what Tim poured into my glass when the lights went out." He'd slapped Tim on the shoulder in shared companionship.

"Only the very best wine, Anthony dear boy," Tim had replied waving one of the now many empty bottles in the air.

All the while, Amanda had remained her silent and aloof self.

Refusing to join in any of the banter. Replying to any direct questions with monosyllabic answers; by the end of the evening everyone had given up trying to involve her in the conversation and largely ignored her.

Wrapped in Craig's arms I ask the one question that has been burrowing away at me all evening.

"Why was she here?"

I feel Craig's pecs tense against my cheek.

"Why was who here?"

"You know who I mean, silly – Amanda. Why did you invite her?"

"Why? Shouldn't I have?"

"Well, she's not part of our crowd."

"Neither's Tim."

"I know. But him being here was the impetus to throw the dinner party. I just don't understand why you chose her to make up the sixth place."

"Because she's a friend. Plus, she also works with Anth. I thought she'd be a good fit."

"You and Anth are both heads of departments."

"So is she, since her last promotion."

"Reporting to you, whereas you and Anth are members of the SMT, and you're a board member."

"Which technically means Anth also reports to me."

"Yeah, but she's your direct report, and you've known Anth most of your life. Long before you started working together. It just seems weird, that's all."

"You said you wanted another female to even out the numbers."

"So why didn't you let me invite Julie? She would have been the obvious choice."

"Because I'd already invited Amanda by then. What's the problem?" He shuffles back from me into a seated position, his head resting against the headboard, and reaches for a glass of water from his bedside table. "She's been to our parties before."

"Yeah — when we've had a house full."

"Granted, but I didn't realise that excluded her from this type of invitation. You and I had a brief discussion over breakfast the other day, I went to work, grabbed a coffee, she was there, and I asked her to come. I could hardly uninvite her after that."

"I know. But I just don't get it. Of all the people — why her?" I roll around to face him.

"Why are you blowing this up into something it's not? Just drop it, Tori. It's no big deal, honestly. She and I were talking. I mentioned that we were throwing a dinner party for one of your friends from London, someone who I've never met before, and who — if I'm honest — I thought sounded like a pompous twat ..."

I recoil instantly. "Why would you say that about Tim? He's not pompous at all."

"Maybe. But he sounds pompous."

"That's ridiculous, Craig. Just because he has a posh accent. Anyway, you're changing the subject. You haven't answered my question." I kneel up, the tension between us rising.

"You're making this into something it's not, Tori. I mentioned it in passing, she said she was free that evening, and that was that. Why are you even bothered?"

"Because she didn't seem to want to be here."

"Eh? She told me she was having a great time."

"That's not the impression she gave everyone else." I pause, wondering how far to push him. "I can't tell you who to be friends with, Craig. But I don't want her back in my house."

I suck air into my lungs and hold my breath while I wait to see how he responds to my demand.

He looks directly at me, his eyebrows raised. "Well this is a new watershed moment in our relationship. You dictating who I can and can't invite into *my* house."

He exaggerates the word 'my'. Technically, this may be *our* home but it is most definitely *his* house. Until now Craig has never made reference to that fact; that I only live here at his invitation. His name is on the mortgage and, although I pay a contribution towards the running costs, legally, until we're married, it would be difficult for me to make any claim to his property.

"Sorry. I didn't mean it like that," I say, backtracking. "You know how much I love you, and how much I love *our* home — there's just something about her, Craig. You don't see how she talks to me when you're not there."

"Like what? What does she say?"

"Oh, I don't know. Just stuff about how lucky I am. Lucky to have you. To live here. As if I don't deserve any of it." I gesture around the room, conscious of the increasing volume of our voices and that Amanda is sleeping in the room next to us. I can only imagine how happy she would be if she could hear Craig and I arguing.

"Well maybe she has a point," he says cheekily. A lightness having returned to his tone. "Obviously, I'm a major catch." He gestures up and down his naked torso, intimating, *'Get a load of this. Me – the major catch'*.

"I know." I tap the end of his nose affectionately. "She just makes me uncomfortable, that's all. I can't quite articulate it. It's more her energy. I feel like she judges me."

"Judges you?" Craig exclaims. "If anything she should be looking up to you. Learning from you. Without you, and all of the effort you put into the cooking and stuff, I would have just about managed a roast dinner, not a three-course extravaganza like you pulled off tonight. I don't know anyone else who is as driven as you Tori, and I don't just mean tonight, I mean in life. You're ambitious, and you're doing amazingly well at work. Everyone loves you. You're sociable, funny, beautiful …." I dip my head at the sudden flood of compliments. "You're the only person I know who is as comfortable in the company of people like Tim as you are when you're hanging out down the pub. Like you're one of the lads. That's a real talent you know."

These are some of the nicest things I think he's ever said to me and I cuddle into his bare chest, wanting to be as close to him as possible. His chest hair tickles my cheek as I wrap my arms tightly around him.

"Honestly Tori, you've got nothing to worry about. I know exactly which side my bread is buttered and I promised you last summer that I would always love you. So if that means that Amanda doesn't come here anymore — then I won't invite her."

My veins flood with gratitude. I shouldn't have had to ask for this, but the fact that he is willing to give me want I want makes me feel secure and loved. I remember the injustice I felt when Chris demanded I give up my friendship with Tim, after our massive row in Hong Kong. So I know I'm being a hypocrite. But this is different. I'm not demanding he doesn't remain friends with her, just that she doesn't come here anymore. I suppose I'm hoping that if she's not present in my company, their friendship will fizzle out.

"Thank you," I whisper.

He cups my head in his hands so that he can look into my eyes. "Tori, *My Girl*."

My smile beams through the dim light of our bedroom. Why would I ever doubt Craig's intention or his feelings for me.

I lean forward and brush my lips over his. As close and as intimate as we are, I never know whether he will reciprocate, but he deepens our kiss, sliding his tongue languidly inside my mouth. He tastes of wine and coffee and as we explore each other's mouths I hear him suck in a deep breath through his nose; all the while his tongue twists and twirls with mine

Wrapped tightly in each other's arms, he sits up off his pillows as I straddle his lap. Cupping my face in his hands, his thumbs slide back and forth over my jaw in his familiar way, and I run my fingers through his hair, cradling the back of his head and fisting handfuls of his thick tresses.

I feel his hardness, still encased in his Calvin Klein's, push up against my groin which is hot, wet, and desperate for him to fill the void within me.

"Oh, Tori," he says breathlessly, his fingers leaving a tingling trail across my cheeks.

He reaches down and quickly pulls my chemise camisón over my head. A chill ripples across my skin as the cool air hits my naked form. I hold his gaze, my hands travelling over the outside of his shoulders, down over his waist, coming to rest on the outside of his hips.

I pause, wondering if tonight he'll allow me to go further and touch him, or whether this will be another encounter where I'm left satisfied but still wanting, or whether he wants to go all the way. But he answers the question for me and hitches his boxers down over his hips to his ankles.

I bend my head and roll my tongue over his nipple, as he nuzzles his cheek against my hair. The pair of us using our faces to caress each other like lions in the wild. His breath is hot against my skin and his day-long stubble tickles my cheek. I inhale his scent, a mix of musk and spices, and feel my desire burn hot inside of me.

Our bodies not yet connected, I unconsciously begin to grind my hips, while I remain straddled across his lap. My body searching for the part of him I need the most, I catch the tip of his shaft with my groin and with one gentle roll of my hips he slides into me. The expanse of him filling me completely, I release a long overdue exhale, "Oh, Chris—"

Our eyes flash open and we both freeze.

What the f—!

The world around us stops turning and neither of us move. The only sound in the room the shallow in out of our breath.

As we hold each other's gaze, Craig's erection softens and slithers out of me. No matter how much my eyes try to plead my apology, there's nothing I can do to stop the distance widening between us as his walls come back up.

Chapter 26

*N*either of us wants to be the first to move. Moving means acknowledging what's just happened.

After what seems like an age, I break the silence. "I'm so sorry, Craig. I have absolutely no idea where that came from."

He continues to stare at me, dumbfounded. His eyes searching my face for a logical explanation. Of course – there isn't one.

"It meant nothing." I laugh nervously, leaning in to kiss him, but he turns his head away.

The pain and confusion I see flash across his eyes stabs my gut like a knife.

"It was just a silly little slip. I wasn't thinking about him. Honestly. I haven't thought about him in years."

"U-huh," he says coldly, rolling me off his lap, rising from the bed and pulling his boxers back up.

"I think it must be because Tim's here..." I babble. "I haven't seen him in so long. And I used to hang out with him when I was with Chris. You have to believe me. In that moment I wasn't thinking about Chris. I was only focused on you. On us."

"Maybe, but I can't just shrug that off." He pulls on a T-shirt and scans the floor for a pair of socks.

"Where are you going? Don't leave, we were having a nice moment there."

"I think *were* being the operative word."

"Please, Craig. Come back to bed. Let me show you it meant nothing."

He pinches the bridge of his nose. "It may mean nothing to you... but saying another man's name in my bed, when I'm making love to you... when I'm inside you... *does* mean something to me. You may not want to acknowledge it, but I've always suspected deep in your psyche, he's still there. You might not think about him, but your unconscious still does."

"But I've not thought about him in years — honestly. Or at least not in a romantic way," I plead, except that that's not strictly true. Chris does drift into my thoughts every now and then. Even during dinner tonight, I was thinking about our time together in Hong Kong. Both the good and the bad. That was the thing with Chris. When it was good, it was beyond good. Eclipsing any highs I've ever felt with Craig, but when it was bad it was horrific.

I'm stark naked and feel deeply exposed but still I kneel up and grab onto Craig's arms as he walks around the bottom of the bed. "I'm not wishing things were different if that's what you're insinuating. It meant nothing. You have to know that I only want you. Please don't make this into something it's not."

"Maybe it was. Maybe it wasn't. But I'm going to sleep in the office. I need some space away from you tonight. Tomorrow is a new day and we'll talk about it then." Breaking my hold, he pads out of the room and gently closes the door behind him.

Defeated, I flop back onto my pillows; a large sob expanding in my throat. I clasp my hands over my mouth to muffle the sound as it escapes, while Craig's footsteps clonking up the stairs into the attic echo through the house. No doubt Amanda can hear him unfolding the sofa bed in the room above her head. The last thing I want is her hearing the sound of my weeping as well. I can only imagine the smug look on her face.

In one way I wish he'd shouted at me. Told me how offended he was or how much I'd hurt him, but by walking out I feel a million times worse. I've nowhere to place the flood of shame and frustration that is coursing through my veins.

I know Craig loves me and he's a good man. He's loving, kind, and funny. Granted, we don't have the hedonistic crazy bedroom antics Chris and I used get up to, but what was it Mel once said to me, all those years ago in our kitchen in Wootton Bassett? *'There's more to relationships than just mind-blowing sex.'* What I have with Craig is what I lacked with Chris: stability.

But the one thing I never thought Craig would make me feel is abandoned. When I was with Chris, that was how he controlled me. The constant threat of abandonment. And for the first time, that is what Craig has just done. Just like Chris used to. But why did my unconscious choose this exact moment to allow Chris's name to escape from my lips? If the pained caused my him wasn't enough, is his unconscious presence in my psyche determined to doom my relationship with Craig to the same fate as my relationship with him? Can I never be free?

Hot wet tears roll uninhibited down my face and soak the cotton of my pillowcase.

$\wr_\circ$

After a fitful night's sleep, the next morning — dressed in sloppy sweats and a loose T-shirt, my hair tied up in a scrunchy — I dance nervously around the kitchen as I agitate the bacon in the griddle pan and turn the buns that are toasting under the grill. My hips sway and my arms twirl above my head while my bare feet pad in time to Prince's "1999" thumping out from the stereo.

"Always did dance like there was no one watching," a voice behind me chortles.

I turn and smile as Tim steps down into the kitchen and plants a *good morning* kiss on my cheek. He too is looking slightly rumpled and less pristine than he did last night. Relaxed jeans, bare feet and an untucked Ralph Lauren pale pink polo shirt.

"Something smells good." He inhales the smoky aroma.

"Good morning. Sleep well?"

"Like a log. I'll go grab a shower in a mo. Amanda's in there at the moment."

As if on cue, she appears in the doorway, her face all bright and shiny, her perfect make-up framed by perfectly arched eyebrows. She's wearing a loose-fitting maxi summer dress in a knock-off Liberty print, and no bra. Completely inappropriate attire for the middle of November in the freezing north.

"Tea?" I say through gritted teeth. Determined to refrain from creating another scene this morning.

"No thanks," she replies haughtily. "I'll just have black coffee."

"Help yourself. There's a fresh pot on the Krupp's." I point to the coffee machine.

"I know where it is," she replies icily, striding across the room and pouring herself a cup. "Where's Craig?" she asks, her undertone already suggesting she knows the answer to the question.

"In his office," I say confidently.

I want her to know that I know she knows... and to make it clear I have the upper hand. "He woke up ridiculously early so went to attack his inbox. He's got such a lot on his plate at the moment."

"Indeed he has," she replies. "He's an amazing boss."

God, I wish I could vaporise her into thin air. Still, after today I won't have to put up with her in my house anymore.

"I've already taken him a coffee. He'll be down in a bit." I smirk. At least the last part is true.

"I thought I could smell something delicious." I jump at the sound of Craig's voice as he appears in the kitchen doorway and smiles directly at me. I exhale and feel my shoulders drop.

"This woman makes *the* best bacon butties in the whole wide world," he adds, hugging me from behind and planting a kiss on my cheek.

"But very questionable soufflés," Tim teases.

"Not my fault." I brandish my fish slice in Tim's direction in mock threat. "How was I to know we'd trip the electric at the most inopportune moment? Now. Here... sit."

Everyone settles themselves around the island as I pass out the bacon sandwiches.

"You're right, Craig. Delicious," Tim says.

I watch as Amanda pulls off every tiny piece of fat from the bacon and ditches the bun, nibbling on the slice of cooked meat.

Give me strength.

Tim's eyes travel over a pile of post neatly piled to the side of the island. Bills, circulars, leaflets for local takeaways and, on the top, a thick quality cream envelope, handwritten in silver ink. "I see Mel's invites arrived."

"Yes. It turned up this week."

"Who's Mel?" Amanda asks.

"A dear friend of mine. Someone you don't know."

Boom! One-nil to me.

"Isn't she your friend from New Zealand? Didn't I meet her at your party last New Year's Eve?"

"Oh, yes. I'd forgotten you were both here then."

Bollocks. One-all.

"She's getting married... in Spain. Next summer. It's a four-day event and, if I know Mel, it'll be one long alcohol-fuelled party."

Take that, Bitch. Two-one to me.

"What's the date?" Craig asks, biting into his sandwich.

He's been working so much lately I've not had a chance to discuss it.

"The wedding itself is Saturday the 29th May, but they're doing it over the second May Bank Holiday, to give everyone a longer week-end. She's having a hen party on the Friday, and Karl's organised a golfing-day-come-stag-do on the same day, which you're obviously invited to."

Craig nods, taking a slurp of his tea.

Without missing a beat Amanda pipes up, "Isn't that the week of our company conference?"

I close my eyes and count to ten.

"I'm only saying..." she continues, "Because you've just banned all holiday leave that week. I remember because I had been thinking of going away. Like you said, Tori, to take advantage of the extra Bank Holiday."

"Shit. I think you're right, Manda." Craig pulls his Filofax from the edge of the island and flicks to the relevant page in his diary, leaving me stupefied. *'Manda' fucking who?*

He meets my gaze and the answer is written all over his face. "I'm really sorry Tori, but Amanda's right. Wednesday/Thursday/Friday of that week is our conference. There's no way I can miss it."

I roll my lips inwards and say nothing. Amanda smirks into her bacon and Tim freezes, holding his mug of coffee mid-sip.

"Well that's that then. I suppose I'll have to decline. It wouldn't feel right to go without you."

"Nonsense. Mel's too good a friend for you to miss her wedding. You should still go," Craig says.

"But I don't want to go alone."

"You won't have to. I'll be there," Tim interjects.

"Is Lydia planning on going with you? I'd hate to be a gooseberry," I ask.

Tim shrugs. "Maybe. You know us. The odd couple."

Odd indeed. Tim's been in a 'secret' relationship with a woman no one has met for as long as I've known him. He keeps her hidden out in the country at 'the barn', while he swans around the world. His job as head of international audit for Merrill Lynch requires him to jump on a plane to any overseas office at the drop of a hat. With a young son from a previous relationship, she prefers to stay put, so he visits her when he has a break in his schedule. No one else gets it, but it seems to work for them.

"See, there'll be loads of people there you know," Craig says.

"Including Chris." I glare at Craig. "I don't want to face him without you there."

...And after last night I wouldn't think you'd want me to, I don't say out loud, but think to myself instead.

My raised eyebrows must convey my meaning as, after a tiny pause, he replies, "Maybe I could fly out late Friday night. Miss the stag-do but make it in time for the main festivities."

I exhale and he gives me a tentative smile. He gets it.

"Or you could fly out first thing Saturday morning, if we can't find a Friday night flight," I add.

He places his hand over the top of mine. "We'll figure it out. I promise I'll be there. You won't have to do this on your own."

"Thanks," I reply, as we catch each other's eye.

Even after my faux pas last night, *my Craig* is back, and with him by my side I know I can attend Mel's wedding and enjoying myself, without the fear of having to face Chris alone.

Part IV

Chapter 27

CRAIG

5 months later, May 1999

*H*ave you heard the craic about Jack Walker?" Anth says, turning the volume down on Craig's car stereo. "No?"

At the mention of the company chairman, Craig's ears prick up.

"Supposedly had his hand in the cookie jar."

"What? Embezzlement?"

Craig's mind flicks to his last dividend payment.

Have I been diddled out of some of my bonus? he thinks to himself.

"Not that kind of cookie jar," Anth says.

Craig spies Anth's raised eyebrow from the corner of his peripheral vision.

The men are on their way home after the Private Practise Software annual conference. The one time in the year when all the regional offices come together to celebrate the previous year's achievements and to set the strategic direction of the company for the year ahead. In the back seat are two other colleagues: Amanda, and another team leader, Dave. Dave lives on the outskirts of

Durham city, so Craig can drop him off on the way through, and Amanda has left her car at Craig's, so that he could take a full carload down to the Belfry, on the outskirts of Birmingham.

"With who?" Craig asks.

"One of the other board member's wives."

"Really?"

"Yes. It may not be true, of course. But if it is, the way it was told to me, it sounded more like harassment than a reciprocated dalliance."

"Well if it is true he won't be the first man in history to have had an affair, but still… shitting in your own backyard is never a good idea."

"Exactly."

"Although I'm not sure I'd believe the rumours. That doesn't sound like Jack. I've always admired him. He's been a great mentor to me."

Jack Walker is one of Craig's greatest supporters, helping him advance his career at every step of the company's growth. A larger than life character, charismatic, strategic, Craig has learnt a lot from the older man, not least how to be a great leader.

"I'm sure if he was found to have behaved inappropriately, he'll be held to account," Craig continues.

"I'm not so sure," Anth replies. "Crossing someone like Jack Walker would be career ending. You'd have to be an idiot to lock horns with him."

"Agreed. You wouldn't want to be on his bad side," Craig adds, sliding the car into fourth gear and accelerating up the slip road and onto the M1 motorway.

Ninety minutes later Craig stops at Tibshelf services for petrol and fresh coffee. Once everyone is suitably refuelled, he weaves back into the heavy traffic. The rush hour volume compounded by the Bank Holiday weekend.

He rolls his shoulders, grips the steering wheel, hard. It's been a long few days and the weather's atrocious. Strong winds and heavy rain.

Anth retunes the radio to something more chilled. Searching for that illusive utopia between high energy, thumping beat, and mellow music to get them home.

They drive through a particularly heavy rain cloud and the water bleaches down the windscreen like a sheet of ice. The traffic forced to slow to thirty miles an hour as the visibility diminishes. Craig leans forward over the steering wheel and flicks the windscreen wipers to double time.

"God, it's wild out there," Amanda says from the back seat after the car is buffeted by another gale-force blast.

"It sure is." Craig looks through his rear-view mirror and smiles at her.

Without warning, the car aquaplanes across a large patch of surface water and Craig struggles to keep it straight, his mind flashing back to his first date with Vicky, almost exactly two years ago. When she accidentally spun his car and missed the wall by millimetres.

His thoughts are interrupted by a shrill *eek-eek-eek*.

"What the hell?" Dave asks from the back seat.

"That, my friends, is the sound of my other half calling."

"Nice. She doesn't mind having the *Psycho* shower scene as her ringtone then? Is there something you're not telling us?" Dave laughs.

"Maybe. She has Right Said Fred's *'I'm Too Sexy for Your Love'* as mine."

Craig hits the *call accept* button on the car phone. "Hi pet."

Vicky's voice comes through the speakers. "Hi sweetheart. How was your day?"

"Long. How about you?"

"Awesome. It's fab here. You're gonna love it. The hotel's gorgeous and it's still twenty degrees even though its 9:00pm now."

"Oh good. It's bloody awful here. Can you hear the rain? It's like a monsoon."

"I was just calling to find out how your presentation went. I know how nervous you were. It's a big deal. Being on the main podium for the first time."

Craig sucks in a sharp breath. As much as he appreciates his girlfriend's concern, he doesn't appreciate his vulnerabilities being shared with his colleagues and subordinates.

"You're on loudspeaker, Tori. I've got Anth, Dave, and Amanda in the car with me. Say 'Hi' everyone."

The three passengers collectively chime their Hi's and Hello's back into the invisible microphone.

"Oh sorry. I didn't realise. Hi, Anth. Hi, Dave. Hello, A-man-da."

Everyone can hear the hostility Vicky has towards Amanda. Craig may have kept his word and not invited her over to his house since the dinner party with Tim, but Vicky knows she can't stop them working together. Not when Amanda's a valued member of Craig's team.

"So how was it?" Vicky continues.

"He was a-ma-zing," Amanda pipes up from the back seat, mirroring the fractious enunciation Vicky used moments earlier.

"Well of course you would be, my darling," Vicky replies, exaggerating the endearment. "You're excellent at what you do."

"Shhh. Don't tell anyone. That's a well-kept secret," Craig replies. He's not enjoying the praise she's heaping on him. She's hardly qualified to comment.

"Where are you guys now?"

"We've just left Tibshelf, but the traffic's horrendous. It'll be hours before we get home."

"Well, take it easy and don't rush. You can sleep on the flight tomorrow. Everything's ready for you. I've laid out your linen suit and part-packed a weekend bag for you but you'll need to add your toiletries and anything else you had with you this week. Your passport and flight tickets are on the hall table, together with a couple hundred quids' worth of pesetas. Just make sure you set your alarm. I've booked a taxi for 5:30 a.m. and I'll see you when you get here. Just don't miss the flight!" she laughs.

"Blimey. You don't happen to have a sister. One that can move in with me and sort my life out?" Dave jokes.

"Sadly not, Dave. It's just Craig and I have been going in different directions these past few weeks. I don't want him to forget anything."

"You're amazing, sweetheart. Thank you."

"Right then, I'd better be going. This'll be costing a bloody fortune. You guys get home safe. Well done on your presentation today and I'll see you when you arrive tomorrow. Bye Anth. Bye Dave."

Craig waits for her to say goodbye to Amanda before he signs off himself, but the line goes dead.

What the hell?!

He'd like to think she got cut off, rather than intentionally snubbing Amanda, but he can't be sure.

I need to have a word with her about that. That wasn't just rude it was borderline unkind. Amanda doesn't deserve that kind of treatment.

He looks through his rear-view mirror, trying to catch Amanda's eye, wanting to give her a reassuring smile, but she's turned to look out the side window and he can't work out if she's bored, pissed off, or indifferent.

He watches as Dave reaches across the back seat for Amanda's fingers, wanting to extend a hand of support, but she snatches her hand away and tucks it under her thigh.

No-one speaks. Everyone feels the tension. A few long moments pass, before Craig retunes the stereo again, searching this time for something more upbeat. Anything to lift the mood and break the uncomfortable silence that hangs in the air. The sound of Kula Shaker's 'Hush' booms out from the radio, and Dave starts singing along to the na-na-na-nahs of the chorus, lifting the energy once again.

"Love Heart anyone?" Amanda asks, opening a tube of the sugary sweets.

"Go on then," Craig replies, and she holds the packet through the gap between the seats.

Pulling one out, he looks at the inscription. *Be my valentine* the looped letters spell out on the flat surface of the small pink disk.

Ignoring any intimation or hidden meaning, he pops the sweet into his mouth, and sucks hard. Meanwhile, in the backseat, Amanda smirks.

Chapter 28

Three and a half hours later, Dave and Anth safely deposited back at their respective front doors, Amanda and Craig pull up outside his house. It's late. Gone 11:30 p.m. and they're both exhausted. It's been a torturous drive, on top of a tiring week. The weather continued to deteriorate as the evening wore on, and the Met Office has upped their weather warning from Yellow to Red, meaning 'risk to life' and advising against all but essential travel. The local radio station has already reported trees down around the region and damage to some properties.

"There's no question of you driving home now," Craig says to Amanda as they battle their way into the house. Both of them hunched over against the wind. "It's not safe. I'd feel much happier if you slept here and went home in the morning."

"Only if you're sure. I don't want to impose."

"You won't be. The spare bed is made up and I won't let you drive when it's this dangerous. Come on. Let's put the kettle on. I bet you're gasping for a cuppa as much as I am."

"Yes, boss." She looks seductively at him, out of the corner of her eyes.

Dumping their bags in the hallway, Amanda follows Craig

through to the kitchen where, ten minutes later, they're sharing a pot of tea.

At midnight, Craig stretches his arms above his head and lets out a long yawn. He glances at the kitchen clock. "Well, if you'll excuse me, I'm gonna turn in. As you've already heard, I've got an early flight tomorrow. Make yourself at home. You know where everything is." He steps down from the kitchen bar stool.

Amanda looks at Craig over the top of the mug she's rolling between her palms.

I've never noticed how beautiful her eyes are, he thinks. I wonder if she has Spanish blood.

A slimmer-shaped face than Vicky's, Amanda's long slim nose nestles between high cheekbones and eyes the colour of sweet, forbidden honey. The pronounced cupid's bow in the centre of her plump lips gives her a permanent pout, as if always anticipating a kiss.

Craig's cock twitches inside his boxers. He suppresses the reaction immediately.

Jesus. I'm just tired. It's been an impossibly long day.

"Do you want me to give you a knock at about 5:15 a.m.?" he asks. "I know it's horrifically early, but that'll give you just enough time to throw your clothes on before I have to kick you out?"

"Don't worry. I'm a light sleeper. I'll hear you when you start moving about," she replies, her voice as smooth as melted chocolate. "But by all means come and find me if you need to. I'll be waiting." She smiles that coy smile of hers, taking another sip of her tea.

"Yes. Well. Right …" Craig mumbles. "Definitely time for me to turn in. Night, night. Sleep tight 'n all that."

Craig tosses and turns, unable to sleep as the storm intensifies outside. The wild and primitive energy stirs something inside him, and a naked image of Amanda lying in the room next door flashes through his brain. Her warm body, hot against the cool cotton sheets. Her long lithe limbs moulded into the mattress, her long dark hair splayed out across the pillow like a fan. He imagines her too lying awake, listening to the wind. Her hand sliding seductively between her legs. Her fingers stimulating her most sensitive spot as he imagines her thinking of him while pleasuring herself. Her need as primal and insistent as the untamed elements outside.

Squeezing his eyes even tighter shut and sucking in a deep breath, he banishes the erotic fantasy and wills his exhaustion to take him.

Tap, tap, tap. The sound of the climbing roses that twist their way up the front of the house tap and scratch against Craig's bedroom window. Outside the wind continues to howl like a wolf and somewhere in the distance a sharp crack, followed by a loud crash, unnerves him.

He goes to investigate, peering out of his bedroom window, and sees a tree has fallen into a neighbour's garden, flattening the fence but thankfully missing the house. A number of bedroom lights switch on down the street, as other neighbours check to see if anyone is hurt. He continues to watch as a few minutes later a police car arrives, its blue light flashing and illuminating the street. Once he's satisfied there's nothing he can do, he crawls back into bed, pulls a pillow over his head, and tries his best to ignore the persistent *tap, tap, tap* at the window. If he doesn't fall asleep soon, he won't have had any rest before his alarm goes off.

Eventually, his breathing deepens and his body relaxes, and he slips into a blissful pool of oblivion.

Tap, tap, tap. The staccato of the roses scratching against the window, and the howl of the wind, continue to invade the periphery of his consciousness. *Tap, tap, tap.* The relentless knocking grows more persistent, rising above the sound of the storm, until he realises the knocking is no longer coming from the window, but from the other side of his bedroom door.

He knows who'll be on the other side, and he has a strong suspicion why she's knocking.

I can hardly ignore her. What if something's wrong? He thinks to himself.

Amanda raps at the door again. "Craig. Are you in there?" she says, her voice meek and childlike.

He tentatively opens the door, as if he were in a hotel. Not wanting a bellboy to see into his room. But the sight that greets him causes his heart rate to quicken and makes him go instantly hard.

Holy shit!

Amanda is stood in the doorway wearing nothing but a sexy black lace chemise, two delicate spaghetti straps the only thing tethering it to her body. One strap has slipped from her shoulder and is draped across her upper arm. The see-through underwear leaves nothing to the imagination and Craig can't help but admire her beauty. Her full yet pert breasts, crowned with dark dusky nipples peek invitingly up at him. Her tiny waist, her washboard stomach and her beautiful smooth mound, all begging to be explored by his fingers, his mouth. *Oh*, how he wants to part her legs and bury his head there. To taste her and make her yield, using nothing more than the tip of his tongue.

Their eyes lock, but neither of them speak. The silence between them full of meaning.

Craig coughs into his fist and opens the door a little wider. "Is everything alright?"

"Not really," she replies in a feeble squeak. "I'm really sacred."

"Yes. It is pretty scary, isn't it?"

They continue staring at each other, knowing they are standing on the precipice. Neither of them wanting to move, but both of them wanting the other to take the first leap.

"Can you keep me safe?" she says eventually, her eyes burning into his as he swallows hard. "Please, Craig. You must realise how much I want you... to keep me safe," she adds as if it were an afterthought.

Before he has a chance to answer, in one fluid movement she

unhooks the spaghetti straps off her shoulders and allows the silk negligee to fall from her body.

Craig gasps.

Her lips pull into a coy smile as she places her palm squarely in the middle of Craig's chest and takes a step forward, pressing her body up against his and crossing the threshold into his room.

He bends his head and places a light kiss on her shoulder as he reaches behind her and quietly closes the bedroom door.

Chapter 29

VICTORIA

Denia, Spain

I'm yanked awake by an intrusion of sound. It takes me a few seconds to remember where I am and realise that it's both the sound of my mobile ringing and someone simultaneously knocking at my bedroom door that has woken me so abruptly. Grabbing my phone, I lunge for the hotel dressing gown, wrapping it around my body as I dash across the room. I hit the *call accept* button on my mobile at the same time as I open the hotel door.

"Hang on, Craig," I say into the handset. "My breakfast has just arrived."

I step back as the liveried hotel porter wheels a breakfast trolley laden with plates and tea things over to the coffee table in front of my balcony. He hands me the chit to sign and I tip him a thousand pesetas as he leaves.

"Right. Sorry about that, darling. Morning," I say, cupping the phone underneath my chin while I pick up the tea pot.

"Morning," Craig replies. "Sleep well?"

I begin to pour myself a much-needed cup of English Breakfast tea, but twist my face when I see the colour of the lukewarm liquid in the porcelain teacup. I leave it to brew and instead give Craig my full attention.

"Like a log. This hotel mattress is up there in the top five most comfortable I've ever slept on. Anyway, how come you're on the phone, shouldn't you be in the air by now?"

I grab my watch from the bedside table and double-check the time.

"Yes, I should be, but here's the thing." I hear Craig suck up a lungful of air through gritted teeth. "There's been a bit of a hiccup."

"What do you mean?"

"There was a really bad storm here last night. All the power went out and my alarm didn't go off. I woke up at 5.45 a.m. to the sound of the taxi driver braying on our front door. He knew I had a flight to catch. Anyway, by the time I pulled my clothes on I was already half an hour late and there were diversions because of trees down all over the place. I was too late."

"Too late? For what?"

"The flight, Tori. By the time we made it to the airport, the flight had closed and they wouldn't let me check in. I'm really sorry, Tori. I'm still in Newcastle."

I sit down heavily on the edge of the bed. "But you can't be. You have to be here. There's still time. We'll find you a flight from another airport. Edinburgh, or Leeds Bradford maybe."

If only I still worked in the travel industry, I could log on and see all the flights leaving from anywhere in the UK.

"But there aren't any. I've already checked with customer services here at the airport. The next flight out from Newcastle doesn't leave until early evening."

"What about flying into Barcelona or Madrid? There'll be scheduled flights going there, rather than charters into Alicante. As long as you land by lunchtime, you could jump on the train to the coast. They have a high-speed rail network all across the country. It could work."

"Tori. Sweetheart." He exhales. "Trust me. I've checked all the options and nothing's going to work. This isn't Heathrow. It's

Newcastle. You can't fly direct to Madrid or Barcelona from here. You'd have to go via London or Amsterdam and nothing will get me there before midnight. I'm really, *really* sorry babes but you're just going to have to go to the service on your own."

My throat closes up and I begin to shake. Fear and adrenaline flooding my body.

"But you can't do this to me," I whimper. "You know how much I need you here. I need your support. I can't do this without you."

I already know how hard it's going to be to face Chris again. But walking in on Craig's arm — as one half of a couple — was meant to be my safety shield. Now the only choice I have is to miss the wedding ceremony this afternoon, or face Chris alone.

"I know, darling. I'm so sorry, but it honestly couldn't be helped."

"Oh well that makes it all alright then doesn't it," I spit, childishly.

"Don't be like that. I couldn't help the storm, or my alarm not going off. I didn't want this either. But I'm sure you're enjoying the time you're spending with Mel. And Tim said he would look out for you."

"But he's not here either. He's stuck in New York," I say, my voice rising.

At the other end of the phone Craig releases another long exhale. "I'm sorry Tori, there's nothing I can do. The best you can do now is focus on enjoying the wedding this afternoon and I'll pick you up at the airport tomorrow teatime. You can do this. I know you're stronger than you think."

"And you trust me?" I ask, thinking back to my unconscious slip-up six months ago, when Chris's name left my lips, seemingly from nowhere.

"Of course I do." I hear him breathe heavily into the handset, as if he's almost holding back tears. "Why wouldn't I? I trust you, like you've always trusted me. You've never doubted me, all the times I've been away on business and stuff, just like you've never given me any reason to mistrust you. And I love you for that."

"I suppose I'm just going to have to put my *big girl pants* on and go on my own. But hey, it's not as if it could be helped or anything, is it?" I don't mean to sound spiteful, but this is the one scenario I wanted to avoid, and through no fault of my own, I find myself having to attend the wedding of my ex's sister – alone.

A heavy silence falls between us. Both of us knowing that no matter what we say next, the situation can't be changed. He knows he's let me down, but as frustrated and disappointed as I am, I can't blame him. It wasn't his fault there was a crazy storm and his alarm didn't go off.

I sigh heavily. "Okay. Well, I'll glam up and put my best foot forward."

"See, that's the spirit."

"Uh-huh. I'll call you tomorrow, once I've checked in."

"Don't miss your flight," he quips and I clench my teeth. "Too soon?" He laughs.

"Goodbye, Craig," I say, pressing my lips into a thin line.

"Goodbye, pet."

I end the call and toss my phone across the bed, before flopping back onto the pillows and massaging my temples with my fingers.

Eurgh!

⁂

I take my time getting ready. I've got a full morning to fill, and wanting to avoid any accidental hotel-corridor-bumping-into-Chris moments, I decide it's safer to remain in my room. Everyone else I know is involved in the wedding anyway, so who else could I hang out with? Not for the first time in my life, I'm unexpectedly all alone, with only my thoughts and my toothbrush for company.

By contrast, the day I had yesterday catching up with Mel was lovely. Dressed in a designer swimsuit and sarong, hanging out at her private villa with the other members of her family for her hen party, while Karl and the men took in a round of golf. I spent the day indulging in pedicures and massages, whilst sipping champagne and dipping my toes in her infinity pool.

It was particularly emotional to see Michelle — Mel's older sister — again. We rushed into each other's arms, instantly dissolving the four years since we'd last seen each other.

'God, I've missed you,' she'd gushed.

'And I you, Mich,' I'd replied, air-kissing her on both cheeks.

'And I know someone else who's dying to see you too. Once she wakes up from her nap, that is.'

My stomach had clenched into a tight knot at this piece of information. I knew there was every possibility that Mel's nieces and nephew would be here, supporting her as a page boy and flower girls, but the thought of seeing Michelle's daughter, Jessica, again, is another reason I'd wanted Craig's support this weekend.

Jess was born four years ago, on the same day I terminated my own pregnancy. A tortuous coincidence, and in the months that followed I projected the grief of losing my own unborn child onto Michelle's tiny baby. Baby Jess became the innocent living reminder of what I'd given up. Other than Chris, no one had any clue how much her existence caused me both joy and excruciating pain. Putting as much distance between myself and the baby was part of the reason I ran away to New Zealand with Chris. I needed to start over. But of course, running away from your past never makes it go away.

'But how could she possibly remember me? She was only six months old the last time I saw her,' I'd said to Michelle while we drank champagne in the sunshine.

'Oh, she knows who you are,' Michelle had replied. 'She has a picture of you on her bedside table. The one of you holding her at her Naming Ceremony. She often points at it and asks, 'When is Aunty Vicky coming to see us again?' I've carried on singing the songs you first sang to her.'

My heart had felt heavy in my chest and a hard lump formed in the back of my throat as I realised how much I'd also missed her. But I was concerned seeing Jess again would bring back all those painful memories. However, I needn't have worried. Jess has grown into a dark-haired headstrong four-year-old, with her own delightful personality and stubborn will. When we were reintroduced, I saw her for the child that she is now, not the baby that I lost.

๛

Sliding my rings onto my fingers and applying a final spritz of perfume, I check my reflection one last time. I'm wearing a dusty pink calf-length crepe dress, cut on the bias so that it falls flatteringly over my curves, but with sufficient weight and volume to swish and move as I walk. I've matched it with a cream pashmina for added modesty inside the church, and the sophisticated elegance of my dress contrasts against the drama of my ridiculously large, oversized dustbin lid-sized Philip Treacy hat. It matches the colour of my dress perfectly and with its three plumes of ostrich feathers sprouting from the brim, I know it makes a dramatic statement. Had Craig been here with me, I'd specifically chosen his light cream linen suit and matched his tie and handkerchief to the exact colours of my outfit. We would have made a stunning couple. As it is, I'd rather disappear into the background, but as I don't have an alternative outfit, I resign myself to using my humongous hat as a shield to hide beneath rather than an attention seeking tool, designed to project a regal air of confidence. Knowing I will come face-to-face with Chris at some point this weekend, I had wanted to exude an air of confidence. At least that was the plan.

I smooth down my dress, check my hat is securely pinned and, opening my clutch bag, double-check I have everything I need. I spy my mobile lying on my bedside table. Picking it up, I pause.

The only person who is likely to call me is the one person I don't want to speak to right now. I'm still cross with him, so I slide it inside the dressing table drawer and snap my clutch bag shut.

Pulling in a deep breath, I straighten my shoulders, hold my head high and leave my room.

Here goes nothing.

As I predicted, I'm the only single female milling amongst the wedding guests as we wait in the hotel lobby for our transport. Standing alone, I mime a few quick *'Hello's'* and *'Hi's'* to some people I recognise. Distant relatives of Mel's. But most of the guests are people I don't know. The older generation must be Karl's family, and I assume the younger couples, people around my own age, are joint friends of Melanie and Karl's, and my relationship with Mel predates these new friendships. I notice more than a few sideways glances, followed by awkward smiles, as they appraise the obvious singleton in the show-stopping hat. I'm sure they're all wondering who I'm related to, or how I fit into the wedding party.

Climbing onto the bus, I'm scanning for a single seat, when a friendly face looks in my direction and pats the empty seat next to her. Gratefully, I sit down.

"Fabulous hat, Vicky."

"Thank you, Susan," I gush.

Susan is Mel's father's second wife, technically Mel's step-mother, although she's never worn that label. I assume Mel's dad will be busy with his father-of-the-bride duties, so like me, Susan has been left partnerless. At least until after the ceremony.

"You have no idea how glad I am to see you." I lean across and give her a hug, as much as our hats will allow.

"Likewise," she replies, her eyes wide and her hands wringing in her lap. She looks as nervous and uncomfortable as I feel.

"It would appear we're the outcasts this afternoon," I say warmly. "So, why don't we look after each other?"

"That sounds like a perfect plan." She pats my knee affectionately.

The bus sets off towards Denia town, our luxury resort being a few miles north-west of the coast. We circumnavigate the dramatic Montgó Massif that forms the southern backdrop to Denia. A huge outcrop of jagged rock that rises up and divides Denia to the north from Xabia in the south, and which forms the easternmost tip of the Costa Blanca.

The bus leaves our resort, driving through barren countryside which is eventually replaced by the palm tree-lined cobbled streets as we arrive into Denia's Old Town. A traditional Spanish fishing port presided over by the Moorish Castle that sits on a rocky crag above. Despite the influx of tourism in more recent years, the town appears to have retained its Spanish authenticity. Much of its architecture looks the same today as I imagine it would have done centuries ago.

We're dropped off in the Plaza de la Constitución, an ancient communal square surrounded on three sides by quaint cafes and exclusive boutiques. On the east side nestles the unassuming church of Our Lady of the Assumption, where the wedding ceremony is to take place.

Susan and I link arms, steadying each other as we climb the stone steps into the church. Leaving the bright sunshine behind and stepping into the dimmer hush of the church, it takes a few moments for my eyes to readjust. In front of us, a long nave leads to an intricately carved altar. Four rich brown stone columns hold up an ornate and heavily embellished ciborium, which protects the statue of the Virgin Mary beneath. Around the fringes of the church are the usual individual chapels of worship found in Catholic churches and dedicated to various revered saints and local holy men. Looking up I take in the huge jade green dome, painted with scenes from the bible which joins the four corners of the building together. The sound of a single harpist playing a classical aria reverberates up into the rafters as the guests file into the church and take their seats.

To my left, a familiar voice asks, "Would you like an order of service?"

My heart skips a beat and my breath catches in my throat.

It's him.

Here. In the flesh.

Slowly turning, I tilt my head, peeking out from underneath my hat; our eyes meet.

He's right here. Right in front of me.

Mel mentioned he was an usher in the wedding party, and I knew this moment would happen at some point today, but I've still been caught by surprise. I didn't know how I would feel. Would I be angry, sad, elated, nervous, or even indifferent knowing our relationship ran its natural course and, despite trying so hard, we couldn't make it work?

What I didn't expect to feel was an overwhelming rush of love. A swell of emotion that has surged up from the deepest depths of my soul and has crashed over me. It takes my breath away.

Smiling from ear to ear and holding out the order of service, he hasn't changed. If anything, he looks more mature, but still the sexy hunk of a man he always was. Dressed in his groomsman's outfit, I don't think I've ever seen him look so handsome. Tailoring, suits him.

"It's lovely to see you again, Vicky," he says, and I try to interpret the cacophony of emotions in his tone. Sadness? Regret? Longing?

"You too, Chris." I dip my head, unable to look him in the eye for fear he too can read my unspoken emotions.

He hands me the wedding pamphlet, and as he does so, brushes his thumb gently over the top of mine. An almost imperceptible gesture, but his touch is like an electric shock, causing me to flinch and look at him a second time. Studying each other's eyes, we say nothing. But holding each other's gaze, we communicate everything.

It's still there. The love we once shared, and we both know it.

Susan, having taken an order of service from the usher on the other side of the aisle, holds out her arm. "Shall we?" she asks.

But I'm paralysed. Transfixed by Chris's intense gaze. Lost in time. Swimming in the pools of each other's souls. It's as if no time has passed and we're back in Tooting Bec Lido, sliding below the surface while the world moves on around us.

I'm the first to break eye contact. I swallow hard, my head spinning from the longing that has risen up from somewhere deep within me and is now raging, unabated, through my body.

"Yes. Let's," I say to Susan, despite my tongue sticking to the roof of my mouth.

I link my arm through hers and we lead each other down the aisle; all the while the heat of Chris's stare burns into my back.

The ceremony passes in a haze. Mel floats into the church, a vision of chiffon and lace. Karl beams proudly at his blushing bride. The congregation sings in all the right places, repeats the relevant instructions from the priest, and everyone says their prayers. One hour later, Miss Melanie Williams officially emerges as Mrs Karl Butcher.

Outside in the square the photographer, aided by Chris, is attempting to bully the respective families into order. Realising that Chris's eyes, despite being tied up with his official duties, are tracking my every move, and knowing that I'm unconsciously doing the same, I turn to Susan and suggest, "Do you fancy sharing a taxi back to the hotel? I don't know about you, but I could do with a drink. If we leave now, we would make it to the bar before the rest of the rabble turn up."

"I knew there was a reason I liked you so much." She smiles. "Come on. Let's go."

She finds her husband and whispers our new plan in his ear before we make our exit and head back to the hotel bar and, for the moment at least, to safety.

Chapter 30

*S*uitably fuelled by Dutch courage, in the form of multiple margaritas, I find my way to my table without crossing paths with Chris again.

The wedding reception is being held outside, in the hotel gardens, which are twinkling underneath a canopy of fairy lights. Circular tables covered in crisp white tablecloths are staggered around an intricate mosaic patio, which is doubling as the dance floor. The pattern of Moorish tiles on the floor reminds me of the ceiling in the hammam Mel and I visited when we went to Istanbul five years ago.

Gosh, that seems such a long time ago. Which I suppose it was. I hardly recognise the young, naive girl I was back then.

I find my name card and sit down; the scent from the centrepiece of lantana flowers and Valencia roses dances up my nose. My fingers fidget of their own accord while I sit quietly on my own, waiting for someone else to join me. If it wasn't for my jitters, I would be more appreciative of the perfection of the setting.

Behind me I hear all the other guests mingle and laugh together. If Craig had been here, I would have insisted we join in and mix with Mel and Karl's other friends, but sitting on my own, I'm not that brave. I close my eyes and allow the harmonic melody of Pachelbel's Canon, which rises elegantly from the string quartet playing in the corner, to waft over me.

In. Out. In. Out. I breathe deeply, to calm the insistent quiver in my gut.

I smile politely as the table fills up and I'm joined by distant cousins of Mel's that I've not seen since Jess's naming ceremony three years ago. Everyone does their best to include me in their conversations, but for the most part I remain quiet and smiling. Chris, thankfully, is seated with his brother, Dean, and Dean's family on the opposite side of the patio. Our seats strategically placed back-to-back, so we don't have to look at each other throughout the wedding breakfast. But it doesn't stop the pull of Chris's energy boring into my back, and like a moth to a flame I'm finding it harder and harder to resist.

In. Out. In. Out. I try to imagine myself back in the swimming pool at home. Steadily cutting through the water. Maintaining my balance. But it still takes a Herculean effort to stop myself turning around and seeking out his face in the crowd.

I push my food around my plate as I listen to Mel's family reminisce and tell stories about old times. Then a toastmaster bangs a gavel and we all turn our attention to the top table, and to Mel's father who gives a heartfelt speech about his daughter's childhood, growing up in New Zealand, and her adventures since. He finishes by formally welcoming Karl to the family, extending his hand for a ceremonial handshake. Karl follows up with an equally touching tribute to his new wife, and an old childhood friend of his rounds off the formalities by delivering the suitably mildly offensive character assassination of Karl, as is the tradition for a best man's speech.

Standing and raising our glasses for the final toast, I can't help but look in Chris's direction. He's looking directly at me, his lips unsmiling but his features softened by the flickering glow of the twinkling fairy lights.

He mouths, '*I'm sorry*', and my legs threaten to give way. I take a gulp of champagne and sit down heavily.

I'm so lost. Floundering and maladroit. Part of me is desperate to talk to him. But his magnetism overwhelms me and frightens me in equal amounts. I'm not sure I'd have the strength to resist him if he were to come any closer.

What if I fall into the well of him again and I can't climb back out? No. For my own safety, I must keep my distance. I cannot allow myself to go back.

The formal part of the day over, the DJ starts the party. After the new Mr & Mrs Butcher finish their first dance, other couples drift onto the floor, leaving me all alone at the table again. Fidgeting for something to do, I roll my champagne flute between my fingers.

And that's when I feel him. I know he's there, standing behind me, and an involuntary shiver ripples down my spine.

But the voice I hear is not the one I was expecting. "May I have this dance?"

I turn sharply. "Tim! When the hell did you get here?" I leap up and throw my arms around Tim's neck.

Out of my peripheral vision I see Chris slink back into the background.

"Just now." Tim air-kisses me. "It's a long story, but I'll tell you while we smooch on the dance floor. You can pretend you're my girlfriend."

"Eurgh." I lightly slap his arm. "Never. But I am pleased to see you."

Tim twirls me onto the floor and we laugh and joke as he tells the tale of his last twenty-four hours. He had planned to arrive on Thursday, but he couldn't avoid his last-minute trip to New York. Apparently, '*it's all gone to cock*', and he had to '*fly out there and sort out the mess.*' He managed to get the last seat on an overnight flight to Heathrow last night, '*...even if I had to rough it down the back in cattle class*', he jokes. But then due to the disruption from the massive storm in the UK, he missed the connection to Alicante from Gatwick, so flew to Madrid instead and jumped on the train to the coast. A few taxi rides later, and he's here. Slightly crumpled, but fashionably late.

"I knew I'd missed the ceremony, but I wasn't going to give up." He waves in Mel's direction and she raises her glass and winks. They exchange a warm smile. "I knew how much it meant to her for me to be here," he adds, turning his attention back to me. "So how come you're here alone? Where's Craig?"

I release a long sigh and feel the sting of tears prickling in my eyes. "It's another long story. But if I tell you, I'll collapse into a snotty mess, so best not to ask."

"Oh, that's a shame. Still, I never thought he was good enough for you."

I pull back from our embrace, tilt my head and purse my lips. "We've not broken up, or anything. He's just not here, that's all."

Tim doesn't know where to look. "Ignore me. Wrong end of the stick."

Despite Tim's faux pas, hearing of his magnanimous efforts to get here, despite arriving late, only accentuates how easily Craig gave up.

The music changes and the DJ slows the pace. A lot of people leave the dance floor; those that remain readjust their stances, the women settling their arms around their partner's necks, the men sliding their hands onto their partner's waists, or for those in more intimate relationships, onto their partner's derrières.

Behind me a deep voice asks, "Tim, may I cut in?" And I suck in a deep breath as I feel the balance of my world knocked off-kilter again.

Chris stands firm, a hand on Tim's shoulder.

Tim squares his shoulders and looks me in the eye. "Do you want him to? I'll stay if you'd rather."

I slowly close then reopen my eyes. I can't put this off any longer.

Giving Tim a weak smile, I reply, "No, it's okay. I'm okay."

"As long as you're sure. Come and find me if you need me."

"Thanks, Tim. I will. And thank you for the dance. I'm so pleased you made it, even if you were embarrassingly late."

He steps aside and Chris takes my hand. The instant his flesh touches mine I know I've fallen into the well of him. Sinking down a bottomless hole with no way out.

Once again I'm falling, falling, falling…

Chapter 31

The sound of Robbie Williams's "Angels" swirls around us as Chris pulls me into him, his energy enveloping me as we sway gently from side to side. My hands clasped together between our bodies, he has his arms around my back, embracing me. I turn my face and rest it against his chest as his chin skims the top of my head. His familiar masculine scent shoots straight up my nostrils and I can't help but inhale him deeply.

A sob catches in the back of my throat, as his jerky out-breath skims the top of my head. He too is on the verge of tears.

Eventually, he whispers, "You look absolutely stunning. But then you always did."

I can't speak. This moment feels too overwhelming. Too perfect. Yet I'm swamped by the waves of sadness and regret that are crashing over me as the past rises up and becomes the present we never had.

"So how've you been, ya olde Goose?"

This time, I'm unable to catch the sob at the back of my throat before it falls out onto his shoulder. No one calls me that. Only him.

Looking around the periphery of the patio I see a lot of people watching us: Melanie, Michelle, Tim, Chris's parents, his brother and sister-in-law. Everyone knows this is the first time we've seen each other since our abrupt break-up when I ran out on him, and I feel the weight of their expectations.

"Chris, there are a lot of eyes on us right now," I whisper. "I feel very exposed."

"I know. Me too. Let's go somewhere more private. Meet me in the rose garden."

There it is again just like it always was. Never a question, always an authoritative command. But somehow, with the way I'm feeling right now, in this moment I'm glad of his dominance. "Give it five minutes then pretend to go to the ladies and I'll meet you there."

Hypnotised by a force that feels more powerful than the both of us, I nod my agreement.

Returning to my empty table, I sit quietly for a few minutes, finishing my drink. When I'm convinced everyone's eyes have switched their focus elsewhere, I collect my hat, pashmina, and clutch bag from the table, avoid saying any formal goodbyes, not wanting to alert anyone to my absence, and sneak away unnoticed. When I reach the rose garden — a haven of roses, bougainvillea, and lilies — he's already there. Standing with his back to me, hands in his pockets. A perfect masculine statue in silhouette.

Like me, he must feel my presence before he hears me, as he turns around when I approach, relief written all over his face.

"Oh, Vicky. You came. I wasn't sure you would."

Reaching for my hands he leads me to a love seat, and we sit down together.

"I'm not sure why I did, or why I'm even here. What good can come from this, Chris? You must realise we can't go back to the past. Our lives have moved on. Things are different now. I'm different now."

"I know. I know. But I couldn't let today pass without talking to you."

We sit in silence, holding hands, our eyes locked onto each other's faces. He pulls on the hairpin holding my French twist in place and my tresses tumble free. Using his fingers, he combs out my hair, tucking a few loose strands away from my face, like he has done a thousand times before. When he's finished, he rests his hand on the curve of my neck, moving his thumb gently back and forth, caressing me. I remain transfixed.

Every touch peels back another layer as he penetrates my protective outer shell. Like an ice-lolly left out in the sun, I'm dissolving right in front of him.

"God, I've missed you," he breathes.

I dip my head.

I've missed him too. Terribly. Especially in those first few months after we broke up. But then I met Craig and things changed. But...

"But, what?" he says, softly. Reading my mind.

I look up at him. Lost. Found. Home.

Very gently he pulls me into him and brushes his lips against mine. The most tender and lightest of kisses.

My whole body aches for him and I want so desperately to open my mouth and let him back in. But I know I can't. If I do that, I won't be able to stop until I've opened my whole being to him and allowed him back into my soul. I have to stay strong. Even so, just the feel of his soft lips on mine causes me to swoon backwards, and he has to steady me before I fall into the rose bush behind.

"Chris, don't," I plead. Breaking our kiss just enough so that we are now nose to nose, our foreheads touching. "I can't. Please don't do this." My voice hardly audible, my breath shallow and fast in my body as I try and control the raging desire that is flooding every cell of my being.

He says nothing and instead pulls me into his firm embrace, wrapping his arms tightly around me. My head, once again, resting against his strong hard chest. The rhythmic sound of his beating heart re-grounding me and holding me safe.

"Let me stay with you tonight," he says quietly.

"No, Chris. You can't. I can't let you. I can't go back. It's too late for us."

"I don't want to go back. I just want to be near you," he whispers. His breath hot in my ear. "I promise I'll behave. No hanky-panky. I just want to hold you." He kisses my cheek while his arms rub my back and I continue to cling to him. "Correct me if I'm wrong, but it feels like you need this."

Silent tears begin to roll down my cheeks and my throat burns from all the emotions I'm holding in. Until now, I thought Craig was everything, and in many ways he is… but he's not this.

Another heavy silence falls between us. I don't have to say anything, Chris already knows the internal battle I'm fighting.

"I can't, Chris. I'm sorry."

"You have nothing to be sorry for. I'm the one that needs to apologise. I'm the one that hurt you. I'm the one that betrayed your trust. I'm the one that pushed you away. It's my fault we're not together, not yours."

Before either of us can say anything more, the sky above us explodes into a cacophony of light, colour, and noise. Our arms wrapped around each other, we turn and watch the fireworks which bang and pop into rainbow after rainbow, lighting up the dark night sky. Sitting quietly familiar and comfortable in each other's embrace, it feels as if we're the only two people in the world; each glittering explosion a reminder of the passion and fireworks we once shared, before each light fades and dies, plunging us back into darkness: a sage reminder of the black, harsh pain neither of us meant to cause one another but did none-the-less.

As the last light dies out, I hear myself whisper, "Okay then. But no hanky-panky, Chris. I mean it." I raise my index finger. He reaches for it and kisses the tip.

"Cross my heart and hope to die," he replies, beaming from ear to ear as he makes the sign of a cross across his chest. Standing and holding out his hands, he issues another command. "Come. Time to go."

Chapter 32

*C*hris pops another bottle of champagne open, and I watch as the cork flies through the air, descending into the garden below my bedroom balcony. Topping up my glass, we both turn towards the moon.

In the last few hours he's removed his jacket, cufflinks and rolled his shirt sleeves up. His cravat discarded, he's loosened his collar and I spy his precious Koru still hanging around his neck: the smooth jade green swirl attached by a leather strap.

"Mellie's told me about your new man," he says, keeping his gaze over the garden and the golf course beyond.

"He's hardly new. We've been together over three years now."

"You didn't hang around did you?" he teases.

"It wasn't like that. I wasn't looking to meet anybody, but then we kinda fell for each other."

"And does he make you happy?"

"Of course."

He takes a languorous sip of his drink. "But I notice he's not here."

"Craig's a wonderful man." I rush to Craig's defence. "We're engaged."

Chris jerks his head back and turns to look at me. "Really? I don't see a ring on your finger."

"Well, more promised to each other than formally engaged. But we are planning on getting married."

"I see. When?"

"I don't know." I break eye contact.

"Hmm." Chris purses his lips, turning his head to look back over the top of the palm trees.

"And what about you? Has there been someone special since we... you know."

"I'm no monk, but no..."

We fall into silence, both of us sipping our drinks as a distraction.

"Chris, you know you will always be my *First Great Love*," I add, more seriously.

"And this — this Craig, is he your second?"

I pause, then reply softly, "Yes." I reach for his hand to hold.

The sound of the DJ playing 'New York, New York' somewhere in the background breaks up our conversation. A sign that the party is coming to a close.

"You actually did me a favour when you left," he says a few minutes later.

I tilt my head, listening.

"It forced me to have to face some of my inner demons."

"Oh?"

"I had to figure out why I behaved the way I did... especially when I knew I loved you."

"I never doubted that, Chris. I always believed you loved me. And you're not completely to blame. I'm not proud of some of the things I did either."

"Yes, but your behaviour was only ever in reaction to something I'd done. You have such a pure capacity to love. My therapist has helped me realise how much I abused that."

"Wait. What? You have a therapist?" I baulk.

"Yes," he laughs. "After I completed the anger management course I decided to continue with therapy."

My eyes wide, my mouth falls open.

"Close your mouth, Goose." He reaches for my chin and lifts my jaw closed. "It doesn't suit you," he teases, his lips smirking, "But yes, I've come to realise how much repressed anger I had. And growing up with a dodgy eye hasn't helped either."

Chris was born with a malignant ocular tumour and had his left eye amputated when he was only a few days old. The silvery scars that disappear into his hairline, and his glass eye a constant reminder of this life-altering childhood trauma. It was the brave surgeon, who agreed to operate on such a tiny baby – ultimately saving his life – who gave him his Koru. According to Māori tradition, for the spirit in the stone to remain, it may never be purchased but instead, gifted in an act of love.

He squeezes my hand. "I'm so sorry for the pain I caused you, Vicky, especially when all you ever did was love me."

I close my eyes and allow his words to wash over me. Even in our darkest moments, I always believed it was only his own pain and insecurities that caused him to be jealous, or manipulative, or abusive. And here he is, atoning for his past, telling me I was right and saying all the things I wished he'd acted on back then. But then, if I hadn't left, he would never have had the impetus to embark on his own journey of self-discovery and healing. We would have continued the destructive cycle of loving each other then hurting one another, over and over.

"My body hurts," I say, wrapping my arms around my own torso.

It's as if his words are releasing all the suppressed pain I didn't know I was holding onto, and I'm suddenly tired and battle-weary.

"Stay here. I'm going to run you a bath." He disappears inside and returns ten minutes later. "It's been such a long day. Go and have a soak. It's all ready for you."

I take his hand and he leads me towards the bathroom.

"Will you still be here when I get out?" I ask. For some reason I don't want to be left alone.

He nods. I close the bathroom door and slip out of my dress and underwear. Sliding into the warm soapy water, I close my eyes and allow the bubbles to ease away my aches and pains.

Half an hour later, I hear a soft rap on the door. "You okay in there?"

I slide underneath the water, wanting to push reality even further away.

"Vicky. Tell me you're okay. You haven't drowned, have you?" Chris sounds concerned, but I can't seem to muster the strength to reply.

"Cover yourself. I'm coming in."

"No, Chris. I'm fine," I shout, but it's too late. I look up and he's standing in the doorway.

Panicked, I swish the bubbles over my bits and cover my breasts with one of my arms. "What are you doing? You can't be in here."

"I was worried."

Since I've been in the bath, he's taken off his trousers, shoes, and socks, and is wearing only his boxers and shirt, the buttons undone to his waist, revealing his bronzed firm torso. My eyes travel the length of his body. His legs are as tanned and roped with muscles as I remember. He takes a seat on the closed toilet lid. "It's not like I don't already know every inch of your body. Here. Close your eyes."

He tilts my head back, and using the hotel shampoo, lathers my hair. Tenderly massaging my scalp with his fingers. I close my eyes and drift away, lost in the sensation. Using a conch shell he rinses the shampoo away, before lathering my hair with conditioner. It's such a tender and intimate thing to do. His fingers rubbing in slow, circular movements across my scalp. It feels simultaneously both sensual and respectful, and with each circle of his digits he's working his way back inside my heart.

I feel both vulnerable, yet cherished, and safe.

He rinses away the conditioner, then combs out my long locks.

"See, that wasn't so bad now, was it?" he says, gently kissing my shoulder. A tiny moment of connection, but the imprint of his lips on my skin feels like a firecracker. "Now, scooch forward," he says.

"No, Chris. You can't," I reply, panicked.

"It's okay, Goose. I'm not going to do anything. No hanky-panky, remember?"

But before I can object further he's stripped out of his remaining clothes and climbed into the bath behind me. Spooning me, he places his legs on either side of mine and I feel the weight of his arms as he wraps them around my waist. He pulls me into him and instinctively I relax back, resting my head against his chest. He feels strong and I feel safe. With my eyes still closed, warm breath tickles my neck as he breathes in and out, and unconsciously my own breath falls into sync with his. We lie there for a few long moments, breathing in and out in unison.

Gently, he begins to swoosh warm water back and forth over my body. I allow the warm rivulets to drain down my torso and over my breasts. I keep my arms wrapped tightly around my body, bathing in the gentle waves that wash over me. I've fallen into the abyss and my senses have taken over. Nothing exists in the world except the feeling of him all around me.

Chris picks up a sponge, pours over moisturising body wash and washes my shoulders. Gently rubbing in slow, circular motions, up and down the curve of my neck. The warm water drains away, down over my torso, alerting every nerve ending in my skin. I half expect him to reach around with the sponge and seek out my breasts which now ache for his caress, but he doesn't; he simply continues to wash my shoulders and down the outsides of my arms.

Next, he digs his thumbs into my trapezius muscles. I flinch when my tight sinews object. Instinctively he lightens the pressure and I place one of my hands on top of his as he massages my shoulders. He bends and kisses the back of my fingers, and I squeeze his hand in response.

Once he's decided my shoulders are sufficiently relaxed, he wraps his arms around me again.

"You're so tense; you needed that," he says softly, and I have to admit I can't remember the last time I felt so comfortable being naked, whilst lying next to someone else who also felt as equally comfortable in their own skin.

"So this doesn't count as hanky-panky then?" I half-joke. I'm not sure how others would define *hanky-panky*, but I'm pretty sure *sharing a bath with your ex* would not be deemed acceptable behaviour.

"Don't know what ya talking about. I've not even touched a boob."

I playfully slap his arm.

Leaning forward, he inhales. "Mmmm, strawberries. Your hair always did smell of strawberries."

Sweeping my tresses aside, he kisses my neck. Slightly more insistent than his soft, light kiss from earlier. With his mouth still attached to the curve of my shoulder, he nips my skin and mumbles, "You have no idea how much I want to give you a hickey right now."

"Don't you dare! Do you know how much trouble I'd be in?"

We both pause. Acknowledging the third person in the room, even if only metaphorically. But as much as I don't want to admit it, I can't remember the last time I felt this level of intimacy with Craig.

"Does he give you everything you want?" Chris asks softly, reading my mind again.

"Yes," I whisper, my own voice not completely convinced. "He's kind, stable, he's my best friend, and I know he loves me."

"And is he passionate? Do you tremble at his touch like you used to at mine?"

"Not everything is about sex, you know." I stiffen, uncomfortable with the direction our conversation is taking.

"I know. But when we were together..." He trails off. "It's never been like that for me with anyone else — ever. Watching you break into a million pieces was my greatest pleasure. I could never get enough."

I remain silent, gently swishing the water back and forth across my stomach. I want to tell him that it's the same for me. That sex with Craig doesn't come close to the spiritual, transcendent out-of-body experience making love with him was like. But telling him would feel like a betrayal to Craig. At first I thought it was because Craig and I got off to such a bad start sexually, but being here with Chris now, I realise that we simply don't share the same kind of sexual chemistry that exists between Chris and I.

Eventually, I whisper, "Me too. It's only ever been like that with you, Chris."

But even as I say it, I also know that what was missing with Chris is what I have with Craig. Craig is stable and solid. He has a great career, a steady wage, we have money in the bank, we live in a beautiful home, and we belong to a fantastic social group. And he's emotionally stable – together we're emotionally stable.

Whereas my relationship with Chris was hedonistic, visceral, and unpredictable. It took me around the world and back and was filled with new experiences that pushed my boundaries both sexually, mentally, and spiritually. But unlike my relationship with Craig, with Chris I experienced the highest of highs, and the lowest of lows, and like Icarus, I learnt that when you fly too close to the sun, or too close to the sea, you will die.

The water continues to swirl around us both, and my mind continues to race. Is the intimacy I desire something I can only have with the man within whose arms I now lie, or the man whose arms wait for me back home? Which is the right choice: passion or stability?

"Your turn to close your eyes." I tap his arm, shuffling forward.

Stepping out of the bath, I wrap a towel around myself, tucking it in like a toga. Turning back around, I see Chris has used one hand to cover his glass eye, meaning his other good one has just ogled an eyeful of my ass. "Oi, you. That's not allowed." I wag my finger at him. "No hanky-panky, remember?"

"Aww, but can you blame me?" He chortles.

I sit on the edge of the bath and sigh heavily.

"What do we do now, Chris? I'm not sure I'm ready for this

night to be over. I don't want you to go, but I'm also not comfortable allowing you to sleep in my bed."

He reaches for my cheek and strokes it with the back of his hand. "Then let's keep going. Let's not go to sleep. I have an idea. Get dressed in something comfy — and wear flat shoes."

I quickly dress in a pair of light blue skinny jeans, a cream cable-knit sweater, with three-quarter length sleeves and a wide-open neck, which causes it to fall over one shoulder.

Chris pulls on his suit trousers and shirt, leaving his waistcoat and jacket behind. Grabbing my hand, he leads me out of the hotel and into the night.

Chapter 33

*G*iggling like two teenagers bunking off school, Chris guides me around the side of the hotel and into the car park. Retrieving a car key from his pocket, he presses the fob and the headlights of a bright red Ferrari flash as the central locking *bleep-bloops* into life.

"Seriously?! You couldn't rent a Ford like a normal person." I shake my head, laughing.

"You know me, Vicky. When it comes to cars, it has to be the best. Hop in."

He holds open the passenger door and I slide into the black leather bucket seat before he runs around to the driver's side. Once settled in his seat he presses a button on the dashboard and the roof unfolds. Revving the engine, he drives us off into the darkness, sending a shower of gravel up into the air behind.

"Even so, you could buy a car for what one week's hire most likely cost."

"True. But there's only so much *wedding* I can take. I needed something to distract me. Over this past week, I've taken this baby as far up the coast as Tarragona and as far inland as Tomelloso. I never realised how beautiful this part of Spain is."

I shake my damp hair and it flies free behind me. Throwing my head back, I hold my arms aloft, feeling the rush of wind between my fingers as I look up at the stars. After feeling so tense all day, I'm now relaxed and at ease.

"So where are you taking me?" I ask.

"You'll see."

The first glimpse of dawn is on the horizon as Chris rams the gears, tearing through the twisty back lanes of the Costa Blanca. Heading initially north from our resort, he joins the CV-736, before turning back south towards Xàbia.

The massive Mount Montgó looms oppressively in front of us. Its jagged edges and craggy outcrops breaking free from the earth's crust as if rising up out of the very confines of hell. Turning the car off the main road, Chris follows a single-track road as far as he can go. When the track ends in a car park, he jumps out, locks up the Ferrari and grabs my hand.

"If we're quick, we'll catch the sunrise from the top."

Following his lead, just as I've done all evening, we scramble the remaining half a mile to the summit, the highest peak for hundreds of miles around.

Laid out directly below us and centred around the harbour, where the fishing boats are already unloading their overnight catches, are the twinkling lights of Denia. To our right, further down the coast and just visible in the distance, we can see the lights of Alicante, and to the north, Valencia. Behind us, the earth is devoid of any major light, the sparse inland plains of Spain's interior punctuated only by the odd isolated farmstead, and stretched out in front of us is the ink-black Mediterranean Sea. Its tideless waves lapping gently to and fro against the shore as the first rays of the dawn aurora bounce off its rippled surface. A new day is about to break.

I feel the comforting weight of Chris's chin on my shoulder as he stands behind me, his arms wrapped tightly around my waist.

"It's breathtaking, Chris. Thank you for bringing me up here."

"On a clear day you can see as far as Ibiza." He points out over the horizon.

We stand in silence, soaking up the vista together. Drinking in the stillness.

The sky temporarily darkens to a deep, rich purple, signalling that the sunrise is only moments away. Then the first haze of red, which turns orange, before a sliver of bright yellow light peeks above the horizon.

Both of us gasp as we watch the fresh day dawn. The sun's brilliant tentacles stretching up and illuminating the ripples on the sea.

"This is how it should have been, Vicky. This is how I should have treated you. You deserved so much more than I was capable of giving you back then. I didn't appreciate you, until I'd lost you."

"Maybe, Chris. But that doesn't change where we are in our lives now."

"I know." He lets out a long sigh that tickles the side of my neck. "I'm just happy I got to see you today and have been able to spend this time with you."

He turns me around, reaches for my hand and, through the open buttons of his shirt, presses my fingers against his heart. I watch as he draws in a lung-filling breath. "There's something I need to say."

"Don't, Chris. Don't say it." I dip my head and squeeze away the tears that pool in the corners of my eyes. "It's too late for us. We can't undo what's already been done."

He ignores my pleas, tilting my chin upwards, his gaze penetrating the very depths of my soul.

"I love you, ya daft old goose. I always have, and I always will."

"No, Chris. Please don't say that." A single hot tear leaks out of my eye and rolls down my cheek.

"But it's the truth. I love you and I know I always will. Nothing and no-one can say or do anything to ever change that."

Crying more hot tears that fall down my cheeks and off the end of my chin, I whimper, "But it's just a fantasy, Chris. We had our chance and we couldn't make it work. No matter how hard we tried. We always ended up hurting each other."

"True." He presses his lips into a thin smile. My harsh truths failing to dampen his confidence. "But it doesn't stop me from loving you."

"And what am I meant to do with that information now?" I weep.

"Keep it safe, my love. Lock it away in the deepest part of you. As long as my heart is beating, my love for you will never diminish."

"Jesus, Chris. I have a whole other life. One that I've worked so hard to create. I love my job, have a great group of friends, a lovely home. And then there's Craig. How am I meant to go back to him as if this night never happened?"

More serious now, he continues, "Then don't. Come away with me. Give us another chance. I know things would be different this time. We wouldn't make the same mistakes we did before. We're older and wiser now."

I lean into him and close my eyes.

What the hell am I supposed to do? Does one night, with what feels like, a soulmate connection with a former lover erase the three years of love and stability that waits for me back home?

In. Out. In. Out. I focus on my breathing again. Trying and failing to quell the turmoil of emotions that are rampaging through my chest. Chris's breathing falls into sync with mine, as he too grapples with his own feelings.

Why the hell couldn't he have been like this when we were together? Sure, there were times when he was. I lived for those moments, and they were the glimpses that kept me bound to him. But how many times did I forgive him only for him to break my heart all over again, and again, and again. Who's to say it would be any different? Yet our chemistry is undeniable.

I suppose the big question is… *Do I still love him?*

I take in a few long breaths as I battle with the definitive choice laid out in front of me.

Go back to Craig, or run away with Chris.

Choose love and stability, or passion and instability.

In, out. In, out.

Eventually I whisper, "I can't, Chris. I can't run away. My life is with Craig now."

He kisses the top of my head and says nothing.

After a long while, he lifts my chin, looks into my eyes and whispers, "It's okay. I only want you to be happy."

We stand silently, gazing into each other's souls, when I spot something dart across the sky.

"Look!" I say, pointing at the falling star as it blazes across the breaking dawn.

"Do you know what I think every time I see a shooting star?" he says as the star burns out and dies.

I look at him blankly.

"That's our baby, Vicky."

"Chris, no…Don't go there," I say, a warning tone to my voice.

Tenderly he lifts my chin, again. "That's our baby girl, Vicky. Reminding us she's still out there. Still waiting to be born."

"And how is that ever going to happen?" A sob catches in the back of my throat.

"It will. I'm certain of it. Not yet. It's not yet her time. But one day, Vicky. One day when the planets collide, she'll come to us. I know it."

I can't take it anymore. It's all too much and I collapse into him. Heaving great big sobs of regret. Tears of sadness, and of release. I let it all go. And all the while he holds me. Stroking my back and kissing the top of my head.

Eventually, when I have nothing left, I wipe my eyes with the pads of my fingers and smile meekly. "Sorry," I snivel.

"Don't be silly. You've got nothing to apologise for." He raises his own hand and this time places it delicately on my chest, above my right breast. I slide my own palm back inside his shirt so we're each feeling the unwavering beating of each other's hearts. Allowing our love to pass freely between us.

The sun has begun to crawl above the horizon. The darkness of night fading with every passing moment. Before the magic is lost and dawn breaks completely, this time I'm the one to lean in and kiss him. With our hands still over our respective hearts, we stand on the top of the mountain and allow our passion to say what we can't. Neither of us wants to let the other go, because we know when we do, it will be time to go on with our lives and leave each other behind.

As our lips move of their own accord, this time I do open my mouth to him, and we deepen our kiss. Our tongues twisting and twirling together in our desperate need to assimilate ourselves into each other's souls. I hear him suck air into his lungs as he feels my heart opening to him, even if only for this one fleeting moment.

Eventually breaking our kiss, our foreheads touching, he gently strokes the outsides of my arms. There is nothing more to be said and I notice tears glistening in the corners of his eyes.

He sucks in another deep breath before whispering, "Come on. It's time to go."

*

Eight hours later as the screen doors open in the arrivals hall at Newcastle Airport, I spy Craig waiting for me, hopping from foot to foot. His sweaty brow just visible behind an enormous bunch of flowers.

Oh, bless him. He looks nervous.

My heart lifts at the sight of him and I rush forward, dragging my wheelie bag and dustbin lid-sized hat box behind me. Dropping my luggage I jump up into his waiting arms, wrapping my legs around his waist and covering his face with a smattering of kisses.

"God, I missed you," he gushes.

"Me too," I reply, covering his mouth with my own. He returns my affection, kissing me passionately, which is unusual. He would never normally kiss me like this in public. Still, I don't object and momentarily lose myself in his embrace. As if allowing myself to sink back into him will cause the memory of last night to fade to black and white.

"I'm so sorry I fucked up," he says, pulling back from our kiss, smiling and smoothing my hair away from my face.

"I know you are. But it's not like you did it on purpose. You couldn't help the storm."

"Yes, I know. But still. I let you down." He pauses, before adding, "I made a terrible mistake and I'm very sorry."

"Apology accepted." I run my fingers through his hair as he sets me back on my feet.

"It'll never happen again," he says, a smidgeon of desperation in his voice.

I draw my eyebrows together. "It's okay. I believe you, Craig. Look, a lot has happened this weekend, and I don't really want to talk about it, but what I do know is, I never want to be without you, ever."

He looks deep into my eyes and I see the acknowledgment of what I've not said. "Yes, I'm choosing you, Craig. You don't need to ask me about it. Yes — Chris was there. Yes — we spoke. Yes — it was intense, but it's over."

"So, no chance his name might slip out again?" He raises a quizzical eyebrow.

"Never. It's you and me from now on."

"God, I love you, Tori. I'm so damn lucky to have found you." He wraps his arms even tighter around my body. His hands rubbing up and down my back as he pulls me closer, as if he's reminding himself of who I am. "I'm sorry if I don't tell you that enough, or I don't show you how much you mean to me. You're my absolute world and for a moment this weekend, I thought I'd lost you."

My mind flicks back to our terse phone call yesterday morning, when I essentially hung up on him after he told me he'd missed the flight. I hadn't realised he'd taken my abruptness so literally.

"Don't worry. I'm not going anywhere. You've got me for life."

"Maybe that's something we should make official, then?"

I jerk my head back. "For real?"

"Yeah, why not? You've been more than patient with me. I think it's about time we discussed it properly."

"Oh, Craig. You're not just saying this because you think it's what I want to hear? You really mean it?"

"I do. The truth — always, remember? And the truth is I want you in my future, Tori... as my wife."

I leap up onto him again and land a smacker of a kiss square on his lips. "And I want nothing more than to be your wife."

"Come on then. Let's get home, and make things official."

Later, I'm unpacking my suitcase while Craig readies the champagne downstairs. We've summoned the gang; at the moment they have no idea why. Although we've agreed to go ring shopping tomorrow, we couldn't wait to share our news with everyone. After almost three years together I'm expecting lots of shrieks of *'about time'* and *'that's the best news'* once we tell them.

I gently lift out the expensive designer dress I wore for the wedding, and buried beneath it is a small black velvet box next to a folded single piece of paper, written on monogrammed hotel stationery. Only one person had the opportunity to hide it there.

He must have written this and slid it inside my suitcase when I was in the bath. Picking up the note, I read:

Vicky,

You know how useless I always was at writing letters, or being able to tell you how I really feel, however these always belonged to you, even if you tried to return them to me once.

I'd like you to keep them, if only to remember the good times.

You will always be my special someone, even if I'm no longer yours.

Chris x

I fold the paper inwards, holding it over my lips, and inhale a deep breath. I can almost smell him on the card.

Reaching down I pick up the black velvet box. I already know what's inside. Even so, I gasp when I open the lid and see the gleaming yellow diamond earrings glinting back at me. The ones he bought in Hong Kong. The design is a yellow marquise tear-shaped diamond, topped by a clear, round, brilliant-cut diamond at the tip. When worn, the teardrop appears to drip from the diamond stud. He surprised me with them on our last day when *'we dined on the top of the world'*, telling me he chose them as they reminded him of the colour of my hair.

From then on, I wore them every day... until the day I left. It didn't feel right keeping them, so before I walked out, I'd placed them in the middle of his mother's dining room table. I knew when he saw them he'd know I wasn't coming back, and I never thought I'd see them again.

Yet, here they are. In my hands once again.

Chris has returned to me the very gift of love I'd used to signify the end of our relationship, as a way of expressing his eternal love for me.

Telling Craig is out of the question, but I don't want to throw them away either. That feels like it would invalidate my entire relationship with Chris. So instead, I pull out my ballerina box from the bottom of my wardrobe, open the lid, and tuck both the earrings and Chris's note inside the wooden keepsake.

Smiling, I head back downstairs, back into the future I've chosen, knowing I can move on with Craig, and lay my relationship with Chris to rest. Safe in the knowledge that the love I once shared with him was, and is, pure and true.

Chapter 34

13 months later, June 2000

*S*tanding in the shaded porch of our family's parish church — a picture-perfect, quintessentially olde English church that could have been lifted straight out of a Richard Curtis movie — I breathe in the heady scent from the hundreds of roses, forming a floral archway over the porch.

My stepdad turns to me and asks, "If you have any doubts at all, there's still time to change your mind."

I pat his hand. "I appreciate you asking, but I've never been happier. All I want to do is get in there and get married."

My real dad knew that his presence today would cause too much upset, the hurt and pain between him and my mother still as raw as the day they divorced, so he magnanimously chose to stay away; therefore it's the man who raised me who has the honour of walking me down the aisle.

Someone opens the heavy wooden church door and, on cue, the organ strikes up. The volume jolting me upright.

This is it. The moment I've waited for all my life.

The thundering vibrations from the organ pipes shake the rafters of the tiny church and muffle the sounds of the congregation shuffling to their feet as they prepare to herald my arrival.

"Good luck," Nessa leans forward and whispers in my ear.

Behind her Becca and Julie complete my bridal party. Whilst I'm a vision of white satin and tulle, they're all dressed in full-length chiffon in an unusual, but classic, deep rich plum. Together, the three of them make a stunning line-up. Nessa's dramatic red hair has been swept up into a classic chignon, Julie's long blonde locks are trussed up into curled waves like my own, and Becca's long auburn pinned curls flow dramatically down her back.

'I need something to take the focus away from this,' she'd said, pointing to her thickened waist when we'd been discussing 'hair options' a few weeks back. At the time I'd felt like I'd been eating, sleeping and dreaming about flower choices, seating plans, and hymn selections as the wedding juggernaut had overtaken my life. Becca's still-thickened waist and oversized breasts are a result of giving birth two months ago. 'An unplanned happy accident,' is how Mark described the arrival of his healthy bouncing baby boy.

'I don't care what the three of you look like,' I'd said at Becca's protestations. 'You could turn up in your pyjamas for all I care. I just want my girls there with me. We'll find you some industrial-sized Spanx and shoehorn you into them if we have to, Becks. You'll look fabulous, I promise.'

Last night Mel telephoned me from Christchurch to wish me luck. 'Not that you'll need it. I'll be with you in spirit, if not in person,' she'd said, both of us gutted that she wasn't able to be here and take her place as my fourth bridesmaid. But following her own nuptials in Spain last year, she and Karl have relocated back to New Zealand. And at eight months pregnant, travelling is out of the question. Michelle, too, is fit to bursting with her second child, and so is also sad not to be here.

The first pews of smiling faces greet me as I stand at the back of the church, waiting for my cue. I can't make out any features, their faces silhouetted from the sunlight that streams in through the stained-glass windows high above, but I feel the joy and love vibrating in the ether.

"Ready?" I say to my wedding party, before sucking in a deep breath and stepping forward, walking in time to the pulse of Jeremiah Clarke's "Trumpet Voluntary" that echoes around the tiny church walls.

Step, together. Step, together. Step, together. I walk reverently down the aisle on the arm of my stepdad, beaming from ear to ear.

It came as no surprise to my 'wedding team' that I'd counted the exact number of steps and how many bars of music it takes to arrive at the altar at the exact moment the trumpet soloist reaches his final notes of the composition.

Step, together. Step, together. Rows and rows of eyes are all suddenly on me, and I modestly return their smiles as everyone *ooh's* and *aah's* as I float past. Straining their necks to get that first glimpse of the bride in her dress. It's impossible to withhold the happiness that radiates out of every pore in my body as I glide up the aisle.

Amongst the silhouetted faces, one face jumps out. He's beaming at me, and my stepdad has to steady me as I almost stumble.

What the hell? How on earth is he here?

A thunderbolt of adrenaline shoots through my body and my gut tightens.

How is this possible? He wasn't invited. Why has he come?

Then my eyes refocus and I realise it's not Chris's face smiling warmly at me, but an unfamiliar family friend of my parents. I release a long exhale.

But why did my mind play such a cruel trick on me just now?

Since our emotional night in Denia last year, Chris has hardly entered my thoughts. These past thirteen months with Craig have been the best yet. Craig and I share an easy and relaxed relationship, and hardly ever argue. I never have to worry that he might fly off the handle at any moment. Both our careers are on the up and up. We go on holiday every chance we get and spend all our spare time socialising with the gang. Craig has stuck to his promise of never inviting Amanda to our home again, and although I know she still works at PPS, she's moved to a different department. One that doesn't report directly to Craig, and so he hardly ever mentions her now. Since getting engaged, we've had no repeats of the slip-ups or hiccups that kept tripping us up in our relationship in the past.

So why the hell has Chris popped into my psyche now? Is it because deep down I think I may be making the biggest mistake of my life? Or is this the universe's way of letting me know that he is giving me his blessing? That it may not be him standing at the front of the church waiting for me, but as he promised, when we stood on the top of Mount Montgó, he only wants me to be happy. Is this his spirit's way of showing me his support?

Gliding down the aisle, floating on the warmth and well-wishes emanating from everyone around me, I look up and see the wide shoulders, strong back, and jet-black hair of the smartly dressed man who is about to become my husband, waiting for me at the altar.

My stomach flips over not from excited anticipation or a wave of love, but because I'm suddenly gripped by a fear that I'll say the wrong name when it comes to saying my vows. It doesn't help that I watched a rerun of *Friends* this past week. The one where Ross says Rachel's name at the altar instead of Emily's.

Oh, God.

Step, together. Step, together. I continue to walk in time to the music, my blood thumping inside my ears as I grip my stepdad's arm even tighter.

It's Chris not Craig. No, Craig. Fuck. No, Chris... Craig. *Fuuuuuuuck!*

I suck air into my lungs, trying to calm the rising anxiety in my throat, while I continue to glide serenely and beam spuriously at the congregation.

Craig, Craig, Craig, I think over and over in my mind.

The final notes of the elaborate trumpet voluntary ring out as I reach the front of the church. My groom turns and, seeing his reaction on his face when he first looks at me, causes a rush of love to flow over me like water washing over pebbles on a beach. I release a long exhale and feel my shoulders drop back into place.

I have nothing to worry about. It's Craig who's here waiting for me. It's Craig, staring back at me with his dark onyx eyes and gorgeous dimples. It's Craig, breathing deeply as he attempts to hold it together and maintain his cool. It's Craig, dressed in full morning suit, a claret-coloured rose in his buttonhole. And it's Craig who lifts my tulle veil away from my face and whispers in my ear, "You look absolutely stunning."

I mouth, '*thank you*' and he gives me a cheeky wink.

Each of our presence calms the other as we turn to face the vicar, and I feel my breath settle inside my body.

This feels right. This *is* right.

Finally, I'm about to become the one thing I've always wanted: a wife to a loving husband. A husband who loves me as much as I love him.

◊

"We're nearly ready for you," our toastmaster tells us as Craig and I wait outside the marquee where our reception is being held. "Just waiting for the last few guests to take their seats," he adds.

A server passes me a welcome glass of Pimm's and I eagerly sip the fruity punch through the straw. Having been outside in the blistering June sunshine for the past two hours, as our wedding photographer captured every possible memory of the day, I'm absolutely parched.

I pass him the empty glass back. "Thanks. I really needed that."

"Do your cheeks hurt?" Craig asks, contorting his face to stretch out his facial muscles.

"Completely," I reply as I too pull a series of funny faces. "One thing I didn't have a plan for, was sore cheeks from smiling so much."

Craig beams at me. "You've done an awesome job, pet. Everything is perfect."

"Thank you... *husband*," I reply, playfully trying out his new label.

"You're welcome... *wifey*." He smiles and gives my bum a little nip.

"Wifey? Err, I don't think so."

"What would you prefer then? Ball and chain, Her indoors, The Mrs, or my Trouble and Strife?"

"*Wife* will do just fine, thank you."

"Okay then, Mrs Fenwick." He squeezes my hand. "You'll always be *my girl* even if you're now also *my wife*."

Mrs Fenwick. I've seen my new name written down — on our marriage certificate and also on the seating plan, but that's the first time I've heard anyone say it out loud. And as soon as the words leave Craig's lips, a rush of energy shoots through my body and fires out of the top of my head. As if I've inadvertently stepped onto some kind of vortex, or all my chakras have come into alignment and are connecting me to something outside of myself. Something transcendent. As if my new name has unleashed my true self. The most authentic version of me.

I stand bolt upright as the column of energy pulsates through me. It's like nothing I've ever experienced before. It feels as if by becoming Victoria Fenwick, I've just released some kind of inner power and I've become the person I didn't know I was always meant to be. Until this moment.

The 'Fenwick' name has always meant something to me. It not only belongs to Craig, but also my grandfather and all of my family on my mother's side, but now it's mine too. And if feels as if, I've finally arrived.

"Ready?" the toastmaster asks.

Craig lifts my hand to his lips and kisses the back of it. "Yes. We're ready."

The toastmaster steps into the marquee and bangs his gavel as we hover in the entrance tunnel. "My lords, ladies, and gentlemen, please be upstanding for your bride and groom. Please join me in welcoming your new Mr and Mrs Craig Fenwick."

Carried forward as if on some ethereal energy, I float into the marquee and take my seat next to Craig as his wife, feeling happier, lighter, and more true than at any other time in my life.

Part V

Chapter 35

*O*nce everyone settles, the toastmaster bangs his gavel again and introduces first my stepdad, who makes a beautiful speech about me being the daughter he always wanted and never had, then Craig, who coughs into the back of his hand, stands, and prepares to make his groom's speech.

After a few heckles of, '*Get on with it*', and '*Rubbish*', to which Craig stares directly at the tables at the back of the room, where a couple of his team are sitting, he clears his throat and begins.

"I'll try and keep this speech short because I know how hangry my wife can get."

This earns him a fresh round of heckles as he publicly acknowledges me as his wife for the first time.

It was Nessa's idea to have the speeches before our wedding breakfast.

'That way they're out of the way and you can all relax,' she'd suggested.

'*Sold!,*' I'd agreed and immediately signed the idea off in my wedding planner. The only thing I've not planned, or had any control over, is both Craig's speech and Clarky's reply as his best man.

I refocus my attention back to Craig as he continues. "I'd like to thank Victoria's family for all their love and support, and for officially welcoming me into their clan. And I know I speak on behalf of my parents when I say how delighted they are to have such a fabulous daughter-in-law."

I glance to my left and right and smile at both Craig's parents and my own.

"It was fate the night I met Tori. I'll never forget the sight of this tanned blonde bombshell stumbling back from the bar in The Quilted Camel, and being completely dumbstruck. If she hadn't tripped up and almost landed flat on her face, I'm not sure I would have had the guts to introduce myself."

He looks down at me and we both smile at the memory of that first meeting.

"It didn't take long for me to realise how special she is and how lucky I am to have found her."

"So why did it take you so long to marry her?" Anth heckles from further down the top table.

As ushers, both he and Mark also had official roles in our nuptials.

Craig looks up from his cue cards. "Erm, I think the phrase you're looking for is, *'Pot calling the kettle black,'* mate."

Anth winks, raising his pint in Craig's direction, before planting a kiss on Nessa's shoulder as she leans back into him. They still don't seem to be in any rush to make their 'unofficial marriage' official.

"I think you can all agree that Tori looks absolutely beautiful today…" Craig continues, and a few guests bang their hands on the tables in agreement. I take a sip of champagne, feeling my cheeks flush.

There's no doubt that my designer wedding dress from Dickens & Jones in London is everything I could have ever wished for. Even so, it was difficult to justify the four-thousand-pound price tag, but Granny Fenwick didn't hesitate and pulled out her cheque book, realising this was 'the one.'

'You only get married once, and you deserve to look your best,' she'd said at the time.

"... but she's also beautiful on the inside," Craig continues. "She's kind, considerate, a great hostess — who makes the best bacon butties in the world."

More jeering and table banging as all our friends endorse Craig's comments.

"But she's also smart, super intelligent, and almost as ambitious as me. In fact, if I'm not careful, I think her career could eclipse mine in the next few years."

That last comment earns the loudest jeers of all, as all my team, including my managing director, stand and applaud, before Craig's team and fellow directors also stand up and heckle back.

Craig uses the moment to take a sip of his drink before bending and kissing my cheek. "You okay?" he whispers.

"Completely. You're totally killing it." I beam back at him.

The crowd quieten once more when he raises his hand to *shhh* them. "But it's not all been plain sailing. Like all couples we've had our issues. I should have realised the day she spun my new car and almost killed us that her driving skills leave a lot to be desired. But then what can you expect from a woman driver."

He winks at me, his mouth twisted into a wry smile, and this time it's all the females in the audience that jeer and heckle at his sexist dig.

"Seriously though, there have been some major ups and downs. Over the past four years we've created some amazing memories together, but..." Craig looks at me. His eyes glassy with emotion. He doesn't need to say anything, but we both acknowledge the struggles that we've had. "...but the important thing is, we worked through them together. And each time we've overcome something, it's made us stronger, and just look at us now."

I smile up at him. He's turned towards me and I know his words are meant for me now, as if the rest of the room has disappeared and there's only the two of us left in the universe. Sensing this, the crowd fall silent and watch as Craig's walls fall away and he lays himself bare.

"As brilliant as today has been, and how much I'm looking forward to spending the rest of my life with you, Tori, you also know how much today is tinged with sadness."

I watch as Craig's Adam's apple bobs in his throat.

"You know, probably more than anyone, how much it hurts that there's one person not here today. Rob would have loved you, my darling, and I would have given anything to have had him here..."

His lips begin to quiver and the whites of his eyes are streaked red as he battles to hold onto his tears.

The crowd wait patiently for him to deliver his next line, but he turns his head even further away and sucks in a deep breath.

I mouth, *"Love you,"* up at him.

A round of supportive applause begins to ripple outwards from the end of the top table where Anth, Nessa, Mark and Becca are sitting, and increases in volume as it Mexican waves across the marquee. A few people stand up in support and applaud. Everyone willing Craig to regain his composure and finish his speech.

But the outpouring of love has the opposite effect. I can tell he's overwhelmed and he turns his back completely to the audience and nips the bridge of his nose as he breathes heavily, trying and failing to hold back the tears he's been holding in which roll silently down his face.

I leap to my feet and, taking the microphone from him, come to his rescue. Plastering a smile on my face I address our guests. "I think what Craig really wanted to say is, *'Thank you all for coming.'"*

The people who were standing up sit back down, and everyone retunes their focus to me.

Still with his back to the audience, I feel Craig reach for my fingers. Clasping his hand in mine, he gives me a *'thank you'* squeeze.

"Today has been absolutely magnificent," I continue. "And I know I speak on behalf of both of us when I say... it wouldn't have been so special if you hadn't all been here to share it with us both. I can't ever remember a time in my life when I was surrounded by so much love."

Craig wipes his eyes clear, turns back around, and takes his place by my side, his hand gripping mine like a vice.

"Moments ago, Craig said I looked beautiful…"

Someone from the back lets out a loud wolf whistle.

I roll my eyes, as the mood lightens once again. "But the reason I look beautiful," I continue, "is because of this man standing next to me."

A couple of female guests sigh and exhale a few '*aahs.*'

"A long time ago, Craig made me a promise. He promised to love me — always. And today I was able to return that promise in the form of our wedding vows."

I turn to look at him and see that he's smiling. "Craig, I meant every word. To have and to hold from this day forward, for better, for worse, for richer, for poorer, in sickness and in health, to love and to cherish 'till death us do part. Whatever the future holds for us, I promise to love you forever, just as you have promised me."

"*Love you,*" he mouths.

"*Love you too,*" I mouth back.

Turning back to address the crowd once again, I continue, "…but a big fat ring on your finger always helps." I hold up my left hand and wiggle my fourth finger, where together with my wedding band, sits my impressive sapphire engagement ring. A single blue stone, surrounded by a cluster of sparking diamonds.

This time the crowd erupt into laughter and applause once more as my punchline delivers.

I allow the ambiance to settle of its own accord, before continuing, "The only thing left for me to say now is what a magnanimous job all my lovely bridesmaids did today."

The thanking of the bridesmaids is something that Craig should have done in his speech. Traditionally the best man's speech is given in response to the bridesmaid's toast, so I'm making sure I'm teeing up Clarky, who's due to speak next.

"You all looked magnificent, even if Rebecca's pants do go from here…" I hold my hand just under my boobs, "…to here." I move my hand to my mid-thigh, earning me more laughs and applause.

Everyone is aware of the juggling act she's managing to pull off today. Her mam is in her and Mark's hotel bedroom with eight-week-old baby Joshua. On hand for when she needs to sneak off and feed him.

"But seriously. Nessa, Becca, and Julie, you three have been magnificent this past year helping me with all the organising for today. And I should also thank Clarky, Anth, and Mark, who I know have been equally as supportive to my darling *husband.*"

The word *husband* earns me a few more *'ooh's* and *'aah's* from the females in the audience.

"Everyone," I hold up my champagne glass, "I'd ask you to please be upstanding and join me in toasting… The Bridesmaids.*"

'The Bridesmaids,' everyone says together as the sound of chairs scrape across the floor as the crowd shuffle to their feet.

I retake my seat as our toastmaster bangs his gavel again and introduces Clarky.

Craig pulls me into a hug. "Thank you."

"I hope I didn't steal your limelight. I just couldn't stand by and watch you *die on stage,* so to speak."

"Not at all; it was perfect."

He leans in and kisses me, as somewhere in the background Clarky begins reading out cards and message from friends and relatives that couldn't be here today.

Chapter 36

*A*nd this one's from someone called Timothy Blatherington-Smythe," I hear Clarky say over to my left.

I look up at the mention of Tim's name.

"Dear Victoria and Craig. Sorry I can't be with you, but wishing you every success in your marriage. Looking forward to enjoying more chocolate soufflés sometime soon."

Smiling, I *humph* out an out-breath like a dog blowing out a puff of air, at the memory of the infamous soufflé fiasco.

I slowly sip my champagne as Craig and I both sit back and relax, allowing Clarky's speech to wash over us. The content morphing into a gentle ribbing of his best mate as he recalls stories from their time together at school, then college, then adulthood.

"Finally," Clarky continues, "Craig has asked me to make an important announcement on his behalf."

I sit up straight and look at Craig, but he shrugs and takes a sip of his drink.

"Now that Tor is a married lady," Clarky continues, "and knowing how much Craig goes away for work, he's aware that she may have entertained the odd evening visitor when she was all alone."

My mouth falls open as the roasting is redirected towards me. Meanwhile everyone else kills themselves laughing.

"So, he's politely asking that anyone who may have a spare key for his back door, please return it now."

I take a big gulp of my drink as everyone's eyes flick around the room, waiting to see who is going to stand up. Obviously it's a set-up, but I'm intrigued to see who's in on the gag. After a long pause, out of the corner of my eye I see Mark cough into his closed fist and everyone jeers. Swaggering his way to the middle of the top table, he places a bronze house key down in front of me and winks.

He's on his way back to his seat when Anth stands up and does the same. Then one by one, almost every male guest makes their way to the front and places a key down in front of me. Meanwhile the hysterics and jeering escalates as the joke goes on and on. Some of the men give me a peck on the cheek, or ceremoniously shake Craig's hand, dishing out words of encouragement as they're enjoying being part of the joke.

It's a great stunt and both Craig and Clarky pretend to be increasingly shocked and offended as each subsequent guest comes forward.

My sides hurt from laughing. There must be at least thirty or so keys stacked in front of me. I have no idea where Clarky has managed to get them all from.

Reaching for my glass, believing the joke over, I'm taking a sip when out of my peripheral vision I spy a slim brunette snaking her way through the tables from the far side of the marquee. Her long dark hair hangs loose down her bare back and her dress is cut so low at the front you can see her navel. If she were to twist too quickly she'd been in real danger of a nip slip. Bloody Amanda!

Craig wanted to invite every senior manager from his work, so even though I wasn't happy about it, I had to accept it would have looked bad for Craig if we'd left her off the invite list.

Amanda eventually reaches the top table and stands brazenly in front of me, her face twisted into a lopsided smile and I have to sit on my hands to stop myself from slapping her smirking chops?

Meanwhile the jeers and table banging around the room intensifies, the punchline of Clarky's joke being the arrival of a woman returning a key.

I force my face into a smile as she stares me down. Expecting her to simply place her key down then walk away, she instead stretches out her arm and dramatically drops her key onto the pile, then, ignoring me, leans over the table and grips Craig's face in her palms. Pulling him towards her, she lands her lips on his and kisses him. He keeps his shocked eyes open and doesn't know where to put his hands, but she carries on kissing him. Moving her lips, trying to entice him to kiss her back while she purposefully smears her bright red lipstick all over his face.

What the fucking hell?!

Her lips still connected to my husband's, she looks out of the corner of her eyes. She wants me to see this. She wants me to *feel* this.

I leap up and wave my arms as if I were trying to flag down a passing car after breaking down on the roadside, seemingly directing my gesticulation at the wider room, when in fact it is directed intentionally at her. "Alright, alright. Very funny." I say it in a jokey way, to cover my seething anger. "That's enough, Amanda. You've made your point. Good one." I grab her wrist and pull her hand away from my husband's face.

She releases him and he takes a small step back as he regains his balance. Turning to walk away, she blows an exaggerated kiss over her shoulder. Everyone laughs, as do I. But behind my fake smile, I'm furious.

While the wave of jovial energy is still bubbling around the room, I turn to Craig and, using my napkin, wipe her red lipstick from his lips, before kissing him — passionately.

Whatever the fuck that was, I want everyone here to know he's mine. He wraps his arms around me and deepens his kiss as we proudly display our union in front of all our loved ones.

Our passionate smooch earns us a few loud wolf whistles and I hear someone in the back of the marquee heckle, 'Get a room'. I know then that this is what people will remember from this moment, and inside my chest my little heart sings.

Ɓↄ

Later, after the wedding breakfast, the party is in full swing, our live band filling the dance floor. I'm quietly loitering by the bar, taking in the atmosphere, when I feel the hairs on my arms stand on end.

"So you finally tied him down," Amanda drawls next to me.

I suck in a deep breath. "More like he finally tied me down," I retort.

"Well I wish I could say *'Good luck in married life'* 'n all that, but then I'm not a hypocrite."

"Amanda, if you're not here to join in and celebrate our nuptials, why the hell did you come? You could have done us all a favour and declined the invitation. That would have been the polite thing to do if all you want to do is dish out snarky comments to me — *the bride*."

"But then I wouldn't get to enjoy this," she replies, her mouth twisting into a wry smile.

"Oh?"

"Yeah. Like I said, I'm not the hypocrite. Your husband is."

"Pardon?"

"Your *husband* is a hypocrite, and you're blind if you can't see it," she says, more slowly this time.

"Excuse me? Are you going to substantiate that statement, or simply slander his character... and my own?"

"Maybe you should ask him to tell you the truth."

I draw my eyebrows together. "The truth about what?"

I watch as she sucks in a deep breath, but before she's had a chance to respond, Craig is by my side. "Tori, this is where you're hiding. I've been looking for you. There's someone I'd like you to meet."

Next to Craig is a smartly dressed grey-haired gentleman with a pink handkerchief poking out of his top pocket.

"Tori, this is Jack Walker. Chairman of the board, and personal mentor to me. Jack, this is my beautiful bride."

"An absolute pleasure," the older man says, dipping his head and kissing the back of my hand.

"Likewise. Craig's told me so much about you. It's lovely to finally put a face to the name."

"No my dear, the pleasure is definitely all mine. You're an absolute dream. Sheer perfection, in fact."

"Wow. I don't think even Craig has said that to me." I give Craig a gentle dig in the ribs. "Better up your game, Husband, or else you may have a rival," I tease, purposefully stroking the older man's ego. "And are you here with your wife, Mr Walker?"

"Jack, please. And sadly not. My wife is not in good health at the moment, but she sends her best wishes." Looking between myself and Amanda and sensing the tension, Jack continues, "I hope I wasn't interrupting anything."

"No, nothing," I cut in. "Amanda was just telling me how much she loves working at PPS. Weren't you Amanda?"

"Yeah," she sighs. "Something like that."

"Well, if you'll excuse me, this is my favourite song. Amanda. Jack." I address each of them in turn, before linking my arm through Craig's and pulling him away, all the while wondering what *truth*, or more likely – *lies*, Amanda was about to reveal.

Chapter 37

CRAIG

Mauritius

"Good morning, Mrs Fenwick," Craig says to his new wife. Her face illuminated by the early morning sun that creeps in through the slatted windows of their honeymoon beach bungalow. He watches as she glides from sleep into consciousness just as gracefully as she glided down the aisle towards him three days ago.

"Mmmm. Say that again," she says, languidly stretching her naked limbs.

"Good morning, Mrs Fenwick."

Craig reaches across and smooths a stray strand of hair away from her forehead.

Rolling towards him she touches his face with the tips of her fingers. "I shall never tire of hearing that. Promise to say it to me every morning for the rest of our lives."

"I promise, Mrs Fenwick," he says again, leaning up on his elbow, trailing his fingertips up and down the contours of her body. "Your granny said something interesting to me."

"Oh?" She shuffles up onto her elbows.

"Yes. That it was lovely that you were finally a Fenwick, like everyone else in your family. I suppose I never really thought about it before, but it must have been weird for you, to be the only one in your family not carrying your grandfather's name."

"True."

When she was born, Vicky's parents were still married so naturally she carried her father's name, even after her mother reverted to 'Fenwick', her own maiden name following their divorce; leaving Vicky the odd one out. Therefore, it seemed the natural choice for Vicky to change it to 'Turnbull' – her stepfather's surname – when her mother remarried.

"It feels like I've stepped into the identity I was always destined to be," Vicky says. "Like my name has finally caught up with who I am on the inside." She leans up and throws her arms around Craig's neck. "Only I never realised before it happened."

"Well, I'm glad you only married me for my name," he teases.

"Don't be daft. You've given me everything I could have ever wished for, as well as a name that fits and feels right."

He leans in and kisses her, their tongues snaking into each other's mouths, feeding each other's desires. Rolling onto his back, he pulls her up onto his stomach, where she lies the full length of his body. Her long limbs entwined with his, he trails his fingers up and down her bare back, feeling her skin ripple under his touch. Her smooth curves feel soft against his firm muscles and manly chest hair.

God, this feels so good. And to think I almost fucked it up, Craig thinks to himself as their kiss deepens. Their tongues twirling and twisting together, a deep guttural groan escaping from the back of Craig's throat as his passion continues to rise and he goes hard. The tip of his cock nudging against her warm silky entrance. Even before they're connected, instinctively she grinds her hips against his as Craig does the same. Both of their bodies rocking together as the pulsating pleasure takes over their senses.

All those years of worrying about being enough for her, or not being born on the right side of the railway tracks, or our backgrounds being too different, when all along all I needed to do was this, he thinks to himself. I simply needed to commit. Give her what she needs, and she'll return it tenfold, just as she's doing now.

Since arriving in Mauritius they've yet to leave their honeymoon suite. A beautiful ocean fronted villa with a private deck for sunbathing, a lounge for chilling, and an enormous bed for lovemaking.

Steps lead down from the deck into the garden, filled with birds of paradise and frangipani; a private path, lined with palm trees, winds its way through the garden to a pure white sandy beach and the crystal blue Indian Ocean beyond. Each evening liveried staff have set up a fully dressed dining table out on the deck, before serving them their dinner. The very definition of private dining.

The cost of the honeymoon was Craig's wedding gift to Tori, but having so many old connections in the travel industry she was able to negotiate a cracking deal, including a room upgrade from a standard room in the main hotel, to this luxurious beach bungalow.

Tori's gift to Craig had been a private helicopter transfer from the airport direct to the hotel, where on arrival, they'd been greeted by a reception line-up, headed by their personal butler, Samuel.

'Good afternoon, Mr and Mrs Fenwick, welcome to the beautiful island of Mauritius. We hope you enjoy your stay,' Samuel had said, his hands pressed together in the prayer position as he'd dipped his head in greeting as the newlyweds stepped down from the helicopter onto the lushes green lawn.

He'd then nodded to one of his team who had stepped forward and, using silver tongs, handed out warm hand towels from a silver tray, followed swiftly by another colleague who offered them two freshly made cocktails.

By the time the newlyweds had sipped their cocktails and hopped onto the golf buggy that whisked them off to their beach bungalow, their suitcases had already been transferred and an invisible team of housemaids had magically unpacked their things. Drawers lined with scented paper were now filled with their undergarments, T-shirts, and swimwear. Craig's jackets and shirts, and

Tori's cocktail dresses were all hung elegantly in the wardrobe. Even her makeup had been laid out in a fan pattern on the dressing table.

'Well that saves me doing my first domestic job — as THE wife,' she had chuckled.

Unlike some of the other hotels on the island, La Residence caters for a smaller number of guests but does so in absolute luxury. Colonial architecture nestled under tall white marble columns and intricately carved wooden panels — cleaned every morning by attendants using tiny paint brushes. The invisible staff shuffle about silently, their uniforms of white linen kurtas over baggy pantaloons. Even the doormen, complete with their pith helmets, look as if they've been deployed direct from the old British Raj.

Craig had always known places like this existed, but this is the first time he's ever had the opportunity to experience how the other half truly live. His parents would be blown away, and like him would need guidance as to the correct etiquette in this very different world. Fortunately, Vicky has gently guided him when he wasn't sure which was the right fork, or wine glass, to use and until two nights ago, he'd never even heard of an amuse-bouche never mind tasted one.

He can't deny he's loved being pampered, even if a part of him struggles to reconcile this type of lifestyle.

"I want you in me, Husband." She grins saucily as they continue to grind their bodies into one another.

"I want to be in you, Wife," he growls, flipping her onto her back and pinning her arms above her head as his mouth nips and licks his way down her neck. The remnants of her distinctive oriental perfume mixed with the heady scent of last night's lovemaking lingering on her unwashed skin.

He takes one of her dark pink rosebuds into his mouth, flicking his tongue across the tip, causing her to release a deep, guttural groan. She draws her legs up and wraps them around his torso, pulling his hips closer while he continues to pin her arms above her head, teasing and flicking her hardened nipple with his tongue.

He's perfectly lined up. One thrust is all it will take to plunge deep inside her, but then the sound of the doorbell *ding-donging* interrupts them.

"Bollocks," Craig says breathlessly. "I think that'll be breakfast. They couldn't possibly be five minutes late, just this once."

"Oh, a full five minutes. I'm so disappointed," she teases.

"Just you wait." He slaps her backside then jumps off the bed and pulls on the hotel dressing gown. Meanwhile Vicky snuggles down underneath the bed covers, hiding her flushed face under the cool white linen as Samuel's team wheels the trolley into the room.

"Good morning, Samuel," Craig asks the older man. "And how are you today?"

"Very happy Mr Fenwick," Samuel replies. "Would you like to take breakfast on the terrace?"

"Yes please."

"Very good, sir."

Samuel's team silently lay out the breakfast of fruit, yogurt, bacon, and pancakes before they all tactfully leave as quietly as they arrived. Once the door clicks closed, Vicky throws on her robe and joins Craig outside; sitting on his lap rather than taking the chair opposite. Sliding a hand inside his robe by the neck, she pulls it from his shoulders, leans forward and gently nibbles Craig's ear.

"Now, where were we?" she says, her lips leaving a delicate trail of kisses down the curve of his neck and over his shoulder.

"About to have breakfast," he teases, ignoring her obvious attempts to re-seduce him.

"Err I don't think so mister. I believe you have some husbandly duties to attend to. Your wife is waiting for her pre-breakfast amuse-bouche."

"Aww, but breakfast is here now, and we don't want it to spoil, do we?"

She turns around and lifts the lid off the teapot, peeks inside and announces, "Nope. Not brewed yet. It's going to need another five minutes at least."

She hitches one leg across his lap, so that she's now straddling him, and her dressing gown falls apart from the waist down, revealing her unabashed lower body. Craig rolls his tongue unconsciously across his lips at the sight of her raw beauty.

Her gaze locked with his, she reaches for the belt of his robe, pulling the knot apart; it too falls open. His erection now on full view, she sucks in a sharp intake of breath.

"Well, I know exactly what I want for breakfast," she says provocatively.

In this perfect position, Craig can't resist sliding two of his fingers inside her warm, soft folds. She moans heavily and rolls her head back at the delectable pleasure and he feels her tighten around his digits. Knowing what she wants, Craig delays her gratification, teasing her, and instead withdraws his fingers, erotically, slowly, and takes great pleasure watching her writhe wantonly in his lap, attempting to draw out the pleasure of his touch as she aches for more.

He waits until she refocuses her eyes back on his, willing him to enter her again, before he seductively licks his fingers, one at a time, tasting her tangy sweet elixir. Then cupping a hand around the back of her head, he pulls her lips onto his, knowing that she too can taste her own juices that linger on his tongue.

Both of them shivering for more, the game of cat and mouse continues. He fully expects her to position herself over the top of him and lower herself onto his shaft, but instead, with expert control, she rubs herself over the top of his cock, allowing him to feel how warm and wet she is, whilst simultaneously denying him his own gratification.

"Two can play at that game, darling," she teases.

Craig groans with a desire that throbs through every nerve ending in his body. They may have been in a relationship for four years now, but the past 72hours, have not only been the best sex they've ever had, it's been by far – the best sex of Craig's life.

Whether it's the romance of the setting, or the aftermath of formally committing to one another – solemnly saying their marriage vows is something that will never leave him – has caused a shift in them both. He's always suspected Vicky had more to offer in this department, but she was waiting for him to open up. Now that he has, there's no stopping her.

Knowing Vicky has Craig exactly where she wants him, desperate for more, she changes tack. Climbing off him, she turns around and bends forward, angling her naked backside towards him, whilst she checks the tea in the pot.

"Oh look. The tea's ready now. Shall I be mother?"

Craig growls in reply, "You absolute vixen."

Unable to contain his desire a moment longer, Craig rises from the chair and lunges for her, but she sidesteps him and instead runs into the lounge, turning and beckoning with a curled forefinger, inviting him to chase her; excitement dancing in her eyes.

"Come 'ere," Craig roars, cornering her on the couch as she shrieks with delight.

He picks her up and she wraps her legs around his waist as he carries her back to the bedroom. Throwing her down onto the bed, her gown falls open. Her legs splayed, she shrieks with laughter.

"I thought you didn't want our breakfast to spoil," she giggles.

"Fuck breakfast."

"Or better still … fuck *me* for breakfast."

"And what the lady wants … the lady must get!" Craig kisses the inside of her knee.

Kneeling in front of her, in one swift movement he wraps her legs around his neck and plunges deep inside her. From this position he controls the depth and speed of their coupling and he takes full advantage of that power. An immense feeling of satisfaction washes over him as he watches Vicky's eyes roll into the back of her head while he fills her over and over, taking his time in long, hard, pounding strokes. Her pleasure completely at his mercy.

"You like that don't you?" Craig pants.

"God yes. Don't stop," she almost shouts, her hands now over her own face, the intensity almost too much to bear.

"I don't intend to. You're mine now. All mine. My girl. My wife. My Mrs Fenwick."

As the words leave his mouth, he feels her orgasm take hold. Her body shuddering and contracting around his as he too reaches his climax and explodes inside her.

"That's right," she says more softly now a few moments later, her orgasm subsiding, her eyes still closed. Still lost in her own internal sensory world, but rolling into Craig's armpit as he comes to lie next to her, she whispers, "I *am* Victoria Fenwick."

Their hot and steamy lovemaking over, both their bodies covered in a light film of sweat, Vicky lies peacefully in Craig's arms. Craig kisses the top of his wife's head and wonders why, despite his overwhelming happiness, something deep inside him refuses to be silenced. Like a distant church bell tolling. A warning, that as much as he wants to ignore it, it refuses to be ignored.

Chapter 38

*I*t's the hottest part of the day and Craig twitches relentlessly with boredom. A skimpy, bikini-clad Tori is lying next to him on the adjacent sun lounger, greased up from head to toe and baking nicely in the hot Indian sun.

"Come for a walk with me?" he asks, rolling onto his side.

Her Walkman headphones clamped to her ears, one knee bent up, she taps her foot in time to the beat.

"IN A LITTLE BIT," she shouts, her volume overcompensating for the music blasting in her ears.

Laughing, he pulls one of the headphones away from her lobe and whispers, "Okay then. But there's no need to shout. I'm sure the folks in Africa don't need to hear your plans for the afternoon."

Sitting up on her elbows and smiling, she pulls her headphones off.

"Sorry. Got a bit carried away. I'm in love with the new Christina Aguilera album. But it's absolutely scorching. How about a dip first? I could do with cooling down."

Not waiting for a reply, she streaks off the sun lounger and runs down the path towards the ocean. "Catch me if you can," she shouts over her shoulder.

Craig gives chase as Vicky shrieks with delight. Catching up with her within a few strides, he grabs her around her waist and picks her up in a fireman's lift as he charges towards the waves.

"Okay, it that's what you want. Time for a swim."

She flays her arms and legs helplessly. "No, no, no. Don't you dare. I was just kiddin. It'll be freezing."

"Yeah well. You should have thought of that before." He slaps her bum playfully.

Reaching the shallows, Craig dumps her unceremoniously in the water, where she lands arse first, before falling backwards, her arms and legs all akimbo.

She emerges a few seconds later, spluttering and pushing her wet hair off her face. Standing at the water's edge, his hands on his hips, Craig bends double with laughter.

"You absolute bastard," she laughs. "It's bloody freezing. You're gonna get it now." Sweeping her arm in an arc across the surface of the water, she sends a wave back in his direction.

"Oh, am I now?"

He easily ducks the splash, but she's not done.

Rushing out of the shallows, she grabs his hand and attempts to drag him back into the sea. He digs his heels in as they continue to wrestle their way back into the lagoon. Moments later, they're waist-deep in the crystal azure waters, wrapped in a romantic clinch.

"You're such a meany, Craig Fenwick."

"No I'm not. You're just too gullible, Wifey." He brushes her hair back off her face.

She looks around. Taking in the idyllic vista. A line of perfect palms framing the pure white sandy beach; in the opposite direction, the rougher more powerful waves of the Indian Ocean crash into the coral reef that acts like a barrier around the island. But in the protected lagoon, schools of striped and spotted tropical fish zip and dart between their legs.

"Gosh it's so perfect here, Craig. I wish it could be like this always. I can't remember ever being this happy." She kisses the end of his nose, then grimaces. "Yuk, salt."

"Sorry," he laughs, kissing the end of her nose in return.

"Yuk. Salt indeed, but now we're even."

"Promise me, Craig, if we ever lose our way or we start to fall out of love with each other, that we'll always remember this moment."

"That's never gonna happen, Tori. But if did — I promise, I will."

They stand in the stillness of the moment for a few long minutes, simply enjoying basking in each other's love.

"Can I ask you something?" she whispers.

"Of course. You can ask me anything."

"It's just Amanda said something weird to me at the wedding."

"Oh?"

Craig's guts contract. He knew it was a risk inviting Amanda to the wedding, but how could he not? It would have been an obvious snub, potentially raising more suspicion. And now that she's in a relationship with Dave, he didn't think there was any risk of their secret coming out.

"What did she say?" he asks.

"Something about how she would be a hypocrite if she wished us a lifetime of happiness."

"Cryptic." Craig presses his lips together.

"Indeed. She said I should ask you to tell me the truth." Vicky looks directly into Craig's eyes. "What did she mean by that?"

"Oh, shit." Craig stumbles backwards as a particularly friendly fish nibbles his ankle, but Vicky remains stoic and waits for him to regain his composure.

"Well?" Vicky presses. "You know I don't like the woman. I like her even less after her inappropriate display during Clarky's speech … I mean, what the hell was all that about? It's like she's always trying to get one up on me."

Craig swallows hard. Vicky had warned him about her, but he took no notice. He never saw the danger until it was too late.

"She's always so snipey towards me. If I didn't know any better, I'd say she fancies you, but then she'd be on to a hiding for nothing. I mean, it's not like that's ever going to be reciprocated — is it?"

Craig closes and slowly reopens his eyes as his mind flits back to the night he'd given in to his primal urges. In one way it was a blessing he missed the flight out to Alicante the next morning. After being rudely awoken by the taxi driver banging on his front door, his eyes heavy with sleep it had taken him a few moments to remember where he was, but then the shock of seeing Amanda lying asleep, her hair splayed all over Vicky's pillow, had brought him back to reality with an arresting jolt.

What the fuck have I done? he'd thought at the immediate realisation of the horrendous mistake he'd made.

'Get dressed,' he'd screamed at Amanda, but not caring about the implications of their situation she'd languidly rolled over and tried to kiss him again.

'Get off me,' he'd yelled. 'I'm sorry about last night. It was a mistake. I should never have let it happen.'

It was only when he'd come back to the house, after missing his flight, still an unshowered, unshaven, sticky post-coital mess, that he'd spotted Amanda's black lace chemise lying on the bedroom floor.

Holy Shit! he'd thought, picking it up and throwing it into a black bin bag. Oh my God, the consequences of Tori finding that don't bear thinking about.

Slumped on the end of the bed, his head in his hands, he'd decided it was time to clean up his act, beginning with washing the bedsheets. If anything, his slip-up with Amanda made him realise that it was time to stop hunting for something that didn't exist. Rob was never coming back, and no one and nothing was ever going to replace that hole inside, even Vicky.

It was time to stop searching for a cure to an incurable heartache and instead finally move forward in his life with the one person who, he'd realised in that moment, loves him unconditionally. She'd been so patient waiting for him to show up and commit to their future.

But now he's in danger of losing her before their marriage has even gotten going.

He wraps his arms around her, and pulls her into a tight hug. "I have absolutely no idea what she was referring to. But I'll ask her when I get back," he says, deepening the lie while at the same deciding it's time he helped Amanda find another job. One that keeps her as far away from his wife as possible.

Chapter 39

3 months later, The Belfry, England

*C*raig hears the bathroom door opening behind him, followed by the familiar scent of Vicky's Coco Chanel perfume floating on the air.

"How do I look?"

"Gorgeous," he replies, without turning around.

"Liar." She gives his black-tie-suited backside a gentle nudge with her stiletto-encased foot. "Get your head out of the minibar and tell your wife how damn hot she looks."

He puts down the mini bottle of Moët he's found and turns round. "Holy crap." His mouth drains of saliva and his eyes jump out on stalks. "You could walk a red carpet looking like that, pet."

She holds her arms aloft and gives him a twirl. "It's not too much?"

Her blood-red, full-length velvet gown skims over her svelte body before flaring out into a puddle train, the thigh-length split revealing a bronzed leg. The boned sweetheart neckline plunges down between her cleavage and the backless design shows off her glowing honeymoon tan.

Her flawless make-up is accentuated by a slick of bright red lipstick to match the colour of her dress, and her heavier than usual eye shadow and false eyelashes make her emerald green irises pop. She's wearing enormous diamond studs in her ears and her hair is swept up into a classic chignon, elongating her neck which tonight is devoid of any necklace. A noticeable change, as Craig can count on one hand the number of times he's seen her without her grandfather's Masonic Orb.

"No necklace tonight?" He runs his fingers over her neck and around the curve of her shoulder.

"I had planned to wear the matching necklace to these earrings, but the extra diamonds were a bit *OTT*. As Coco Chanel once said, *'Before you leave the house, look in the mirror and take one thing off.'* Plus Granny's lent me this for the evening." She wiggles the middle finger of her right hand which currently sports an enormous ruby ring. A single cushion-cut claret stone surrounded by a cluster of yet more glittering diamonds.

"No-one's going to notice me tonight. You'll outshine everyone," Craig says, proudly.

"I doubt it. My sole purpose tonight, is to show you off."

Craig pops the champagne and pours two glasses.

"To us." He smiles as he chinks his flute against hers.

"To us," she replies, before taking a sip, leaving a slight smear of red lipstick on the rim of her glass. "Right, let's get your dicky-bow sorted." She picks up the limp length of cloth and comes to stand behind him, both of them facing the mirror. "I can only do it from behind."

"Isn't it always better from behind?" he adds, sliding his hand inside the split of her dress and up the inside of her leg.

She gives him a gentle slap on the shoulder. "Oi you, behave. We don't want to be late."

ℛↄ

Two waiters stand on either side of the entrance to the ballroom, silver trays in hand. Craig and Vicky take a glass each as they glide past, pausing momentarily to scan the room. They nod and smile at the few board members and other senior managers they know.

PPS has just swallowed up another large competitor in the marketplace. A purchase funded by their equity partners, Thames Capital Management, who are hosting this 'close of sale' celebratory evening.

Craig has been down in London, the week before last, to help with the finer details of the negotiation. Then in the evening, Jack Walker invited him to dinner with the Health Minister, to discuss the future technology needs of the NHS. Clearly Craig's star is continuing to rise.

The takeover deal was officially signed this afternoon, and after much handshaking, backslapping, and cigar smoking, tonight is a staged event intended to integrate the two businesses in a sociable and non-threatening way. The wives and girlfriends are intentionally on the guest list to keep things light, and smooth over any undertones. Despite the promises made in the deal, Craig is under no illusion that, starting Monday, the job of taking the other business apart, transitioning their customers over and stripping out any unnecessary workforce, begins.

"Looks like we're on the top table," Vicky whispers in Craig's ear after studying the seating plan. "You're next to Jonathan's wife, and then he's sat on her other side..."

Jonathan Hiddleston is the company CEO and Craig's immediate boss.

"...and I'm next to Jack Walker, and his wife is on his other side. Get your game face on, babes. I'll bet my granny's ruby ring you're about to be unofficially interviewed."

"Best not get arseholed and do anything stupid then." Craig wraps his arms around her waist and kisses her shoulder as they head off in search of the powerhouses.

Right now, he couldn't feel prouder to have his beautiful wife on his arm. As well as her obvious glamour, he knows she won't need babysitting. She can hold her own in any conversation and is highly knowledgeable in topics as diverse as art, travel, politics, and business.

She's the perfect wife to make me look good, he thinks to himself.

As Mark once said years ago, *'Play your cards right mate with her and you'll be set for life'*, and now it seems he was absolutely right.

A short while later, comfortably seated at their table, the conversation flip-flops between business and current affairs. Bill Clinton has not long been sworn in for a second term as President of the United States, and his ambitious plans to reform the structure and access to healthcare in the US could lead to further expansion opportunities for PPS.

Jonathan's wife, a sixty-something housewife with greying roots and worn-out eyes, offers very little to the conversation that snaps between Jonathan and Craig, so they largely ignore her. She sits mutely between the two of them, silently sipping her drink, as Jonathan continues to ask Craig about the output of his division and how he's handled some of the key challenges over the past six months. Craig takes the opportunity to update him whilst sharing some improvements and developments he's successfully implemented across the wider business.

The meal over, Vicky whispers in Craig's ear, "Back in a bit. Just off to powder my nose."

"Of course, darling."

As Vicky gathers up her skirt, Jack Walker leaps up from his seat, pulls out her chair and offers her his hand.

"Thank you," she says. Her manners, as always, impeccable.

Jack Walker hops into Vicky's vacant seat and Jonathan swaps with his wife, so that the three men are sitting side by side.

"So Craig, where do you think we should place our strategic focus for the next three years?" Jack asks the obviously leading question.

"Well, until we're the largest provider in the UK there's still opportunity to grow here. Although other than JW Software there are fewer decent acquisition opportunities here in our home market, so the next question has to be which country to break into next."

"Interesting." Jack raps his fingers against the side of his glass of whiskey as he catches Jonathan's eye. "So where would you suggest we focus next? The US?"

"The US market is massive, but also extremely fragmented with different legal structures across the various federal systems. Different requirements for different insurance funders would mean huge complexities for our platform. In my opinion it would be an extremely expensive market to break into and gain traction within. Certainly as our first jump abroad."

"Hmm. But surely it would be foolish to ignore a market of two hundred and seventy million users. Four and a half times bigger than the UK," Jack says.

"Agreed," Jonathan adds, raising his glass.

"I think a better way to tackle North America would be to break into Canada first. Yes, the market is smaller. Thirty million users, smaller even than the UK. But it's less complicated than the US. Their Medicare system is more uniform and would allow us to iron out any kinks in both marketing and execution, building a name for ourselves across the pond before making a hard push south of the Canadian border. We can open the Canadian market without going to the expense of opening a legal entity there. We would need a small sales team on the ground, obviously, but we could run the implementation and support functions from here. We already operate twenty-four-hour support as it is, and we could trade on the back of the free trade agreement between the EU and Canada. Then once we've broken ground, we could take the next step and open a physical infrastructure in Canada, including registering a Canadian company and opening bank accounts etc., then we could enter the US market tariff-free through the free trade agreement between the US and Canada."

Jack sits back, drink in hand, absorbing everything Craig has just said. "Well, well, well. It appears you've articulated the exact strategy we've already been considering. Great minds think alike, eh?"

"Well, you know." Craig dips his head and swirls the ice in his glass. "I'm ambitious. I want us to build a global company. Maybe run a country division one day."

"Or take over completely?" Jack laughs.

"Yes," Craig answers matter-of-factly, eyeballing Jack.

"Interesting. I always thought you were rooted to your precious North-East."

Craig sucks in a deep breath.

This is it. The opportunity my parents always hoped I'd get someday. The chance to set up a life-changing career move. One that *gets me out.*

"Oh don't get me wrong. I love where I live. The people are great. The craic's great and the beer is as cheap as chips — but given the opportunity I would love the chance to travel. See a bit of the world."

"And what about your charming other half? How would she feel about moving? Potentially sacrificing her career in support of yours?"

"Like me, she'd jump at it. Without a doubt. She's already lived abroad, and London before that. Tori's just turned thirty, and we're planning a family at some point in the next decade; we've already talked about her becoming the primary caregiver — at least for those first few years. We're both ambitious, but she also wants to be a mother, and she's happy to take a temporary sidestep in her career, when that time comes."

"The downside of being a woman, eh?" Jonathan interjects. He's been listening intently.

"Yes indeed. For all women have some fantastic assets..." Jack raises a bushy eyebrow, "... there's no getting away from the inconvenience of the childbearing years. You are indeed a lucky, *lucky* man Craig Fenwick. She's an absolute charm. Been telling me all about her travels over dinner. Such a delight."

Craig watches as Jack's eyes drift off towards the exit of the ballroom. "You can ask her yourself how she would feel about a potential move when she comes back."

"I will. Now if you'll excuse me, I need to use the little boys' room." Jack excuses himself and disappears out of the ballroom.

Chapter 40

ifteen minutes later Vicky returns. Sitting down sharply, she fidgets with her hands, twisting them over and over in her lap as she glances nervously over her shoulder, back to the entrance of the ballroom. Craig notices red blotches have crept up her neck and her hair looks as if it's been repinned in a hurry. With shaking fingers she reaches for a tumbler of water and drinks it down in audible gulps.

"Hey. What's up? You okay pet?" Craig reaches across her lap for her hand to hold.

"Yes I'm fine." She brushes his hand away and wraps both of hers around the tumbler.

"Okay. No need to be tetchy. You don't look fine, that's all."

"I am, honestly." She flashes him a fake smile. "See, game face on."

Jack reappears at the table. He leans on the back of Tori's chair and Craig catches a glimpse of him stroking the nape of her neck with his thumb. Tori visibly stiffens before leaping up.

She throws her napkin down next to her wine glass. "Gentlemen. Ladies." She bobs her head at the other guests around the table. "I appear to have been struck down with an almighty headache, so if you'll please excuse me, I'm going to retire for the evening. Craig, shall we?"

Confused, Craig stands and offers her his arm.

૧૭

"What the fuck was all that about?" Craig whispers as soon as they're out of earshot.

"Don't Craig. Just leave it."

"Well I wish I could, but what's with the diva act all of a sudden?"

"No reason."

"Then why am I escorting you out of the room when I should be back in there securing my future promotion with Jack and Jonathan?"

Walking through the lobby, the lift doors open and, stepping inside, Vicky frantically presses the button, trying to make the doors close faster.

Craig's eyes bore into the side of her face, while she keeps her gaze on the display panel as the lift begins to move, watching as the numbers increase.

Arriving at their floor, she holds her finger on the Doors Open button. "You're right, Craig. You should go back down. I don't want to ruin your opportunity to shine."

Walking out of the lift, she marches off down the corridor without a backwards glance.

Slamming his hand between the closing doors he shouts at her back, "What's gotten into you? Why are you trying to sabotage the evening?"

The doors re-open and he chases after her.

"Well that's just fucking lovely. You think that's what I'm doing? For your information you could not be more wrong."

Walking into their suite she kicks off her high heels and tosses her clutch bag into the middle of the bed.

Craig places his hands gently on her shoulders. "So why don't you come back downstairs with me," he says softly. "Give it ten minutes. Say you've taken some headache tablets, then come back down and we can pick up where we left off. I was just explaining to Jack my thoughts on a US expansion plan, and like you said, I think he's sounding me out — well, us out — for a potential move to the US or Canada. Imagine that, Tori? Moving across the pond."

She closes her eyes. "I'm sorry Craig, but there's absolutely no way I'm going back downstairs."

"Why the hell not?!"

Unzipping her dress she turns her back on him. "I'm not stopping you going back down... in fact I think you should. If you go now, you'll catch the coffees and can continue your conversation with Jack."

"But I think he wants to sound you out as well. Make sure you're on board with the idea."

"Of course I am. I'd follow you anywhere. You know that."

"Yeah. But they don't. They need to hear it from you."

What the hell? Why is she trying to sabotage my career? Maybe she lied when she said she'd be happy to take a back seat when we have kids?"

"Craig, I don't know how to say this more clearly — I'm not going back. Not tonight anyway."

"But why not? You've still not given me a valid reason."

"Craig, honestly, just leave it."

One hand on his hip, Craig runs his fingers through his hair. "No, I'm not going to fucking leave it — you're being completely unreasonable. Just tell me what the hell is the matter."

Ignoring him, she steps out of her dress, which pools at her feet, before she slips on the hotel's bathrobe. Stretching out on the bed, she reaches for the TV remote, pointing it angrily at the TV on the wall behind Craig.

"You're in the way. Please move."

"Not until you tell me why you're behaving like this."

Kneeling up on the bed, she throws the TV remote across the room. It smashes into the wall and the back breaks off, sending the batteries flying across the floor. "Fine. If you really want to know. Jack Walker — *the* most powerful man in that room tonight — has just molested me."

"What? Jack? No! He would never do anything like that."

"Oh he wouldn't, would he? You trust his character and integrity more than my word?" She's still kneeling up on the bed, her head cocked to one side, her hands on her hips.

"No. That's not what I meant." Craig raises his hands in defence.

What?! She's being ridiculous. Why would she say he has done something like that — unless she wanted a reason to pull me out of there. She knew tonight was an opportunity to position myself for my next career move; maybe she didn't want me to continue my conversations because she knows it means my career will overtake hers.

"And why should I have expected anything other than *that* reaction." She jabs her index finger in Craig's face. "How stupid of me to think for just one tiny moment that you — *my husband* — would believe *me*, a member of the female sex, never mind *your wife*. You realise you've done what every member of the male species always does — defend your own kind over the word of a mere woman. I thought you had more respect for me."

"I just meant... it makes no sense," Craig stutters. "I can't imagine Jack doing anything like that."

"Like what, Craig?" Her eyes narrow into slits. "Like, pushing me up against a wall, grabbing me around my neck, forcing his disgusting lips on mine while he slid his hand inside my skirt, ramming his fingers inside my knickers. Inside me. You mean anything like that?"

Frozen to the spot, Craig's jumbled thoughts race through his brain.

Holy shit! What if she isn't lying? Did Jack really just do that?"

"Are you absolutely sure you didn't say anything to him. To... you know... lead him on in anyway? I just... it just... it doesn't make any sense, that's all. Are you absolutely sure?"

Her hands raised, she shakes her head vigorously. "What the

fuck. What do you mean *am I sure?* Yes, I'm fucking sure that sleaze-ball has just sexually assaulted me. I didn't fall over and land on his fucking fingers."

She's shaking so violently, Craig knows he should reach out and comfort her. Tell her that it's going to be alright, but he too is in shock. That's when it dawns on him.

Oh my God — she's telling the truth. How could I have doubted her? Jesus! What kind of husband am I? Not only did I not protect her, I questioned her integrity. How could I possibly have thought she'd make this up to get one over on me?

Her chest heaves, her eyes bloodshot, yet still Craig remains frozen to the spot. Unable to offer her any comfort while he's still processing what she's saying, or the implications of Jack's actions.

"What do you want me to do?" he asks quietly.

She sucks in an audible breath. "Do what the fuck you want Craig. The fact that you're even asking me—" She breaks off before finishing her sentence, her voice cracking.

They catch each other's eye, and her disappointment in him pierces his heart like an arrow of clarity.

I need to show her I believe her. I have to put this right.

"Stay here. I won't be long," he says, marching out of the room.

Running down the corridor he smashes the button for the lift with the side of his fist. When it doesn't come immediately, he crashes through the panic bar for the stairs, galloping down them two at a time. He's running at full speed by the time he reaches the ground floor.

Charging into the ballroom, he sees Jonathan and the other directors smile and acknowledge his re-arrival.

Jack rises from the table. "Ahh Craig, dear boy, we were just about to retire to the lounge. Would you care to join us? I believe Jonathan has managed to rustle up some magnificent Cubans for the occasion."

Craig doesn't stop to think. He swings his clenched fist before Jack has a chance to react. Craig's knuckles crunch as flesh meets bone, spinning Jack's head to the point of snapping, and spraying blood across the clean white tablecloth and the other guests around the table.

The women scream and the men leap up, lunging for Craig, trying to pull him away.

But he isn't finished.

He shrugs off the other men and reaches for Jack's slumped torso, picks his head up by the hair and smashes his face into the table again.

"You absolute bastard," Craig screams, spittle collecting in the corners of his mouth. "You won't get away with this," he shouts like a man possessed. "People like you think it's okay to take what you want. To destroy other people's lives. Well I'm not letting you get away with it, not this time."

Despite the satisfaction of knowing he's done what needed to be done – something that he should have done years ago to right the terrible wrong done to Rob – as he's being dragged away Craig also knows he's just ended his career and changed the trajectory of his life. Potentially irreversibly.

Chapter 41

VICTORIA

3 months later, December 2000

*T*rap quietly on the attic door that leads to Craig's office.

"What?" he shouts back, annoyed at the interruption.

I poke my head inside the room. "Please come. Everyone is expecting you."

"Just leave it, Tori. I've told you, I'm not coming."

"But why? It's Joshua's christening. What am I going to say to Mark and Becca if you no-show?"

"Tell them I'm not well." He scrubs his unshaven chin.

"But I think a day out with your friends would do you good."

"And since when did you know what's good for me?"

I let out a long sigh. "I don't want to argue, darling, and I know you're feeling down—"

"You have no idea how I'm feeling," he bites back.

"That's not what I meant. I just wish you'd come. I mean how much longer are you planning to hide away up here?"

"As long as I want."

Craig swivels his chair back around to face his computer monitor, signalling that as far as he's concerned our conversation is over.

Defeated, I gingerly retreat, realising that not for the first time since the fallout from the night at the Belfry, I'm going to have to go it alone.

∩⊃

"More wine?" Becca asks, holding the bottle over my half empty glass.

I shake my head. "No, I'm fine thank you. I'm driving."

"Like shite you are. Leave your car here and get a cab home. I've just got Joshua off to sleep, bundled my mother out the door, and survived an afternoon of ten tiny terrors trashing my house." She gestures at the chaos all around her, at the same time as taking a big slug of her wine.

Their beautifully decorated Christmas tree twinkles in their bay window but look in any other direction and it's a different story. The dining table is littered with half-sucked finger food, mashed pieces of cake, and the carpet around our feet is strewn with piles of building blocks, plastic cars, and cloth books. Becca maybe the first of our group to have had a baby, but within her wider family she's much further behind on the 'baby train'. Her house has been filled to the brim with toddlers and small children all afternoon.

Becca lets out a long sigh. "I *need* at least one bottle in me before I can tackle this carnage." She points at me. "And I'm buggered if I'm going to let you drink tea while I get bladdered!"

"Well when you put it like that Becks," I laugh, allowing her to refill my glass, before she does the same to Nessa, who has also stayed back to help clear up. Mark and Anth, meanwhile, have escaped down to the Red Lion before they get commandeered.

Nessa busies herself putting building blocks back in their box. "So how are things at home Tor?" She looks up and catches my eye.

I shrug. "As well as can be expected I suppose. I mean, it's been a massive adjustment and the last few weeks have been particularly brutal. I think Craig just needs a bit more time, you know."

Following the Jack Walker incident, our lives have changed

beyond recognition. On the evening it all happened, after Craig had been bundled into a side room by a combination of PPS directors and hotel staff, Jonathan wanted to call the police and have him arrested. But when Craig threatened to expose Jack Walker and have him charged with sexual assault, it was decided it would be best to deal with the matter internally. The negative PR on the company's share price could have been catastrophic. The following morning, Craig and I were required to give our accounts of the previous evening's events to the hastily called extraordinary board meeting, and I was put in an impossible situation.

If I chose to accuse Jack publicly — an accusation he strenuously denied — as there were no other witnesses to the assault it would be his word against mine, and Craig would be charged with actual bodily harm. And unfortunately for us, half the board witnessed Craig's attack on Jack. That would leave them no option but to dismiss Craig for gross misconduct, meaning as well as a criminal conviction, he'd lose his job and forfeit any benefits, including his one and only major asset — his PPS share options.

Alternatively, if we agreed to sign a non-disclosure agreement restricting us from ever accusing Jack of lewd conduct, and Craig were to relinquish his position on the board, then they would offer him a very generous redundancy package, allowing him to keep his accrued benefits and leave quietly without the threat of any criminal charges.

Essentially they were forcing him to exit stage left, with a boosted bank account and a gag order prohibiting either of us from ever revealing the truth.

More brutal than Craig's punishment, though, was the board's decision, the following week, to close the North-East office and relocate all of the functions that had been based there to other locations around the UK. Consolidation, they called it. A reduction in unnecessary costs. Streamlining the business in readiness for the next stage of growth — when in fact it was all a ruse to legitimise removing Craig from the company. As the most senior manager in the North-East office, with him gone, rather than replace him with someone new, it's given them the opportunity to pull out of the region altogether.

"How's Anth doing?" I ask Nessa, knowing he too is a casualty of the cutbacks.

"Great. Starts his new job at Sage in the new year, and his redundancy payout means we can finally finish the house. What's left is going in the wedding fund." She raises her eyebrows at us both.

"Really?" Becca asks. "Have you guys *finally* set a date then?"

"Oh, I wouldn't go that far. But PPS closing has been a positive thing for us."

"I wish I could say the same for Craig," I sigh.

Becca purses her lips. "He's taken it hard, hasn't he?"

I nod, my eyes filling with tears. I can't even tell my girls the truth. That it's my fault we're even in this situation. If only I'd kept my gob shut and not told Craig what Jack did, then everything would have been alright.

"Last Friday was the worst. He came home and actually sobbed." The girls both put down their glasses and listen intently. "It's weird because in years gone by, we'd have been on the Quayside that day. For black-eye Friday. But not this year. Last Friday was his final day at work, and he was the only one left. Said it was soul-destroying. Locking up for the last time. It seems like every Friday for the past few months it's been someone else's leaving do, but last week was his turn and there wasn't even anyone left to share it with. He said he looked around the office for the last time, at all the empty desks and chairs, messages still scrawled on the whiteboard... and that's when it hit him. Everything he's ever worked for, all the talent he's amassed, all the good work they all did together — basically everything he's ever created, it's all gone." I suck in a deep breath. "I mean, how do you make sense of that?"

"The best thing he can do now..." Becca busies herself picking up mushed finger food off the floor, "...is get back out there and find a new job. No point wallowing, wishing things were different."

"I agree," Nessa chimes in. "Anth got straight on it and look how quickly he's found something. Something better, and on more money."

"Yes, but Anth's an out and out programmer, whereas Craig really needs a senior management role, or a directorship. It's a few years since he's done any programming himself, and things change so fast, he's worried he doesn't fit what people are looking for these days. Plus, he needs some time to sort his head out. He's struggling, mentally."

Both of them look at me when I share this nugget.

"But it's to be expected." I jump to his defence. "He's just had the wind taken out of his sails."

"But if he's not working how will you pay the bills?" Becca asks.

"He's got a years' worth of wages in the bank, so we'll be alright for now. Plus he got to keep the Audi."

Both of them raise their eyebrows at this new piece of information. Neither of them had any appreciation of the sizeable sum he was given, or the reasons behind it.

"Alright for some," Becca mutters under her breath.

"I wish Anth could stay home all day," Nessa sighs. "I bet you're being spoilt rotten. Does he have your tea on the table every day?"

"Yeah. Something like that." I drop my eyes to the carpet.

"Well I hope he's feeling better soon," Becca adds. "Such a shame he wasn't able to make it today. He was missed. It's been ages."

"I know. So do I." I smile meekly back at them both.

They don't know the half of it, but how can I tell them the full story?

Arriving home a few hours later, I sing-song my familiar, "Hi, honey, I'm ho-ome," but when I don't get a reply I steel myself and head up into the attic.

Knocking and then nudging open the door to what was once Craig's office but has now become his gaming room, he spins around in his chair and stares at me with dead eyes. "You're back early."

"Not really, darling. It went dark hours ago. It was a lovely christening, by the way. Joshua slept through most of it. Everyone was asking after you."

"Uh-huh," he replies without any expression.

"So how's your day been?"

He shrugs and says nothing.

I suck in a deep breath. "Listen darling, I've been thinking. Maybe tomorrow, when I come home from work, you'd like me to help you make a plan. The job market is always flooded with new opportunities every January, and I know you'll want to get your C.V. into as many hands as possible, ready for when the boom hits."

"What C.V.?" he snorts, pushing aside the pile of *Evening Chronicles* where I'd circled in red pen potential roles I thought he might be interested in. "I've already told you. I don't have a single qualification to my name. Who's going to hire me?"

"And I've told you..." I glare back at him, frustrated, "...you've got so much to offer. All your skills are transferable, and your experience is what counts. Just look at me. I made the transition from travel into marketing without a single marketing qualification to *my* name."

He rolls his eyes and leans back in his chair; sliding a hand inside his sweatpants he scratches his balls.

"Aren't you at least going to try?" My throat burns and I try to ignore the quivering in my gut that flips over like a snake.

Blanking me, he swivels back around to his keyboard and types out a message to the other gamers he's playing alongside in some online fantasy world.

I crinkle my nose. "Craig, don't you think you should take a shower? It's been days, darling."

He turns sharply back around again. "Look Tori. I'm not in the mood for another one of your lectures. I just want to be left alone, okay? Stop trying to fix my life. Trying to fix *me*. I'm not in any hurry to go back into another dead-end job, so stop trying to force me."

He glares at me, and although he's never said it, we both know that he blames me for this situation. Well, not directly. But if what happened hadn't happened, he wouldn't have felt the need to defend my honour and we'd likely be packing our bags about now, preparing to move across the Atlantic.

When I think back to that night, I was still processing what had happened when Craig was pressing me to tell him what was wrong. It had all happened so quickly. I came out of the ladies and there was Jack Walker, a smirk twisted across his face. He stepped forward and I instinctively stepped back, trying to keep a respectable distance between us, but in doing so I'd literally backed myself into a corner. Towering over me, before my brain had had a chance to catch up with what was happening, he was kissing my neck, whispering something about me being *the most beautiful woman he'd ever met,* and pressing his bulk up against me. I could taste the whiskey on his breath. Before I had a chance to stop him, his hand was inside my skirt — his fingers inside me. And in that moment, I was back in Istanbul.

Almost a decade has passed since Mel and I were abducted, but all those feelings of anger, disgust, and shame at being violated came rushing back. I was angry at myself that I hadn't spotted the signs earlier. Accepting his harmless flirtations as just that: harmless.

I was outraged. And when I'd slapped him across his face and screamed *'what the hell do you think you're doing?'* my outrage was replaced with frustration and injustice when he'd replied *'but I thought this is what you wanted?'* as if he was somehow the victim and I the perpetrator.

Even more infuriating, but as is always the case with men like Jack Walker, he's retained his position of power. He's never going to be held to account, and Craig and I are the ones paying the price.

"Okay darling," I sigh. "Do you fancy a cuppa? I'm about to put the kettle on."

Silence.

"Okay. Well. I'll leave you be, then. Try and come to bed before midnight tonight sweetheart."

He continues to ignore me and I slink my way out of the room, closing the door and resting my forehead against his closed office door. A single silent tear escapes out of the corner of my eye and rolls down my cheek.

I pad quietly back down the attic stairs and, for the first time since I met Craig, I'm compelled to go and find my journal and write down my pain.

He's pushing me away and I don't know what to do?

I want the old Craig back.

I feel so alone...

Chapter 42

*S*omehow Craig and I manage to navigate Christmas and New Year without our façade slipping. Both of us presenting a united front to the external world, assuring those who keep asking him about his plans for the future that he's '*thinking about his next move,*' or '*giving himself time to decompress from the pressure he's been under*', but as soon as our front door closes behind us, he returns to the attic, I go back to my journaling, and we slip back into our individual survival modes. The distance between us growing wider every passing day.

It doesn't help that my job is busier and more stressful than ever. These days I wake at 6.00 a.m. and head into work by 7.30 a.m. I try and make it home for 6.30 p.m. but more often than not when I do get home Craig is still in bed, having slept all day. He'll usually refuse my offer of a home-cooked dinner, preferring the lure of the Red Lion to drink with whoever he finds there. Hardened locals rather than our usual crowd, as these days Becca doesn't allow Mark out during the week anymore on account of the baby, Anth is focusing hard on his new job at Sage and spends most of his weekends DIY-ing, and Clarky started an MBA last September which, on top of his day job, doesn't leave much time for weeknight socialising. Therefore, most evenings I eat alone, try and switch off with a little bit of telly before crawling into bed at 10.00 p.m., exhausted. Mentally and physically.

I try not to worry, but even when sleep claims me, I always have one ear listening out for Craig. Waiting to hear him stumbling back home sometime after 11.30 p.m., after he's been kicked out of the pub; rather than come to bed, my heart sinks a little more each time I listen to his footsteps climbing the stairs up into the attic, knowing he'll then spend the next six hours gaming through the night before crashing, usually fully clothed, in the spare room just before dawn. Him *'not wanting to disturb me'* as his justification for sleeping separately.

How the hell did it come to this? Right now, I couldn't be further away from the vision I'd had for us as a married couple after our nuptials last summer. By now, I'd expected us to be seriously talking about our timeline for falling pregnant, but not before we'd taken a few more exotic holidays together. Before we married, we had talked about our respective careers and our financial goals, to building our long-term security. But since losing his job he's drinking his way through his redundancy pay and becoming more and more verbally aggressive every time I suggest he sorts himself out.

Desperately wanting to avoid a repeat of the dark moments in my relationship with Chris, I find myself walking on eggshells around a disengaged, disenfranchised, depressive slob, who has no motivation or drive to want to turn his life around.

Who the hell *is* this person? This is not the man I married!

I want my husband back… so bad. But I've no clue how to reach him. As each day passes, I feel more and more alone. More and more disconnected. Not just from him… but from myself.

He used to bring out the best in me, and now that he's disappeared, I am too.

I want to believe the man I married is still inside the shell of the man I'm living with, but with each passing day it's becoming harder and harder to hold onto that fantasy.

But I *have to* win him back.

But what if I can't? What then? Who will I be then?

No, I can't allow myself to think like that. The 'what ifs' are *not even* an option.

๙๖

I check my watch, then hold down the number one key on my mobile: the preprogrammed shortcut for Craig's mobile. I listen as the line connects, before his voicemail clicks in. I leave him a short message:

"Sorry babes. I'm stuck at work and I'm not sure what time I'll be in. At least 8, possibly 9. There's a chicken casserole in the fridge if you want to heat it up for your tea. See you soon." I hesitate, my thumb hovering over the *call end* button before I add, "Love you."

Sighing deeply, I return my attention to the report on my desk and the spreadsheet on my screen. I can't leave until I've submitted my budgets for next year, and right now, no matter how many different ways I attack the numbers, they refuse to add up.

My phone beeps and I glance at the screen. I've missed a call off my mam. I hit the redial button and she answers immediately.

"Hi Mam. What's up?" I mumble, my pen clamped between my lips.

As I listen, I slowly put down my pen and give her my full attention, my eyes growing wider the more I listen.

"I'm still at work, but I'll get there as soon as I can. Try not to worry. I'm on my way. Love you."

Hanging up, I hastily bash out an email to my managing director explaining why my budgets will be late, but I know he'll understand. Then as I shut down my PC and gather up my things, I type out a quick text to Craig:

Call me when you get this. T x

๙๖

It's three-thirty a.m. before I crawl home. Flicking on the kitchen light, I jump at the sight of Craig sitting at the table.

"Jesus, Craig. What are you doing sitting in the dark?"

"Waiting for you." He jumps up and begins pacing the room. His fingers fidgeting, his pupils dilated.

"I've been trying to reach you all night," I say, exhausted. "Why haven't you answered any of my messages? I could have done with your support."

"Oh, sorry. I never realised. That's why I've been sitting waiting for you. We need to talk."

"Oh?" I sigh, wearily. "Well if you'd returned any of my texts—"

"I have some news," he interrupts, without asking me where I've been all night and seemingly oblivious to how exhausted I am. I look at him again and realise as well as half-cut, he's also high.

"News?"

"Yes. And I'm hoping you're going to be happy for me. I've finally taken your advice, Tori; I've made a decision about what I want to do next."

"Good," I sigh. "But must we talk about this now? It's the middle of the night, darling, and I've had a hell of a day."

"Charming," he spits. "All you've done is nag me for the last two months that I need to sort my shit out. Get myself back out there and I've finally found something I want to do and you'd rather go to bed than hear about it."

Actually, what I really want is for him to take me in his arms, kiss the top of my head, ask me what's wrong, then tell me everything's going to be alright. But instead I lean my back against the sink and watch him pace the room.

"Okay then, darling. Tell me. What is it that's so important it can't wait until morning?" I put my hand out to steady myself. Tiredness and emotion overwhelming me.

"I want to go travelling."

I jerk my head back. "What?"

"Yes, travelling."

I blink a few times in quick succession, unable to make any sense of what he's just said. But then nothing about today makes sense.

"Ever since we first met, I've listened to you talk about all the amazing places you've been. You've seen and done so much. Bungee jumping in New Zealand. Throwing away money in the casinos in the South of France. Naked massages in Hammams in Istanbul. Riding the No.6 bus to Stanley Market in Hong Kong. Even as a child your parents took you to places I've only ever dreamed about. The Maldives, South Africa, Disney, Bali… the list goes on and on."

I close my eyes, my lids drooping under their own weight. "U-huh," I mumble. He's not wrong, I have travelled — probably more than most — but what has this got to do with our lives now?

"Whereas, where have I ever been?" he continues. "No-fucking-where, that's where. Scarborough, in a caravan, as a kid with my parents. Tenerife, once, for a lad's holiday. A long weekend in Amsterdam for my stag do, a couple of package summer holidays in Spain with you, and Mauritius on our honeymoon… and that's it."

"O-kay." I stutter. "So I've travelled, and you haven't, but…" I slowly close and reopen my eyes. I can hardly string two sentences together, my mind so foggy with exhaustion.

"But what?"

What I want to say is, *'But where has all this suddenly come from? This was never the plan when we got married.'* Instead, I placate him. "Nothing, darling. But can we please talk about this in the morning? A lot has happened today."

"Yes, of course. But I've spent the afternoon at the travel agents and I've already booked my tickets."

"What?!" My eyes flash open. "You've already booked a flight?"

"Yes. I thought you'd be proud of me. Isn't one of your philoso-phies, *never leave the moment of a decision without taking the first action towards it?* Well, I took your advice. I made a decision, then acted."

Without talking to me first, I think to myself.

"I know everyone will think I'm being ridiculous," he adds.

"Or having a midlife crisis," I mumble under my breath.

"But the more I've thought about it, the more excited I am. Honestly, Tori, I've never looked forward to anything else as much in my life since... well, never."

Even marrying me? I wonder.

"Craig, I need to sit down." I plonk down in a chair and he takes the seat on the opposite side of the table.

I drop my head into my hands. How can he be doing this to me? Any discussions we've ever had about places we've fantasised about visiting, we always talked about as holidays or trips we would take together. Never did we discuss a possibility of one of us heading off on a solo trip.

He reaches across the table and wraps his fingers around my wrist. Both of us jump, as if we've been burnt. It's our first physical touch in months and our bodies are not used to the feel of each other's skin.

"Please understand, Tori; I figure if I don't do this now, then when? When I retire and I'm too old to enjoy it? When the monies run out and I'm forced to take on some dead-end job to pay the bills? I'm so excited. I've been waiting all night to tell you all about it."

"And you never thought about this being something we might do together?" I look at him, and he drops his head in shame.

I'm not sure what hurts more, the fact he's gone and booked a ticket without discussing it with me first, or the fact that he sees this as something he wants to do on his own. If it were me, I wouldn't want to be doing anything like this without him. The experience just wouldn't be the same.

"I didn't see the point in asking you when I knew you'd never get that much leave approved," he shrugs.

"Why? How long are you planning on being away?" I ask, when in fact I don't want to hear his answer. What I want is to put my palms over my ears, shut out the world, and scream until I'm blue in the face.

"I leave on the 16th April. First to Hong Kong, like your mate Tim once suggested, then Singapore. Then down to Thailand, then Oz,

Fiji, and finally Vancouver for a few weeks in the Rockies, before flying home."

I stare at him, stupefied. What the hell?

My chest feels as if it's being crushed by a vice, and the room begins to spin. I can't catch my breath. "I thought you meant you were planning a few weeks away, not a round-the-world fucking gap year. You're thirty Craig, not eighteen. How long are you planning on being away?"

"Only twelve weeks. It'll fly by, I promise. When it came down to it, it was cheaper to book a round-the-world ticket than a return ticket to one place. This way I can hop from one country onto the next. I haven't booked any accommodation yet, I thought you might help me with that. I'm sure you'll know some of the best places to visit."

I fall silent, squeezing the tears out of the corners of my eyes as the reality of the decision he's made slams into me like a runaway train. *He's leaving and he doesn't want me to go with him.* And at no point has he thought about how this may affect me, affect *us.*

"Say something, please," he begs.

"I'm not really sure what you want me to say, Craig," I whimper, my eyes blurring once again as tears well up.

"Tell me you're happy for me. Tell me I have your blessing. All you've been saying lately is that you want me to *make a decision,* any decision, to take charge of my life and *do* something. Well now I have."

"Yes, but I meant... get a job. Get your life back on track. Not do something like *this.*"

"But this is me getting my life back on track. For the first time ever, I'm doing something that *I* want to do."

"At the expense of me," I say softly.

He looks away and presses his lips into a thin line. "It's not like that. I'm not doing this to deliberately hurt you."

"No, I'm just an inconvenient casualty."

He lets out a long sigh. "This is exactly what I hoped wouldn't happen when I told you. That you'd make it all about you. Well this isn't about you, Tori. It's about me, and what I need."

"And what do I need?" I challenge.

His selfishness is a serrated knife through my heart. In making this plan he's not once considered the impact on me, or our marriage. Surely this separation is only going to drive us further apart, rather than bring us back together. How can I possibly give him my blessing?

But then I look down and see the single gold band of my wedding ring sitting next to my sparkling sapphire and diamond engagement ring, and I close my eyes and release a long, slow breath.

I chose him. I wanted him to be my husband. I wanted to be his wife. I love him, and when I married him and made my vows, I meant every word.

For better, for worse.

I suck up a lung-filling breath, grit my teeth and clench my jaw. I will not stop loving him — I can't stop loving him — just because the *worse* came before the *better*.

I will not pull away just because it's gotten hard. Craig needs me right now, and I refuse to treat him like others have treated me.

I am not my father.

I am not Chris.

I refuse to abandon Craig in his time of greatest need, then look back a decade from now, full of remorse and wishing I'd acted differently. I will stay true to my promises. I will support him, no matter the cost. Surely, that is the very definition of unconditional love.

I suck in a deep breath and slowly close and reopen my eyes. "If this is what you want. You're right. I have travelled. And I never appreciated that that is something you feel you've missed out on. Perhaps this is a good thing. Maybe by going away now and getting it out of your system, you'll come home refreshed and ready to restart our life together... like we planned."

This time he reaches for both my hands, and I let him hold them. "You're incredible, Tori. Do you know that?"

His lips pull into a smile wide enough to reveal his dimples. I'd almost forgotten they existed. I smile weakly in return, even though my eyes fill with tears and my gut tightens in pain.

"Just promise me one thing, Craig. That's all I ask."

"Yes, anything."

"Come back to me."

I look down at my hands then back up and meet his gaze. "This won't be easy for me. And I don't think you've realised you'll be away for our first wedding anniversary."

His eyes stretch wide. I knew he'd forgotten.

"But if you truly believe this is not just what you want, it's what you need, then I want you to go."

Even before the words have left my lips, my heart breaks into two. The life force within me bleeding into my chest cavity as real as if I were slowly bleeding to death. But then I look again at his face which for the first time since that evening at the Belfry, is reborn. His features flooding with life and a renewed energy. His previously dead eyes, alive and sparkling with possibility. This is the Craig I've been missing. Only I never imagined that his way back to life would mean sacrificing my own needs.

He glances at the clock, finally registering the time.

"So where have you been? You can't have been at the office this late."

"No, Craig. I haven't been at work. And if you'd answered the phone or checked your messages, you'd know how much I've been trying to reach you."

"Why? What's happened? Is everything alright?"

"No. No it's not." I can't hold it in anymore and collapse my head into my hands and weep.

"I've been at Dryburn Hospital all evening. Granny had a stroke. She died a few hours ago."

Chapter 43

*E*xplain something to me," Julie whispers in my ear as the pair of us, dressed head to toe in black, order drinks from the Golf Club bar. "How come you're here, grieving the passing of our beloved grandmother, while your husband is, where exactly?"

Wow! I don't think I've ever heard Julie be so cutting. Her job as a psychotherapist means one of her superpowers is withholding judgement.

"I know. Don't have a go at me. It's hard enough as it is."

She puts a comforting arm around my waist, and I feel the familiar burning at the back of my throat as my emotions threaten to erupt and spill over.

"And that's not helpful either," I say, my eyes swimming. "Being nice is even more likely to set me off."

I seem to be permanently one cutting comment or kind compliment away from a tirade of tears.

We take our drinks into a quiet corner, away from the prying eyes or wagging ears of the rest of our family and friends, who are all here, showing their respects, at Granny Fenwick's wake.

Julie raises her eyebrows at me and waits for my explanation.

"I don't expect you to understand. I'm not sure I understand it myself. But what other choice did I have? Throw a hissy fit and demand he didn't go? He'd already booked his tickets, so what would that have achieved, other than a massive fight between us. If I'm honest, he's been in a rut for so long I focused more on the fact he'd finally made a decision about something he actually wants to do, rather than what the decision was."

"Or how it affects you?"

"Or how it affects me." I repeat, glancing away.

"I think we're all a bit surprised that he still left when he did. It would have been nice if he'd postponed leaving until after the funeral at least."

I look down at the floor. "Yeah, yesterday wasn't great. I was trying to act happy for him, when inside…" I release a long sigh and Julie squeezes my hand. "I just need the next three months to whizz by and for him to come back – fixed."

"You're incredibly brave, Vicky. Not many wives would have given their blessing."

I shrug, holding my palm out flat. "I think of him as a butterfly. If I were to try and hold onto it, I would crush it." I close my palm and reopen it again. "I have to allow it its freedom to fly away and trust it will come back to me."

"That's a great analogy. Let's hope you're right."

"It doesn't make me miss him any less though." I look away and bite my lip. I've cried so much these past few weeks, I have a permanent taste of salt on the end of my tongue.

"The best advice I can give you is to approach these next few months like an Army wife would. They have to adjust to long periods of separation. But they get through it and come out the other side."

"I guess. At least I'm joining him for the last two weeks of his trip… in Canada. Two weeks' holiday without any work or distractions. It'll give us a chance to reconnect, before we come home, and normal life takes over again."

"Exactly. And in the meantime, try and stay positive. Focus on the day to day and stick to a routine. Otherwise you'll drive yourself mad with worry."

I look down and admire my new ring. My granny's precious ruby, which she'd made clear a long time ago, was gifted to me in her will. The same ring I'd borrowed for the black-tie dinner at the Belfry. The same night that the course of my life went awry. But wearing it keeps her close to me and I wear it now with as much pride as my grandfather's Masonic Orb that hangs around my neck. She and Grandad came from tough stock. The generation that lived through two world wars, a depression, years of rationing; yet through all their hardship and sacrifice, I never once heard them complain. They just knuckled down and kept going.

"It looks nice on your finger," Julie says, rolling her thumb and forefinger over the diamond studs slotted into her ears. Her own gift from our granny's jewellery collection.

A beam of sunlight lands on Granny's ruby ring; the refracted light breaks into a rainbow on the table in front of me, and from somewhere deep inside I hear her voice, telling me what I must do. *'Victoria, stop feeling sorry for yourself. Get on and make the best of it.'*

ℛ

Later that day, the sound of my front door closing behind me echoes through my empty home. Suddenly my house feels ten times bigger with only me in it. I wrap my arms around my own body, trying to hug myself.

I throw my house keys into the bowl on the hall table and press the red flashing button on the answer phone. Craig should have arrived in Hong Kong by now but I'm still waiting for a message to tell me he's landed safely.

Beep. The answerphone begins to play.

'Well, that's just charming, how dare you not be in when I call.'

The corners of my mouth curl into a smile. Instead of the sound of my husband's voice, I hear Tim's familiar cutting tone fill up my empty hallway.

'I can't talk long so here's the deal. I'm off to the Caymans for two whole months, the bank's a bloody mess out there and I'm leading the

cavalry to sort it out. Anyway I'm going to be bored rigid, so I'm asking anyone and everyone to clear their schedules and come and join me. Come for a long weekend, a couple of weeks, whatever. I have a massive beach-front villa, a private chef, and an unlimited expense account. It would be fab-u-lous darling if you and Craig could come and join the party. Fund your own flights, then everything's on me once you get here. Ping me an email in the morning and let me know if you can make it. I'd love to see you both.'

Tim's timing couldn't be more perfect. A cheeky week away is the perfect tonic to my perpetual gloom — assuming I can wrangle a week off work, of course.

℟

Ten days later and I'm in a different place — literally. As I looked out of the plane window when I took off from Heathrow two days ago, I made a conscious effort to leave all my worries behind on the tarmac, and take the opportunity over the next seven days to recoup and recharge.

Forty-eight hours later and I'm already beginning to feel more like my old self.

Tim winks at me, grabs my hand, twirls me around and dips me backwards, earning us a ripple of applause from the other party-goers scattered around the fringes of the makeshift dance floor on the beach outside his villa. I hold my breath as the tinny notes from the steel drums reverberate up into the star-studded sky.

"Ti-im…" I grit my teeth as he holds me in place a tad too long to be considered socially acceptable.

"Sorry." He plonks me back up on my feet and holds out his hand. "Shall we?"

Linking my arm through his he leads me off the dance floor and back onto the cool sand, where my feet, encased only in delicate ballet pumps, sink into its soft undulating ripples.

Tim weaves us between a pair of fairy-lit thatched bar shacks, their wooden slats painted in Caribbean pastels of blue, pink, and yellow, and we retake our seats around the firepit. Beside us, Tim's team, along with their invited guests, discuss the day's diving or shopping expeditions.

Tim nods in the direction of one of the barmen who bobs his head in acknowledgement. He begins immediately to make up our drinks, flaring his bottles into the air.

I turn my head towards the black expanse of ocean and close my eyes. The soft soothing sound of the waves washing up and down the pure white sand of Seven Mile Beach drifts in on the breeze. My hair blows about my face and my silk maxi wraps around my legs. I suck in a lung-filling breath and can taste the salt on my tongue.

Every in-breath in this perfect paradise refills my soul. Mother Nature herself reigniting my spirit.

I reopen my eyes and Tim is smiling, watching me. His face glowing in the soft light from the firepit.

"God — this place is pure magic. I wish life could be like this all the time," I say.

"It should be. This is the life a woman like you deserves. I'm not one normally to judge other people's relationships – I mean look at me – but it doesn't seem like your husband is taking very good care of you at the moment."

"A-ah." I cut him dead with a raised index finger. "That topic is off limits, remember? I'm here to recharge, not to add more fuel to my problems by talking about them. If I want your opinion, Tim, I'll ask."

He flicks a non-existent bug off his chino shorts. "It's your life."

"Yes it is," I add, defiantly.

A smartly dressed waiter in pressed white shorts and a turquoise polo shirt appears next to us and passes out two large rum punches. I chink my glass against Tim's before taking a sip through the straw, allowing the sharp, spicy liquid to slide over my tongue. I never used to be a big fan of rum, vodka being more my spirit of choice, but since arriving in Grand Cayman, I've discovered a taste for the local Tortuga Rum.

"And like so many other women who marry for love," Tim is

clearly not going to let this drop, "chasing the *happy ever after* dream, reality bites when your man either can't keep you in the lifestyle to which you are accustomed or when your career overtakes there's. No man can cope if his wife's status outstrips his own. No wonder your darling husband has run away to the east where – trust me – he'll be treated like a God by anything with a vagina, and for that matter, a penis. I don't think you appreciate how subservient they are out there. Especially to a western man with money."

"Really Tim? Is that what you think makes a good relationship? I always knew you were a complete cynic about love, but unlike you I refuse to accept that money and status is more important than love and loyalty. I have news for you... the 1950s called. They want their oppressive misogynistic pre-feminist view back."

That makes him laugh. "Touché."

"Seriously though. Where did all that come from? And for your information, Craig has never had an issue with me making my own money. He helped me find that job, for fucks sake. He's always liked the fact I'm independent, have my own mind and don't need him – or anyone else for that matter – to take care of me."

"Except you do, don't you? Or else you wouldn't have landed here with a face as long as a horse because your marriage is falling apart."

"And how is the lovely Lydia? Does she appreciate all the designer handbags you buy for her?" I cut through his evaluation of my love life with a jab at his own. I know any mention of his illusive girlfriend is guaranteed to put him back in his box. "I thought I might have finally had the opportunity to meet her this week, so I'm curious — did she not want to come here, or did you not invite her?"

"Aww come on Victoria, you know it's complicated." He gives my knee a gentle squeeze before rubbing his palm up and down his own thigh.

"Enlighten me," I reply, sharply. If he's going to grill me, I'm not letting him wriggle out of my interrogation.

"You know the set-up. I'm happy enough when we get together. And she's happy living the life I provide for her and her son."

"So if that's the case, why haven't you slipped a ring on her finger yet? Why do you continue to live such separate lives, especially when you pay for hers? I don't understand why she's not the one here sharing this magical place with you. Why do you need my company this week, instead of hers?"

He pauses, and sucks in a deep breath, "...because she doesn't want to."

"Hmm." I take a long sip of my cocktail. "Doesn't want to travel, or doesn't want to marry you?"

He meets my gaze and for the first time in all the years I've known Tim, I see a vulnerability behind his eyes.

"Shit — you've asked her, haven't you? And she's turned you down."

He leans forward, rolling his glass between his palms, and stares into the flames that crackle and spit in the fire.

I squeeze his knee and whisper in his ear, "Well it's her loss. This place is simply wonderful and I'm pleased she's not here, so that you could invite me and I could have the chance to hang out with you. I'm very grateful. Thank you."

He smiles meekly and, placing his hand behind my neck, pulls my face towards his. I breathe in sharply, steeling myself.

Shit! I don't want to kiss him. But how do I rebuke him without offending him?

Our mouths draw closer and my breath freezes inside my body, then at the last moment he dips my head and plants a kiss on my forehead, cementing our friendship once again.

"Thanks Victoria," he says, warmly, "For all I tease the hell out of you, you really are lovely, and Craig's a fucking dickhead if he can't see it."

Chapter 44

*T*he following evening, as we're getting ready to head out to the famous Wharf restaurant, Tim calls me down to the Great Room. A massive open-plan space in the heart of his villa. He's leaning nonchalantly against the bar, the telephone handset laid beside him, while he chalks up his snooker cue, waiting for his turn in the game that is underway in front of him. The rest of the men are all either making drinks behind the bar, or clustered around the snooker table, whiling away the time while all us women finish getting ready.

Taking a sip from his beer, Tim points to the handset. "It's for you." He smirks, one eyebrow raised.

"Hello?" I twist the telephone cord around my fingers, hoping upon hope that this is finally the call I've been waiting for from Craig. Neither of our mobiles are tri-band, and so don't work in the Americas, but I texted him before I left the UK and gave him the landline of the villa where he could reach me.

"Well hello stranger," a familiar Kiwi voice greets me from the other end of the line. "Long time no speak."

"MEL!" I scream into the handset. "What the bloody hell? How did you know I was here?"

"You weren't the only one on Tim's invite list. He called me a few weeks back trying to bribe me to come along as well."

"Oh, that would have been brilliant. We would have had an absolute riot, just like the old days."

"Yeah, well, Tim seems to have forgotten that I'm married—"

"And?" I cut her off. "So am I."

"But I also have a one-year-old to look after. I'm afraid my days of gallivanting all around the globe on a whim are long gone."

"And how is the gorgeous Hannah? In the photos you sent in your Christmas letter she looks like an absolute angel."

"Ahh, don't let that fool you. She's a stubborn little madam who knows what she wants. Cruising all around the furniture at the moment. It won't be long before she's off. Then God help us. She's gonna take over the world, that one."

"Must take after you," I reply fondly. "God, I miss you, Mel. The years are whizzing by so fast. How can it be two years since your wedding?"

"And almost a year since yours. How's married life treating you? I keep waiting for my update letter, but you're almost as bad as my little brother at keeping in touch."

"Yeah. Hmm." I press my lips together. "Sorry about that. But I don't have anything really newsworthy to share at the moment."

"Really? That's not what my sources tell me. It sounds like there's been lots of change going on in your world recently. If I'm not mistaken it sounds like your husband's left you in the lurch."

I glare across the room at Tim, who simply shrugs and takes a sip of his cocktail.

"Hardly. Regardless of what Tim might have told you, yes Craig is off travelling at the moment, but only for a few months. It's not like we're getting divorced or anything. He's just had a really tough time of it lately and he needs to do this for himself."

"And what about you? How are you bearing up?"

"Fine," I lie. Who am I kidding? "If he hadn't of gone off to Asia, then I wouldn't have had the opportunity for this cheeky week away.

It's been lovely to catch up with Tim. He doesn't change. And I'm flying out to meet Craig in Vancouver in nine weeks' time. For the last leg of his trip. And I can't wait. But this break is exactly what he needs."

"Humm. Perhaps. Well look, I just wanted to let you know that, I know I'm on the other side of the world, but I'm still your friend. If you ever want to talk about it..."

"Thanks Mel." I feel my eyes swimming again.

"Why don't you take some time this week and write me a really long letter, tell me everything that's been going on. I might not be able to give you any advice, but at least I can be a sounding board."

"You were always trying to get me to write my stuff down."

"Because it works," she shouts down the line, laughing.

"Thanks M—" but before I've had a chance to finish my sentence the line goes dead and we've been cut off.

I stand and stare at the silent handset.

"Everything alright?" Tim asks.

"Yeah. We were cut off, but it was so lovely to hear from her."

"Good, but you'd better get back upstairs and finish getting ready. We can't be late, otherwise they'll let our reservation go."

"Righty-ho." Tucking my silk kimono around me, I pad quickly back upstairs, when moments later Tim shouts for me again.

"What now?" I stomp back down. "I thought you said I needed to hurry up."

"I know. But it's for you ... again." He holds out the handset once more, a doubly mischievous grin on his face this time. "And I think you'll want to take this one."

I grab the handset, feeling more than a little irritated. I don't want to be responsible for us missing our table. The Wharf is booked up weeks in advance and Tim had to use his charm and connections to get us all in tonight.

"Hello?" I say into the mouthpiece.

"Hello, wifey." My stomach flips over at the sound of Craig's voice, even if he's using the one term of endearment, I asked him not to. Right now – I don't care.

"Oh my God, how are you doing? It's soo good to hear from you. Where are you?"

"You're never going to believe it Tori, I'm currently at the swankiest party on the top floor of the Union Bank. It's the highest building in Singapore. The views from the top are a-ma-zing."

I can hear the *thump-thump-thump* and muted chatter of a disco in the background.

"What?! How the hell did you wangle that?"

"It's a long story. But I'm having so much fun. I wish you could see me."

I grit my teeth. I wish I could see him too. However, my heart is buoyed by how he sounds. So full of life. Like the old Craig. I've not heard him so animated since, well... since everything went wrong.

"It sounds like you're having fun."

"I am. I've totally fallen in love with Asia. It feels like home, which is weird. Especially as I've never been here before, but it feels like everything fits... if that makes sense."

"It does," I reply.

I know exactly how he feels. I felt the exact same in New Zealand. Like you belong to the land and it's part of you.

"You'll never guess who's here with me," he continues.

"How the hell would I know?" I laugh.

"Only the Head of Rentokil Asia, and the Vice-President of Executive Partnerships for Microsoft. Honestly Tori, it's amazing. You should see the spread they've put on. Here, speak to some people..."

Before I have a chance to object, Craig has passed the phone to a complete stranger, *'Here... say hello to my wife. She's in the Cayman Islands,'* I hear him say in the background.

"Hello? Who's this?" The person at the other end sounds more than a bit drunk. It's only then that I realise it must be almost daybreak in Singapore. They must have been partying all night.

I force out a laugh. "Hello, my name's Victoria. I'm Craig's wife. It sounds like you're all having a great time."

"Yes we are. It's wild. The girls are so naughty."

"Err, okay. I wonder if you could pass me back to Craig, please."

I wait patiently while I listen to some fumbling as the phone is either dropped or plonked on a surface.

"Craig? Craig, are you still there?"

I look at Tim and shake my head, mouthing, *'Crazy'*.

"Tori? You still there?" Craig shouts over the background noise as he puts the phone back to his ear. "Look, I need to go. This will be costing a bomb, but I just wanted to say I lo—"

I hold my breath, but the line's gone dead.

I love you. Is that what he was about to say? It's been so long since I've heard it, I'm beginning to doubt he ever loved me at all.

I hold the phone to my breastbone, and wish he could sense how much I still love him. All I want is to know that he loves me as much as I love him.

Tim comes over and takes the handset from me, replacing it back on its cradle, and gives my bum a gentle slap. "Now you really do need to go, or else we will be late."

"I'm going. I can't help it if I'm so popular."

I've only just closed my bedroom door when Tim shouts for me a third time.

"Are you having a *giraffe*?" I smirk, running back down the stairs and taking the handset from him again.

"Hello … again," I laugh into the receiver. "So what was it you wanted to say before we were so rudely interrupted?"

"Hey, ya olde goose. How ya doing?" the voice at the other end replies, causing my heart to stop instantly and my breath to freeze inside my body.

Chapter 45

I reach for the nearest bar stool, my legs threatening to give way, and perch my shaking body against it. Just the sound of Chris's familiar nickname for me has knocked the wind right out of me.

Tim appears beside me with a glass of water and rubs my back. "You okay?" he whispers. "Do you want me to handle this?"

Tim answered the phone to Chris, and there's never been any love lost between the pair of them.

I shake my head, and mouth back, *'No, it's okay.'*

"Gentleman, let's take our drinks outside." Tim waves an authoritative hand in the air and the other men follow him out onto the deck.

"Chris. This is…so unexpected," I stutter.

It's two years since we last saw each other at Mel's wedding and we've not spoken since. As emotional as that evening was, I came home having finally achieved some closure on our relationship, and the next day Craig proposed. At the time it finally felt like all the pieces of my life were falling into place. But the familiar timbre of Chris's voice has rereleased a whole flood of unchecked emotions that are currently racing through my veins.

Why is the sound of his voice pulling me back to a place I don't want to go?

"I know. But I'm here at Mellie's and she's given me the abridged version of what's going on with you at the moment. I couldn't stop myself from picking up the phone to say something."

I squeeze my eyes tight shut. Is this really happening?

"Don't, Chris. Don't go there."

I can't cope if he's about to give me his opinion on my failing marriage, or declare his undying love for me all over again.

Ignoring my protestations, he continues, "Don't panic, Goose. I'm not about to jump on a plane and turn up on bended knee or anything daft like that."

I plonk my elbow onto the bar top and drop my forehead into my hand.

"I just wanted to call and remind you how special you are, Vicky. I'm not going to drag up the past and apologise all over again, but when you were mine, one of my biggest regrets is not putting you first every single day. Even when we were forced to be apart, I regret not putting a bigger effort into showing you how much you meant to me. You deserve to be somebody's number one and shouldn't have to chase after that love. It should be given to you, because you deserve nothing less. You have such an amazing heart, with so much love to give, it hurts me thinking that somebody else could be hurting you, like I know I hurt you."

The line goes quiet while Chris waits for me to respond.

"You still there?" he says, softly.

"Yes, Chris. I'm still here. I'm listening. It's just a lot to take in. Especially when we haven't spoken for so long."

"I know. I seem to have a habit of knocking you off your feet when you least expect it. But let's just say as I've gotten older I've gained more perspective. Look, I don't know Craig from Adam and he could be the most amazing husband to you, but from what Mellie's telling me, it doesn't sound like he's being very husbandly at the moment, and that makes my blood boil. I want to shake some sense into him, make him appreciate what he's got to lose, and I reckon I'm the only one qualified to say that."

It's then that my tears start to fall and my shoulders wrack with big heaving sobs. He's so right. If only he'd treated me better when we were together, then maybe I wouldn't have left. But I moved on and found love again. Yet right now, Craig is treating me the exact same to how Chris once did. How can I be in this situation – again? It's just not fair.

"Hey-hey. Don't cry, Goose. I didn't want to upset you. I wish I could reach out and give you a hug—"

"Or run me a bath," I interject.

"There you go. That's the spirit." I can hear the smile in his voice.

"Look, I'm going to go now, but just think about what I've said. I know you deserve the world, and if he's not giving it to you — and it sounds like he isn't — then why are you putting up with it? The Vicky I know wouldn't stand for it. You didn't stand for it from me, and I paid the ultimate price. That's all I'm saying. You're worth more. Don't ever forget that."

"I won't, Chris. Thanks for calling."

"Okay then. Take care of yourself."

"I will. Bye."

"Bye, Goose. Love you."

The line cuts dead and I'm left staring into the handset. Did he just say he loves me, as in he's *in love* with me? Or was it more of a 'love you', like a friendship 'love you'?

I'm more confused now than ever.

Despite all our conversations of *moving on,* or *letting each other go,* is Chris still in love with me? Meanwhile, the *second great love* of my life – my husband – the person who I want to be chasing after me and showing me the kind of consideration and care that Chris just has, didn't ask me one question about how I'm doing.

I feel the weight of Tim's had in the small of my back. "Everything okay?"

"Not really, Tim. My life's a fucking mess." I wipe my nose on the back of my hand.

"Drama queen. I think that's a mild exaggeration my dear. I would have thought it's every woman's dream to have two men calling her within moments of each other. The crowd here think it's pretty impressive." His laughter echoes up into the wooden beams of the vaulted ceiling. "I have an idea," Tim continues. "Why don't we bin off the group tonight and instead I'll whisk you away to Rum Point. We can take a water taxi across the sound. Then watch the sunset in a suitably stereotypical romantic repose, whilst all the while we drown your sorrows in copious amounts of rum. Give the gang here even more to gossip about."

"But you were really looking forward to dinner at the Wharf."

"It's not important. I can do it another time."

"You'd do that? Why are you always so nice to me?"

"Because that's what friends do for each other. Come on. Dry your eyes. Go and fix your make-up and be ready in fifteen. I'll tell the group of the change of plans. I doubt they'll mind. They'll probably enjoy having a night out without their boss in tow. Especially when I give them my corporate credit card and no limit on their bar bill."

*

Forty-five minutes later Tim and I are reclining in a hammock outside the beach bar at Rum Point. Looking west across the water of the North Sound, the sun seems to melt into the lagoon as it drops below the horizon, its rays shimmering across the flat surface of this sheltered bay.

Tim has his arm wrapped around my back as I nestle my head into the crook of his armpit.

"You really do pick them, don't you?" he says.

"Oh God. Is it your turn to give me your insight into my marriage?"

"Yes."

Tim brushes some non-existent sand off the hammock while I swallow hard.

"You're such a bright, intelligent young woman; I don't get why you're putting up with so much shit."

"Says the man whose other half is also in another country and doesn't want to be with him."

"Touché. But seriously, I can't get my head around it."

"Oh, don't start, Tim. I'm not in the mood," I say, rolling my eyes. I've just about had my fill today.

"Tough tits darling, because it's high time you listened to someone who isn't going to brush over how appalling your husband's behaviour is, or help you justify your own choices in support of his. Whatever is causing his mid-life crisis, you don't deserve to be treated this way. You deserve better."

"That's all everyone keeps telling me, yet no one seems to have any actual advice on what to do about it. I just keep thinking back to what it was like when we first met. It was nothing short of amazing."

"But it's always the same at the beginning of any relationship, when you're shagging like rabbits."

"Maybe," I shrug.

How do I tell Tim it wasn't like that for us? After the hedonistic bedroom antics of Chris's seduction, Craig's courtship couldn't have been more different. His sexual restraint I took as a sign that his love for me was different. More meaningful. Not driven by primal needs, but something deeper, which I interpreted as *love.* But if that were the case and his affections weren't superficial, why then has he had to abandon me to search for the thing that is missing for him? That can only mean – I alone am not enough for him.

"But what I find more surprising, is why you're putting up with it?" Tim continues.

I suck in a breath and wish I could share with Tim the catalyst for all of this – Jack Walker's assault – and the guilt I harbour for telling Craig. If only I hadn't of told him, everything in my life would have remained as it was. But telling Tim would be in breach of the gag order. And I don't have the money or the energy to fight a court battle if the truth ever came out.

When I don't say anything, Tim fills the silence. "I don't understand why you don't just ditch him. File for divorce and be done with it."

I turn and glare at him. "Never! I could *never* do that."

"Why not?"

"Do you have *any idea* how much money my parents spent on our wedding? How humiliating it would be if we just gave up. We've not even been married a year."

"But if it's beyond repair, then cut your losses and move on."

"But you don't get it, do you. I could *never* get divorced. I've seen first-hand the harm and destruction a divorce does to people. I would never do that to him. I won't be that person. I meant every word in my marriage vows and I intend to live by them. Divorce means more than admitting my marriage has failed. It means breaking my promises. And I refuse to do that."

"Rubbish. But if that's how you see it."

"Can we not talk about this anymore, please?"

I'm so tired and weighed down by everyone else's opinions; I just want everything and everyone to go away.

Tim rubs the outside of my arm and kisses the top of my head. "It's just so shit what's happening to you. I know you love Craig, but he didn't endear himself to me."

I turn and glare, demanding Tim expand on what he's just said.

"I couldn't be sure, which is why I've never said anything to you. I didn't want to burst your love bubble on a suspicion, but that night I came for dinner I got the distinct impression there was something going on between him and the other girl who was there. Not your friend with the boyfriend. The other girl. The one who worked with him. I forget her name."

"Amanda?"

"Yes, that was her."

"Why? What happened?"

"I caught them in the kitchen."

"What? Kissing?!"

"Not exactly, but it looked like it was going that way if I hadn't have walked in when I did. But then the lights went out, and you remember everything after that."

"Yeah. The soufflés were ruined."

"One of the many memorable moments from that evening."

"Hmm... she made a quip at our wedding which made me suspicious, but I confronted Craig, and he swore that it was all rubbish. And I believed him. I mean, we were on our honeymoon. If I stop trusting him, then we're doomed."

"True."

"And I mean, look at us two now." I make a circle with my hand in the air above us. "Plenty of people could judge this for more than it is. Although Chris never trusted you, you know. He always thought you had the hots for me."

"Well, as much as you know how much I love you," Tim puts his arms around me and gives me a squeeze, "Your hideous Geordie accent would eventually drive me crazy and I'd have to dump you."

"Don't flatter yourself. Your arrogance would make me dump you first." I laugh.

"And she's back." Tim tickles my ribs. "I've missed the jibes from my favourite non-related little sister."

"Oh bugger off. Go and buy me another cocktail." I hand him my empty glass and he dutifully climbs out of the hammock and heads towards the bar, leaving me mulling over every conversation from today.

Why does everyone else seems to know what's best for me, when all I want is the one thing that seems to be slipping further and further out of my reach — Craig's love.

Chapter 46

The following morning, as the men head into Georgetown for work, I'm invited to join the wives and girlfriends for a scuba dive. I've always wanted to dive the famous Cayman Wall, a sheer drop-off that plunges vertically five kilometres deep, down from the island's continental shelf to the sea floor below: the deepest trench in the Caribbean.

Flipping backwards off the boat and into the shallows I feel immediately relaxed and supported as I sink into the womb-like warmth of the tropical waters. Turning my attention to the sea floor, some ten metres below me at this point, I begin my descent. The deeper I swim, the more detached I feel from all my worries about my marriage and the torrent of everyone's opinions on my situation. Everything back on land seems to have faded to black and white as I'm bedazzled by the rainbow colours of the reef below me. I'm mesmerised and feel myself softening into a meditative state. The only reminder that I'm still alive the sound of my breath sucking in and out through my regulator.

My diving buddy is one of the other wives, Corrine. A warm and friendly woman, we've met a few times previously at some of Tim's legendary dinner parties back in London in the years before I left for New Zealand.

She hovers in the water next to me and gives me the 'Okay' sign. I signal that I'm fine as we swim on together. Reaching the infamous 'Cayman Trench' we hold hands as we gingerly peek over the top. Checking in with each other once more, over we go and begin our descent of the vertical reef.

Weightless, swimming sideways along the face of the wall, I'm spellbound. Looking up, my retinas are bombarded by the vivid palette of the coral that waterfalls over the edge of the drop-off. Shoals of tropical fish dart in and out of hidden crevices, sunbeams cutting through the water from the surface above, twinkling and illuminating this underwater paradise. Turning my head in the opposite direction all I see is nothingness. A vast expanse of deep blue water below me, disappearing into a never-ending black abyss as the shelf continues down further than the eye can see. Magnetised, I swim deeper and deeper, chasing a tiny fish, or following a line of coral that snakes its way down the rock face.

Down, down, I go.

Fifteen metres.

Twenty metres. My mind lost in time and space, my only focus the sparkling colours of the various angelfish darting in and out of the coral, always seemingly just beyond the reach of my fingertips.

Twenty-two metres.

Twenty-five metres. I know the 'bottom' that's been set for this dive is thirty metres, and I'm not qualified to dive deeper than that anyway, so I take care to check my instruments regularly.

A bolt of adrenaline shoots through me when, out of my peripheral vision I spot a reef shark cruising along the face of the cliff. It's only about three feet long but it's the same shape as a great white. Even though my logical brain knows reef sharks are unlikely to attack humans, but it's the first time I've ever seen a shark in the wild. Startled, my eyes stretch wide open, causing the airtight seal around my mask to break and a blast of sea water to splash my face. The shock and the sting of the salt in my eyes blurs my vision, and I accidentally inhale through my nostrils instead of my mouth. This forces water up my nose and into my throat, yanking me out of my meditative state. Coughing and spluttering underwater is unnerving and I flay my limbs and shake my head wildly as I try and clear my airway.

Keeping my eyes closed, I suck in a deep breath through my mouth and count to five.

Keep calm, I tell myself. You know what to do.

Still with my eyes closed I take my regulator out of my mouth, press the purge button to force a puff of air through the mouthpiece, to clear it of all my spit, before I put it back in my mouth and take in a few relaxed breaths. Then, dipping my head forward, I gently pull my mask away from my forehead, allowing a controlled trickle of water inside and down the visor, which clears the fog and condensation on the inside. Reversing my action, I tip my head back, place my palm over the top of my mask and breathe out through my nose, which forces the excess water back out of the bottom of my mask, resealing it once again around my face.

There, done. I open my eyes.

The whole reset routine took less than a minute, so I'm shocked when I realise I've been picked up by a downward current and have drifted a further five metres down and away off the wall, which is now about fifteen to twenty metres in front of me. I'm in open water and in potential danger.

I check my depth. Thirty-two metres and still sinking — fast.

I look around frantically for Corrine but can't see her, or any of the others, anywhere. They must be back up on the top of the shelf, which is now too far away for me to see.

I check my depth again.

Thirty-five metres. Shit!

I kick — hard, attempting to swim at a forty-five-degree angle back and up in the direction of the wall. But the current is too strong, and despite my best efforts I'm barely holding my depth. The current pulling me down deeper. Sucking in a huge breath, I kick harder still, using my arms as well as my legs to try and swim upwards, but within seconds I'm exhausted, and burning through my air supply.

It's then that I realise the amount of real danger I'm in.

I check my depth again. Forty metres.

I've already passed the safety depth set for this dive, and at the speed I'm being pushed down, it will only be a matter of minutes before my buoyancy will be completely compromised and I'll no longer be able to float. I'm already consuming more air than I should be as my body tries to compensate for my increased depth. Plus the deeper I go, the more time I'll need to decompress in a 'safety stop' on my way back to the surface.

There's a real possibility I'll either sink into the abyss and never be seen again, or run out of air on my way back to the surface. If I dump my weights and use the last of my air to inflate my Buoyancy Control Device I'll surface too quickly and pop up like a cork, and if I don't make the necessary safety stop at five metres, I'll suffer the consequences of decompression, which is potentially fatal anyway.

Realising my fate I should feel panicked, but instead a sense of calm descends over me. Maybe this is how it's all supposed to end. Maybe it's time to stop fighting and let the current take me away. I could easily close my eyes and slip away without any fuss. That would make the pain stop. I wouldn't need to worry about Craig or how the hell I'm going to fix our marriage anymore. I'd never have to think about Jack Walker, or what he did, ever again. Chris, Tim, Mel and all my friends back home could stop worrying about me. Sure, they might be sad for a while, but their lives would continue, after I'm gone.

And Craig would be free.

He could go on and do whatever he wants. Travel wherever he wants. Live wherever he wants. Find whatever it is that's missing without the responsibility of me or our marriage holding him back.

My feet stop kicking of their own accord, and I fold my arms restfully across my chest, allowing my eyes to soften. The only sound in my ears is the slow, shallow breath of the last of the air in my tank.

As I feel myself drifting peacefully away, a single tiny tropical fish appears in front of me, flicking its tail fin back and forth like an excited puppy dog wagging its tail. It's a type of damselfish. A sergeant major, I think. Vertical black stripes cover a white body tinged with a yellow hue down its back. It hovers in front of my face and stares me down.

I try and swish it away, but it's undeterred and comes back to hover directly in front of my mask.

How has it swum this far out? The wall is at least fifteen metres away. And where is its school? Surely I must look like the weirdest, scariest thing in its world, yet it's here. Fearless.

I lift my hand, and it allows me to tickle its tummy as it swims between my fingers.

It turns away from me and swims to my right. Initially, when I don't follow, it comes back and hovers in front of my face again.

Okay, I get it, I chortle inside my head. *I'll follow you.*

It leads me horizontally through the open water and twenty seconds later, I feel the grip of the current ease and I'm no longer being pulled down. Now the little fish changes direction and heads back and up, towards the wall. It takes five or six minutes to swim back to the cliff, and I grip the rock face to rest, my body exhausted from the exertion.

I look down at my instruments. I'm back at thirty metres depth, but my PSI monitor is already on red, meaning I have mere minutes of air left. If I'm going to survive the dive, I'll need to make an additional safety stop on my way back, and I definitely don't have enough air for that.

While I'm still wondering how I'm going to make it back to the surface alive, the little sergeant major swims in circles around my head, before beginning a vertical ascent up the rock face. Every time I stop, it comes back and entices me on.

Focusing on taking slow, easy breaths, and using the minimum of exertion in my legs, I continue to follow the little fish upwards where the colours once again become more vivid as the sunlight reflects through the water.

Twenty-five metres.

Twenty metres.

I can see the top of the wall now, the multitude of crustaceans water-falling over its edge.

Swimming upwards again, I spot the rest of my dive group above me. Like a bob of black seals, their torsos encased in their half-wetsuits. I can see the relief on their faces when they see me swimming towards them. They were clearly worried and by the looks of it, beginning to think through their options for a search and rescue.

The little fish leads me up and up, only stopping when we reach the top of the wall. It stops and I stop too. Both of us floating in the now current-free water as we stare at each other once again. I raise my fingers and allow it to swim around my digits and tickle my skin. Then without warning it turns, darts, and disappears into a sea anemone.

I turn my head the other way, and find I'm surrounded by my dive buddies, who are all signalling simultaneously, asking if I'm okay.

I look down and see that my tank is completely empty and give the signal to Corrine that I'm out of air. She passes me her emergency scuba octopus, allowing me to take in a few long breaths from her tank. Only now do I appreciate how long I've been running on empty. Fresh oxygen floods my veins and sharpens my senses.

Corrine wraps her arm around my waist and, taking the necessary decompression stops, we make our way safely back to the surface.

≈

Back in the boat, we shed our weights and dive gear, and take our seats at the stern before the captain starts the engines and takes us back to harbour.

Looking out over the beautiful lagoon behind us, Corrine turns to me, her face white as a sheet. "That was so scary. One minute you were there beside me, and the next you'd completely disappeared."

"I know. But it doesn't matter now. I found you again, and you got me back to the surface."

"How come you're so calm? If I'd just had a near-death experience, I'd be an absolute wreck."

I pat her knee, and laugh. "And what good would that do? Maybe I'm just thankful to still be here."

I'm alive when I didn't expect to be and that has to mean something. It means I still have a chance to save my marriage and get my life back on track.

"Well, I don't know about you, but I'm heading to the first bar when we get back on dry land. I'm shaking like a leaf," Corrine says.

"You're on. And it's on me. You have just saved my life after all?"

Except she wasn't the one who rescued me, even if she did get me back to the boat. It was actually a little stripey fish that saved me. What? — or who? — it represented; I have no idea. But I do know it wasn't a coincidence. Somebody wanted me to have a second chance. Without it, I'd be dead. And I'm not, which means I'm meant to be alive. I'm meant to fight for what I want. And I'm damn well going to. Craig may not be *in love* with me at the moment, but I'm going to show him how my love can be enough for both of us.

After we finish our cocktails in the harbour shack, we take a slow walk around the shops and boutiques of Georgetown.

After purchasing the obligatory Hard Rock Café T-shirt, and sending a couple of postcards to my parents — both sets, my mam and stepdad and my *real* dad and his wife — I can no longer ignore the pull of the glittering jewellery shops on Church Street.

"It doesn't cost anything to look," I say, grabbing Corrine's arm and dragging her inside. "And I think we've earned a little treat, don't you?"

Stepping over the threshold, we both blink a few times as our eyes adjust. Display cabinets filled with every possible combination of glittering gems run around the perimeter of the store. After walking past a display of emeralds, then sapphires, then a range of multicoloured jewellery — rings, earrings, and necklaces made from a combination of diamonds, rubies, emeralds, and sapphires — I'm drawn to a cabinet in the corner, which is filled with pure white diamonds.

Earrings the size of knuckles, engagement rings filled with stones bigger than I've ever seen before, all draw me in for a closer look.

Corrine is eyeing up the diamond bracelets and points to one that she particularly likes.

"Can I try that one on please?" she says to the sales assistant, whilst nudging me in the ribs. "No harm in looking, eh?"

The sales assistant unlocks the cabinet and lifts out the diamond bangle. A slim design of eighteen-karat yellow gold, set with twenty-two tiny round diamonds embedded in the channel setting across the top. It's absolutely stunning and I lean forward for a closer inspection.

The sales assistant passes it to Corrine and she holds it up to the light and looks at it from different angles. "I think you should try it on, Victoria. Your wrists are much slimmer than mine and this is too delicate for me."

"Delicate, but strong," the saleswoman interjects, taking the bracelet back from Corrine. "See how the bridge under the diamonds is made up of triangles?" She turns the bracelet on its side so we can see the design which is indeed made up of fifteen intricate contrasting white gold triangles, allowing the light to penetrate the stones from all angles. "Triangles are the strongest geometric shape in the world. That's why they're used so much in engineering. Any pressure is distributed evenly throughout all three sides. They're unbreakable, just like the diamonds. The brighter the stones, the more pressure they've been under when they were formed. You don't get that kind of sparkle without having been crushed first."

"Sold!" I say enthusiastically, holding out my right hand and inviting the sales assistant to fasten the bracelet around my wrist, knowing I'll never take it off.

This bracelet has instantly become my warrior symbol to remind me how strong I am.

I've already been through so much; being raped at college, the abduction in Istanbul, Chris's attack in Hong Kong then his abandonment the night before I terminated our pregnancy. Coming back home from New Zealand and starting my life over, finding a new career, settling into a new city, a new group of friends, daring to fall in love again. And despite Jack Walker's assault and Craig leaving me I'm still here.

From now on, every time I look down at the sparkling diamonds on my right wrist, I will be reminded that each adversity has only served to make me stronger.

I will *never* give up.

I will get my marriage back on track.

I will help Craig find a way back to me.

Never again will I think about slipping away.

I am strong enough for the both of us and I'll show him as much when I get to Vancouver.

I'll show him how much I'm prepared to fight for him.

To fight for us.

Part VI

Chapter 47

CRAIG

7 weeks later, Koh Pha Ngan, Thailand

*C*raig throws back the plain cotton sheet, climbs out from underneath his mosquito net, and rolls off his cot. It's too hot to sleep. Not that he wants to sleep anyway. His veins still throb from the four buckets he downed at last night's Full Moon Party.

Grabbing a cool can of Coke from the tiny fridge in the corner of his bungalow — a luxury he's grateful he paid extra for, even if the generator cuts out fairly frequently — he pads barefooted across the wooden floor and heads outside onto the deck. Sitting on the bottom step, he digs his feet into the cool white sand and wiggles his toes.

What the fuck am I going to do? he thinks, looking out over the moonlit sea.

He pulls the ring pull on the can and the gas inside escapes with an audible fizz. Lifting the can to his lips, the cool sweet liquid slides down his gullet but does nothing to settle the persistent turmoil in his gut.

A few stray revellers remain dotted about the beach. Huddled together in small, circular groups, using driftwood as makeshift seats, faded glow sticks hanging from their wrists and around their necks. Others are paired up underneath the palm trees dotted around the fringes of the beach. Their silhouettes writhing and moving as they suck out the pleasure from each other's bodies.

A couple of familiar faces wave in Craig's direction. He raises his can in acknowledgement. New friends, acquired mere days ago, their shared experiences bonding them forever.

He expected to like Asia, and his initial city visits to Hong Kong and Singapore lived up to all his expectations. The power-hungry energy reminding him of the capitalisation he once craved, but as soon as he arrived on the beaches of Thailand he never expected to fall in love like he has. There's a reason Thailand is called *The Land of Smiles,* and as soon as he arrived, he decided to bin off the rest of his round-the-world ticket in favour of spending the remainder of his time in blissful oblivion.

Here he's been able to shed all of the labels and expectations that he never realised until now were weighing him down. Here he's known simply as *'Craig, the man from England,'* not *'Craig, the board member,'* or *'Craig, the husband,'* or *'Craig, the man who's lived his life to fulfil the expectations of others, by marrying the right girl and climbing the social ladder.'* Here he's free to be who he chooses, and he's never felt simultaneously more at peace and more troubled.

Five years ago when Tori stumbled into his life, he wasn't expecting to fall for her, and yes — they've had their issues — but when he married her, the future he'd envisioned from that point forward was with her. But that was then. And this is now.

Craig brushes away a few specks of sand from his shin, noticing how the grains feel underneath the pads of his fingers. It's these types of details that he's never noticed before. It's as if he's been asleep for the last decade — and he's just woken up.

But what the fuck do I do now?

The rhythm of the lapping water from the Gulf of Thailand mirrors the breath inside Craig's body. If only the peaceful waters could calm the internal rolling and twisting in his gut.

"Oh Rob," Craig sighs up to the heavens. "I've royally fucked up this time. I wish to hell you were here to tell me what I should do."

Craig laughs as he imagines what Rob would likely say. 'Oi, dipshit, what the fuck are you playing at? Sort your life out. You're not a kid anymore.'

Craig curls his lips into a smile as he raises his can to his mouth and takes another slug of his Coke. Even after all this time, his heart still feels the loss of his brother.

Maybe that's why I've never found peace... until now, he thinks, realising that it's only in the past five weeks he's experienced moments of real inner calm. As if somehow his experiences here in Thailand have finally begun to exorcise his inner demons.

Looking back, he realises everything he's ever done was to distract himself from feeling these emotions. Whether he was using drink, work, money, Tori, sex with Tori, no sex with Tori. It was all a mask. And finally that mask has fallen away and he's closer to knowing his real self for the first time in his life. The problem now is that the person he's become is no longer the person everyone else expects him to be, and he has no idea how to reconcile the two.

Rob would have turned thirty-four this year.

I wonder who you would have married, Brother? Maybe you'd have had kids by now and I'd be an uncle. There's so many things I wish I could have experienced with you. Not least this place. You'd have loved it.

Craig looks out over the horizon, and watches as the sky turns from a dark, ink black to a warm mauve, signalling the imminent arrival of a new day. Craig continues to stare out over the water and watches as the great orange orb breaks above the horizon. Its rays bleeding across the ripples of the sea.

Another day has dawned. Another opportunity for him to either do the right thing, or continue to ignore the hard truths and live one more day as his true self.

He has no idea what time it is; his watch, together with his passport, phone, and wedding ring, are all safely locked away in a safety deposit box back at reception, but he knows it'll be the middle of the night back home, and for the first time in days his thoughts drift back in earnest to his wife.

He squeezes his eyes tight shut and suppresses the guilt that rushes up his gullet as he imagines her sleeping alone. Desperate for any word from him.

Poor Tori. She doesn't deserve any of this. He twists his thumb and index finger around the space where his wedding ring should be. He knows he should switch his phone back on, but as soon as Tori receives the read receipts for all the texts she's no doubt sent in the past week, he knows she'll ring him straight away. And he can't face her barrage of neediness. Not yet anyway. If only he could roll back time, he'd do things differently.

The longer he remains unplugged, the longer he can keep her at arm's length, and the longer he can delay entering his old world.

But he's torn. His heart split into pieces; he doesn't know how to put it all together again.

The person he should want to be sharing this experience with is back at home, pining for him and desperately hanging onto the fraying threads of their marriage. The person he really wants to be sharing this experience with died thirteen years ago in a tragic car accident, ripping a hole in his heart that has finally begun to heal, largely because of the person he *is* sharing this experience with. The petite, dark-haired beauty lying back inside their shack, her long mane splayed out over her pillow like a Spanish fan as she sleeps on peacefully, oblivious to the fact that as she's helping him heal one part of himself, she's destroying another.

Chapter 48

VICTORIA

8 days later

*C*M y knees bob incessantly as I look out the oval-shaped aircraft window at the snow-capped mountains of the Rockies which contrast against the kingfisher blue straits that separate Vancouver Island from the mainland. I've always wanted to come to Canada and I cannot wait to be reunited with Craig and for us to spend the next two weeks exploring this vast landscape together.

Since returning from the Cayman Islands, I've habitually crossed off each day on my kitchen calendar.

Forty-five more sleeps.

Thirty-two more sleeps.

My excitement at the anticipation of being reunited, combined with my nerves of *which Craig* will be there to greet meet – the Craig I married or the Craig who left me – increasing with every red stroke of my marker pen.

Three more sleeps.

Two more sleeps.

By the time the countdown reached *one more sleep,* ironically, I couldn't.

I hope it's the Craig I married who will be there at the airport. The other Craig – the one who has slowly become more and more withdrawn over the past six months — I'm hoping has been left somewhere on a beach in Thailand. Regardless, I don't care. The next two weeks are our chance to reboot our relationship.

I've not had a conversation with him for two weeks, since he was on his way to a Moon Party in Koh Pha Ngan, but I've had a couple of texts confirming our respective arrivals in Vancouver.

> I arrive the day before you. I'll sort somewhere for us to stay the first night and I'll see you in Arrivals.
> Craig.

All very formal and no kiss. But I tried not to read too much into it.

I alternate between snapping my fingers and shaking out my hands.

"Right, what do I still have to do?" I say to myself.

"Not long now," the middle-aged woman next to me says with a smile.

"I know," I reply, my eyebrows twitching.

I imagine him standing at the barrier waiting for me, clutching a bunch of flowers, just like he did all those years ago when he met me off the train at Durham station after the reunion with my father.

I'm expecting there to be *some* distance between us initially. We weren't exactly loved-up when he went, but I'm hoping the romance of Lake Louise and other beauty spots along the way will help us find our way back to each other.

I'm still me, he's still him, and I still believe in *us.*

Looking down into my compact mirror, I check my reflection one last time. Satisfied that I've successfully masked the twenty hours of travel on my face, with practiced precision I lean forward and slide my contact lenses into my eyes, blinking rapidly as they settle. No more looking through glass filters; now I can see clearly.

"Ladies and gentleman," the captain announces over the tannoy, "we will shortly be arriving in Vancouver, where the local time is two minutes to four in the afternoon and the weather outside is a balmy nineteen degrees Celsius. Whether you're ending your journey here or travelling onwards to your final destination, I'd like to thank you for choosing British Airways and wish you a safe and pleasant rest of your day. Cabin crew, ten minutes to landing. That's ten minutes."

Shit! My tray table is covered with all my make-up and contact lens stuff.

The chief purser follows up the captain's announcement with his own instructions. Asking everyone to return to their seats, fasten their seat belts, and return their tray tables to the upright position.

I hastily swipe everything into my washbag, just as a frumpy stewardess gives me a hard stare. I nod nervously and click my tray table back into place. It's too late to stand up and put it back in the bag in my overhead locker so instead I tuck it down the side of my seat, between my arm rest and the side of the aircraft.

Bobbing in my seat and sitting on my hands to still them, I will us onto the ground.

Here we go…

ℛ

Twenty minutes later the plane arrives at the gate and I push my way past the exiting passengers, running as fast as I can to beat the queue at passport control. I arrive at the border, but when I open my handbag, my blood runs cold.

Shit! I rummage frantically through it while the passport control officer tuts as the queue behind me builds.

I clutch my passport in my hand, but I can't find my glasses anywhere — then I remember.

My throat burns as, with tears in my eyes, I blurt out to the passport control officer, "I've left all my toiletries on the plane."

Ignoring me, he simply holds out his hand. "Passport please."

What should I do?

I could leave my washbag. Trying to find it would only delay my reunion with Craig, and I'm not the least bit bothered about any of my make-up or face creams, but without either my glasses or my two-week supply of daily contact lenses, I'm scuppered.

I take a step back, clutching my passport to my chest. "I'm really sorry," I say, shaking my head. "I have to go back to the plane."

Waving me away he calls the next person forward as I elbow my way in the opposite direction, back through the advancing crowds, ignoring all the disapproving tuts and sharp sniffs. With my head down, I pelt as fast as I can back through the airport and towards our arrival gate.

Arriving back at the gate, I race back up the tunnel and reach the aircraft door just as a crew member is about to close it.

"Stop!" I scream, raising my hand and catching the purser's eye. He pauses closing the door mid-swing, and I collapse against the fuselage, unable to speak, clutching my hand to my throat.

"Can I help you, madam?" He steps out onto the apron. "Are you hurt? Is everything alright?"

"I'm fine." I lift my head and gulp down a lungful of air. "I've just been a complete *div* and left my washbag with all my contact lens stuff down the side of seat 43K."

He holds out a hand and hauls me to my feet. "You're not a *div*," he smiles, his eyes twinkling. "You're just the lady who's excited to finally be reuniting with her husband, aren't you?"

A hot flush creeps into my cheeks.

"One of my colleagues overheard you talking to the couple next to you. It's all very exciting isn't it?"

I nod, my eyes brimming with tears.

"Well then, we don't want to keep him waiting now, do we?" He steps back and gestures for me to reboard the plane.

"Thank you!" I smile and bolt past him.

Half an hour later and I've finally made it through passport control, collected my rucksack, and safely stowed my washbag back inside my hand luggage.

My hands still shaking, my breath shallow in my body, I'm half running, half walking as I push my trolley through the opaque sliding doors of the arrivals hall. The point of no return.

As if emerging from the womb, I'm instantly blasted by a barrage of noise and light which momentarily disorientates me. Sunlight streams through the floor to ceiling windows of the vast hall, and crowds of people shriek and hug as they reunite with loved ones. Smartly dressed limo drivers hold up placards with the names of their booked passengers written on them, their eyes scanning every new face that appears every time the opaque doors open.

Walking slowly forward, I keep waiting for Craig's familiar face to step out of the crowd but when I reach the end of the guard rail, separating the arriving passengers from the waiting public, my gut clenches.

He's not here! How can he not be here? He promised.

Panic builds in my body, and my palms begin to sweat as I look around frantically from face to face.

I must have missed him.

He's likely to be really tanned. Maybe he's lost weight. Perhaps he's grown a beard.

He must be here somewhere. He has to be here. He *has* to…

What if he never got on the plane? A voice inside my head whispers, sending a shiver down my spine. But I hold myself ramrod straight and refuse to acknowledge that idea. He would never do that to me. Even he couldn't be that cruel. Could he?

I pull up against a tall white pillar and wipe my eyes with the heels of my hands, inhaling a long breath.

Take your time, he's here somewhere, I instruct myself, looking slowly around the vast space, searching every face.

Thanks to my washbag fiasco, I'm at least half an hour behind everyone else who came off my flight, which now landed over an hour ago. And with no way of reaching Craig, our phones not being tri-band and therefore useless in North America, perhaps he's the one panicked. Desperately searching the airport looking for me.

I dig out my phone and power it up, hopping from foot to foot while I wait for the screen to light up. I know there won't be any new messages, he was due to leave Bangkok before I boarded my plane in London, but I need to check his last message and make sure we haven't got our dates muddled. Scrolling through my messages only confirms my worst fears: this is definitely the right day, and he definitely confirmed his flight was due to arrive yesterday.

I collapse down onto my hunkered knees my heart racing, my chest heaving as I try to keep it together.

What am I going to do? I'm in a strange country. Abandoned. All alone. With no way of reaching him. He didn't show and I have no idea why. I finally allow my mind to acknowledge my earlier fear — he could still be in Thailand and if he is I have no way of finding him, or knowing if he's okay. He could be hurt — or worse — and there is nothing I can do about it.

These past few months his communication has tapered off to almost nothing as he's kept his phone mostly switched off. We've only spoken a couple of times and he's only replied to my almost daily text messages, every ten days or so.

I suppress the urge to vomit, clamping my hand over my mouth, and that's when my new diamond bracelet catches the light. Sucking in a deep breath, I shake my hands, knocking out my nerves, and stand back up.

I can do this. I just need a plan. I have enough love for the both of us, remember.

Looking around me, I read the airport signs looking for directions to the customer services desk.

I'll check there first to see if he's left me a message. Then I'll head across to the Air Canada desk and see if they'll confirm if he was on yesterday's flight. As his legal next of kin, there's a good chance they'll release the information to me. Failing all of that, I'll check into an airport hotel and use my prepaid phone card to call home and see if he's been in touch with anyone back in the UK. Maybe he's called Clarky, or Anth, or his parents, knowing that I'd eventually reach out to them. There has to be a reasonable explanation for all of this. Just one I'm not yet privy to.

I gather up my things and I'm heading in the direction of the customer services desk when I do a double take.

He's here.

Partially obscured by another white pillar at the far side of the hall, I spy him, leaning nonchalantly against the structure. Tanned, slimmer, clean-shaven; his hair is slightly longer, but his eyes are exactly the same.

My face breaks into a wide smile and my heart flips over. I wave frantically, wanting to let him know I've seen him, and expecting him to rush towards me. He's looking directly at me but he stands firm, his face blank.

I don't care, my relief obliterating any expectations I had of how our reunion would play out. Pushing my trolley as fast as it will go, I run towards him. But the faster I go, the more the trolley wants to scoot sideways. Seeing me advance, he pushes off the pillar and stands firm, still making no attempt to come towards me.

Eventually I abandon the trolley and run the last few yards up to him, but he doesn't open his arms and welcome me in; instead his hands remain firmly pushed down into his pockets. I want to jump up onto him, but fearing he won't catch me, I come to a dead stop in front of him, grinning like an awkward Cheshire cat.

He looks down at his feet, then eventually meets my gaze. But I don't see the warm, open love I was secretly hoping for — this moment of reunion becoming the exact point we'd both leave the past behind and start afresh. Instead I see walls, sadness, and loss.

After a few long moments that feel like agonising minutes, I rock up onto my tippy toes and give him a soft peck on the cheek. "I've missed you."

He coughs into his closed fist. "Yeah. Me too." His eyes flick from side to side, as if he's looking for the emergency exits. "Shall we get a cab?"

"Sure," I say, forcing a lightness I don't feel into my voice. "Have you just got here? I was beginning to panic when I couldn't find you."

"No. I've been here for hours," he says without any emotion. "I was sat over there. In the café, watching you."

I jerk my head back. If he was watching me this whole time, then surely he must have seen how frantic I was? Unless...? No. Surely he wasn't enjoying my distress? Once again I banish that thought before it fully forms inside my head.

Before I have a chance to ask any more questions, he turns and walks in the direction of the exit, leaving me pushing my trolley in his wake.

Chapter 49

*S*itting side by side in the back of the cab, Craig turns away from me and looks out the window as the cityscape whizzes past outside. I stare at his hand lying in his lap, willing for it to reach out for mine, but instead he's unconsciously spinning his wedding band around and around. Pulling it off over his knuckle then pushing it back on again, and I can tell from the lack of a tan line on his chestnut brown finger, and how uncomfortable it appears to be, that he's not worn it for some time.

Maybe he decided it would be safer to keep it locked away rather than risk losing it at the beach, I internally justify to myself.

"So how was your flight?" I ask, my eager tone overcompensating for his lack of enthusiasm.

He shrugs.

"Mine was loooong. I thought I'd never get here," I babble, trying to fill the silence between us. "I watched four films back-to-back."

More silence. The air inside the taxi as thick as custard.

"God, I've missed you, Craig. I've been counting down the days. Aren't you a tiny bit pleased to see me?"

I can't hold back any longer and reach for his hand to hold. He doesn't pull away, but fails to return my grip. I keep my fingers clasped around his, but turn my face to look out of the window.

I'll take what I can get, even if something as insignificant as *not* pulling his hand away means there is a tiny fragment of connection left between us.

"Does this hotel have a restaurant?" I place a hand over my grumbling tummy. "I'm starving."

"No," he replies flatly. "It only does breakfast. We'll need to eat out. What do you fancy? Italian? Chinese? Thai?"

"Thai?" I snort-laugh, more out of relief that he's finally asked me a question, rather than what he's just said. "I would have thought you'd fancy a change from all those coconut curries."

"I happen to love Thai food." He looks at me, his eyes hard.

"Yes. Silly me." I squeeze his fingers hoping he'll return the gesture. He doesn't. "I'm easy. We can have Thai if that's what you want."

I suck in a long breath, before continuing, "I have some news."

He finally holds my gaze, but there's no joy sparkling in his irises which look back at me dark and dull. His body may be in the best shape of his life, but mentally he looks like he's carrying the weight of the world on his shoulders. This is not the face of a man who's just stepped off the proverbial merry-go-round for twelve weeks of unplugged R&R. Even if we're not in a good place as a couple, I expected him to return to me feeling better about himself.

"Anth and Nessa have finally set a date for their wedding. Can you believe it? Saturday 15th September. After all these years they're finally going through with it."

"Yeah. I already know."

"Oh?"

"I called Anth a couple of days ago and he told me then. He's asked me to be his best man."

"You called Anth? Two days ago?"

"Yeah. And?"

"Nothing," I shrug, not wanting to rise to his bait, when in fact it's not nothing. He thought it was completely cool to call one of his mates mere days ago, when I've been waiting and waiting for him to call me. Believing he needed his space, and not wanting to put any of my needs onto him.

We pull up outside a nondescript concrete hotel downtown, with a neon sign over the doorway.

He follows my gaze as I take in the grubby looking entrance. "I didn't think it was worth blowing the budget, if we're only going to crash here for a few nights. I assumed we'd hire a car and head off into the Rockies tomorrow or the day after."

"Yes, of course," I say, grabbing my hand luggage from the back seat while he pays the cab driver.

The hotel has no lift, so by the time we arrive at our room I'm out of breath from carrying my pack up the four flights of stairs. He pushes open the hotel door and I follow him into the small but clean functional bedroom. The way things are going I wouldn't have been surprised to discover the room had twin beds, with him citing some feeble excuse about it being fully booked, but thankfully it has only one double bed.

"I assume you'll want to take a shower." He nods in the direction of the bathroom before flopping down onto the bed, pulls out his portable CD player and slides on his headphones.

"Good idea," I say, but he's not listening, his eyes already closed, his feet twitching to the beat of whatever he's listening to.

Our conversation clearly over, I slink into the bathroom and lock the door.

Standing naked in the shower, the warm water running in rivulets over my slim form — I've lost ten pounds in the last few months — I finally allow the tears I've been holding in, to flow.

This is all wrong. *All wrong.*

Yes, in my hopeful fantasy I had wanted him to be waiting for me, clutching a bouquet of flowers, and I would run into his arms, and we would be ripping each other's clothes off by now. And yes, I was fully prepared for a slightly cooler reunion. But nothing could have prepared me for the stony reception I've actually received.

Where is the man I fell in love with?

Covering my mouth to muffle the sounds of my sobbing, I replay all the key moments from our relationship, like a cinefilm, in my mind.

The moment we first met on the quayside all those years ago when I'd almost fallen flat on my face, and he'd come to my rescue. How he'd made his first move by inviting me out into the garden at Nessa and Anth's with two bottles of alcopops. How kind he'd been, and how safe he'd made me feel when I spun his new car and almost killed us the night we went to the cinema and watched *Romeo + Juliet*.

How patient he'd been when the condom had snapped and I'd had a panic attack, and how open and vulnerable he'd been when he'd opened up about his pain at losing his brother.

Making our promises to each other in the cottage at Bamburgh the night of Becca and Mark's engagement. His eventual proposal, a fumbled but sincere moment when I landed back from Mel's wedding in Denia. Our wedding, and how right it all felt. The power that raced through me the moment I became Mrs Fenwick and took my mother's maiden name as my rightful own.

If it wasn't for his help, I would never have reconnected with my father; although that relationship is still a work in progress, it's no longer the empty void it once was.

Hell, if it wasn't for Craig, I wouldn't have landed my dream job, and seen my career soar over the past five years.

How is it possible that only a year ago we were the happiest we'd ever been – standing together in the lagoon in Mauritius promising to always come back to that moment if we ever lost our way – how have we gone from that, to this?

I simply refuse to accept that just because things turned sour so quickly, they can't turn right again just as fast.

I have two weeks to remind the stranger lying on the double bed next door, how good we were once.

I'll be kind.

I'll be funny.

I'll be loving and I *will* find my husband again.

Over the following two weeks we holidayed around British Colombia, staying a couple of nights in Whistler, then heading up to Jaspar, via Kamloops, before heading south and twisting our way back down through the Rockies. Initially it was awkward and discombobulated between us, but after a few days adjusting to being in each other's company again, we settled into a platonic, if somewhat lukewarm, friendship. Our connection pleasant and companionable, if devoid of any romance or sexual intimacy. But right now, I'll take that.

Once I get him home, then everything will go back to how it was before: the firm belief that kept me moving forward.

Every day we hiked in the Rockies, admiring the views, eating, drinking, and even occasionally laughing together, making new memories — or so I liked to think.

Any conversation about his trip to Thailand, or Singapore, or Hong Kong, or why he'd decided to bin off his trips to Australia and Fiji and spend the rest of his time in Asia, specifically Thailand, he deflected. He said it was because of the beauty of the place, and how much he loved the culture. Telling me in great detail about Bangkok, Bottle Beach, Koh Samui, Pantong, Phuket, Koh Pha Ngan, but never about what he'd done there or who he'd met.

I'm not so naive to think that he hasn't succumbed to some of the illicit pleasures offered on every street corner in the seedy tourist spots he's visited, but knowing how low his sex drive is generally, it isn't something I've allowed myself to dwell on. I always knew it was a risk, but like the butterfly in my hand, I had to believe he would come back to me, and we could start over.

Two weeks after Julie dropped me off at Newcastle Airport for my flight out to Vancouver, the screen doors open and Craig and I arrive home. We're immediately met by loud shrieks and a crowd of people running towards us, as Anth, Nessa, Mark, Becca, Clarky, Julie, and Craig's parents are all waiting for us, waving their home-made banners in the air.

Craig turns to look at me, his brows knitted together.

"Surprise!" I shrug my shoulders, my lips pulling into a wide smile.

The crowd surround him, shaking his hand and slapping his back. Welcoming him home as if he's just won a major sporting tournament, or successfully completed some heroic challenge. He's dragged away from me, the lads all bombarding him with questions and fist-bumping each other.

I stand back and watch as, surrounded by his friends, the old, animated Craig emerges. His smile wider than I've seen in almost a year. His energy effervescing. He squeezes Mark's shoulder and tickles the chin of the now toddling Joshua, that Mark is holding in his arms. "My, haven't you grown little fella. You just wait until you hear the stories I have to tell you."

One scenario I hadn't considered when I was thinking about our reunion in Vancouver and wondering which Craig I would be greeted by — the bubbly warm Craig, or the withdrawn distant Craig — was that he could be both. Right now I'm witnessing the warm bubbly Craig greet his friends and family. So why am I still getting the cold and withdrawn Craig?

Someone touches my arm.

"Hi." It's Julie. "How are you?"

I turn and press my lips into a smile. "Fine. A bit tired. It was a long flight."

"Hmm, I bet. And how are things… between you two?"

"Better."

"Good," she says, matter-of-factly, grabbing Craig's trolley and pushing it alongside mine towards the exit.

Chapter 50

*T*hat smells delicious, Mrs. F," I say to Craig's mam the next day as she leans over the hob, stirring the bubbling beef juices in the roasting tin.

"Thank you, Mrs F." She pats my hand, her eyes twinkling.

As the two Mrs Fenwicks in Craig's family, calling each other Mrs F has become our affectionate nickname for one another.

"Do you need me to do anything?"

She points to the oven. "Take the tatties through to the table. I'll bring the gravy through once it's done. Then we're all set."

Bob is already carving the beef, chatting animatedly to his son, as I bring through the roast potatoes. Placing them on the mat in the middle of the table, I bend and give Craig a kiss on the cheek. But my gesture is like a pin pricking a balloon, as the touch of my lips on his skin pops his enthusiasm instantly. I take my seat next to him, flapping out my napkin and trying to ignore the wall that he's erected between us again.

"Well isn't this lovely?" Craig's mother bustles, stepping into the room, carrying the jug of gravy.

"Beef?" Bob asks me, holding aloft a carved piece of meat.

"Yes please." I hold up my plate and he plonks the slice down.

The passing round of tureens continues as everyone focuses on the food, attempting to ignore the obvious atmosphere in the room.

Eventually, Craig's mother asks. "So, come on then, son. Tell us everything."

"Well it wouldn't be appropriate to tell you everything, Mam." He raises an eyebrow in her direction as I sink back into my chair, wishing the ground would swallow me up.

What the hell has he been up to?

"I hope you're not insinuating what I think you are, son." Bob gives Craig a disapproving stare. "That's not how you were raised."

"Oh nothing like that, Dad," Craig laughs. "I just mean some of the parties and drinking was pretty extreme. At the full moon parties we drank these crazy whiskey cocktails called buckets. And they were literally buckets with straws. Had me blind drunk on more than one occasion."

"Well, I'm pleased you made it home in one piece," Craig's mother says, taking her frustration out on a piece of beef.

"So am I." I gaze sideways at Craig, desperately trying to engage him.

"I just wish I'd used the opportunity to travel more," Craig continues, sliding a fork full of food into his mouth.

I cock my head, listening. This is news to me.

"There's so much more to see and do over there. And although I spent most of my time on the islands, I really wish now that I'd taken the time to travel up north. There's so much more to Thailand than just beaches and palm trees. I missed Songkran—"

"Songkran?" I ask, interrupting him.

"The Thai equivalent of New Year. Happens every April. It's a five-day festival meant to symbolise renewal, but in reality involves a lot of water hurling. Supposed to be great fun. I was in Hong Kong at the time; if I'd realised, I'd have flown to Thailand sooner. But there's so many other festivals and things I wished I'd had the chance to see. Chiang Mai, right up in the north, for example, is famous for its mountains and temples. And that's before you even consider going to Vietnam, Laos, or Myanmar." Craig looks towards his confused father. "Burma, Dad."

Bob nods his head.

"Then maybe we can go together?" I chew on a potato. "Make it our next holiday. You can show me some of the places you've already unearthed, then maybe we can go and explore Chiang Mai or one of the other places together."

"It's not something you can really squeeze into a two-week holiday. Plus I don't think it's your kind of place, Tori."

"Oh?"

"I mean, it's not really a five-star resort type of place."

I laugh nervously. "Not every holiday has to be like our honeymoon, darling. Haven't we just tramped around Canada for two weeks?"

"Yeah. But this is different."

"How so? Please enlighten me because I'm beginning to lose my patience. I've spent the best part of these past three months, Craig, trying to understand what it is that's so alluring about being away from your family. Away from me."

I glare at him, my jaw set, my eyes brimming with tears.

Both of Craig's parents suddenly become much more focused on the food in front of them. The sound of knives scraping across plates adds to the tension in the air.

"How is it different, Craig?" I press. "What is in Thailand that you don't have here... with me?"

He looks at me, closes his eyes, and swallows. "I don't know, Tori. I wish I did."

"Well at least you're home now and it's all out of your system." Mrs F. pats Craig's hand. "And that's the main thing."

"Yes. I'm looking forward to things going back to normal," I say, my jaw clenched.

If I my presence alone can't bring him back to me, then Plan B is to get him back into work and to the lifestyle he had before. Maybe reintroducing some structure into his life – even if it means forcing it on him –is the best thing for everyone.

It's Craig's turn to slink back into his chair and look deflated.

"You've had a full six months off, like you wanted," I continue. "And I knew you'd be keen to start looking for a new job as soon as you came back, so I've already taken a stab at your C.V. and circulated it around a number of companies and recruitment agencies. A couple of them are already interested and have asked you to call them next week."

I hear Craig exhale; his head dropping to his chest. Defeated.

Meanwhile his mother chimes in, "Well isn't that just lovely? How thoughtful of you, Tori. You're so clever. You should be grateful you have such a beautiful wife who cares so much about you, pet."

"Yes, I agree," Bob says. "What you need now, son, is a bit of stability. Time to put all that Thailand business behind you and get your life back on track. You were doing so well before all of this..." he flaps a hand in the air, "... came over you."

"Couldn't agree more, Bob." Craig's mother beams at her husband.

I know Craig seems beaten right now, but my hope is that once he finds a new job and gets himself back into the corporate world, he'll feel better about himself and hopefully... better about us too.

I silently slide my hand under the table and reach for Craig's to hold. He gives my fingers a little squeeze and my heart lifts. It's the first sign that he's beginning to accept that this is the right path for him.

Chapter 51

2 months later

*B*ecca and I watch from the sidelines as Anth and Nessa take their first dance as husband and wife. Nessa's long auburn locks are braided into a plait, threaded with gypsum, which hangs loosely down her back; and her bohemian empire-line lace wedding dress skims over her delicate curves, the soft puddle train pooling around her feet.

I remember the moment four months ago when she'd emerged from the changing room.

'*That's it,*' Becca had said, leaping up from her seat in the waiting room, glass of bubbles in hand.

'I've never seen you look more beautiful,' I'd added, standing up and kissing Nessa's cheek. 'Anth is one very lucky man.'

I didn't think it possible at the time, but watching the two of them now, bathed in each other's love, she looks even more beautiful.

Anth, together with the rest of the men, are all equally as smart in their traditional morning suits. Their blush-pink cravats chosen to match the colour of mine and Becca's bridesmaids' dresses.

The wedding ceremony was held in the historic Kings Hall within the bowels of Bamburgh Castle before the slightly bossy photographer guided us all outside and made us tramp all over the ramparts, determined to capture the perfect shot.

It's been a stunning day all round. Crisp blue skies. Wisps of threaded white clouds. Just enough breeze to catch our dresses and give movement to the photographs that will soon adorn Anth and Nessa's wedding album.

After a solid hour of posing, eventually it was Nessa who called a halt to the proceedings, politely reminding the photographer that taking the perfect picture was not her priority, and as the photographer had shuffled away with his tail between his legs, Anth had leaned over his wife and kissed her again, adding, '... *and that is exactly why I love you. You always say and do the right thing. Right, everyone, I think there is a party going on that requires our attendance.'*

'Hurrah!' we'd all chimed in unison and followed them back into the candlelit medieval hall where the drinks were already flowing.

Standing amongst the suits of armour and ancient tapestries it's impossible to ignore the sense of history surrounding me. Wars lost and battles won. Ill-fated love affairs and passion found. If only the walls could advise me on how to win back my own lost love.

I take another sip of my drink while I watch Anth tenderly kiss the end of his bride's nose. They're swaying gently from side to side, lost in their own private world while the soulful tones of Etta James' *'At Last'* reverberates up into the rafters. There couldn't be a more perfect song to celebrate their marriage.

I'm so happy for my friends, but their joyous union only highlights how lost Craig and I still are. But there has been progress. Despite him slipping back into his old ways of gaming all night and sleeping all day, I have managed to secure him a new job. A head of customer support role in a telemarketing company, which he's due to start at the beginning of October. It's nowhere near the career defining role as his previous position, but it's a start and I know that as soon as they see his potential, he'll start his climb up the corporate ladder once again.

Now that a few more couples have stepped onto the floor, Mark wanders over from the bar. "Come on Becks, time to throw some shapes. Let's show everyone how it's done."

"To this?" She holds up her finger, listening to the mellow ballad.

"Yeah. It's the only chance I get these days to feel you up."

A smile creeps across Becca's lips. She holds out her glass to me and asks, "Would you mind?"

I nod my acknowledgement as Mark takes Becca's hand and guides her onto the floor, where they throw their arms around each other and sway to the sound of the next cheesy love song.

Determined not to be left standing on my own, I stride over to the bar where Craig is chatting to Clarky, plonk both mine and Becca's glasses down and grab Craig's hand. "Come on you. Time to smooch with your Mrs."

He too is consciously trying to maintain our pretence in front of our friends, so he follows me onto the floor. I throw my arms around his neck, as his hands settle on my waist and we begin to sway in time to the slow beat.

I lean up and try to land a light kiss on his lips, but he turns his face away. "Not here Tori."

"Jesus, Craig. If not here – at a wedding – then when?"

The evening at the Belfry didn't just end his career at PPS, it killed any physical connection between us. He's not initiated even a peck on the cheek since.

"Don't make a scene," he says, a warning tone to his voice. "Just chill – will you."

"But how much longer am I going to have to wait?"

"I don't know."

After the mind-blowing sex on our honeymoon, I never expected us to maintain that level of intensity once *real life* kicked back in, but I also never expected to find myself in a relationship devoid of any intimacy just over a year later.

"But you've always known that has never been the most important thing to me, and I don't really see you that way anyway."

I jerk my head back.

"So who were you making love to during our honeymoon?"

"You of course. But I'm sorry. I don't know what's changed."

"But it can change back again. I know it can."

"I'm not sure I want it to."

We stop swaying to the music and stand stock still in the middle of the dance floor, our eyes locked onto the other.

"What do you mean?"

"I don't know. I only know I can't change who I am. It's just the way it is."

"But it's not just our sex life, Craig. Why will you not let me make you happy anymore? You're my absolute world, darling, and I would do anything for you. But I can't show you how much I love you if you keep pushing me away. Behaving like I don't exist, except when we're out in public. Or spending all your time in the attic. And you need to move back into our bedroom. I know we can get back to where we were. I mean, what's the alternative? We're married, remember, or have you forgotten your vows already?"

He takes a step back, breaking our embrace. "I need the gents, sorry," he says, marching off without a backwards glance, leaving me to retrieve my drink from the bar and find a place to hide around the periphery of the room.

A little while later Becca comes over to join me, Mark now propping up the bar next to some of Anth's other mates.

"Everything alright?" she asks.

"Yup. Totally." I take a sip off my wine.

"They're the perfect couple, aren't they?" She nods at Anth and Nessa, who are now dancing to a more upbeat number. The pair of them still completely focused only on each other.

"Makes you wonder why they waited so long before making things official."

"I think they did it for their families more than for themselves. They've been committed to each other from the moment they met."

"And have you and Mark thought about making things official anytime soon?" I give her a gentle prod in the ribs.

"We're different. We've got a kid together, which means I'm lumbered with Mark for the rest of my life, whether I like it or not," she laughs. "We'll get around to it eventually, but a bit like Nessa and Anth, since we got engaged, we've not really worried about getting married. I mean, when you're certain you're committed to each other what difference does a piece of paper make?"

"I agree... in part. But when I stood at that altar and made my vows to Craig, I meant every word. That's what marriage means to me... promising to love each other, no matter what."

"Even if only one of you is doing all of the loving?" She looks at me out of the corner of her eye.

"But love is not conditional. It shouldn't mean: I promise to love you, only because you're loving me in return."

I dab the corner of my eyes. My tough veneer in danger of cracking. It's true, I know I'm doing all of the loving at the moment, and have been for more than a year now. But what's the alternative? Give up? Divorce him? Tell him that I didn't mean what I said when I married him and that he's no longer enough for me? No — I refuse to entertain that idea. I didn't survive almost drowning whilst diving the Cayman Wall to give up now.

Becca clasps my hand. "I'm here for you. Whatever you need. Craig's my friend too, but in all honesty, I think his behaviour this past year has been nothing short of despicable. You deserve better."

Her words mirroring Mel's, Chris's and Tim's from when I was in the Caymans, and Craig had not long left for his travels. Six months later I never expected that things could have gotten worse. But right now, Craig seems further away from me than at any other time before.

"Don't, Becca. I know you mean well, but if you keep being nice to me, I *will* fall apart."

I glance towards the bar, expecting to see Craig standing amongst the male crowd, but he's not there.

I frantically scan the room. He must be here somewhere, chatting to Anth's family or some other friends, but I can't see him. He's disappeared. My gut tightens and a panic descends over me and I'm back in Vancouver airport, desperately searching the crowd for his smiling face. He can't have left. Abandoned me.

"Have you seen Craig?" I ask Becca.

"I'll go ask Mark." Becca wanders off.

Could he still be in the gents? I think to myself, gulping down the dregs of my wine before heading in the direction of the loos to check.

Waiting outside, I politely ask one of the exiting men if there's anyone else inside, and when they confirm not, I bolt upstairs, hoping to find him in our room. But when that too is empty, a hot panic rushes through my veins, and my breath becomes shallow and fast in my chest.

Where the hell is he? He can't just have walked out. Not here. Not now. How many times is he going to behave as if I don't matter a dot to him? And today of all days. In front of all our friends. It's all going to come out now. If he's missing and I don't know where he is, I won't be able to keep up the façade any longer. It'll become clear to every else how broken we are.

Only his disappearance this time feels more serious than before. It feels permanent. As if our chat on the dance floor earlier was the final straw.

I have to find him. I *have* to. Before he decides to leave me forever. I need to apologise for what I said. Tell him there's no pressure. That he can take as much time as he needs. I will wait. I will always wait.

My heels click-clack on the stone staircase as I run frantically back into the Kings Hall, where I scan the room once again, but he's definitely gone. My throat closes up, and I can't catch my breath. The walls start to close in on me and the room begins to spin. How can I stand up when the world keeps shifting beneath me. I fall to my knees while garish faces from ancient portraits look down their haughty noses and laugh at me.

You don't know where your husband's gone.
You don't know where your husband's gone.
What kind of wife are you, if he's left you all alone?
You don't know where your husband's gone.

I have to get out of here. To run away as far as possible. To where, I have no idea, but I can't stay here and face everyone's sympathy or concern. I'm too embarrassed. Too ashamed.

In blind panic, I bolt out of the door, grabbing the nearest bottle of wine on my way past.

Chapter 52

CRAIG

*H*ere." Clarky passes Craig a bottle of Bud.

The two men are sitting amongst the marram grass of the sand dunes below the castle. Their gaze fixed on the black horizon out across the North Sea. The darkness punctuated by two intermittent lights, as the beacons from the lighthouses of Lindisfarne to their left, and the Farne Islands dead ahead, turn and warn against the dangers of crashing against their rocks.

Having spotted Craig lurking in the doorway of the Kings Hall, and sensing his reluctance at re-joining the party, Clarky had grabbed a couple of beers and dragged him outside. Walking in silence for over half an hour, they'd weaved their way down through the outer walls, until eventually they'd parked their arses on the cool sand and, sitting side by side, stared out into nothingness. Clarky waits for Craig to begin to explain what's going on, but Craig is completely empty. He feels nothing. He daren't allow himself to feel. Feeling things has only brought him pain.

"So are you going to start talking or would you prefer to have this conversation telepathically?" Clarky jokes.

"I'm not sure what to say, mate. Other than I'm a meteoric fuck-up."

Clarky takes a slow sip of his beer, sensing Craig has more to say, giving his friend the space to purge himself.

"I just don't know what to do, Paul. I think I've made the biggest mistake of my life and I can't see a way to reverse it. I'm trapped in a box with no way out."

"Nowt like being overly dramatic now, is there," Clarky half-laughs. "Alright then, so let's not worry about fixing problems just yet. Why don't we take a step back and you can tell me what's happened?"

"Nothing. That's the problem."

Craig turns and looks at his friend, before dropping his head into his hands. Clarky places a consolatory hand in-between Craig's shoulder blades.

"I can't explain it."

"Try."

"I don't understand it myself."

"Then tell me what you do understand, and let's see if we can figure it out together... whatever *it* is."

Craig looks up and meets his oldest friend's gaze. "I thought I had it all figured out."

"U-hum," Clarky mumbles, unsure where Craig's rambling is going.

"Life, I mean. It's a simple formula really. Do well at school. Stay out of trouble. Get a job. Get another job. Earn more money. Buy a house. Find a woman. Settle down. Ask her to marry you. Pump out a couple of kids. Visit Disneyland at least once in your lifetime. Retire, then die."

"Well, when you put it like that," Clarky snorts.

"But what if that isn't the plan? At least, not the plan for me?"

"But these past few years you've seemed happy. When you met Tor, you two seemed perfect together."

"I know. But that was before..."

"Before what? Are you actually going to tell anyone what happened while you were away?"

"That's the thing, mate. It didn't just happen before I left to go travelling; it started way before that."

"What started? Another woman?"

"No. Well, yes. But that's not what this is about."

Clarky's eyes stretch wide. "What? You've had an affair – really?"

"Not a full-blown affair, but yes. There have been others. After the first time I should have realised I was walking a path that wasn't my destiny, and my soul was screaming for a way out but instead I ignored my gut and did what I thought was the right thing. Only now I've dug myself into an even deeper hole and I can't find a way out. Not without hurting a lot of people."

The light from the Farne Islands flashes past, illuminating the walls of the castle behind them.

Craig points towards the lighthouse. "It's like everyone expects me to move towards that light. And that would be the right thing to do; it would keep everyone else happy." Then he changes direction and points towards the dimmer light in the distance; the light shining out from Holy Island. "Yet something inside me is pulling me over there. But I haven't got it all figured out yet. I don't really know what *over there* means, and I don't have the luxury of time or space to be able to decide. Because everyone else wants me to keep moving towards that light there." He switches his focus back to the light from the Farne Islands.

"But you can't live a lie."

"I've been trying to, for years now. Only it's taken reaching rock bottom for me to realise. It all meant nothing. Everything I thought I was, was all a cover up."

"And has this epiphany helped you realise what you *do* want, or rather who you *do* want to be, rather than keep reminding you what you *don't* want?"

"I'm not sure. Maybe? Something inside me has shifted and I can't shift it back. But if I don't—" Craig drops his head and pinches the bridge of his nose. His shoulders shaking in wretched empty sobs.

Clarky rubs his back. "Look, you're one of my oldest mates and you know I'll support you no matter what, but everybody can see that you and Tor are deeply unhappy. All we want is for you guys to find a way to be happy again. Be it together, or separately. She's my mate too, and watching her struggle so much these past six months, I'll be honest mate, has been horrible. We've all kept schtum because we were hoping you'd work it out between you. But you're clearly making each other miserable."

A gentle breeze rustles through the grass and Craig shivers.

"The only piece of advice I have for you is to be honest. Starting with yourself. If you keep running from the truth, you'll only end up causing more pain and upset in the long run."

They sit in silence for a long while, allowing the cool sea breeze and the flashing lights in the distance to roll over them.

"Thanks, Paul. This has been really helpful."

"Sup up," Clarky says. "We've been gone well over two hours. I'm sure people will be wondering where we are."

The men finish their beers, stand up and brush the sand from their trousers. Making their way back through the dunes towards the Gatehouse, an almighty crash disturbs the stillness of the night air. The unmistakable sound of metal crumpling into metal, followed by the blare of a car alarm. Quickening their pace, they make their way around the side of the castle and towards the sounds of shouting.

Coming around the corner, they're met by pandemonium. People shouting and gesticulating wildly. Others running, while car alarms wail frantically. Someone has smashed into two parked cars, their headlights flashing in protest. In the middle of the commotion is Craig's Black Audi A4, its front end crumpled into the back of a red BMW, while behind the Audi is a silver E-Class Merc, its front grill hanging off and its bumper all buckled.

"Jesus Christ!" Craig runs towards his car, opens the driver's door and finds Vicky slumped over the steering wheel, her head bleeding, a bottle of wine clasped between her knees.

Chapter 53

VICTORIA

I look up through the blur of alcohol and tears and see Craig's stony face staring down at me.

"What the hell?" he growls, the whites of his eyes streaked with red blood vessels.

"I'm sorry," I weep. "I'm so sorry."

"Somebody get her out of here." Craig turns away and squeezes his forehead with one hand, sucking air in through gritted teeth, his shoulders slouched, his other hand on his hip.

More people have joined the crowd, including the owner of the Merc.

"What the f—?" the angry wedding guest exclaims, his hands either side of his head when he sees the damage I've caused.

"Tor, are you alright?" It's Becca. She leans inside the car, unclips my seat belt and presses a cotton handkerchief to my bleeding forehead. "Let's get you out of here." She goes to help me out of my seat, but the open bottle of wine rolls into the footwell, its contents leaking all over the floor. "Mark, pass me your jacket…NOW!" she screams.

Mark does as he's told, and Becca grabs the bottle and wraps Mark's jacket around it. "Here. Hold this. Don't drop it. And for God's sake don't let anyone see. We need to get her out of here."

Clarky steps forward. "Go! I'll deal with Craig, and sort out the shit here."

Before I have a chance to object, Mark and Becca are bundling me away from the chaos and back into the castle. We pass a confused Nessa in the entrance hall.

"Is everything alright?" she asks, her face plastered with concern.

"Everything's absolutely fine," Mark replies. "Tor's just had a bit too much to drink and is not feeling well. We're taking her upstairs to sleep it off."

"Don't you worry about a thing," Becca adds. "There's been a little accident outside, but Clarky and Craig have got everything under control. You just need to concentrate on enjoying the rest of your day. Go and find your groom and have another dance." She pats Nessa's arm. "Oh, but if you do see Julie anywhere, could you ask her to pop up to my room? No panic, but I'm sure Tor will want to have a chat with her." Becca winks at Nessa as Mark bundles me towards the stairs.

Once inside Becca and Mark's room, Becca pulls off my shoes and wraps me in the counterpane from the bottom of the bed, my body now shivering uncontrollably in shock.

"Put the kettle on," Becca instructs Mark. "We need to get some black coffee into her."

I can't look at either of them. "I'm sorry. I'm so sorry," I mumble over and over, rocking back and forth on the end of their bed. "I couldn't find him. I didn't know where he was. I thought he'd left me again," I say over and over in an incoherent ramble.

Becca comes out of the bathroom with a clean flannel and dabs the cut on my brow. I wince, but she holds my head and applies a light pressure, stemming the bleeding.

"Mark, can you grab my washbag? I'm sure I have some plasters in there."

"How bad is it?"

"Not bad enough to need stitches, thankfully."

"Thank God."

I look down and, seeing the drops of blood on my beautiful pink chiffon bridesmaid's dress, my face crumples.

My head in my hands, I sob big, heavy wet tears. "I've ruined it. I've ruined everything."

"It's fine, Tor. Everything's going to be fine." But out of the corner of my eye, I see Becca and Mark exchange a worried look.

"Here." Mark passes me a white teacup, filled to the brim with strong black coffee. Its aroma snaking its way up my nose and cutting through my alcohol-induced haze. "Drink this."

There's a knock at the bedroom door, and Mark lets Julie into the room. She rushes towards me, kneeling on the floor in front of me and placing her hands on my knees. "Goodness me. What on earth's happened?" She looks first at Becca, then Mark, then back to Becca, waiting for an explanation.

"Tor's had a little accident... in Craig's car," Mark says, jerking his head in the direction of the open bottle of wine on the corner of the dressing table.

Julie bobs her head. "I see." Turning her attention back to me, she asks, "And how did you come to be in Craig's car?"

My body still shaking, I pull my knees up to my chin and pressing my eye sockets into my kneecaps. I don't know what to say. I've made such a horrendous mess of everything.

When I don't answer, Julie continues, "Okay. I think someone might benefit from a bath, don't you?" Her tone as soothing as a mother comforting a distressed child. "Becca, maybe you could go and put the plug in, and Mark... perhaps there's somewhere else you'd rather be?"

"Understood." Mark, who's been sitting in the dressing table chair, stands up. "I'll go and see if I can help outside." He turns to Becca. "I've got my mobile on me. Just call me if you need anything."

An hour later, wrapped up in a hotel bathrobe and tucked up in Becca's bed, my hands wrapped around yet another cup of coffee, Becca sits on the side of the bed next to me, while Julie has pulled up one of the easy chairs. She reaches for my hand to hold.

"Let's start at the beginning, shall we? Can you remember now why you were in Craig's car?"

"I needed to get home," I blurt out. "To put the washing on."

"I see," Julie replies, her voice maintaining a steady tone, while Becca's eyebrows shoot up into her hairline.

"Yes. I remembered Craig had left a pile of his washing on the kitchen floor, and I thought if I could get home, then I could put it on and everything would be alright."

"And is that the only reason?"

"No. We've got no milk in the fridge. I didn't want him not being able to make a cuppa if he arrived home before me. I didn't want him to have any more reasons to hate me."

"I see."

I'm aware I'm slurring my words, despite the coffee which has gone some way to clearing my senses.

"Vicky, I'm going to ask you something and I want you to answer me truthfully: Are you high? Have you smoked something, or have you taken any pills?"

"No, nothing. Honestly Jules. I promise you I've only had a few glasses of wine. I've definitely not taken anything. Well, other than what the doctor gave me."

Becca's eyes look like they're about to pop out of her head.

"Okay. And do you have those pills on you?"

I point to my clutch bag on the dressing table. Becca grabs it and passes it to me. I rummage inside and pass the blister pack of pills to Julie.

"And why has your GP prescribed these?" she asks, her voice clinical in its analysis.

"To help me sleep. I've been so tired lately. But they haven't helped at all. I feel more tired since taking them."

"Vicky, do you realise what these are?"

"Sleeping tablets?"

"No. Well, aiding sleep is often a by-product. This is Diazepam. One of the strongest and most addictive antidepressants on the market. How long have you been taking these?"

"Just over a week. My GP would only give me a two-week supply."

"Thank goodness," Julie exhales. "Any longer and you'll be trying to get off these for the next ten years."

"My periods have stopped, you see..." I add.

Becca's eyes grow wider still and Julie taps her steepled fingers together at this new piece of information.

"... so I wanted to get that checked out."

"And there's no chance you could be pregnant?" Julie asks.

"Hardly. I've not had sex in over a year."

Becca's eyes stay wide, but now her mouth drops open as well.

"The doctor said it was most likely because I've lost so much weight. Then I told her that I've had trouble sleeping, and that's when she gave me these."

Now that I'm saying all of this out loud, I realise how bad it all sounds.

"Yes, you have lost a lot of weight, and clearly you've not been sleeping, but do you think there could be something else that's affecting you?"

When I don't answer, she continues, "Think really hard, Victoria. What do you think is the underlying cause of all these physical symptoms?"

A new wave of exhaustion washes over me and my shoulders shake as more sobs wrack my body.

Becca leans over and pulls me into a hug. She strokes my hair and rests her chin on the top of my head. "Look, I've held back from saying my piece for far too long. Craig may be one of Mark's best mates, but you're my friend and I can't stand on the sidelines any longer. You need to hear my opinion. What he's doing to you is beyond cruel. You don't deserve this, Tor. You've just said it yourself – you've lost so much weight you're a bag of bones, and your periods have stopped. That in itself should be enough to make you realise how wrong this all is. Never mind the fact you're currently popping pills that artificially change the biochemistry of your brain to help you cope. This is not right, pet."

"But I love him," I whisper. "I would do anything for him. I already have one failed relationship behind me, I can't fail at this one as well. I won't get divorced. It would destroy me."

My face crumples into an ugly cry. Julie leans forward and holds my hand. "But marriage isn't meant to be a life sentence of pain and suffering either. When was the last time you thought about what *you* need? Everyone can see the sacrifices you've made, and how much you've wanted to support him, but where's the boundary? Is it when you've lost more than ten percent of your body weight? Is it when your periods have stopped, or as Becca says, is it when you need prescription medication to cope? Or when you hurt yourself, or someone else, through reckless behaviour? You could have really hurt yourself tonight, Vicky, or worse — someone else."

I sniff hard, wiping my nose with the back of my hand.

"I don't think it matters now anyway. When he opened the car door tonight and saw me inside… I've never seen him look like that before. He wasn't just angry, he was disgusted. I disgust him."

A fresh tear rolls down my cheek and I quickly wipe it away.

"Oh, come here, pet." Becca pulls me into a hug. "There, there," she soothes. "I'm sure it'll all feel better in the morning. Once you've had a chance to sleep it all off."

"But I have to talk to him. Explain. Apologise and tell him I made a mistake."

Becca and Julie exchange a look.

"Don't worry about that now," Julie says. "The best thing you can do now is get some rest."

I sit bolt upright. "Where is he?"

"That's not important," Becca says.

"It is to me! Pass me my phone." I hold out my hand.

"I don't think that's a good idea, Vicky." Julie takes my phone from my clutch bag on the dressing table and slides it inside her own, snapping the clasp shut. "Listen to me. If I give you your phone now, you're likely to say or do something you'll regret. Let me look after it for you tonight. Craig's with the boys. Sorting out the crash. Let them deal with that, and we'll look after you here. If he messages you, I promise I'll let you know."

"But he hasn't, has he? Messaged me?" I flop back onto the pillows, a fresh wave of tears rearing up inside me as Julie slowly shakes her head.

The harsh reality is I'm not Craig's priority and I haven't been for a long time.

"God, I've made such a mess of everything. I just wish I could turn the clock back," I say.

"This isn't all your fault," Becca tempers, her lips pressed into a thin line. "He has to take some responsibility. But the pair of you can't go on like this. It's not good for either of you."

"I know," I sigh.

And she's right.

Starting tomorrow, something has to change.

Chapter 54

$\mathcal{I}$ spend the night in Becca's room. She sleeps next to me, I suspect to stop me from doing anything else idiotic, none-theless I appreciate her company. The last thing I want right now is to be left alone with my own thoughts.

Mark sleeps elsewhere. I assume with Craig in my room, but no one will tell me for sure. Nor will anyone allow me to go and see him. Julie keeps my phone overnight and tells me to focus on getting a good night's sleep.

Like that's possible.

Every time I close my eyes all I see is the look of disgust on Craig's face when he opened the car door and found me slumped over his steering wheel.

Oh, what have I done?

My stomach contracts and twists as I roll around the bed, sleep evading me, and I have to fight the urge to scratch at my throat with my fingernails. Turning my pain in on myself, like I've done before.

The next morning, breakfast arrives; all the while I'm kept in Becca's room, away from prying eyes, idle gossip... and my husband.

Julie brings me my clothes and overnight bag from my room and returns my phone to me. I ask her if she's seen him, but she avoids giving me a straight answer.

I check my messages, but Craig hasn't tried to get in touch.

My fingers hover over the keys, my mind trying to form a text, but I have no idea what to say.

I look up with pleading eyes, as if my girlfriends can tell me how to fix my broken marriage.

"He's hitched a lift with the tow truck," Julie says. "Maybe leave it until you get home. Give you both a chance to think about what to say... or do, next."

I slump back against the pillows and close my eyes. "And can I hitch a lift home with one of you?"

Becca pats my hand. "It's already sorted. You're coming home with Mark and me."

"Then I think you should make another appointment with your GP," Julie adds. "I can't be your therapist. We're related. But I think you would benefit from talking to a professional."

"Either that, or just dump him," Becca mumbles under her breath.

We make our exit quietly. I send Nessa an apologetic text, hoping upon hope that I didn't ruin her special day. She and Anth have already left for their honeymoon, but she replies telling me not worry and to look after myself.

I steel myself, expecting Craig to be waiting for me, his face as stony as it was last night, but when I arrive home, the house is empty. Pulling out my mobile I bash out a text.

> I'm so so sorry for last night. I don't know what came over me. I'm home now. See you soon?

....I type, adding a question mark at the end. I have no idea where he is, or when he's planning on returning home. All I know is he will have to come home at some point.

My fingers hover over the send button before I add.

Love you x

I throw my phone into the middle of the kitchen island and drop my head into my hands. I want to be here when he returns, but pacing back and forth for a full forty-five minutes, my nerves twisting into an ever-tighter ball and a sense of dread weighing down on my chest, eventually I grab my swimming bag and head to the pool.

&

The sharp smell of chlorine hits the inside of my nostrils before I've even emerged from the changing room. Hooking my toes over the edge of the pool, I take a deep breath and dive in. My steepled hands puncturing the water as I plunge head first into another world. Like piercing a veil between my physical reality and the world inside my head. The water envelops me, and even though I'm aware of the sting from the cut on my forehead, and my arms and legs moving rhythmically through the water, I feel detached. The only world that exists to me now are my thoughts. is the one inside my head.

I close my eyes and sink deeper into the time when Craig and I were so in love, the day he pulled me out of his car after I almost crashed it into a wall, and kissed me in the pouring rain. He wasn't angry then. In fact, the complete opposite. I remember the feel of his lips on mine. A coil of heat uncurling in my belly.

In. Out. In. Out. My breath fills my chest as I drag my body forward.

He slides his hand down over my bum and grabs a handful of flesh, releasing a deep, guttural groan from the back of his throat. Our lips part and he slides his tongue inside my mouth. I taste him on my lips and drink him in. I'm both lost and found.

In. Out. In. Out. My fingers touch the side of the pool; I turn and go again.

He smooths my rain-soaked hair away from my face and says to me, *'Hey, hey. It's okay. We're both okay, aren't we?'*

I bury my face in his chest. 'But I was so stupid. I shouldn't have been trying to impress you. I should have been more careful.'

He holds my head between his hands and tilts my face upwards. I blink hard against the falling rain as he continues, *'I know. But you're safe now. I've got you. You're My Girl.'*

In. Out. In. Out.

'I've got you. You're safe.'

Kick. Splash. Kick. Splash.

'My Girl. Tori Turnbull. The craziest, smartest, most bull-headed amazing woman I've ever met. Never think you have to do anything to impress me. Just be you.'

In. Out. In. Out. Touch the side. Go again.

Just be me.

But who am I? And who are you?

I thought I knew.

Kick. Splash. Kick. Splash. In. Out. Touch the side. Go again.

To have and to hold, from this day forward.

In. Out. In. Out.

For better, for worse. For richer, for poorer.

To love and cherish, till death us do part.

In. Out. In. Out.

That's who I am. Or so I thought. The person who makes a commitment to love and cherish until the day I die.

The side of my face touches the water as I sweep an arm overhead.

Maybe that woman doesn't exist. Not anymore.

But she was real once; she can be real again.

Kick. Splash. Kick. Splash. In. Out. Touch the side. Go again.

If I'm not her... then who am I? Do I even exist?

I suck air into my lungs, but my chest is gripped by a vice. I can't breathe. I'm drowning.

With an outstretched arm, I lunge for the side, gripping on for dear life. Planting my toes against the side of the pool, I rip off my goggles and weep.

How has it come to this? When did I disappear?

He made me relevant. *He* saw the real me when I was broken and hiding away from the world. *He* breathed life back into me, soothed my broken heart, and helped me find my feet again. I believed in him because he believed in me.

Almost immediately, *I* become *we*, then *we* built a life together and now I don't know how to exist without him.

Is that why I chose him instead of Chris? Because I was too scared to exist without him – because I didn't know how to. When I made that choice I willing gave Craig my whole heart, merging every part of my identity into his.

I wipe my eyes with the pads of my fingers, but the tears keep coming.

I don't want to be *me* in this world without *him*.

Because I don't know how to be *me* in this world without *him*.

A shriek from the other side of the pool interrupts my thoughts. A young family are laughing and playing together. The father throwing their young son into the air and catching him. The mother coaching their older child, a hand under their belly, holding them up as they learn to swim on their own. That was meant to be me. That's the future I was promised.

I turn my head the other way, my heart heavy with wearisome thoughts. I hear the voices of Becca and Julie in my head, '*What he's doing to you is beyond cruel. You don't deserve this, Tor. It's not right pet.*'

'But I love him. I've already failed at one relationship, I can't fail again.'

I can't be alone again… alone again… alone again, my thoughts swimming inside my head.

'But where's the boundary?'

I rinse out my goggles and pull them back over my head. Pushing off once again, I resume my stroke.

In. Out. In. Out.

Maybe there hasn't been a boundary because I've never existed independently from him. Because I've never needed to, and now I'm terrified to.

I love him, of that I am sure. But I can't make him love me. No matter what I try. Despite what I want to believe, one love isn't enough for two. Not for this to work. So all I have left is to... *just be me.*

That's all there is.

That's all there ever was really.

Now it's time to find out if that is enough.

If I'm enough.

...and if I'm not, then who knows.

Chapter 55

I walk home from the baths, my combed-out hair wet and limp down my back. Grabbing a few supplies from our corner shop, I brace myself as I walk through the back door. But Craig's still not home. I don't know whether he's been home and gone out again, but a quick check in his 'man drawer' shows that the tin where he keeps his excess cash hasn't been touched, meaning he hasn't taken any money out to go to the pub and it doesn't look like anything else has been disturbed.

I check my mobile again — nothing.

With no option but to wait for the storm to hit, I flick the switch on the kettle and I'm making a cup of tea when the back door opens behind me. I turn slowly, wanting to delay the inevitable frosty confrontation that is no doubt coming. But he remains in the doorway, his bulk filling the space, as if he too is unsure of what to do next. He's freshly showered, and freshly shaven, his overnight bag in one hand, his suit carrier from the wedding yesterday hooked into his index finger and slung over his shoulder.

"I took a shower at Clarky's. He came and got me from the garage."

I bob my head in acknowledgement. "He's a great friend."

"Yes. Yes he is."

"Tea?" I ask, holding the kettle mid-air.

He hovers in the doorway, the fresh September air blowing in from outside. When he doesn't answer, I pull down his favourite mug and begin to make him one anyway.

I pass him the freshly made cup of steaming tea. "We need to talk. I think it's about time you and I had an honest conversation. No more pussy footing around the issues. The truth from now on."

"I agree." He pulls out a chair at the table and sits down.

I come and sit opposite him, cupping my hands around my mug. We stare at each other, sipping our tea, neither of us wanting to be the first to acknowledge the monumental conversation that we know is hanging in the air between us.

I suck in a deep breath, trying to calm my gut and steady my breathing, but all of a sudden it feels as if the walls are closing in on me again.

Leaping up from my chair, I blurt out. "I need to get out of here. Come for a drive with me. We can go in my car."

He lifts his mug to his lips and blows across its surface. The steam snaking upwards. Keeping his head tilted forward, he gazes up at me. "Okay. But after yesterday's debacle, I'm driving," he says, his eyes hooded. The same way they were when we first met. His dark irises connect with mine and he gives me a meek smile. And like an unstoppable chain reaction, my heart expands instantly and air rushes into my lungs.

It's not over yet. There's still hope.

I pass him my car keys, and he flips down the roof on my little MG before sliding into the driver's seat. It's a gorgeous autumnal day. Bright and crisp. The colours on the trees every shade of rust and copper, the air filled with a no-nonsense briskness.

I pull my scarf tighter around my neck as he turns the car south over the top of the moors, towards Teesdale. Much of the heather has been burnt off, turning the landscape black and charred, but primed for next season's re-growth.

"Where are we going?" I ask.

"I thought we could take a walk to High Force."

"Good idea. I bet it's in flood."

"Probably."

"You're not planning on pushing me off the top, are you?" A snort-laugh escapes from my nose, but he ignores my attempt at humour. Both of us still dancing around the elephant in the room.

He parks up, and we walk in stony silence along the trail to the breathtaking waterfall a mile up the valley.

Twisting our way through the woodland, I look down at my feet, steeling myself. If he's not going to start the conversation, then I will.

"I really am sorry about crashing your car."

"I know you are."

"I have no idea what came over me. One minute we were on the dance floor, then when you disappeared and I had no idea where you'd gone, and I couldn't find you — I freaked out. I was so embarrassed. I'm your wife. I'm supposed to know everything about you. What you're thinking. What you're feeling. But I don't know anything anymore. I know it seems totally illogical now but I thought you might have gone home and I needed to get there. I was worried you'd be cross we had no milk in the fridge." I drop my head. "I know it sounds ludicrous now."

"Yes it does," he replies, giving nothing away in his tone.

A heavy silence falls between us again.

"I've never told you how Rob really died," he says quietly.

"What?" I say, shocked. "You told me he was killed in a car accident."

He stops walking and turns and looks at me. "Yes, he was. But I never told you it was a drunk driver that smashed into him."

My hands fly up to my mouth as I shake my head realising the implications of my actions last night. He'll never forgive me now.

"Oh, my God. That's terrible. Why have you never told me that?"

"There's more…"

He sits down heavily on a wooden bench positioned to enjoy the views of the river below. The waterfall, further upstream, is still hidden by the curve of the trail, but the unmistakable sound of the river plummeting twenty-two metres over the crop of whinstone into the plunge pool below fills the silence between us. I gingerly sit down next to him and take his hand. He doesn't pull away.

"It's my fault he's dead. He was out looking for me when the crash happened." He drops his head, ashamed.

I watch as a myriad of micro emotions roll across his features, before he winces, sucks in a deep breath, and continues. "I was with Claire — my girlfriend before you."

I bob my head in acknowledgement.

"Let's just say it was the first time we were… you know — intimate. Anyway, I was MIA and Mam was worried. No one had mobile phones back then, so Rob went out looking for me and that's when he was sideswiped by some rich bastard in a Jag. Twice over the legal limit, on his way back to the office after a business lunch. He walked away without a scratch but Rob was you know—."

He bends even further forward, dropping his head into his hands as the painful memories wash over him again.

"That pompous asshole even tried to say it was Rob's fault… when in fact it was all mine."

"But that's ridiculous. It's not your fault Rob was killed," I say, softly.

So much makes sense now, I think to myself. So many pieces of the jigsaw suddenly slotting into place. No wonder he's struggled to let go in the bedroom, if all the while he was having to reconcile his own passions and primal desires with the guilt that being with his first girlfriend contributed to his brother's death. And no wonder he harbours a distrust of anyone with inherited wealth, or privilege; earned or otherwise.

How on earth has he managed to balance his own ambitions and success with his internal feelings of shame and blame.

Maybe he hasn't. Not deep down, anyway.

Maybe the night he landed one on Jack Walker, he wasn't just defending my honour; he was punching every person who believes they can take what they want from him, without consequences. Just like the businessman who killed his brother yet walked away without a scratch.

Perhaps he was even thumping the part of himself that he didn't want to become.

Of course he'd want to turn his back on his life and runaway when the opportunity presented itself. And no wonder he's been struggling to come back, not just to me, but to *this* life when it was so full of buried pain.

"I wish I'd known. I wish you'd told me."

"Why? Would it have changed anything?"

"Maybe. Who knows?"

He lightly squeezes my hand.

"You must know how sorry I am for last night, Craig. I wasn't in my right mind. I'll never do anything like that again. Even without knowing what happened to Rob, I really am very sorry."

"Me too."

I sigh. "How the hell did we end up here?"

He shrugs.

"It seems madness that after everything we've been through, we don't seem to know each other at all."

"I know."

"I still love you though." I give his hand another squeeze and he squeezes my fingers in return. "I've never stopped loving you, but I can't go on like this."

"Me neither,' he says.

"So how do we fix this? Fix us? I'm assuming you do want us to be fixed?"

"Let's keep walking." He stands and kicks a stone off the path.

I follow along beside him. The trail turns the final corner and we both stop in our tracks when the waterfall comes into view. The roar of the river free-falling over the edge, echoing the pounding inside my head. The river is indeed in flood, and the second spout that only opens up a couple of times a year is also crashing down onto the rocks below.

Eventually, he sighs. "I don't hate you, you know."

"Is that meant to make me feel better because I'm still waiting for you to tell me you love me or that you want to fix our marriage."

I fidget with my hands when he doesn't respond, putting them in my pockets, then pulling them out again. Meanwhile he stands stock still, staring at the ever-flowing water. It just keeps coming and coming. A sheer force of nature. Unstoppable and more powerful than any human desire.

"I can't control my heart, Victoria. No one can."

I don't have the strength to hold my head up anymore and drop down onto my hunkered knees. I begin to shiver as a wave of grief crashes over me. He's *never* called me that before. I've always been Tori — *his* Tori, *his* girl.

He kneels down next to me and goes to put his arm around me, but then thinks again and retracts his hand.

"I don't know what else to say, Tori. It's like we were always in the same boat. You and me side-by-side. Through the highs and the lows of the last five, almost six, years. Things have been sometimes good, sometimes bad, but we made a good team you and I."

He smiles weakly and I close my eyes. For all I asked him to tell me the truth, I don't want to hear what he has to say.

"And then one day you'd moved into a boat next to me. But I wasn't worried because you were still there, right beside me. Then ever so slowly, you sailed a little bit further away. Drifting gently in the opposite direction. But I could still see you, and that made it okay. Then one day I couldn't see you anymore. Your boat disappeared — and I don't know where you went or how to get us back in the same boat. But then I realised," he pauses, "… I realised I didn't need you in my boat anymore."

"This is all Jack Walker's fault." I stick my bottom lip out. My unconscious clutching at any straw.

"No, it's not. I agree that that was hideous, and what he did to you was unforgivable, and it was definitely the catalyst that sped things up for me, but I was unhappy a long time before that. I just didn't know it."

Gently, I take his hands in my own and look directly into his eyes, desperately searching for any remnants of the connection that once was.

"But I'm right here, Craig. Right in front of you. I've always been here. I never went anywhere. You were the one that climbed out of our boat and drifted away from me. But I don't care about any of that. I don't care about the past. I love you. All of you. Even the wounded and dark parts of you. I've just been waiting for you to come back to me so we can heal all of this — together." I kiss the back of his hands in turn, twist my head and lay my cheek against them. "But if you're not in love with me anymore. I need you to tell me you *want* to be in love with me again? To climb back in the same boat?"

He looks down at me and I turn my gaze once again to meet his. I know he can see the desperation in my eyes, but his eyes look dark and distant. It's like I'm invisible to him. I don't want to beg, but my insides are screaming, *I'm right here Craig. Loving you. I've never stopped loving you. Can't you see me? Please love me. Please don't leave me.*

"I don't see how that's even possible. I can't control what's in my heart."

A single tear rolls down my cheek and this time I don't rub it away.

"It's not about the *how* you will fall back in love with me again. I'm only asking if you *want to*. Decide first, and we'll work the *hows* out together."

"But I'm not the same person you fell in love with."

"I think you are. Only now I know more of you. I want this to work, Craig. I want you to love me, like I love you. Regardless of all the mistakes we've made, I still believe in us."

He lets out a long sigh and sits back on a boulder behind him, patting the space next to him. Indicating for me to join him. I take up the invitation.

"I wish I had your belief. But I don't. I'm sorry but I can't see a future with you. Not anymore. One thing I am sure of, is I can't give you what you want."

"Yes you can. Because all I want is to be married — to you. I don't care about anything else. I don't care where we live. How much money we earn. None of it matters to me. I'd follow you to the ends of the earth if you'd let me. All I want is your happiness Craig, but you've got to let me back in."

I sit quietly. Waiting.

"But what about what you want? You can't live your life through me."

His words punch me hard in the gut and I bend double as if I've just been physically winded.

You can't live your life through me.

He's right and hearing him say it, finally I have to acknowledge that our relationship is not going to work. Not while I needed to be *his girl* in order to define who I am.

"I never meant to hurt you," he whispers.

I want to believe that that part is true, even if he's just cut me with a thousand razor blades. I turn away, digesting the finality of what he's saying.

All this time I've been fighting to get the old Craig back, but what if that person was never real to begin with? I've been trying to change my husband back into the person he was before, but maybe it's time for me to change instead. To face the unthinkable and ask the one question I've avoided thus far.

I suck in a deep breath. "What is it you want, Craig?"

"Freedom," he says simply.

"Freedom from what specifically? From me? From our marriage? Freedom to be with someone else?"

"Freedom from who I was trying to be while I figure out who I truly am."

And there it is — at last.

His truth.

The harsh reality is that both of us were using the other as a crutch. Neither of us sharing our true selves with the other, even if we didn't realise it when we first met and fell in love.

All this time I was trying to be the perfect woman, the perfect girlfriend, the perfect wife. To mould myself against him so we would be the perfect couple, when all along he wasn't being true to himself either. While he was telling me to *just be me*, he didn't know who he was either. It was all an illusion. He was trying to fill a void of guilt and shame created by the death of his brother, and I was using our relationship — our marriage — as a way to validate my self worth.

How could our marriage have ever succeeded when both of us were presenting a façade to each other? Each of us using the other to cover over deeper wounds and insecurities.

If he has any chance of finding true happiness, he can't do it with me by his side and as painful as I know facing the next chapter of my life alone will be, if I have any chance of finding that illusive everlasting love, I must face my own fears and let him go.

I squint my eyes against the sun as it breaks through from behind a cloud. When I open them, the most magnificent rainbow has formed across the plunge pool and is framing the waterfall behind. Two different elements, the light from the sun and the water from the spray, combining to create something beautiful. Something ethereal. Something so pure it can only survive for a moment in time.

The vibrancy of the colours takes my breath away, and a lump forms in the back of my throat. I blink, and as quickly as it appeared, it's gone. The sun having disappeared back behind the cloud again.

All it takes is one element to change and the magic is lost. It's neither the light nor the water's fault, the beauty reliant on the other showing up at the exact right moment, but rainbows are never permanent. Perhaps so we learn never to take them for granted.

"I'm sorry I've put so much energy this past year into trying to 'fix you'."

"I know. And anybody else would be grateful for everything you've done for them. Helping them find a new job, doing everything you could to try and motivate someone who didn't want to be motivated. But I'm not that person anymore. That Craig's gone, and I don't want to bring him back."

"I understand. So what do we do now?"

He wrings his hands together. "I want to do that other trip I talked about. Take another three, maybe six, months, perhaps even longer, and explore the other parts of Asia I never went to. Chiang Mai, Laos, Vietnam. I can't explain it; I was somebody different when I was over there. But I was riddled with guilt at the person I was becoming. Because I knew that man was hurting you. But if I go back, I'd like to find him again. He felt more real to me than anything else in my life has before."

"Then you must go. No question. You need to find *that* Craig. Find a way to be happy. Truly happy."

We fall into silence again.

"But where does that leave you?"

"Alone," I reply matter-of-factly, and he winces.

I can tell he doesn't want to cause me anymore pain, but he's stuck between a rock and a hard place. If he stays and tries to make me happy, he'll never be who he was destined to become.

"Look, Craig. I'd be lying if I didn't say a part of me wants you to shower me with flowers and affection. To choose me and promise to love me forever—"

I catch my breath in my throat. Letting him go might be the right thing to do, but it doesn't make it any easier.

"I can't lie, the idea of going on without you is too painful for me to even process right now. But I don't want to be the reason you're miserable. If loving you means I should let you go…" I continue, my breath coming out in short staccato puffs of air, "...then that's what I need to do."

"Are you sure?"

"Yes," I whisper. My heart still not wanting to believe what I'm doing in my final act of love. "I'll contact a lawyer tomorrow and start divorce proceedings," I add, my voice hardly audible over the roar of the waterfall. "That way you'll be completely free from any obligation to me, legal or otherwise. Then who knows what the future holds for either of us."

"I've only ever wanted to do the right thing by you, you know."

"I know and I believe you. And all I've ever wanted is for you to be happy."

"And I've let you down... so much. You deserve so much more than I was ever able to give you."

"Don't say that Craig. You were always enough for me. More than enough. I'm just sorry I wasn't ever enough for you."

I notice that, without realising, I've begun to refer to our relationship in the past tense.

"I hate that I'm breaking my promises to you," he adds.

"You aren't, I'm releasing you from them. There's a difference. Consider everything we've ever said to each other a promise unmade rather than a promise that either of us broke. Only we know the truth of our relationship. We know what our love meant to each other, at least at the time. Let's not spoil it by tainting it with words like *failure*, or *broken*. I still believe we were meant to meet, meant to fall in love, meant to get married, even if it wasn't meant to be forever."

"You really are incredible, Tori. Do you know that?"

He takes my hand and pulls me to my feet.

"Yeah, well. That maybe so, but it still leaves me alone and unloveable."

"You're not unloveable. Far from it. And like you said, who knows what the future holds. There's someone out there for you. I know it."

But I wanted that someone to be you, my heart pleads.

He pulls me into an embrace, and his familiar scent shoots up my nostrils, and that's when the tears finally come in earnest.

Knowing that I'm doing the right thing doesn't make our break up any less painful. Inside, a part of me is still screaming; *don't leave me, stay and love me — please. I'm nothing without you.*

Tomorrow morning I know I will wake up alone, childless, and single. With no idea where my life is going, other than in the exact opposite direction from where I'd pictured it being by my thirty-second year.

But then out of my peripheral vision I notice a beam of sunlight dance across the diamonds in the bracelet on my right wrist.

I breathe in. I can do this. It will be hard, but I need to remember; I'm stronger than I think.

As Craig continues to hold me, his chin resting on the top of my head, I allow myself to soften into him one last time, knowing that once we break our embrace, this chapter of my life — this *great love* — will be over.

Chapter 56

18 months later, March 2003

I wake up in a pool of sweat. My PJs stuck to my skin and my duvet in disarray. It's still dark outside. I check the time on my phone: five a.m. Sitting up, I swipe my hair away from my face.

Last night he invaded my dreams again.

It's eighteen months since we separated, the day after Anth and Nessa's wedding, and a mere three weeks since our divorce was finalised, but still I dream of him. Almost every night.

In my dreams we're still together, still married and still madly in love.

Each time I wake, it takes me a few moments to readjust to the present. To remind my conscious that I'm alone and he's gone.

Never in my life did I think I'd have to walk away from a man I loved not once, but twice. I left Chris to save myself, and I released Craig from his promises – despite still being in love with him – as he needed to save himself.

In each case, I know it was the right thing to do, but it doesn't stop my heart from bleeding. My poor, poor broken heart. What she's had to endure, and still she yearns for that illusive happy ever after.

I want desperately to move on in my life and put my relationship with Craig behind me, but every time I dream of him, it cuts open those same wounds. It's exhausting, but I'm powerless to make it stop.

Ironically,, it never feels like I'm dreaming of him, more like he's invading my subconscious. Like his soul keeps returning to visit me. As if there are some unspoken words or unsaid emotions between us. It's unsettling, and rather than leave me satiated and content, each vision reopens the unanswered questions and pain caused by the ending of our marriage.

Every time I wake it takes me a few moments to reconcile all the decisions I made, why I made them, and to readjust to my new reality. Yet I still wonder, should I have fought harder? Or ask myself, what else I could have done?

I long for the visions to stop. How else can I move forward?

But how can you dictate what you dream about?

Except last night's dream was different.

We were standing in front of each other as usual. Just the two of us, suspended in an unearthly plain. Both of us surrounded by a brilliant white dazzling light, beaming smiles on our faces. His eyes were bright and happy as he gazed deeply into mine and I felt only pure love passing between us. Like it had been when we first met. It's at this point, normally, I would wake up, arms outstretched, reaching out for him, only to discover the space in front of me dark, empty and cold.

Except in last night's dream I didn't wake. Our souls remained coupled as we stood facing one another. Slowly he lifted his hands to cup my face, leant forward, and kissed me. Cupping my head in his hands in his particular way. Gently stroking the sides of my face with his thumbs as our lips connected.

We kissed slowly, tenderly, in the way only two people who

know each other intimately do. I remember the familiar feel of his soft but firm lips on my own, causing my knees to weaken as I softened into him. After our long, lingering kiss he'd gently tilted my face towards his and looked intensely into my eyes, all the while his loving smile beamed bright, causing his dimples to form in his cheeks.

In that moment I felt his love more strongly than ever and my heart swelled in my chest as I breathed him in.

I closed my eyes, and felt the gentle imprint of his lips on my right eyelid.

'*One,*' he'd whispered.

'*Two,*' he'd said, kissing my left eyelid.

I'd held my breath, waiting for him to say three.

When he didn't, I opened my eyes. '*Three,*' I'd said quietly.

'*Three,*' he'd repeated, tilting my head towards his, leaning his face down and delicately kissing my lips, before he'd released my face, turned slowly and walked away.

The brilliant light swallowing him up as he'd disappeared into the distance.

...then I woke up.

I may be covered in sweat, but rather than feel bereft with longing, as I've done every time before, as I hold my phone in my hands and the neon green numbers confirm the time as 5:02, I feel calm and serene.

Regardless of how short our marriage was in the end, the love that we had shared was pure and good. Of that, I am sure.

Chapter 57

*H*ere hon, let me help you up." Mark helps a heavily pregnant Becca to her feet.

She strokes her distended belly. "Tor, that was delicious, but I need to pee again. Bladder the size of a teaspoon."

"No problemo." I wave my wine glass in the air. "You know where you're going. Have a lie down if you need to. You've done really well tonight, considering."

"Thanks Tor. You're a gem."

"I miss my belly." Nessa strokes her still slightly rounded abdomen.

"And what a magnificent belly it was." I grip her hand and give her a wink. "How are the little rug rats?"

Nessa gave birth to twins three months ago.

"Exhausting." Anth uses his thumb and index finger to manually stretch his eyes open. "We have a new mantra in our house: '*Sleep is for wimps*'."

"But I'm sure it's all worth it," I say as Anth and Nessa share a loving smile.

Tonight is their first night out since their bairns were born, and the combination of eyebags and idiotic grins, tells the story of their overflowing exhaustion and joy at the arrival of their fully formed family.

"I'll pop over tomorrow afternoon. Once I've dropped Tim back at the airport. Need to keep my cuddle quota topped up."

"Anytime, Aunty Tor. You're always welcome," Nessa says with a warm smile.

"And how've you been?" Julie directs her question across the table to me. "Since, you know…"

"Since my degree absolute was issued." I fill in the blanks for her.

"Well, yes."

"Fine. Great, actually."

Over the past eighteen months, I've had to face my greatest fear — finding out who I am on my own. It hasn't always been easy. Of course, they've been times I've missed the closeness and intimacy of being in a relationship. And each time another one of my friends has had a baby, I've shed a silent tear, but following my dream last weekend, something in the ether seems to have shifted. I'm no longer wanting or grieving. It's as if I've reached the end of a journey and am no longer fearful of either the past or the future.

I'm strong. I'm independent and I'm finally comfortable just being me. I am enough.

"I can't quite put my finger on it," I continue. "But yeah, I'm really good, thanks. I've just landed a really interesting account at work. My team are all great. All my clients are happy. I'm off to Milan again next week for work. So I'm looking forward to some good wine and proper pizza. The 'olds' are all well. And all the paperwork's finally through and the house is mine."

I sweep my hand in the air, indicating that the house that started out as Craig's bachelor pad, before it became our marital home, is now my safe haven. Since Craig left, I've given his personal belongings back to his parents and slowly made the space mine. Every room now has a 'Vicky' stamp on it. Oversized arty ballet prints on the walls. Fresh flowers in every room. Lots of cushions in soft, muted tones. Big sofas to sink into. Gone are the VHS videos of *The X-Files* and *Star Wars* and instead my video library is stuffed full with romantic comedies, the entire boxset of *Friends* and recordings of both The Kirov and Royal Ballet's performances of Romeo + Juliet.

"Indeed, congratulations on your divorce, darling." Tim raises his glass. "I never thought you made a very good doormat. You're much more attractive now you're back in your own driving seat."

When I told him I was hosting a divorce party, he insisted he be here. Which is no mean feat, now that he's based in Hong Kong and continues to split his time between there, his apartment in New York, his holiday home in Grand Cayman, and of course, visits out to Lydia at 'the barn'.

Becca comes back from the loo, and returns to her seat and I take a moment to look around the seven people gathered around my table. The kind and generous faces of all my friends who have had my back while I've navigated the latest transition in my life, and I'm so thankful for them.

Anth picks up the bottle of red and tops up Clarky's glass, then, without thinking, asks, "How was Thailand? We've not caught up since you got back."

Everyone freezes and Julie flashes Clarky a warning look, then flicks her gaze to me. Meanwhile everyone else suddenly seems more pre-occupied with their napkins, or their glasses of wine.

Tim leaps up, his chair scraping across the floor. "Think I'll go check on the puddings," he says before disappearing into the kitchen. Clearly he wants no part in this conversation. His disdain for Craig having never softened.

Nessa reaches for my hand and gives it a consolatory squeeze. I appreciate everyone's concern. There was a time when any mention of Thailand, its culture, or its people would cause me to burst into tears. The loss of not just my marriage but the future I'd once dreamed of, when thrust in my face, or catching me off guard, still too raw for my emotions. But after my dream two weeks ago, I'm at peace.

"It's okay," I say. "Honestly everyone, it's absolutely fine. At least I'm not the only singleton around the table." I wink at Julie but she looks away.

Turning my attention back to Clarky I ask, "Did you have a nice time Paul? I assumed you must have seen Craig while you were there?"

"Actually," he replies, sheepishly, "Jules and I were there for his wedding."

Julie locks eyes with me. "I'm sorry honey. I wanted to tell you, but I didn't want to upset you."

I burst out laughing and everyone looks on, worried. I suspect they're mentally checking where they've left their car keys and that they're safely out of my reach.

"I'm sorry," I say regaining my composure. "I'm not laughing at you. It's just I'm not sure what's caught me more by surprise. Finding out Craig's married, or that you two went together. Explain yourselves." I wave my hand in the air while everyone else holds their breath.

Clarky and Julie exchange a look that means only one thing. Love.

"It's a bit of a long story," Clarky says. "But yeah, I'm mad about this woman."

"It's been a very slow burn," Julie says, as if trying to justify their relationship.

"You could say that," Becca chimes in.

"You knew?" I glare at Becca with furrowed brows.

"Everyone knew, honey. It's been fizzling for years!"

"But with what you've been through, they were just being sensitive," Anth adds.

How did I never spot the signs? My mind races through all our parties and gatherings. How many times did they arrive separately, but share taxis home? Were they sharing a room at Nessa and Anth's wedding? Come to think of it, even as far back as the races, the day Clarky came to collect me, I wondered how he had Julie's number but never questioned it any further at the time.

"I get it. Well, you make a lovely couple." I raise my glass. "To Paul and Jules."

"Paul and Jules," everyone repeats.

"Now, back to your other bombshell. Spill. Craig's married?"

"Yes." Clarky still can't look me in the eye, preferring to study the wine in his glass as he rolls it between his fingers.

"It's okay. I'm absolutely fine. I only ever wanted him to be happy."

It's easy to forget that, although Paul Clark was the best man at mine and Craig's wedding, he and Craig grew up together and he's Craig's oldest friend. It makes total sense that if Craig were getting married, he'd want Clarky there. I already knew Craig was in a relationship with a Thai national, a piece of information that the girls sensitively shared with me a year ago. Whether it was someone he'd met before we separated is unclear, but either way, it doesn't matter now.

"They seem very happy together," Julie adds. "I never knew that she too lost an older brother. In a motorbike accident, apparently."

I bob my head. "Tragic. But something I'm sure that bonds them in a way no one else can understand. I'm happy for him," I say, realising I mean it.

"Ta-da!" Tim appears in the doorway from the kitchen, carrying a tray of eight perfectly risen chocolate soufflés.

"Oh wow." I stand up and help to serve the ramekins to my guests. "For God's sake, eat them before they sink."

"Now these look a lot better than the last time I tried your eggy delights," Tim laughs. "They were a *di-saaars-ter*, darling."

"I agree," Nessa adds, smiling. "These look much more scrumptious." She picks up her spoon and dives in.

Sitting back down, I'm about to taste my triumph when I pause, my spoon hovering over the top of my pudding.

"Do you mind me asking..." I lock eyes with Julie. "When exactly did they get married?"

"Two weeks ago. Why?"

A shiver runs down my back and the hairs stand up on my arms. At the exact same moment he was marrying again, saying his vows to his new bride in a sun-drenched ceremony on the other side of the world, he was in my dream, saying goodbye to me. Letting me know that he had loved me once but that he was moving on, as am I.

I know I'll never dream of him again, and that there are no more ties, legally, physically, emotionally or spiritually, holding us together.

He is free, as am I.

♫

The next morning, Tim goes and collects the post from the mat behind the front door. Bringing the pile of letters through to the kitchen, I discard the bills and circulars onto the pile on the edge of the island, while he turns a postcard over and over in his hands. Studying it.

"Weird. It has no message," he says, passing it to me.

I take the postcard from him, and like him, turn it over and over, looking for clues.

It's postmarked from Fiji. A picture of a moonlit beach. The waves in shadow, illuminated only by the ripples of moonlight bouncing across a beautiful sea. Piercing the centre of the picture — a single shooting star cuts through the dark night sky.

Resting the card against my lips, I smile inwardly. Knowing whose hands have also touched this paper, I can almost smell him on the card.

"Any idea who it's from?" Tim asks.

"No. None." I shrug my shoulders. "Weird."

"Weird indeed."

Making my excuses, I head out of the kitchen and into my bedroom. Opening my wardrobe, I slide the postcard inside my ballerina box, alongside the yellow diamond earrings and my sapphire and diamond engagement ring, that I've also placed in there for safekeeping.

One day, I may wear them again. When and where I have no idea, but for now they're safely stowed away with my most precious memories of not just my first great love — but also the memories of Craig, the second great love of my life.

Epilogue

VICTORIA

Leeds, England. May 2005

My hands shaking, I grip the steering wheel of my luxury 4x4. Checking for oncoming traffic, I pull out of the multi-storey car park and join the line of cars snaking their way along the Leeds inner ring road.

When I turned up for the meeting this morning, even though I wanted them to say *'yes'* to my proposal, I was ready for some push back and never expected them to be so enthusiastic about my ideas. It feels as if I'm finally on the receiving end of some good luck, and the dark cloud that has been hanging over me has finally lifted.

Is this small victory the end of one enormous, tortuous roller-coaster? This positive outcome a small but significant step forward in the next chapter of my life?

This deal will inevitably change the trajectory of my business, and the course of my life. About fifty percent of new businesses fail within the first three years, and with what we've just been through, today's good news means we can look forward to positive business growth.

I can't wait to share the news with my employees.

I pull up at the pedestrian crossing to give way to those waiting patiently at the side of the road. Watching the crowd of people filing numbly in front of my car, I catch my breath.

It can't be? But it is: it's him!

My eyes follow him as he ambles, unaware, in front of me. The last person on the entire planet I'd expect to see walking in front of my car. The sight of him again after all this time causes me to freeze in my seat, the windscreen in front of me the only barrier between us as he saunters past a few feet away. Never, on this day of new beginnings and fresh starts, when it feels as if something massive has just shifted in the ether, did I expect to be confronted so directly with my past.

I remain frozen but for the continuous and intense shaking of my hands on the steering wheel. I hold my breath.

He shouldn't be here. He should be on the other side of the world, focusing on his new life, as I am on mine. What on earth is he doing in this northern industrial city where neither of us has ever lived, or, as far as I'm aware, has any connections?

I take in his familiar gait and relaxed manner as he steps up onto the opposite kerb, and watch out of my rear-view mirror as he turns left down the pavement, walking away, still unaware of my presence.

If I don't act now, this moment will be gone forever, and I may never see him again. Is there a reason the universe presented him here, directly in front of me, today of all days? On a day when I feel like I'm gliding into a new era of my life, why have the planets chosen this moment to collide and serve up my past?

If I ever wanted closure, or answers to my unasked questions, I realise that *this is it*; I must seize this opportunity before it is gone forever.

I quickly check my reflection in my rear-view mirror, running my tongue over my teeth, and smacking my lips together to even out my lipstick. Satisfied with my appearance, my tyres screech in protest as I yank the steering wheel to the kerb, stopping abruptly at an awkward angle. Horns honk around me, but I don't care. I leap out, cup my hands around my mouth and shout his name.

He's about a hundred yards away now, the muscles in his strong, wide shoulders rippling under his cotton shirt as he continues to walk in the opposite direction. But the familiar pitch of my voice calling his name must resonate. He stops and turns, tilting his head as if confirming his mind is not playing tricks on him and that it really was the familiar sound of my voice he heard.

He spots me amongst the flow of passing pedestrians moving around me, smiles widely, and quickens his pace back towards me. The adrenalin and buzz I felt from my earlier business meeting returns and intensifies as I realise this is it: the moment we never had when we broke up.

I have no idea what he will say, what questions I'll be brave enough to ask, or what will happen as a result of us bumping into each other again. Seeing him so unexpectedly and in such an odd way feels as if greater forces have reunited us.

But why?

As he approaches, I suck air into my lungs and attempt to organise the tumultuous thoughts racing through my mind. His smile grows the closer he gets.

"Hi," he says, running his hand through his hair. "Well, this is a pleasant surprise. What on earth are you doing here?"

"I could ask you the same thing," I reply, taking in the slim gold wedding band on his left hand.

"How are you? You look well," he says casually.

"Good! You?" I point at the black and white image of James Dean down the front of his tie. "It always was your favourite."

"Well, you know." He thrusts his hands in his pockets and casts his gaze down to the pavement.

"What are you doing here? I thought you were living in Asia now?"

"For half of the year. I'm a highly sought-after IT consultant now." His lips curl into a wry smile. "I spend six months over here, working as a contractor, then we can afford to spend the rest of the year chillin' back at home in Thailand."

"Sounds like the perfect balance. I'm happy for you."

Keeping his head tilted, his gaze meets mine. "You were right about that, Tori. You always said I had transferable skills and would easily find a new job. You were right about a lot of things."

Silence.

"I hear you have a baby now. A little girl." I say enthusiastically and watch as his face lights up at the mention of his daughter. "You always said you wanted a girl. A *daddy's little princess*."

"Yeah, she's gorgeous. Everyone loves her."

"I'm really pleased for you, Craig. Pleased you found what you were looking for — even if it wasn't with me."

Unconsciously, I place my hand protectively over my own imperceptibly rounded belly, knowing that I, too, am on the cusp of having everything I've ever wanted.

He sucks in an audible breath. "I never meant to hurt you, you know. I know I did and I'm really sorry."

"It's all good — honestly."

"No, I mean... there was a time when I thought I was the right man for you, but... well, thank you. For everything."

"No need to thank me. I should also thank you. It was hard at the time, but I have no regrets. You?"

"None."

"Good."

As painful as the end of our relationship was, ultimately it was healing for both of us and has allowed us both to go on and create lives filled with love and joy. We needed to break each other, in order to heal our respective wounds, even if that meant we were no longer compatible as a couple.

"Actually Craig, there's something I've always wanted to ask you."

"Oh?"

I suck in a breath before blurting out. "Did you ever sleep with Amanda?"

All the colour drains from his face and he looks down at his feet, guilt written all over his features.

"I'm sorry," he says eventually, meeting my gaze. "Like I said. I never meant to hurt you. It only ever happened the once and it was a mistake. I realised that immediately. Afterwards, I tried so hard to be the husband I thought I should be for you. If anything that one-night stand was another symptom of my deep unhappiness with myself. But I ignored it, like everything else at the time. I'm sorry," he says again.

"Thanks for being honest."

"The truth — remember."

"Always," I smile. "At least it explains why she hated my guts."

"And you're happy now?" He asks, changing the subject.

"Yes. More than I ever thought possible."

"Good." My eyes travel to his wrist and register that something is different. "Your leather straps. Where are they?"

"It was time to let him go. Time to live my own life, you know?"

"Oh, that's really good, Craig. I'm sure Rob would approve."

We both stand and stare at each other. Each of us registering the end of our bond.

He glances at his watch. "Well, I'd better be getting back."

"Yes, of course."

I never expected to see Craig again, so had no idea how I would feel, but I'm secretly pleased that, standing in front of him now, my heart is not doing somersaults, and my tummy is devoid of any butterflies. If anything, looking at him now it's hard to believe that I used to think he was sex on legs. I smile inwardly at these thoughts. How things have changed.

"Well, it was lovely to bump into you again, Tori."

"Likewise. Take care," I say, realising I mean it.

"… and you." He leans forward and gives me a gentle peck on the cheek before he turns and walks away.

I know I shall never see him again, and that this chapter of my life is well and truly closed. I have complete closure. He has nothing more to give me, nor I, him.

I return to my car, and as if the planets are intervening once again, Kelly Clarkson's new single *'Since you've been gone'* booms out through my car speakers. I turn it all the way up and tap my fingers along in time to the beat, smiling unconsciously.

My heart feels as light as air as I sing along to the lyrics.

Life is good.

The End

Keep reading to find out what happens in the final instalment, *A Star Unborn*

Order 'A Star Unborn' now

A forgiving heart, a life-changing loss, an unconditional love.

Successful and ambitious **Victoria Turnbull** has had enough of relationships–too many times she's made painful sacrifices for love–but that was before she lands in the lap of a tall, quiet Welshman at her best friend's New Year's Eve party.

Recently divorced **Gavin Williams** is calm, caring and kind. He falls instantly for the enigmatic Vicky, but it's only when a hurricane blows through the Caribbean, cruelly ripping the lovers apart, that Vicky finally realises she has everything she's ever wanted in Gav, except the one thing she truly desires—a baby.

Surely a decade-old hidden secret won't stop her from having a child with the man she loves, until she discovers getting pregnant is one thing, staying pregnant... another.

· · ·

Then when Gav's past slams unexpectedly into Vicky's present and she's left reeling from a thirteen-year-old confession from former flame, **Chris**, everything she thought she knew about love, life and her past decisions, is thrown into turmoil.

With two *Great Loves* vying for her heart, will Vicky stay true to herself, or will her shameful secret stop her from having a family with the man she was always destined to be with?

From the **majestic mountains of Snowdonia** via the **sun-drenched beaches of the Cayman Islands, the formality of Singapore, the laid-back vibe of San Diego**, and **the stunning vistas of New Zealand**, 'A Star Unborn,' the thrilling finale in '*The Three Great Loves of Victoria Turnbull series,*' is a beautiful and emotional love story about what it means to continue loving, even in the face of great loss.

A perfect read for fans of Jojo Moyes, Taylor Jenkins Reid and Nicholas Sparks.

Order 'A Star Unborn' now

રી

Dear Reader,

I want to say a massive thank you for firstly buying and then taking the time to read one of my books - it means a lot!

If you've enjoyed reading about Victoria's second *Great Love* in this trilogy, then I'm unashamedly asking for your help. I don't have the weight of a massive publishing house behind me to help get the story out there, and the best way for me to reach more readers is via your support.

One of the most powerful things you can do is leave a short review on Amazon and/or Goodreads. It doesn't have to be long, just a single sentence will let others know what you thought. Do not underestimate the influence your review can have on a book's success.

- Leave a review on Amazon.com
- Leave a review on Amazon.co.uk
- Leave a review on Goodreads
- Leave a review on Bookbub

... or head to your local Amazon or online store and follow the process from there.

If you're feeling super generous, please recommend this story to all your friends, post about it on your social media platforms, and suggest it to your book club (if you have one). Did you know you can invite me to Zoom into your book club meeting by emailing me on hello@isabellawiles.com

If you'd like a FREE copy of the prequel to this series, hop over to www.isabellawiles.com and follow the instructions to download the e-book of *A Life Unstarted* (or purchase the paperback from Amazon) and learn more of Vicky's backstory, how she became friends with Mel, and some of the high-stakes antics the pair get themselves into before Vicky met and fell in love with Chris.

Needless to say, Victoria's story will continue to unravel as she continues in her quest *'to love and be loved'*. Read on for a taster of *A Star Unborn*, the final instalment in *The Three Great Loves of Victoria Turnbull* series.

Much love,

Isabella x

A Star Unborn - Chapter 1 Excerpt

VICTORIA

North-East England, 30th December 2003

Every muscle in my body shakes but sucking in a lung-filling breath, and rather than giving into the weaknesses of my frame, I deepen my Goddess pose.

"That's it ladies. Breathe in your power," the yoga teacher encourages before dragging in an audible breath through flared nostrils. She changes position and we all follow her lead, straightening our outstretched legs and reaching our hands up to the corners of the ceiling. "Now feel your Stars twinkling bright, and on your next out breath, return to your Goddesses. *Feel* your inner power."

I straighten my arms and legs into a four-point Star pose, lengthening my muscles before—on my next breath—returning to my Goddess stance, bending my knees into a deep plié once again, and opening my arms from my chest, my fingers splayed. A mix of tension and power rushes through my thighs. My muscles still shaking, I remind myself: *It's only fear and weakness leaving my body. I'm in control and I am strong.*

Out of my peripheral vision I spy Vanessa, who's given up on the pose and is shaking out her arms and legs. With a free hand she sweeps away a tendril of red hair which has broken free from her ponytail, before she sinks down to her mat and curls up in Child's pose.

We catch each other's eye and smile, before I close my eyes, returning my focus inwards as I blow out another long breath through pursed lips.

I will not lose focus. I am strong. I am my own Goddess, I say to myself over and over.

"See you tomorrow," Nessa says as we roll up our mats at the end of class.

"Tomorrow?" I ask, faking innocence.

"*Durr*. Don't pretend you don't know. New Year's Eve, round mine. You're the only one who hasn't confirmed. But you have to be there."

"Why? What difference would it make if I skipped this one?"

"Are you friggin' kidding me? You're becoming a recluse, Tor. Working far too hard. Let your hair down for once. What is it the proverb says? *All work and no play makes Jack a dull boy?*"

"Maybe I enjoy being dull," I fire back at her.

"Don't be ridiculous, Tor, you're normally the life and soul of every party. You've missed so many this past year; make an exception for this one."

Seven years ago, when I moved back to the town I was born and raised, I used to go swimming with Nessa and my other girlfriends twice a week, and every other spare minute was spent hanging out in The Red Lion, or drinking down on Newcastle's vibrant quayside, our partners in tow. Most weekends, and sometimes more nights in the week than not, we'd be there, drinking, watching whatever match was playing, and taking the mickey out of each other. It was our religion, but these days everyone's lives have moved on. My high-powered job, Nessa's energy zapping but cute-as eleven-month-old twins consume all of her spare time, and all the other girls' lives are equally busy. So when everyone does come together now, it's usually for an event. A birthday, a christening, a formal dinner party, and there are only so many do's I want to attend on my own.

I'm not ashamed or unhappy at the way my life has turned out– far from it–but it's exhausting having to muster the extra energy to confidently walk into a room alone, before having to explain to someone new, the reasons why.

Nessa places an arm around my shoulder as we make our way outside. "It wouldn't be a New Year's Eve party if you weren't there. You started the tradition, remember? You and Craig. Your New Year's Eve parties were legendary."

"Different times." I shrug. My breath forming clouds of condensation in the freezing air outside.

"I'm not taking no for an answer, Tor." She glances sideways at me.

Order 'A Star Unborn' now

Book Club Questions

Below are some sample questions you may wish to use as starting points for a discussion about *A Promise Unmade*.

Warning: contains spoilers.

- In order for Vicky to release Craig from his promises, she had to redefine her beliefs around unconditional love. Do you agree with her new definition of *loving someone sometimes means letting them go?*

- One of the most shocking moments in the story is Jack Walker's assault. Do you believe if that had happened today – post #metoo movement – rather than have happened in 2000, the outcome would have been different?

- In the middle of the story, Vicky is reunited with Chris. How has Chris's character changed from *A Flame Unburned?* Do you believe Vicky made the right choice at that point in the story? And if not, why not?

- One of the recurring motifs throughout the story is the use of water to represent emotions that Vicky was either unable to express, or that mirrored her deeper authentic self. Did you pick up on this theme and if so, how many places in the story use the symbolism of water to reflect this deeper meaning?

- What are your thoughts on Craig? Do you have empathy for him, or dislike him?

- Craig had a lower sex drive than Vicky, creating conflict in their relationship. What are your thoughts on the differing ways in which Chris and Craig express their love for Vicky?

- By the end of the story, it's clear that neither Vicky or Craig were presenting their true authentic selfs to one another when they first met and fell in love. At what point in the story did you realise this? If you re-read some of the text with this additional insight, how many places is this now obvious, even if it wasn't before.

Not part of a book club? Then hop online to Izzy's Reading Bees and start a discussion, and invite other readers to comment and add their thoughts to your own.

About the Author

By day, Isabella Wiles is the CEO of her own Management Consultancy, something she loves but considers both a blessing and a curse. A curse because it takes her away from home, but a blessing because by night, whilst waiting for endless planes in faceless airports, or while stuck on trains with rubbish Wi-Fi, it allows her the opportunity to indulge her secret passion – writing compelling women's book club fiction.

She has written hundreds of business articles, reviews, and multiple bestselling works of non-fiction under the name Nicola Cook, which are published internationally and translated into multiple languages, however *The Three Great Loves of Victoria Turnbull* series is her first foray into writing romantic women's fiction.

She initially published a version of *A Flame Unburned* in 2018 under the name *Belonging*. Following a complete overhaul of her initial work with the support of a new editor, in 2021 she released a re-edited edition of her debut novel under the new title *A Flame Unburned* together with the prequel novella, *A Life Unstarted* (available FREE to download from www.isabellawiles.com), followed by the final two books in the trilogy, *A Promise Unmade* in December 2021 and *A Star Unborn* in December 2022.

When she is not sitting on trains or stuck in airports, she lives in the north-east of England with her long-suffering husband, their two children, a looney Basset Hound and two equally unhinged goldfish.

Be sure to follow Isabella and receive advanced notification of upcoming new releases.

Join Isabella's online readers club
Facebook.com / groups / IzzysReadingBees /

f facebook.com / isabellawiles

⊙ instagram.com / isabellawiles_author

♪ tiktok.com / isabellawiles_author

BB bookbub.com / authors / isabella-wiles

g goodreads.com / Isabella_Wiles

Acknowledgements

Like any musician grappling with their *difficult second album,* my greatest fear was that my follow-up to *A Flame Unburned* would fall short of the exacting standards of you – my reader. Hopefully that is not the case and my creativity and craft have delivered another story that's kept you turning pages long into the night. It took a long time to wrestle this story out of me, but many *many* drafts later, I'm pleased that the story on the page is the one I intended to tell. And that wouldn't have been possible without the support of a small army of helpers.

I cannot express how grateful I am to my Storygrid developmental editor, Kim Kessler, for her guidance, expertise, and humour as we broke apart my shitty first draft and rebuilt this story from the ending, forwards. These past eighteen months have been so tough creatively, and I honestly would not have got to this point without you, Kim. You are a genius at what you do, and I'm so grateful for your continued support.

Thank you also to Zoë Markham, from Markham Correct, for your beady eye copyediting the final draft, and for all your hilarious comments in the margin. Your attention to detail is unsurpassed and you do make me giggle. I mean, who doesn't know *'drop down on your honkers'* means dropping down on bent knees, and not falling forwards, flat on your boobs! I thought that was obvious. Doh!

Thanks also to Stuart Bache and his team at Books Covered for yet another outstanding cover.

To my merry gang of fellow scribes, Imogen Clark, Meg Cowley, Debbie Ioanna and Holly Lyne, thank you for the constant cheer-leading and general camaraderie. Your collective knowledge of both craft and publishing is like having my own personal encyclopaedia on tap. Thank you also for checking in when I drop off the radar, to make sure I'm okay. Sometimes I'm not, and it's comforting to know you are always there for me.

Thank you also to Jay & Jo Scott-Nichols for collecting a mountain of research during your family holiday to Asia, and to Karyn Brown for fact-checking all my Thailand references. Karyn, your emails were hilarious and I promise, will never be shared!

Thank you again to my Alpha readers, Kate Freeman, Sarah Miller and Bianca Robinson, for reading my hideous early drafts. I'm sure you'll agree that this story is very different from the first version I penned. Never-the-less I'm immensely grateful for your insights and feedback. Keep it coming.

In this book, I particularly want to thank all my *besties*, not for any specific help in the creation of this book, but as someone who has been divorced and come out the other side, I'm not sure I would have survived that period of my life without you all being there for me; dusting me down, picking me back up and being my strength when I didn't have any. Thank you Angela Blake, Karyn Brown, Jacqui Cook, Rachel Farrell, Caroline Gallagher, Kathryn Hardy, Tiffany Hodkinson and Sarah Miller; and more recently Claire Love, Rachel Hicks and Michelle Sheini. You all mean the world to me. And 'yes' – you did all make it into the story. Your essence is meshed into the characters of Nessa, Becca, and Julie.

I would also like to thank Michael Reay, Lee Dial and the rest of the team at Precision Building & Joinery, for not only for building our beautiful home while I was writing this book, but for creating my amazing library – or as you've named it Michael, 'The Tart's

Boudoir'. It's the perfect space to nurture my creativity and in which to write – thank you.

However, my biggest thanks has to go to my incredible husband and my children. Thank you for your unending love and support. Thank you for giving me the space and time to write. And thank you for your constant belief in me. I love you three more than you will ever know.

Thank you,
    Izzy x

Resources

If you are a victim of sexual abuse, dealing with relationship issues, or having suicidal thoughts – below are a list of organisations in the UK who can help.

Women's Aid
www.womensaid.org.uk

Samaritans
www.samaritans.org
Tel: 116 123

Sexual Abuse Support
www.sexualabusesupport.campaign.gov.uk

Rape Crisis
www.rapecrisis.org.uk
Tel: 0808 802 9999

Relate
www.relate.org.uk
Tel: 0300 003 2324

ISBN E-Book: 978-1-9996529-9-9
ISBN Paperback: 978-1-915137-00-5
ISBN Large Print Paperback: 978-1-915137-01-2

Published by Aurora Independent Publishing.

The contents depicted in this book do not reflect the views of the author, publisher or related sales and distribution parties.

A Promise Unmade is written in British English.
Cover design: BooksCovered
Developmental Editor: Kim Kessler at Storygrid
Edited by: Markham Correct